The Fatal Series by Marie Force
Now available in ebook
Suggested reading order

Fatal Affair (available in print)

Fatal Justice (available in print)

Fatal Consequences (available in print)

Fatal Destiny (available in print with *Fatal Consequences*)

Fatal Flaw (available in print)

Fatal Deception (available in print)

Fatal Mistake (available in print)

Fatal Jeopardy (in print Fall 2015)

Fatal Scandal (in print January 2016)

And stay tuned for *Fatal Frenzy*,
the next book in the Fatal Series from Marie Force

Coming in ebook Fall 2015
Available in print Spring 2016

Praise for the Fatal Series
by *New York Times* bestselling author Marie Force

"Another awesome political/police adventure... The suspect wasn't easily found and the ending was perfect. This series is fantastic in so many ways, making it a definite must read for mystery fans."

—*Night Owl Reviews* on *Fatal Mistake*, Top Pick

"It is a marvelous romance/mystery novel and one that is deeply emotional and so very entertaining."

—*Book Binge* on *Fatal Mistake*

"Force pushes the boundaries by deftly using political issues like immigration to create an intricate mystery."

—*RT Book Reviews* on *Fatal Consequences*, 4 stars

"Marie Force's second novel in the Fatal series is an outstanding romantic suspense in its own right; that it follows the fantastic first installment only sweetens the read."

—*RT Book Reviews* on *Fatal Justice*

"The Fatal Series is a MUST read, it's fun, suspenseful, sexy and heartwarming."

—*Guilty Pleasures Book Reviews*

MARIE
FORCE

FATAL
mistake

Book Six of the Fatal Series

BONUS CONTENT INCLUDED

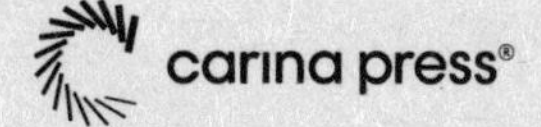

Recycling programs for this product may not exist in your area.

ISBN-13: 978-0-373-00271-9

Fatal Mistake and After the Final Epilogue

Cover image: Randy Santos

This edition published by arrangement with Harlequin Books S.A.

www.CarinaPress.com

Printed in U.S.A.

FATAL MISTAKE

Book Six of the Fatal Series

ONE

This, Nick Cappuano thought, *is as good as it gets*—a cool, crisp autumn night at the ballpark with all his favorite people and the hometown D.C. Federals cruising toward a spot in their first-ever World Series. Going into the top of the ninth inning, the Feds were up two to one with three outs standing between them and the big show.

"I can't believe this is really happening," Scotty said. The twelve-year-old vibrated with excitement.

"Don't get ahead of yourself." As a lifelong Boston Red Sox fan, Nick had learned to be realistic about these things. "We don't want to jinx them."

"All they need is three outs, and it's a done deal."

"Shhh," Nick said, cuffing the boy's chin and making him smile. He'd been living with them for two months now, the best two months of Nick's life. He and his wife Sam had filed formal adoption papers to make the boy an official member of the Cappuano family.

Speaking of the devil. His gorgeous wife made her way across the luxury skybox he'd collaborated with his close friend, retired Senator Graham O'Connor, to secure for the big game. With a water bottle in hand, Sam plopped down on Nick's lap, looping her arm around his shoulders.

"Having fun, babe?" Nick asked.

"So much fun. Freddie and Gonzo are already taking bets on the World Series."

"They shouldn't do that," Scotty said gravely. "Nick says they'll jinx the Feds."

"Can you even stand this?" Graham asked, grinning widely as he joined the Cappuanos. "It only took three seasons to make the World Series! And to think, last year, they were giving away tickets to fill seats."

"Tell him, Scotty," Nick said. "You're going to jinx them."

Graham ruffled the boy's hair. "I'm liking our chances with Lind on the mound to close this thing out." The Feds' lights-out closer, Rick Lind, was a big reason the team was sitting pretty in the top of the ninth inning in the seventh game of the National League Championship Series. The six-foot-six-inch pitcher's hundred-mile-an-hour fastball was a thing of pure beauty.

"If only the Sox had made it too, this would be even more exciting," Scotty said.

The Sox had flamed out of the pennant race in late September. "We have to take what we can get," Nick said.

Lind struck out the first two batters in the Giants' order with six sizzling fastballs the hitters never saw coming. Sam and Nick joined the rest of the ballpark by standing to cheer the home team.

"Holy cow," Scotty said, on his feet now that only three strikes stood between the Feds and the World Series. "This is the most exciting night of my entire life!" He paused, glanced at Nick and frowned.

"What?" Nick asked. The roar of the ballpark made it hard to hear, so he tipped his head closer to the boy.

"Your convention speech was way cooler and so was

what happened afterward." That was the night Scotty told them that he'd like to live with them permanently, which ranked as one of the best moments in Nick's life—and Sam's.

Smiling, Nick slung an arm around Scotty. "This is pretty darned cool too. It's okay to push it into first place."

Scotty shook his head. "It's a close second to that night."

"I'll give you that."

Scotty looked up at him with a loving smile that nearly stopped Nick's heart. He'd had no idea it was possible to love so deeply until Sam and Scotty had come into his life. He kept his arm around his son as the third Giants hitter stepped into the batter's box and Lind went into his famously contorted windup. How he ever managed to throw strikes out of that windup was a mystery to every baseball fan in America.

"He looks like Big Bird on acid," Sam said dryly, cracking up everyone in the box.

The fans stood as one, roaring as the game came down to two more pitches from the best closer in baseball.

The snap of the second strike hitting the catcher's mitt could be heard seven levels up in the skybox. Nick glanced at the scoreboard in center field where the pitch speed had been posted at 103 miles per hour. *Holy shit.* Lind was pulling out the biggest of the big guns for this final inning.

The volume in the park was earsplitting by the time Lind threw the second strike of the at bat.

To Nick's left were Sam, her partner Detective Freddie Cruz and his girlfriend Elin, Detective Tommy

"Gonzo" Gonzales holding his son Alex, Gonzo's fiancée—and Nick's chief of staff—Christina Billings, Sam's dad, Skip, and his wife Celia, Graham and his wife Laine, Terry O'Connor and his girlfriend, D.C. Medical Examiner Dr. Lindsey McNamara, the O'Connors' daughter Lizbeth and her family, and Sam's sister Tracy and her family.

Also enjoying the box seats were Sam and Nick's assistant, Shelby Faircloth, and Nick's friend Derek Kavanaugh, who'd brought his baby daughter Maeve. Nick was glad to see Derek getting out again after the devastating loss of his wife Victoria. Derek was talking to Shelby, who held Maeve and laughed with Derek at the baby's antics. Derek seemed more relaxed than Nick had seen him since his life imploded, which was a welcome relief.

The entire group was laughing and cheering, and Scotty had gone from vibrating to bouncing up and down. While he, too, was a lifelong Red Sox fan, something he and Nick had bonded over from the beginning of their friendship, Scotty had become a big fan of the Feds this season. This was especially true since the baseball camp he attended in the District over the summer, at which he'd met the team's all-star center fielder Willie Vasquez.

Willie was now bent at the waist, staring intently at the action unfolding on the mound as Lind wound up and delivered another pitch that was fouled off. The frenzied energy in the stadium deflated a bit as the ball sailed into the seats near left field. But the roar began anew as Lind wound up, delivering a breaking ball that was again fouled off.

Nick glanced down to find Scotty biting his nails as

he stared at the diamond below where the catcher, first baseman and shortstop were conferencing with Lind on the mound.

When he caught Nick watching him, Scotty dropped the hand from his mouth. "This is so stressful."

"Imagine how the players must feel."

"I may not be cut out for professional sports."

The kid was endlessly amusing, which was one of many reasons he and Sam loved him so much. "Well, luckily you have plenty of time to make career decisions, buddy."

"That's true."

When the conference on the mound broke up, Scotty joined the rest of the crowd in clapping and calling out encouragement to Lind.

As the pitcher stared down the batter, Sam's hand clutched Nick's arm—tightly.

He glanced over to find her riveted by the action on the field as Lind delivered. The crack of the bat had thousands of people gasping as the batter raced toward first base, beating the shortstop's throw to the bag.

"It's okay," Nick said, resting a hand on Scotty's shoulder. "It's only one man on." He didn't say that a home run would give the lead to the Giants, because Scotty didn't need to hear that—and he already knew. To Sam, Nick said, "Um, that's starting to hurt."

"Oh, sorry." She released her grip on his arm, but only slightly.

Scotty was biting nails on both hands as Lind walked the next batter in four pitches, indication that his legendary control had been broken by the unexpected hit. Once again, the catcher, first baseman and shortstop approached the mound, this time with the team's pitching coach and manager, Bob Minor, in tow.

"I can't even stand to look," Scotty said, turning his face into Nick's chest.

Nick patted Scotty's back, hoping to provide comfort. "Stay strong, my man. We only need one out."

With adrenaline and anxiety duking it out in his own bloodstream, Nick had to remind himself this was *only a game*, a thought he refrained from sharing with Scotty.

"Time to look again," Nick said as the next batter approached the plate.

Scotty returned his attention to the game, clapping and shouting his encouragement to the team.

Sam's grip again tightened on Nick's arm, but since he loved being her main squeeze, he didn't complain.

Two fouls and three balls later, Nick was looking for something to squeeze. The tension in the ballpark was palpable, especially after the runner on second stole third, landing in a diving slide that took the Feds completely by surprise.

"Crap," Scotty uttered, echoing the sentiments of Feds fans everywhere.

With runners at the corners and one out standing between the Feds and the World Series, every player was on full alert, and every fan was on their feet.

"Come on, come on, *come on*," Scotty chanted as Lind went into the windup.

Another foul into the seats behind home plate.

"I don't know how much more of this I can take," Scotty said.

"Spoken by a Red Sox fan who has only lived

through the decade of success," Skip said from the other side of Sam.

"That's not my fault," Scotty said, making the others laugh.

"Hang in there, pal," Sam said, leaning in front of Nick to address Scotty. "You want to hold hands or something?"

"Nah, my hands are too sweaty."

"I don't mind." Sam extended her hand to Scotty, who grabbed it gratefully.

She and Nick shared a smile, and then she let out a whistle that nearly deafened him. Who knew she could do that?

"Come on, Lind!" she screamed. "Get it done!"

"I think we've made a fan out of her," Nick said to Scotty.

"That's what we get for dragging her to games all summer."

"I can hear you two talking about me."

Nick's retort was swallowed when Lind let loose with another fastball. The crack of the bat silenced the screaming crowd as the ball arced to center field where Willie Vasquez waited patiently. Only because Nick had switched his focus to the giant TV screen in the box, did he see Vasquez take his eye off the ball for a fraction of a second to check the runner on third base.

That fraction of a second was all it took for the stiff breeze to intervene, sending the ball sailing over Willie's head. It took another fraction of a second for Willie to realize what'd happened. By then, right fielder Cecil Mulroney had grabbed the ball and returned it to the infield. But the damage was done. Both runs had scored, and the Giants had taken the lead.

The same fans who'd been cheering so loudly a few minutes ago were now booing even louder, and trash rained down on the outfield from the bleachers.

"I don't understand," Scotty said, his eyes swimming with tears. "How could he miss that? It was an easy fly."

"He took his eye off the ball," Nick said, shocked by the turn of events. "That's all it takes."

As the grounds crew scrambled around the outfield, cleaning up trash that continued to come from the seats above, security wrestled with enraged fans in the bleachers. Nick was glad to be in a skybox, away from the frenzy erupting around the stadium.

Vazquez stood alone in center field, seeming dazed by what had happened.

A tap on Nick's shoulder had him turning to Eric Douglas, one of the Secret Service agents assigned to his detail. They'd been tailing him in the waning days of his reelection campaign, ever since Sam pinned Victoria Kavanaugh's murder on former presidential candidate Arnie Patterson and he'd vowed revenge on her family. "Senator, we'd like to get you and your family out of here," Eric said.

"Not until the game is over," Nick said.

"We'd like to go now. Just in case the situation escalates."

"I can't take Scotty out of here now, Eric."

Sam's pager went off, as did those belonging to Gonzo and Cruz. She checked hers. "Wow, the entire MPD is being put on tactical alert."

"What for?" Nick asked, as a feeling of unease came over him.

"The expectation of rioting." She pointed to the field. "Look."

As he glanced at the action below, uniformed police officers stepped onto the field, armed with serious-looking weapons.

"Special response team," Sam said with a note of pride in her voice.

"They were already here?"

"Hell, yeah. These days we've got to be ready for what happens if the team wins—or if it loses. People go batshit crazy either way. They must be expecting big trouble if they recalled everyone."

His stomach plummeted at the thought of the city erupting in violence and his wife being smack in the middle of it.

"I'm going to drop Christina and Alex at home," Gonzo said to Sam as he hustled his family from the skybox. "I'll see you at HQ."

"Me too," Cruz said, holding Elin's hand as they headed for the exit. "Thanks for the great seats, Nick."

"Gotta go," Sam said with a kiss for Nick and a hug for Scotty. "Try not to take it too hard, buddy. No matter what happens, there's always next year."

"Yeah, I know. Thanks for bringing me to the game. It was exciting to be here, no matter how it ends."

"That's the way to be," she said. "I'll see you guys at home."

"Um, Mrs. Cappuano," Eric said. "We'd prefer that you remain with us."

"I'm sure you would," Sam said with her trademark cheeky grin. "But I've got a job to do, and so do you. You take care of my guys. I'll take care of myself."

Nick tried very hard not to get in the way of her job, but he had a bad feeling about what might happen in the city if the Feds lost. "Sam—" The steely stare she directed his way killed the thought before he voiced it. "Be careful out there, babe."

"I always am." Nick's eyes were glued to her as she said goodnight to her dad and Celia and hugged her sister. He wanted to go after her and find a way to make her stay. But when duty called, as it often did, Sam always went.

"Senator?" Eric's second inquiry was more urgent than the first.

Nick glanced at the field to find the outfield covered in trash and team security surrounding Willie Vasquez as they led him to the dugout, presumably to get him out of harm's way. Didn't the fans know the Feds had three more outs and only needed one run to tie and two to win? It could still be done.

He glanced at Scotty, who watched the scene on the field with a mix of confusion and anger. "I don't understand. Why are they doing this? The Feds still have three more outs. The game isn't over."

"I don't get it either, buddy. Listen, Eric wants to get us out of here in case there's trouble."

"Before the game is over?"

"Yeah, he wants to go now."

"Will they get to finish the game?"

"As soon as they get the fans settled. We can watch the end on TV at home." All at once, Nick was anxious to get the hell out of there, and more important, to get Scotty the hell out of there.

"Okay." Scotty took a last look at the field before he let Nick guide him toward the exit.

The rest of their party followed them to the elevator, which the Secret Service had secured for their descent. How they did that—and the many other things they did with seemingly effortless authority—was a source of constant fascination to Nick.

"I'll make sure Shelby gets home," Derek said in a low voice that only Nick could hear over the conversation in the elevator.

"Oh, thanks. That'd be great. You seemed to have a good time tonight."

Derek focused on Maeve, who had a spit-soaked fist jammed in her mouth. "What's a good time anymore?"

Nick ached for his heartbroken friend. "It's nice to see you out."

"Thanks for asking me. I don't mean to be a downer."

"You're not. You know we all want to help. Any way we can."

"And I appreciate that. I don't know what I would've done without my friends and family the last couple of months."

"Any thoughts about going back to work?" Derek was deputy chief of staff to President Nelson, who, like Nick, was up for reelection next month.

"After the election, if he wins and if he wants me back. I can't even think about wading back into the action at this point."

Nick patted his friend's back. "He'll win, and he wants you back. He's already told you that."

Derek shrugged. "Not sure my heart's in it anymore."

"Give it some time. Don't make any big decisions."

"That's what everyone says."

Over Derek's shoulder, Nick watched Shelby play peekaboo with Maeve, making the little girl laugh.

Her laughter drew a small smile from her dad. "Life goes on, right?"

"You're going to be okay, Derek."

"Keep telling me that. Maybe one day I'll believe it."

"You got it."

TWO

THE SECRET SERVICE agents moved swiftly to usher Nick and his friends to their vehicles. Nick and Scotty were escorted to the large black SUV that had been getting them around for the last two months. Watching Scotty buckle in, Nick was amused by how well the boy had adapted to not only a new family but also the nuisance of around-the-clock protection.

"Sorry about all this, pal."

"All what?"

"Having to leave the game before it's over, the Secret Service, all the hassle."

"Seriously? It's *awesome*. My new friends at school think I'm someone important because the agents follow me around."

"Is that right?"

"Uh-huh. Don't worry, it's cool."

"Would you tell me if it wasn't?"

Scotty took a moment, thought about that. "If I thought there was something you could do about it. It's not like you're thrilled with the Secret Service hanging around."

Nick had been quite vocal about his dislike of being shadowed everywhere he went. "It's annoying as all hell. I didn't appreciate my freedom until it was gone."

"Imagine what it'd be like to be president."

"Yeah." He'd thought about that quite a lot since the

convention and the subsequent buzz about him running for president in four years.

"Do you ever wonder… Nah, never mind."

"Wonder about what?"

"People talk, ya know?"

Nick eyed him warily. "And? What do these *people* say?"

"That my new dad might be president someday and what would that be like. You know, for me."

Scotty was so sweet and considerate, not unlike the twelve-year-old Nick had once been. Nick had lived in constant fear that his grandmother would get tired of having him around and send him to a foster home, so he'd been on best behavior at all times. "What do you tell them when they ask you?"

"That I have no idea. How could I know what that's like until it happens?"

"Good point. Would you want to find out?"

Scotty's big brown eyes got even bigger. "Are you going to do it?"

"I don't know yet. But like you said, there's a lot of talk. It has me thinking about what ifs."

"What does Sam say?"

Nick's laugh was a low rumble. "Mostly she sticks her fingers in her ears and says 'Lalalala, can't hear you.'"

Scotty cracked up. "I can so see her doing that. It's because of her job, right?"

"In part. If anyone would chafe against the restrictions, it'd be her. She'd go nuts being followed around all day. I can't, for the life of me, picture her living like that."

"True."

"And since I can't live without her…all the talk might be a moot point."

"What's a moot point? What does that mean?"

"It means there's probably no point in talking about it when it can't really happen without Sam being on board."

The divider window opened and Eric turned in the passenger seat to face them. "Sorry for the delay, Senator. We're stuck in traffic."

"Any word on the game?"

"It's over. The Feds went down swinging in the bottom of the ninth."

Scotty let out a tortured groan. "We were *so* close."

"They'll be talking about this one for years to come," Eric said with a sympathetic smile for Scotty.

"Poor Willie," Scotty said. "He must be so upset."

"I'm sure he is," Nick agreed.

"I'm going to write him a letter. When we get home, I'm going to write to him and tell him I don't blame him. Accidents happen, even to Major League ballplayers."

Nick's heart swelled with love. "I think that's a brilliant idea, buddy."

They shared a smile that made him so very grateful for the boy who was now his son. Soon enough the adoption would be official. Nick couldn't wait for that day.

SAM ARRIVED AT HQ pissed off about being called into work on a night she'd planned to spend with her guys. They got so few free nights together, especially during Nick's campaign, that she tended to be greedy about every one. She sauntered into the situation room where Chief Farnsworth, Deputy Chief Conklin and Detective

Captain Malone were consulting with the lieutenants who ran the Special Response Team and Patrol Division.

She took a seat next to Detectives Dani Carlucci and Giselle "Gigi" Dominguez, the two third-shift officers under her command. "Well, this blows, huh?" Sam said.

"You said it, LT," Gigi said. "All over a stupid baseball game."

"Too bad people don't go nuts over homelessness or something that matters," Dani added.

"I was just saying that same thing to Christina," Gonzo said as he took a seat behind them.

Freddie came in with Detectives Arnold, McBride and Tyrone.

"The gang's all here," Sam said, nodding to each of her detectives.

"The Feds have lost the game," Farnsworth announced to groans. "The Special Response Team is handling crowd control in and around the stadium along with the FBI and other federal law enforcement agencies who were already on standby in case we needed them. It's my belief that we're going to need them tonight. Everyone listen up as Deputy Chief Conklin hands out assignments."

Conklin gave out the special radio channel the Operations team would monitor during the night and mentioned the cameras the Special Response Team had trained on the stadium were showing increasing unrest in the area. He went through the roster, doling out orders. Everyone became a Patrol officer on a night like this, when the city was overtaken by the unruly masses working out their frustrations over a game gone wrong. "That's it, people," Conklin concluded, after he'd given other tactical instructions. "Let's hit the streets and be careful out there."

Sam waited until the others filed out of the room to approach the brass. Her partner, Freddie Cruz, had been sent out with McBride and Tyrone, leaving with a quizzical look for Sam.

"You forgot someone," Sam said to Conklin.

"No, I didn't." He glanced at Farnsworth. "I'll let you handle this one, sir."

Farnsworth waited until Conklin and Malone left the room before he met Sam's intent gaze.

"What gives?" she asked.

"I need you here, helping with Command and Dispatch."

"With all due respect, sir, that's a bunch of happy horseshit. Tell me what's really going on."

His steel gray eyes hardened. "I could point out that you're being insubordinate, Lieutenant Holland. Again."

"You could but you won't. What's the real story? Why am I being wrapped in swaddling clothing all of a sudden?"

"You know why."

"Arnie Patterson is in jail! This is getting ridiculous! My husband and son have Secret Service agents following them around everywhere they go. I'm being kept off the street."

"Because you refuse to take the threats seriously. Whether you choose to believe it or not, Patterson has a ton of supporters. Your investigation squashed their dream of seeing him in the White House. They blame *you.*"

"Um, hello, he's a murdering, scheming scumbag, and *he* squashed their dreams."

"You know that, and I know that, but try and tell *them* that."

Arnie's disciples had taken to the internet and social media since his arrest to denounce the detective who'd tied the murder of Victoria Kavanaugh to Arnie Patterson and his sons. Most of their vitriol had focused on Sam as the detective who'd uncovered the scheme, even though the FBI had made the actual arrests.

"Until the furor dies down," Farnsworth said, "you're off the streets."

"Even if there's a homicide?"

"We'll cross that bridge when we come to it."

"I need a nice juicy murder to sink my teeth into. It's been weeks and weeks with nothing good to work on."

"You're sick, Holland, you know that?"

"That hurts my feelings."

"What feelings?" he asked with a laugh. "Help with Dispatch, help with Command, help with the reports and don't step foot outside this building without my knowledge, you got me?"

The man she'd once called Uncle Joe rarely pulled rank on her. In fact, he let her get away with everything except murder itself in running her investigations and her division. Because he was often so accommodating, she decided to accommodate him. For now. But this coddling shit couldn't continue much longer without her losing her mind.

"Fine," she said to his back as he left the room. "But after tonight, we're having a conversation about my clipped wings."

He waved to indicate he'd heard her, and Sam kicked the trash can out of frustration. She hated being sidelined due to worries about her safety. Why didn't anyone think she was capable of taking care of herself? She'd been a cop almost thirteen years! And here she was relegated to desk duty on one of the most intense nights the department had seen in years. It wasn't fair.

And while it might not be fair, it was happening, so she put aside her frustration to go figure out where she was needed. In the Dispatch area, she was drawn to the bank of televisions repeatedly broadcasting the ball sailing over Willie Vasquez's head as the commentators talked about a moment that would land in the baseball history books, right next to Bill Buckner's famous bobble that cost the Boston Red Sox a World Series victory in 1986. "This might even be worse than Buckner," one of the broadcasters said grimly.

Her gaze shifted to the next television where Metro Special Response officers were in crowd control formations outside the stadium. Other images included a car on fire, another lying on its side, a shattered storefront and angry mobs of people in the streets.

All over a freaking baseball game.

Choking back her dismay over what was happening to her city as well as her inability to do anything about it, she buckled down to help out in central processing, which was overwhelmed with people being dragged in off the streets by increasingly irritated police officers.

Wanting to drown out the roar of the voices in the station as well as the disturbing images coming from the TVs, she put in her earbuds and let Bon Jovi take her away from it all as she typed reports and tried to stay focused on the menial tasks involved with processing hundreds of arrests.

An hour later, a nearby flurry of activity caught her attention as a man wearing a navy blue jacket with bold yellow FBI letters on the back scuffled with an unruly prisoner who continued to resist arrest right up to the last minute. Sam tugged out her earbuds and went to offer assistance in subduing the man.

The agent caught her gaze, and Sam gasped at the sight of Special Agent Avery Hill's golden brown eyes. "Agent Hill," she said, haltingly after they succeeded wrestling the man into central booking. "We meet again."

"Unfortunate circumstances."

"Are there any other kind in our line of work?" That drew a slow, sexy smile from the man who'd been less than circumspect about his crush on her. Sam cleared her throat as a flurry of nerves made her feel stupid and dismayed. She hated the effect he had on her as she had absolutely no interest in him. "What're you doing here? I thought you were relocating to the West Coast or Outer Mongolia or some such place after we closed the Kavanaugh case."

"That was the plan," he said in the honeyed Southern accent that made the toughest of women want to swoon. Not Sam, though. She liked to think she was immune. "Director Hamilton had other plans for me." His self-deprecating smile exposed an adorable dimple on his left cheek. "Meet the new agent in charge of the Criminal Investigation Division at headquarters."

"Oh," Sam said, thunderstruck by the news. "So you're staying in town?" And closer now than he'd been when he worked out of Quantico. Awesome. Wait until Nick heard this news. He'd tuned into Hill's interest in Sam the first time he met the agent and was none too happy about it.

"Appears that way." He gestured to the guy he'd

brought in. "I offered to transport for Officers Beckett and Dempsey. They had a full car. They should be right behind me with the paperwork."

"Lots of that to do tonight."

"I'm surprised to find you here and not on the streets."

"You and me both," she said with a snarl. "Freaking Arnie Patterson and his freaking threats have gotten me a pair of severely clipped wings."

"Oh, that sucks."

"No kidding. You helped to nail him too. I don't see him threatening you."

"You're much more famous than I am," he said with a teasing grin.

"Screw you."

He raised a brow and seemed to be considering the offer. "Well, I'd better get back out there. Word is the president is calling in the National Guard to help with crowd control. Never seen anything like it in my life."

"All over a baseball game."

"I know. It's insane."

"Congrats on the promotion."

"Thanks." He headed for the main door, but stopped and turned to find her watching him go. That was embarrassing.

"Could I ask you something?" he said, zeroing in on her in that intense way he did so well.

"I guess."

"Your assistant, Shelby."

"What about her?"

"A while back, she asked me to have coffee with her. Since I'll be sticking around, I was thinking I might take her up on the invite."

Sam had no idea what to say to that. "Oh."

"Would that a problem for you?"

"I, um… I don't see why it would be." As long as Shelby kept him far, *far* away from Sam and Nick's house, that would be fine, right? Sam made a mental note to address that with their assistant pronto.

He nodded. "See you around, Sam."

"Right," she said as he went out the door and into the night. "See you." As she went back to her workstation to continue processing arrest reports, she also tried to process the latest info on pesky Agent Hill. She'd thought him long gone to assignments out West, but instead he was not only staying in town but also thinking about going out with their assistant.

Far too close for comfort, she decided.

A few minutes later, Hill came back into the station, seeming a bit shaken. He came right over to the bull pen where she was working. "Lieutenant, I need a word in private, please."

"My office."

They walked in silence to the detectives' pit where Sam gestured for him to go into her office. She shut the door behind them. "What's up?"

"I just got a call from my friend Ray Jestings, the owner of the Feds."

"You're friends with the guy who owns the Feds?"

"We grew up together in Charleston. He married Elle Kopelsman."

Sam blew out a low whistle at the mention of one of Washington's most illustrious families. The Kopelsman family was the closest thing Washington had to royalty. As the owner of the *Washington Star* newspaper, Harlan Kopelsman had campaigned tirelessly for years to bring Major League Baseball to the nation's capital and then died of a massive stroke midway through the team's first season.

Elle was Harlan's daughter, a blonde-about-town who'd made a name for herself as a socialite and philanthropist. When her father died, she took over the *Star* and her husband took control of the team.

"Anyway, Ray told me that Vasquez's wife is frantic because she can't reach him, and according to the team, he left the stadium quite some time ago."

"They let him leave without security? Are they for real?"

"Apparently, he refused the offer of security, and Ray didn't argue with him in light of what they're dealing with in and around the stadium."

"Can you get me the make and model of his car and the plate number? I'll put our people on the lookout for him."

"That's what I was hoping you'd say. I'll get the info for you."

While he called Jestings, Sam tried to formulate a plan for how to go about looking for the missing ballplayer without adding to the unrest in the city.

"Okay," Hill said when he ended the call. "It's a black Lincoln MKZ." He rattled off the D.C. plate number.

Sam relayed the info to Dispatch and asked for an all-points bulletin for the car.

"No APB for him?" Hill asked when she put down the phone.

"You know the rules about 'missing' adults. Until they're missing at least twenty-four hours, there's not much we can do, unless we're dealing with a mental health condition or something like that. He might've gone underground until the furor dies down. I wouldn't blame him if he did."

"Without telling his wife or team where he'd be?"

"Maybe he doesn't want them to know. He's probably embarrassed as all hell and going off to lick his wounds."

"Do you really believe that?"

Exasperated with the cat-and-mouse game, Sam propped her hands on her hips. "Why don't you tell me what *you* believe, Agent Hill?"

"I believe this guy is single-handedly responsible for the Feds losing the game and their first trip to the World Series. I believe there're a lot of people in this city who'd love to get their hands on him. I believe the fact that he's missing and not answering calls from his wife is a sign that he's in some sort of trouble."

"If we put out the word he's missing, it might make things worse."

"You don't trust your people to keep a lid on it?"

"I wish I trusted *all* of them to keep a lid on it, but the temptation would be tremendous. I'm afraid to even do an attempt-to-locate bulletin with the city going ballistic at the moment. All it would take is one patrolman telling his girlfriend, and the next thing we know it's all over Twitter and Facebook that Willie is missing. I have to weigh what's best for the entire city over what's best for Willie."

"Will you be okay with that decision if something happens to him?"

Sam thought about that for a moment. "Yes, I suppose I'll have to be. I'll put my detectives on the lookout for him, but that's as far as I'm willing to go."

"I'm going to look for him too."

"Hill..."

"You can't tell me not to, Lieutenant. You're not the boss of me."

Smiling, she shook her head. "You sound like my nephew Jack. That's his favorite thing to tell his mother."

"How old is he?"

Sam instantly regretted sharing something personal with him. "Almost six."

He winced. "It's been a while since I was compared to a six-year-old."

"I was just going to say be careful, and don't take any chances. Things are crazy enough out there."

"Why, Lieutenant, it almost sounds as if you care."

"I've got enough paperwork to do without adding your bloody carcass to the pile."

He grinned and shook his head. "I'm touched by your concern. I'll let you know if I find anything. You'll do the same?"

She gave a short nod of agreement, even though sharing info with the FBI usually went against her entire belief system. In this case, however, it seemed only fair since Hill had notified her of Vasquez's potential disappearance.

They walked out to the lobby together and went their separate ways without another word. But as always, being around Hill left her feeling off balance and out of sorts. After she'd confronted him about his propensity to stare at her, he hadn't denied being attracted to her.

While the attraction was definitely one-sided, knowing he had a thing for her was weird. Maybe she'd give Shelby a push—or even a shove—in his direction. Whatever it took to get his eyes off her and on to someone else before his staring issue caused her more trouble with Nick.

She sent a text message to all her detectives, letting them know that Willie Vasquez had left the stadium without security and was out of touch with his family and the team. She asked them to keep a lookout for the ballplayer, but to keep his potential disappearance to themselves. It wasn't necessary to explain the need for discretion to any of them. They carried gold shields because they "got it" without having to be led to it.

Determined to shake off the encounter with Hill and her concerns about where Willie Vasquez might be, she put her earbuds back in and turned up the volume on Bon Jovi to drown out her disturbing thoughts. She pounded away on the computer all night until she was so stiff from sitting in one position for hours that she had to stand up and stretch. Through the main door she could see the first hint of pink and orange lighting the sky, signaling the end to what had felt like an endless night of chaos, violence, arrests and paperwork.

One of the dispatchers called her over. "What's up?" she asked.

"Possible homicide." He handed her a slip of paper with an address on Independence and Seventh. "Body in a Dumpster."

"Got it." Sam took a quick look around and saw no sign of the brass. If she couldn't *find* Chief Farnsworth, she couldn't *ask* Chief Farnsworth, right? "Give me ten minutes to get out of here before you tell anyone else about this, got me?"

"Yes, ma'am."

They might be able to sideline her for a riot, Sam thought as she went to her office to retrieve her jacket, keys and radio, but murder was her business. No one was keeping her from that. On the way out of the building through the morgue entrance—where there was minimal chance of being stopped by the endlessly observant chief of police—Sam called Freddie.

"What a night," he said without preamble. "I've never been so tired in my life."

"Better find some caffeine because we just caught a possible murder."

His groan was so loud that Sam held the phone away from her ear. "Meet me at Independence and Seventh, behind Air and Space."

"Be there in fifteen. I thought you weren't allowed out to play."

She bit back the nasty retort that burned the end of her tongue. After all, it wasn't his fault she'd been pulled off the streets, even if she was usually more than happy to take out her aggravations on her partner. "I'm not."

"Yet you're going anyway?"

"Yep." The single word dared him to challenge her. Fortunately, he knew better. "See you there."

As she ended the call with him, her phone dinged with a text message from Nick.

Are they letting you out of there anytime soon?

Just caught a murder.

Oh crap. I guess we'll see you when we see you.

Sorry. How's the boy?

Glum, but looking forward to next season.

Tell him I love him, and I'll see him tonight. You too.

Love you too, babe. Be careful out there.

Always.

She said what she usually did, but she had even more reason to be careful now that she had a son to consider.

Months after Scotty had agreed to come live with them, Sam was still getting used to the fact that he was now a permanent member of their family. She'd wondered if the responsibility of it all would weigh on her, but it didn't. Rather, it filled her with elation and a sense of purpose she'd craved for years.

Maybe she'd never get to have a child of her own. Since Scotty had come into their lives, the ache of that possibility didn't seem quite so acute. She only wished they'd met him when he was much younger than twelve, so they could've had more time together. Regardless, she and Nick would take what they could get where he was concerned.

Driving from HQ to Independence Avenue, Sam got a firsthand view of the carnage that had been left in the wake of the riot. Trash and broken glass littered the streets, and a smoky haze hung over the city. She'd heard that the fire department had received a record number of calls overnight.

It was heartbreaking to see the damage and the wary residents venturing on to the streets to start the big cleanup job.

Something was fundamentally wrong with a society that put so much importance on the outcome of a game, Sam thought as she became increasingly infuriated by what she saw. Smoking hulks of cars, some turned on their sides, blocked her way, forcing her to take a roundabout course to her destination.

Thirty minutes after she left HQ she arrived at Independence Avenue and parked as close as she could get to the back of the National Air and Space Museum, part of the Smithsonian complex. She flashed her badge to the Patrol officers guarding the scene and was waved through.

"What've we got?" she asked the Patrol sergeant.

"A couple of my guys were dragging some crap that was blocking the street to the Dumpsters and found this." He signaled for her to follow him to a set of garbage bins behind the hulking frame of the museum.

Sam shooed away several seagulls as she approached the most fragrant of the four bins and glanced inside to find a man, facedown. "Did you guys touch him at all?"

"Only to check for a pulse."

Since they hadn't identified him, Sam realized she would have to. The vic was well dressed, Sam deduced, based on the quality fabric of the gray suit he wore. From her back pocket, she tugged out a pair of latex gloves. "Did you call the M.E.?" she asked, as she looked for blood on the pavement and found none.

"On her way."

"Good. Give me a boost."

His brows furrowed. "Excuse me?"

"Into the Dumpster," she said, aggravated that she had to explain herself. With her people she never had to explain. They knew. That's why they were detectives, and this guy was still pounding the pavement in Patrol. "You go like this," she said, lacing her hands together. "Then I put my foot in, and you hoist me over. Weren't you ever a kid, Sarge?"

"Very funny," he grumbled. "Pardon me if I've never had an LT ask me to hoist her into a Dumpster before."

"First time for everything," she said with a big grin. "Fun never ends on this job."

"You got a crazy idea of fun, lady."

"I hear that a lot. Ready?"

Frowning, he laced his fingers together and bent at the waist to get low enough for Sam to put her foot into his hands. He propelled her up with more velocity than Sam was expecting, sending her flying into the Dumpster, thankfully clear of the body. She couldn't help but wonder if the sergeant had enjoyed tossing her into the giant trash can. And they said rank had its privileges. Sure it did.

Speaking of rank… The stench of rotten garbage hit her immediately, sucking the air from her lungs. If she'd eaten anything recently, it would've come right back up as she gingerly reached into the victim's back pocket to retrieve his wallet. Since it was still there and still full of cash, she concluded that robbery hadn't been a motive. Placing her fingers on his neck she found him cold to the touch. He'd been there a while.

She flipped open the leather billfold and drew in a deep breath that she instantly regretted due to the stink.

"Who is he?" the sergeant asked.

With a sinking feeling in her stomach, Sam stared at the District driver's license, unable to believe what she was seeing.

"Lieutenant?"

She looked up and met his gaze. "I want everyone out of here. Seal off this alley to even our people and get the M.E. in here the second she arrives."

"You got it." He walked away to see to her orders. Left alone with the remains of Willie Vasquez, Sam's heart broke for the ballplayer, his family and all the fans who'd loved him, especially her own son, who would take this hard.

"Ah, Willie," she whispered. "Why'd you take your eye off the ball?"

THREE

Freddie Cruz arrived a few minutes later, amused to find Sam inside a Dumpster. "Wish I could have a picture of the LT in the Dumpster for the bulletin board in the pit."

"Close your yap and take a gander at who our victim is." Over the top edge of the Dumpster, Sam handed him Willie's billfold.

Freddie took a quick look and then met her gaze, stunned. "Crap."

"This might be a good time for an actual swear word, Detective."

"Shit."

"Better."

"On the way over here, I was listening to WFBR and more than one caller said they'd like to have five minutes alone with Willie. You could hear the rage coming through the airwaves."

"Interesting. We'll have to take a look at that angle." Sam watched as he placed the wallet in an evidence bag. Next she checked to see if Willie had anything else in his pockets that might prove useful to them. A careful search of pants and coat pockets yielded nothing. "Any sign of Lindsey?"

"Not yet. Want a hand out of there?"

"I'll wait with him until she gets here. You got your phone?"

"Yeah," he said warily. "Why?"

"Hand it over. I left mine in the car."

"Do I have to?"

She shot him a perturbed look.

"Well excuse me if I don't want my phone in a Dumpster," he said as he handed it to her.

She needed to call Hill, but Freddie wouldn't have his number. She'd do that as soon as she got back to her own phone. "I don't want my person in a Dumpster, and yet here I am. Where's Gonzo's number on this thing?" she asked, fiddling with it while trying to keep her balance on top of a mountain of trash. The phone nearly flew out of her hand, but she caught it just in time, giving Freddie a sly grin.

"Do *not* drop it. If you do, you owe me a new one."

"Yeah, yeah. Gonzo? Now?"

He walked her through the steps of finding Gonzo's number.

"I don't know why they call these freaking things smart phones. I never feel more stupid than when I try to use one of them."

"There is *so* much I could say to that. So, *so* much."

"And yet you wisely choose not to."

"I heard they're keeping the 2G network alive just for you and that old flip phone of yours."

"Couldn't resist, huh?"

"Nope."

The phone rang and rang. Just when she was about to give up on Gonzo, he picked up.

"What's up, Cruz?"

"It's Sam."

"Oh, Lieutenant. Sorry. What's going on?"

"We've caught a homicide. Willie Vasquez."

"Get the fuck outta here."

Now that was the kind of language she expected from her officers at times like this. "Keep a lid on it. I'm not looking for the city to erupt again."

"Right. Of course. What can I do?"

"I know you're just off an overnight, but Cruz told me they're airing out the game on the radio. I need you to monitor sports talk this morning. Get a handle on what's being said about the game, about him, about the fans. Take note of anyone who seems a little too angry, if you catch my drift."

"Will do. What else?"

"Dig into his life. I need all the usual info, including financials."

"Got it. Where'd you find him?"

"In a Dumpster behind Air and Space."

"Whoa," Gonzo said. "Tossing him in the trash. That makes a statement, huh?"

"Sure does. Freaking sports in this country. Totally out of hand."

"No kidding. I'm on it and will report in when I have something. So Farnsworth released you from time-out, huh?"

"Um, not exactly."

Gonzo's bark of laughter made Sam smile. "I love it," he said.

"Get to work, Detective." She ended the call and passed the phone back to Freddie, who handled it gingerly before jamming it into his coat pocket. "Where the hell is McNamara?"

"Here I come," Lindsey called. "Sorry for the delay. The streets are a mess. What've we got?"

Sam filled Lindsey in and then told Cruz to help the M.E. into the Dumpster.

As she came over the top, Lindsey's nose wrinkled at the scent. Her ponytail bobbed from side to side as she landed next to Sam. She took a series of photos of the victim. "Help me turn him over."

Sam held her breath at the stench as she took his feet while Lindsey worked the shoulders. His face was unmarked, but a huge pool of blood covered what had once been a white dress shirt.

Lindsey took more photos. "Looks like a stab wound," Lindsey said, moving in for a closer look.

"Only one?"

"I can't tell for sure until I get him back to the morgue."

"No defensive wounds on his hands," Sam said. "No other visible injuries." After she encased his hands with paper bags to seal in any evidence, Lindsey signaled for her team to bring over the stretcher and body bag. "Let's get him out of here."

Sam and Lindsey worked together with Cruz's help to lift Willie out of the Dumpster into the waiting hands of two members of the medical examiner's staff.

One of them was a young man with blond hair and blue eyes that bugged when he recognized the victim.

Sam repeated her tight lid orders to Lindsey and her team. "Don't tell anyone about this. That means *no one*."

"Y-yes, ma'am," the blond kid said. He and his partner zipped Willie into a body bag.

With her hands on the edge of the Dumpster, Sam jumped down to the alley, narrowly missing Cruz, who scooted out of her way. He'd been watching the removal of Willie's body and hadn't seen her coming.

She flashed him a grin as he recoiled from the smell of her.

"Commandeer a Patrol car to take me home to change," she said to her partner.

"Do I have to go with you?"

She dropped her keys into his hand. "After you get my phone out of the car, you can bring it to HQ."

"Oh, thank God," he said as he walked away to break the bad news to one of the patrolmen.

Sam reached up to help Lindsey down.

When she was back on terra firma, Lindsey pulled off her latex gloves. "This is going to be huge."

"Aren't they all?"

"Some are bigger than others."

"True." Sam's mind raced, putting together a dog-choking to-do list. She'd wanted a juicy murder to sink her teeth into. This was about as juicy as it got. Maybe there was something wrong with her, but she lived for this shit.

Before the word got out about their victim's identity, she needed to consult with the department brass about making sure the city was as locked down as it could be to prevent more rioting and violence. However, the minute she contacted Farnsworth she'd probably be put back in time-out. That couldn't happen, she thought, mulling the dilemma as she walked with Lindsey from the alley to Independence Avenue.

She saw Freddie point to her, and the Patrol officer he was talking to shook his head. Sam nearly laughed at the pained expression on the officer's face.

"I'm going home to change. I'll see you at the morgue shortly."

"I'll get right on it," Lindsey assured her. "Thanks, Doc."

Lindsey shook her head, dismay stamped into her expression. "Just think, this time yesterday he was getting ready for the biggest game of his career, and now he's dead."

"Sad to think that one error in a distinguished career could've led to this."

"Some disgruntled fan probably decided to teach him a lesson."

"Probably," Sam said, although she'd learned to look beyond the obvious when investigating murder. "See you back at HQ."

"See ya there."

After Lindsey got into the passenger side of the medical examiner's van and it sped away, Sam called Cruz over. "Get Crime Scene here and have them do a thorough search of all the Dumpsters and nearby trash receptacles. We're looking for the murder weapon, most likely a knife. Remember—tight lid. This can't get out until we're ready to let it out."

"Yes, ma'am," Cruz said, sucking up as always, but she could count on him to manage the scene until the CSU detectives took over. He handed her phone over. "I'll meet you back at HQ in an hour." When she was satisfied that he had the situation under control, Sam went to make the day of the Patrol officer Cruz had tapped to drive her home.

Once settled in the back of the Patrol car with an extremely disgruntled patrolman driving her home with all the windows open, Sam made the call to Hill.

"What's up?" he asked when he answered.

"WV is dead," she said, keeping her voice as low as possible so the patrolman wouldn't hear her.

"What? I can't hear you."

"The person we spoke of during the night... Dead."

"Oh, fuck. Seriously?"

"Yes."

"How?"

"Stabbed in the chest and tossed in a Dumpster behind Air and Space."

"Christ."

"I'm on my way home to shower after digging him out of the Dumpster, and then I'm heading back to HQ. I could use your help on gaining access to the team if you're game. No pun intended."

"Sure, yeah. I can help with that."

"Let me get with my brass and figure out how we're going to play this one, and then I'll get back to you."

"Thanks for letting me know."

"I'm sorry to say you were right about this."

"Hell of a thing to be right about."

"Judging from his appearance, he's been dead a while."

"Where do we even begin to get to the bottom of this one?" Hill asked, his tone weary.

"I haven't the first clue, but we'll get it done. We always do."

GONZO ARRIVED AT the apartment he shared with his fiancée, Christina Billings, and his young son. Alex crawled to the door when he heard Gonzo come in. The crawling was new, and while keeping track of the baby had become more complicated since he'd figured out how to get around on his own, Gonzo loved watching his son grow and thrive.

"Dada," Alex said, raising his chubby arms. Gonzo's heart melted as he scooped up the dark-haired little boy who looked just like him and spun him around.

"Careful," Christina said, emerging from their bedroom in one of the sharp, sexy suits she wore to work as Nick's chief of staff. Her blond hair was tamed into a sophisticated twist that Gonzo loved to mess up when she got home from a long day on Capitol Hill or on the campaign trail. "He's got a belly full of oatmeal that won't look good all over you."

"Ohhh," Gonzo said to Alex, "Mama saves the day." Rather than swing the little guy around, Gonzo tickled his belly, drawing a deep chortle from Alex. "I love that laugh."

"And you go to astonishing lengths to make him do it," Christina said, sliding into sky-high heels as she smiled at them.

"Want me to take him to Ang?" Gonzo asked. Sam's sister Angela watched Alex for them during the day.

"It's on my way. I don't mind dropping him off." She came over to him, caressed Gonzo's scruffy jaw and kissed him.

Alex made a kissy face that made them both laugh. "Long night, huh?" Christina said.

"Very long and not over yet." Because he trusted her with his life as well as his son, he told her about Willie.

"Oh my God, you're kidding."

"Wish I was."

"God," she said again. "What's wrong with this world?"

"Too many things to list when you've got somewhere to be."

Her wistful expression had him wondering what she was thinking, but Alex yanked on his hair, wanting his attention. Gonzo kissed his son's neck until he was giggling madly. "You need to go see Ang and the kids, buddy."

"Jack," Alex said. Angela's son's name had been the boy's first word, which had been an endless source of hilarity to all of them. No *mama* or *dada* for his boy. Nope, he was already out making friends.

"You'll see Jack after school, but baby Ella will be there," Gonzo said as he handed Alex over to Christina. "Thanks for watching him, babe." He still felt guilty when his work kept him away from home for long hours.

"You know I love him as much as you do."

"I know." He kissed her cheek and then her lips. "We need a night alone. Soon."

"I'd be all for that. Name the time and place, Detective."

"I'll work on that."

"Will you be here later?"

"I gotta sleep at some point, but I'll be working from here for a while today. Not sure what's going on, schedule-wise. Let me know if you need me to get Alex from Angela's later."

"We've got a free night on the campaign tonight, so I may be home at a decent hour. I'll text you."

"Sounds good. Love you guys."

"Love you too," she said on the way out the door with his son in her arms. She'd been such a trouper about stepping up for Alex—and for him—since he'd learned about the son he'd fathered with a woman he'd been with exactly once. Lori Phillips. The name had barely registered with him when he first heard about the baby. Now it gave him nightmares as a custody battle loomed.

He'd kept a lot of the details from Christina, not wanting to worry her in the midst of Nick's reelection campaign when she was so busy and distracted. Thinking now of Lori, he recalled the message he'd received yesterday from his lawyer Andy. He'd put off returning the call because he'd been in such a great mood before the baseball game and hadn't wanted to hear whatever bad news Andy might have for him.

Now, however, he placed the call to Andy, knowing he couldn't put it off forever, as much as he wanted to. "Hey, Tommy," Andy said when he came on the line a minute later. "So I've heard back from Lori's attorney. Apparently, she's successfully completed rehab, ended her relationship with Rex and moved into a two-bedroom apartment."

Each bit of information hit Gonzo like knives to the heart. He had no illusions about why Lori was working so hard to get her life together.

"Tommy? Are you there?"

"I'm here. Waiting for the really bad news."

"Here it is—she intends to file for full custody." The breath left his lungs in a whoosh. His legs buckled, and he dropped onto the sofa. "You can't be serious. He's lived with me for more than six months. All that time she's had hardly any interest in him."

"I don't think that's exactly true. She's been in rehab for a lot of those months."

"And in the meantime, we've become a family. My fiancée has become his mother."

"She's not technically his mother, and you both know that."

"Still…"

"I get it. Trust me, I definitely see this from your point of view, but the fact remains that Lori is his biological mother, and she does have rights."

"Rights," Gonzo snorted. "What about my son's rights?"

"He has them too, and the court will take them into consideration."

"So you see this going to court?" Gonzo asked, a sinking feeling invading his abdomen.

"I do, unless you and Lori are able to come to some sort of arrangement on your own."

That was highly unlikely, Gonzo thought, as he hadn't even spoken to the woman in months.

"How do you wish to proceed?" Andy asked. "I could set up a meeting with Lori and her attorney. Give you two a chance to hammer this out amicably."

"Do you recommend that?"

"It's always advised to keep things as friendly as you can for as long as you can. Perhaps you can work out something that works for both of you, short of going to court."

"I don't want anything less than full custody."

"You need to be prepared for the fact that she wants the same thing."

"She can't possibly have as strong a case as I do as the parent who has cared for him all this time."

"Maybe not, but she is the child's mother, Tommy, and the court will be pleased by the changes she's made. It shows that she has good intentions."

"Where were her good intentions when she hadn't

even bothered to give my son a name months after he was born?" Gonzo couldn't keep the bitterness from creeping into his tone.

"Should I set up the meeting?"

Gonzo thought about it for a long moment, weighing the pros and cons. "Yeah, go ahead. See if you can make it for after the election. Christina has enough on her plate between now and then."

"I'll see what I can do and be back in touch. Hang in there, okay?"

"I'm trying. Thanks, Andy."

"No problem. Talk soon."

Gonzo put his phone on the coffee table and reached for one of the teddy bears Alex slept with. The scent of baby shampoo and powder clinging to the bear brought tears to his eyes. Thinking of a long, protracted, expensive battle with Lori only added to his weariness. All he wanted was a peaceful life with Christina and Alex and any other children they might be blessed with. Was that too much to ask?

Apparently, he thought bitterly. He could never regret the one-night stand that had brought Alex into his life so unexpectedly last winter. At the time, he'd been stunned to learn he had a son with a woman he barely remembered. Now he couldn't imagine a day, let alone a life, without the boy at the center of it. He'd fight for him with everything he had for as long as it took to ensure their family stayed together.

The thought of telling Christina that they might be in for a fight with the baby's mother filled him with pain.

They'd both submitted to the fantasy of letting Alex think of her as his mother. Why wouldn't they when his real mother barely showed an ounce of interest in him?

Christina was amazing with him, as devoted to him as she was to Gonzo. They'd barely begun dating when Lori dropped the bomb on him about Alex, but Christina had rolled with it from the beginning. It was simple, she always said, she loved him, and she loved his son.

Gonzo got up and flipped on the radio, tuning it to WFBR, the station owned by the Feds. Then he went into the kitchen to brew a pot of coffee that would be critical to remaining awake after the night without sleep. He got busy on his laptop digging into Willie Vasquez's life and listened to the hate spewing forth from angry fans on the radio. But all the while, his thoughts were on the little boy he loved and the looming fight to keep him where he belonged.

FOUR

SAM ARRIVED HOME in time to catch Nick as he was about to leave for the Hill. When she came in the door, his gorgeous face lit up with that sexy grin she loved so much. “This is a nice surprise,” he said, approaching her, his intentions obvious.

She held up her hands to stop him from getting any closer and started stripping out of her foul clothes right inside the front door.

“Scotty and Shelby?”

“Left ten minutes ago.”

Removing the holster that held her service weapon, she put it on a table next to her badge and cuffs.

Nick’s eyes widened and his mouth fell open as he took in the striptease. “To what do I owe this unexpected show?”

“I’ve been Dumpster diving.”

“Seriously?”

“Yep. That’s where someone tossed Willie Vasquez after they stabbed him to death.”

All the color drained from her husband’s cheeks as he gasped. “No…”

“Afraid so.”

“Oh my God. Scotty…”

“I know. That was my first thought too.” She picked up her clothes and sneakers. “Sorry, but I’ve got to take a shower.”

"Sure," he said absently, still processing the news. "Go ahead."

"Come up with me."

He checked his watch and then followed her upstairs to their bedroom where she dropped her clothes and sneakers into the washer located in their bathroom, dumped in twice the usual amount of detergent and set the water to the hottest setting.

Then she turned the water to boiling in the shower. "I'll be quick," she said to her husband.

"I'd rather you be thorough."

That drew a laugh from Sam as she stepped under the hot water and got busy scrubbing every square inch of her body. The last time she'd scrubbed her skin so hard was after Clarence Reese blew his brains out while standing right next to her. Thinking about that awful day made her shudder as she turned her thoughts to the latest case.

Where to even begin figuring out who killed Willie when every person in the metropolitan area had motive after his blunder cost the home team an easy victory the night before?

As she worked conditioner through her long hair, she pondered that question and others, including whether she'd even be allowed to work the case. That was a battle she'd willingly fight as the most seasoned Homicide detective in the city. Farnsworth would be crazy to trust such a potentially explosive case to anyone but her, and while the chief could be stubborn at times, he was far from crazy.

By the time she emerged from the shower, she was fortified and ready to do battle with her superiors on behalf of Willie Vasquez. Whoever killed the star ballplayer had better be ready to deal with her, because she was coming after them, and she would find them.

Nick was sitting on their bed when she came out of the bathroom wearing a white robe and her hair wrapped up in a towel.

Even though neither of them had time, she plopped down next to him and reached for his hand. "Are you okay?"

"I'm thinking about Scotty."

"I have been too."

"Is there any chance of him hearing about this at school?"

"I don't think so. We're keeping it quiet until we notify Willie's family and figure out how to proceed."

"I'm going to pick up Scotty at dismissal time so he won't hear it from anyone else."

"Do you have time to do that?" His schedule was insane as the campaign wound toward the election.

"No, but I'm going to anyway. I'll let Shelby know." He turned to face her. "There's something else I need to tell you."

"That sounds ominous."

"It's not really, but I have a feeling you're not going to like it."

She braced herself, preparing for whatever he might say. "Hit me."

"I got a call from the White House this morning."

"It still blows my mind to be married to someone who says things like that."

His face lifted into the half grin that often made her want to swoon. Not that she actually swooned. Badass cops did not swoon. She only thought about it. "Focus, babe."

She focused on his smoothly shaven jaw, the dark brown hair that curled at the ends, the sexy hazel eyes and the sinfully beautiful mouth. Taken all together, his features made for one hell of an appealing package. "Okay, sorry."

"Nelson is taking a quick trip at the end of the week. He invited me to go along."

His words permeated her brain. "A quick trip to where?"

"I'm not allowed to say."

"Not even to me?"

"Not to anyone."

"Is he going to Afghanistan?"

"I can't tell you that, Sam. I'm sorry. I want to. I know you tell me stuff I'm not supposed to know all the time, but I can't do it with the president's security on the line. I hope you understand."

Sam didn't need him to confirm where they'd be going. Virginia had suffered significant losses in the war zone in the last year. It stood to reason that President Nelson would ask members of the commonwealth's congressional delegation to go with him.

"How will you get where you're going?"

"On *Air Force One*." His eyes lit up as he said the words. "How freaking cool is that?"

"Pretty darned cool," she said, even though her insides had gone cold at the thought of her beloved husband flying into a war zone on a gigantic airplane that bore the flag of the United States of America. "Won't it be dangerous?"

He thought about that for a second, probably trying to find a way to answer her question without giving anything away. "Maybe a little, but the trip is top secret.

No one will know. Even the reporters that come with us won't know where we're going until we're there." Tipping his head, he eyed her. "What're you thinking?"

"It scares me to think of you flying into somewhere dangerous."

"I'll be on the most secure airplane in the world, babe. Nothing to worry about."

"Sure," she said. "Whatever you say."

He put his arm around her and drew her in close. She nuzzled her nose into his neck, drinking in the scent of the cologne he'd recently applied. It was one of her favorite smells in the entire world. "Would you stay home if I asked you to?"

"Would you stay home today if I asked you to?"

"Yes," she said with a sigh, his point clear. "But you'd never ask me to."

"No, I wouldn't."

"It scares me."

"It scares me every time you walk out that door, knowing there're people out there who hate you just because of the badge you carry. Not to mention your psycho ex-husband who hates you because you love me. It scares me to know that you can nearly get shot in the face when you stop to buy a bagel."

Nick pressed a line of kisses over the fading scar on her face, earned during a robbery she walked in on over the summer. When she'd jumped the guy from behind, he'd pistol-whipped her face, laying open her cheek.

"I don't like it when you pit your much bigger fears against my smaller, mostly insignificant fears."

His chuckle rumbled from his chest as he pressed another kiss to the top of her head. "I'm not a hundred percent sure I can go yet. It'll take some juggling of campaign events."

Was it wrong of her to hope he couldn't get out of them? "But you want to go. Right?"

"Babe… It's the president and *Air Force One*. Yeah, I want to go—but not just because of the super cool plane. Where we're going, why we're going… It's important or I'd never do it."

"I understand."

"Do you really?"

"Not yet, but I'll try to get there by the time you go."

"While you were in the shower I was thinking about Scotty. With Willie being murdered, I might need to stick around for him."

"It's a quick trip, right?"

"They said we'd be gone about forty hours total."

"I can handle things here for forty hours."

He squeezed her again and kissed her. "You're the best wife ever."

"We both know that's not true."

"You're the best wife I've ever had."

Sam laughed and slugged his arm as she got up. "I walked right into that. Can you and your detail give me a lift to HQ on the way to the Hill?" It was out of their way, but she knew he would do it if he could.

"Happy to, but where's your car?"

"Cruz is meeting me there with it. I didn't want to stink it up."

"So how'd you get home?"

"I stunk up a Patrol car."

"You're all heart, babe."

"Aren't I?"

"I'll wait for you downstairs."

"I'll be quick." In the bedroom across the hall that served as her closet, Sam found a clean pair of jeans folded neatly on a shelf that was now devoted to jeans. The unusual organization stopped her short. Who had done that? Ugh, Tinker Bell!

Sam needed to tell Shelby to expend her organizational energy elsewhere. She liked her mess exactly the way it was. She pulled on a wool sweater and found socks and a pair of hiking boots to complete her ensemble. If she would be putting in long hours, she'd be doing it in comfort.

She ran downstairs and heard Nick talking to someone. He was in the kitchen with Shelby, going over one of her famous lists.

"Morning," she said to Sam. "Coffee?"

"Yes, please." It was rather nice to have freshly made coffee waiting for her. She'd give Shelby that much credit. "No organizing my closet, Tinker Bell."

"I didn't do hardly anything in there."

"The jeans were folded."

"Oh my God," Nick said, scandalized. "You didn't!"

"I did," Shelby said with a teasingly glum expression. The tiny blonde wore a pink sweat suit that resembled high fashion on her. "My apologies. It won't happen again."

"Good," Sam muttered, not amused by their teasing. "Ready to go?" she asked Nick.

"Whenever you are. I've got Scotty after school," Nick said to Shelby. "I'll take him back to the office with me for a couple of hours."

"He'll enjoy that."

"What kid wouldn't?" Sam asked. "All that legislating and backstabbing." She shivered. "So exciting." As

Shelby giggled behind her hand, Nick shot his wife a playful snarl and headed for the living room.

"Let's go, Lieutenant."

Taking advantage of a second alone with Shelby, Sam lowered her voice. "You asked out Agent Hill?"

Shelby seemed shocked by the question. "How do you know that?"

"Yes or no. Did you?"

"Maybe. Now tell me how you know."

"He might've mentioned it to me."

"You saw him? Where?"

"At work. Duh. Where do you think I saw him?"

"I bet he looked good enough to eat."

"I refuse to dignify that with a response. You may be hearing from him."

"Oh my God. Seriously? Tell me everything he said."

"As fun as that return to high school would be, I've got to get to work. Keep him far, far away from here. You got me?"

"Why don't you like him?"

"Come on, Sam," Nick called.

"Far away. That's all I'm saying." Sam left the room before Shelby could continue the conversation. She grabbed her coat, strapped on her weapon, shoved her badge and notebook into her back pocket, and put her cuffs in her coat pocket before she ran out the door.

Nick was already in the black SUV with the tinted windows. One of the agents waited for her at the curb, holding the door for her.

When she got in, Nick was on the phone with Christina.

Sam buckled in as they pulled away from the curb. Even though she'd made fun of the lack of excitement at his office, she loved watching him in senator mode. He consulted with his chief of staff about the invitation to join the president for a quick trip.

"I'll tell you when I get there," he said, glancing at Sam.

"Why does she get to know where you're going, but I don't?" Sam asked.

Nick held the phone away from his mouth. "Because she has a security clearance, and you don't."

"I need to get me one of them." Agent Hill had rubbed his top-secret clearance in Sam's face, using it as an excuse to insert himself into the Kavanaugh investigation. Despite his staring issues, he wasn't a bad guy and had been invaluable to her during that case. Not that she'd ever tell her husband that. He saw red where Agent Hill was concerned.

She checked the clock on her phone. It had been an hour since they found Willie, and it would be a while yet before Lindsey had anything for her. So she would start at Willie's home address and then head for the ballpark with Hill. As always, the media would be on her like white on rice the second the word got out about Willie's murder, but she could handle the reporters. She'd stonewall them the way she always did for as long as she could.

Nick ended the call with Christina and tucked his cell phone into his suit coat pocket. "What're you thinking about over there?"

"Where to start to find a murderer when everyone in the city had a motive."

"That's a tough one, but you'll figure it out. You always do."

"If I'm allowed to run it."

"Why wouldn't you be?"

"Farnsworth doesn't want me on the streets with Arnie's people running loose."

"Can't say I disagree with him, babe. A lot of Arnie's followers are among the affectionately termed 'loony fringe.' I wouldn't put it past them to take a shot at you looking to vindicate him."

"Be that as it may, Arnie's ass is staying in jail. We've got him screwed, glued and tattooed."

Nick chuckled. "I'd never heard that expression until I met you."

"See how I've broadened your horizons?"

His hand landed on her thigh. "Speaking of broadening horizons… Have you given any more thought to what we talked about the other night?"

She'd thought of little else until she found Willie Vasquez dead in a Dumpster. "Some."

"And?"

"I don't know yet."

"Do you want to talk about it some more?"

"At some point."

"I'm not pressuring you, babe. You know that, right?"

"I don't feel pressured."

"Good." He squeezed her thigh and removed his hand. "I'd never want that."

Her body tingled at the reminder of their most recent interlude in the loft he'd put together to remind them of their honeymoon in Bora Bora. Their sex life had heated up even more than usual over the summer, and they'd been doing a lot of experimenting ever since. "I know." She paused for a moment, choosing her words carefully. "I need to tell you something."

"What's that?"

Even though it went against her nature to be forthcoming with potentially troublesome information, she'd learned the hard way to be truthful with her husband. It saved her a shitload of aggravation where he was concerned. "Hill has been promoted to agent in charge of criminal investigations. He's moved to D.C. permanently. He grew up with the Feds' owner, Ray Jestings, so we'll be calling on him for assistance with the investigation. I wanted to be upfront with you about his involvement, so there's no trouble between us over it."

Nick's expression never changed, but his lips tightened, a sure sign that he was annoyed.

When they arrived at HQ, the agents brought the SUV to a stop outside the main entrance. "Thanks for telling me about Hill." He looked over at her, slaying her with those amazing hazel eyes that saw right through her. "You've come a long way, babe."

"What does that mean?"

"Not that long ago, you would've kept that tidbit to yourself and hoped I wouldn't find out you were working with him again. While I wish he'd go away and never come back, I'm glad you told me yourself."

"Even an old dog like me can learn a few new tricks. I can be trained."

Rolling his eyes, he let out a guffaw of laughter. "You? Trained? That'll be the day." He leaned over to leave her with a kiss. "I love you."

She patted his face and kissed him back, even though they were outside HQ and inside her no-PDA-zone. The tinted windows on the SUV preserved their privacy.

"Love you too. I'll see you when I see you. Take good care of our kid later. He's going to need a shoulder."

"He'll have both of mine for as long as he needs them."

"He's a lucky boy."

"I'm the lucky one. Be careful. Watch your back."

"I will. Don't worry."

"What? Me worry? Go to work, babe."

Even after almost a year together, she still hated to leave him. But she had a job to do, and so did he, so she got out of the car and waved as the SUV sped off toward the Capitol.

FIVE

SAM HEADED FOR the main doors at HQ, through the courtyard that would be mobbed with reporters once the word got out about Willie.

She was holding a mock news conference in her head, thinking about how she might approach the press without igniting another riot, when she smacked into a hard wall of white chest that sported a gold badge. Shit.

"In my office, Lieutenant. Right now."

Sam let out a huff of aggravation as she followed the chief to his suite, which was located behind the Dispatch area.

The chief's receptionist gave Sam a sympathetic smile when she passed the desk, which only made Sam more anxious about the reaming she was in for.

He stood at the door, stone-faced as she walked past him.

The slam of the door behind her made her startle. "What part of 'don't step foot outside this building without me knowing about it' did you not understand, Lieutenant?"

"I looked for you. I couldn't find you."

"Since I was here all night, I'd say you didn't look very hard."

"I didn't want to bother you with something I could easily handle."

"Which is how you ended up in a Dumpster with a dead body."

"Yes. It's Willie Vasquez. The body, that is."

His face went blank for a second before he recovered his mojo. "You're kidding me."

"Wish I was."

"Ah, God." All at once he looked exhausted and every bit his sixty-plus years. "We just got things under control, and now this."

"My first stop will be his home, followed by the ballpark to speak to the team leadership."

"I don't want you on this one, Sam. Assign it to one of your people."

"Sir, with all due respect—"

"I said assign it to someone else."

"And what am I supposed to do? Sit in the office and twiddle my thumbs?"

"There's plenty you can do without being on the street."

"You know that's not true. There's no way I can run an investigation of this magnitude without being out there doing what I do."

He went around his desk and sat down, seeming as if the weight of the world rested on his formidable shoulders.

"You know I can take care of myself, Uncle Joe," she said this softly, using her old name for him for the first time since she'd been under his command.

"Something's always happening to you."

"And yet here I am, still providing a daily pain in your ass."

"I wouldn't have it any other way. You know that." Their rare foray into sentiment was no doubt due to the long night they'd both put in, but Sam wasn't above using it to her advantage. "I also know you care about me, and I appreciate that. But you've got to let me do my job. I'm the most qualified detective to handle a case like this. You know that as well as I do."

Watching him as he weighed the decision, she noticed he'd aged since she'd last looked closely. When had that happened? The observation left her strangely unsettled. Men like her dad and Uncle Joe were supposed to stay forever young and live for as long as she needed them, which was always.

"I don't think I've ever told you that Marti and I weren't able to have kids of our own," he said, further startling her. "We had you and your sisters, our nieces and nephews… You all were our kids. I think we've done a good job, you and me, of navigating the personal as we deal with the professional. But if you think it's ever easy for me to send you out into harm's way, you don't know me at all, Sam. Someone threatened one of my officers, but they also threatened one of my kids—one of my favorite kids. Don't forget that."

She stared at him, astounded and moved and uncertain of what she should say, which didn't happen very often. "I… I won't forget. I won't ever forget."

"See that you don't." He combed his fingers through wiry gray hair in a gesture filled with exhaustion and resignation. "Run Vasquez, report directly to me, watch your back and don't take any foolish chances, you got me?"

"Yes, sir."

Because of what he'd said, because he'd been her Uncle Joe a lot longer than he'd been her chief, because she loved him, she went around the desk, put her hands on his shoulders and kissed his cheek. "I love you too."

As she walked toward the door, he said, "I never said I loved you." His gruff tone was more in keeping with what she'd come to expect from him.

"You didn't have to." She smiled all the way back to the pit.

READY TO DO battle on Willie's behalf, Sam strolled into the pit to find it empty except for Cruz, who was sprawled out in his office chair, sound asleep. Was there something wrong with her that she took perverse pleasure in booting the chair and sending him flying into the wall of his cubicle? The look on his face when he came to and realized she'd caught him asleep in the pit was priceless.

"Up and at 'em, Sleeping Beauty. We've got work to do."

"You enjoyed that, didn't you?"

"I don't know what you're talking about. Where is everyone?"

"Home sleeping if they're smart."

"Aren't you the lucky one to be teamed up with the LT?"

"The luck never ends. Don't you need sleep like the rest of us mere mortals?"

"I'll have lots of time to sleep when I'm dead. In the meantime, let's hit the morgue."

"If I'm going to be expected to work twenty-four hours straight, I need food. Real food. Not sprouts and weeds and that crap you consider food."

He needed a hit of grease to restore his equilibrium. Since she needed him performing at top capacity, she decided to indulge him. “I’ll feed you after we hit the morgue.”

“That ought to do wonders for my appetite.”

In the morgue, they found Lindsey working on Willie’s autopsy, assisted by her deputy, Dr. Byron Tomlinson.

“Give me something, give me anything,” Sam said as she strolled into the examination room with Cruz in tow. He took one glance at the Y-shaped cut in Willie’s chest and looked away.

“So far all I can tell you is we’re looking at a single stab wound to the chest that severed his aorta,” Lindsey said.

“Look at the angle.” Byron pointed to the wound. “Judging by the angle of entry, my guess is the perp is a lefty.”

“Could they have come at him from behind?” Sam asked.

“Not likely,” Lindsey said. “I’m thinking it was a seven-to-nine-inch blade. They wouldn’t have been able to get the angle needed to reach the aorta from behind. I’m leaning toward a front-facing attack, a one-shot deal that took him out very quickly.”

“And it would’ve made a big mess,” Byron added. “The aorta blowing would’ve been like a geyser when the knife was pulled from his chest.”

“Let’s hope CSU gets us a murder weapon.” Sam reached for her phone to place a call to the Patrol lieutenant, then cursed under her breath when she got his voice mail.

“That would help,” Lindsey agreed. “We’re running toxicology and other labs now. We’ll let you know if we get any hits.”

"Thanks, Doc. We're on the street, so hit my cell."

"I thought you were grounded," Lindsey said.

"Not anymore."

Chuckling and shaking her head, Lindsey gave her a thumbs-up. "I don't know how you do it, Holland."

"Charm, Doc. It's all charm."

Cruz snorted loudly as he followed her from the morgue, earning him a glare. "Something wrong with your nose?"

"Nothing a little sleep wouldn't fix."

"Don't act like you'd sleep if I sent you home." He and his girlfriend Elin spent half their lives screwing like bunnies, or so it seemed as he showed up sleepy and dopey-looking to every crime scene, no matter what time of day or night.

"I'd sleep." He gave her the slow, lazy grin that drove the girls crazy—other girls, of course. Not her. "After."

"Ewww. Spare me the details and drive me to Georgetown."

"What's in Georgetown?"

"Willie's condo."

"You promised there'd be food."

"And there will be. Soon. We have to notify the family, and I can't do that on a full stomach."

"Right. Me either."

He understood. There was nothing either of them hated more than having to tell people their loved ones had been murdered.

"What's the address?" he asked as he drove her car out of the parking lot.

Sam consulted her notebook where she'd jotted down the details from the license in Willie's wallet. "3032 K

Street, Northwest. What did you do with Willie's wallet?"

"Inventoried and photocopied everything and locked the wallet with the cash in the evidence locker."

"Good. Get Gonzo on the phone."

"Anything else you want me to do while I'm driving you around, your highness?"

"That'll do for now, but thanks for asking."

He grunted out a laugh and had Gonzo on speaker half a minute later.

"Speak to me," Sam said. "What've you got?"

"You gotta stop calling me on Cruz's phone. You're freaking me out."

Despite the horrible errand they were headed to do, Sam flashed a big smile in Freddie's direction.

"You make her day when you say that stuff," Cruz told his friend.

"I can only imagine."

"Where are you right now?" she asked. "Almost to HQ."

"Ask Malone to figure out who owns the cameras in the area behind Air and Space and adjacent locations. I'm assuming they belong to the Smithsonian, not us, so we need to get warrants. I want as much film as we can get from the ballpark too. Especially the players' parking lot and anything you can get from the Potomac Avenue area."

"Got it. Will do."

"Gimme what you've got on Vasquez."

"Pulling over so I can refer to the notes." Less than a minute later, he said, "Born in Santo Domingo in the Dominican Republic on February 10, 1985. Parents are Carlos and Belinda Vasquez. Willie was a stand-out baseball player from the time he was a child and was drafted right out of high school by the San Diego Padres. He bounced around several National League teams before being picked up by the Feds at the trade deadline during their inaugural season in 2010. Since joining the Feds he's come into his own, hitting .325 in 2010 and .327 in 2011. This season has been his best so far with 42 home runs, 102 runs batted in and 162 hits. He was a two-time All Star and by all accounts most likely a future Hall of Famer."

Sam took notes as Gonzo rattled off Willie's accomplishments on the field.

"Married for five years to Carmen Peña Vasquez. Two kids—Miguel, age four, and Jose, age two."

"Shit," Sam muttered, noting that Freddie gripped the wheel a little tighter.

"Yeah. Sucks big-time."

"Financials?"

"Not yet. A lot of his accounts were in the Dominican Republic. I've left messages."

"What're they saying on the radio?" Sam asked.

"People are extremely pissed. The guys on WFBR, the Feds' radio station, are really fanning the fire."

"We'll have to pay them a visit at some point."

"I can do that if you'd like."

"That'd help. Work it until sixteen thirty and call it a day. Meet up at HQ at zero seven hundred."

"Will do. I'll let you know what I find out. Um, Lieutenant, could I speak to you about something unrelated to the case?"

"Sure."

"Off the speaker, if you don't mind. No offense, Cruz."

"None taken." Freddie fiddled with his phone and handed it to her.

"What's up?"

"I wanted to let you know that I might need some time off in the next couple of weeks. The situation with Alex's mother looks to be heading to court." He filled her in on the latest developments.

"I'm sorry, Gonzo. That sucks."

"Yeah. I haven't said too much to Christina about it yet because of the campaign and how busy she's been, so I'd appreciate it if you kept it quiet for now."

She got that he was asking her not to tell Nick, in particular. "I understand. Let me know if I can do anything to help."

"I might need some character witnesses, beginning with a decorated police lieutenant and her senator husband."

"Whatever we can do. You only have to ask."

"Thanks. It's okay to tell Cruz what's going on. I can use all the support I can get, but I wanted to let you know about the time off."

"I'll tell him, and don't worry about the time. We'll cover for you."

"Thanks, Sam. I'll get back to you after I hit the radio station."

"Talk to you then."

She handed the phone to Freddie.

"Everything okay?"

"He said I could tell you that he's heading into what could be an ugly custody battle with Alex's mother."

"Oh, crap. Can she do that? Show up months later and stake a claim?"

"She's his mother, and from what Gonzo said she's apparently gone to great lengths to clean up her act."

"He must be freaking out."

"Just a little, and he's not saying much about it to Christina until after the election."

"I won't say anything to anyone. Don't worry."

"You could say something to him. He's going to need his friends."

"I will." He drove the car into the parking lot and flashed his badge at the security guard. "Detective Cruz and Lieutenant Holland to see Mrs. Vasquez."

"What's this in reference to?"

"It's personal."

The guard studied both their badges before returning them to Freddie. "You're that cop who's married to the senator."

"Really? I didn't know that. Let us in. Now."

"No need to be cranky about it. You'll be met in the lobby by a member of security and escorted to the Vasquez residence."

"Excellent."

Freddie put up the window and waited for the security arm to rise before he drove on.

"I wasn't being cranky."

"You're never cranky."

"Why do people think I need to be told who I'm married to?"

"Because they're afraid you might forget?"

"That's always a possibility, I suppose."

The banter helped to keep their minds off the dreadful task that awaited them inside. He pulled into a visitor parking space and cut the engine but made no move to get out of the car.

"I hate this," he said.

"I do too, but sitting here another five minutes isn't going to make it any easier. Let's get it over with and get back to figuring out what happened."

Another Keystone cop met them in a lobby that was all marble and greenery and opulence. The security guy wore a well-tailored black suit and an earpiece. As Sam wondered if the earpiece made him feel more important, she noticed two other men and a woman, all in suits, all with earpieces and handheld radios. An awful lot of obvious security for a richy-rich condo building, she thought, wondering who else lived in the building.

"Right this way," the security guy assigned to escort them said. "We figured it was only a matter of time before the angry fans found out where Mr. Vasquez lives, so we've ramped up security today."

Sam appreciated that he didn't dick around and try to stonewall them the way private security usually did. "Probably not a bad idea."

"Is everything all right with Mr. Vasquez?" he asked with genuine concern.

"I'm not at liberty to discuss that." He'd find out soon enough that everything was not all right with Mr. Vasquez.

"I understand." He led them past a reception desk to a bank of elevators and used a key inside to access the top floor. The elevator didn't make a sound as it whooshed them to the penthouse that made up the seventh and eighth floors.

"Please wait here," he said when the elevator opened into a hallway with two doors. He proceeded to the door on the left, knocking softly. He spoke in low tones to the domestic who answered the door and then gestured for

Sam and Freddie to come. They were ushered into what could only be called a palace with a breathtaking view of Washington Harbor, Georgetown, the Key Bridge and Arlington National Cemetery across the river. The maid showed them to a sitting room and said she would get Mrs. Vasquez.

"Wow," Freddie whispered as he took in the plush digs. "Baseball has been very, *very* good to him."

"Seriously."

A pretty, petite young woman with dark hair and red, puffy eyes came running into the room. "Are you from the team?" She spoke with a heavy Hispanic accent and looked more like a teenager than a wife and mother. "Did they send you? Were they able to find my Willie?"

"Carmen Vasquez?" Sam asked.

"Yes." She came over to Sam and gripped her arm frantically. "Tell me you found him. Please tell me."

Sam wished in that moment to be anywhere else in the world. "Come have a seat."

"No, I don't want to sit. I want to know what's going on."

A little dark-haired boy came toddling into the room, dragging a blanket behind him. Judging by his size, Sam gauged him to be Miguel, the older of their two sons. "Mama…*¿Qué te pasa? ¿Por qué estás triste? ¿Dónde está papá?*"

His mother picked him up, whispered to him and handed him over to the maid.

Sam glanced at Freddie and saw the same unbearable sadness etched into his expression that she was feeling. She'd learned over the years to say it quickly, to put it out there and get it over with. But this time the words got stuck on the lump in her throat.

Sensing her distress, Freddie stepped forward. "*Señora Vasquez, lo siento pero tengo que decirle que su marido fue encontrado asesinado.*"

Carmen screamed and clawed at Freddie's chest. "*Por favor dime que no es verdad. No, no, no.*"

"*Lo siento. Ojalà pudiera.*"

Thankfully, Cruz was standing close enough to catch Carmen when she fainted. He eased her onto a sofa. "Go find the maid," Sam said to the security guy, who watched the scene unfold with big eyes and shock etched into his expression. He didn't need to speak Spanish to understand what'd just happened. "Get a cold cloth and some water. Hurry."

By the time Carmen regained consciousness a minute later, he had returned with the items Sam requested.

Freddie ran the cloth over Carmen's tearstained face. "*Toma una respiración profunda.*"

"*Por favor, dime que no es verdad.*" Her voice was little more than a whisper.

"*Lo siento.*"

"No," Carmen said as she broke down again. "*Por favor, no.*" She glanced at Sam and thankfully switched to English. "He can't be dead. Not my Willie. It wasn't his fault. He made a mistake. People make mistakes all the time. How could they kill him over it?"

"I don't know," Sam said, "but I promise we'll do all we can to find out what happened." She stopped short of assuring the other woman that she'd definitely get the murderer. For the first time in her illustrious career, she'd come across a case in which tens of thousands of people—perhaps even hundreds of thousands—had a motive for murder.

Carmen fixed her gaze on Sam. "I know you. Have we met?"

Sam shook her head. "I'm married to Senator Cappuano from Virginia. That's probably how you know me."

"Yes, we saw you at the convention. Willie admired your husband."

"My son admired your husband. He was very kind to him at a camp this past summer."

"That's my Willie." Her eyes welled with new tears. "He's kind to everyone. He never hurt anyone." She looked up at Sam with watery brown eyes. "How..."

"He was stabbed in the chest. The medical examiner believes he died very quickly."

With her hand over her mouth to muffle her sobs, Carmen shook her head as if to deny what Sam had told her.

"Is there someone we could call for you? A friend or family member?"

Carmen took a moment to collect herself, to wipe the tears from her face and to sit up a bit. "Yesterday, I would've been able to give you a list of friends, mostly Willie's teammates and their wives or girlfriends. When he didn't come home last night, I called them all to see if they knew where he was, and none of them answered. The only one who took my call was Ray Jestings."

"When did you last speak to Willie?" Freddie asked.

"Before the game. He called about twenty minutes before it started."

"Did he express any worries or concerns about the game, other than the obvious stress of the play-offs?" Sam asked.

"No, he was very calm all day. Determined. Focused.

He spent the morning playing with the boys and left for the ballpark around two."

"Did you attend the game?"

Carmen shook her head. "My younger son has been sick, so I stayed home with the boys." She paused, her eyes filling again. "I'm glad now that I wasn't there. I was so upset when it happened. I knew how awful he must be feeling, and when they started throwing trash at him..."

Sam ached at the thought of having to tell her he'd been found in a Dumpster. They'd be keeping that detail to themselves—for now.

"Did he have problems with anyone on the team?"

"No, they all loved him. They even made him one of their captains this season. He was so proud of that. He'd worked so hard for so long... He made one mistake. *One*. And someone *killed* him for it?"

"We don't know anything yet," Sam said.

"But that's why! They killed him because he missed that ball! How do I tell my boys that their papa died because he didn't catch a ball?"

Sam didn't want to think about her own son finding out about the ballplayer's senseless death, let alone Willie's sons. She sat next to Carmen and took her hand. "I've been doing this a long time, long enough that I've seen the worst of humankind—and the best. The one thing I've never understood is how anyone can take a life. I hope I never reach the point in my career where that makes sense to me. I've also learned that the most obvious motive often has nothing to do with what really happened. There's a good chance this will never make sense to you. If we do our jobs, you'll know how it happened, but you may never know exactly why."

"What am I supposed to do now? He was my whole world. Willie and our boys. They're my world." When she sagged, Sam put an arm around her, something she rarely did with strangers.

"I need to know if Willie had a cell phone."

"Yes, he had it with him all the time in case I needed to reach him."

"It wasn't on him when we found him, so I'll need the number." Sam dropped her arm from around Carmen's shoulders to write down the number as Carmen recited it for her.

"Could we call your family or his?" Freddie asked. "You'll want them to know what's happened before his death is reported on the news."

"I'll call my brother," she said, defeated as acceptance began to settle in. "He'll take care of telling Willie's family, and he'll come here to be with me."

"Where is he?" Freddie asked.

"In the D.R."

"If you'd like me to wait here with you until he arrives, I'd be happy to do that," Freddie offered, glancing at Sam.

After the night without sleep, they were running on fumes and would have to quit soon anyway. She gave a short nod to grant her approval.

"Do you want me to call your brother for you?" Freddie asked.

"Yes, please. I don't think I could say the words."

"I'll say them for you," he said.

Before she left, she took Freddie aside. "You came here hungry. Want me to have something sent over for you?"

He shook his head. "Thanks, but I've lost my appetite."

She could understand why. "When the brother gets here, go home. Meet me at HQ at zero seven hundred. You did good with her, Detective."

"Glad you thought so. I was dying inside."

"Me too."

He handed over her keys. "Where're you going from here?"

"The ballpark."

ON THE WAY to the Federals' stadium, which was named after a credit card company Sam had never heard of and could never remember the name of, she called Dispatch. "This is Lieutenant Holland. I need to speak to the officer in charge of Patrol at the moment."

"Just a moment please, Lieutenant."

She waited on hold for a long time, listening to weird instrumental music that made her long for her earbuds. Finally, the call went through.

"Stahl."

If she hadn't been driving, she would've rolled her eyes to high heaven. "I asked for Patrol, not the rat squad."

"What do you want, Holland?"

"I want to speak to the officer in charge of Patrol."

"You got him."

"What're you doing there?"

"Covering for the lieutenant who worked all night on crowd control, not that it's any of your business."

"Oh that's right, you Internal Affairs types don't get the recall messages that the rest of us get. I hope you had a good night's sleep while our city was being torn apart."

"Is there a purpose for this call? If not, I've got better—"

"Be quiet and listen to me." Was it possible to *hear* a person's face turn purple? Sam smiled at the images that danced through her mind. "I need a thorough sweep of the entire Southwestern quadrant of the city, from Potomac Avenue to Independence. We're looking for a large quantity of blood. It would be hard to miss."

"And you expect me to devote our currently limited resources to a witch hunt for you?"

"We're looking for a murder scene, you stupid ass. Get Patrol on it, or I'll get Farnsworth on you."

"That's right, all you have to do is snap your fingers, and he jumps. Are you sleeping with him, Holland? Because that would explain a lot—"

Before he could say anything else that would make her understand how someone could commit murder, Sam ended the call. "Fucking bastard." For insurance purposes, she placed a call to her superior officer and mentor, Detective Captain Malone.

"Holland? I heard you caught a homicide."

"What in the name of hell is Rat Face Stahl doing in charge of Patrol?"

"Good morning to you too. He's filling in. We're extremely short-handed today after everyone worked all night."

"Why can't they work all day too? We are."

"Not everyone has your squad's dedication to duty, Lieutenant."

"Are you patronizing me, Captain?"

"Would I be foolish enough to patronize you? What can I do for you?"

She told him what she knew so far about the Vasquez murder, which wasn't much, and what she needed from Patrol officers.

"I'll see to it. We're going to need to put our heads together about how to go public with this."

"That's the other thing I wanted to talk to you about. My next stop was going to be the ballpark, but if I go there we'll tip our hand and the team is apt to take control of the story. I'd really like to see their reactions when they hear the news. So I was thinking, I'll go over there and break the news to the team, while you all handle the media at the same time. And P.S., I'm going to take Agent Hill with me. He knows the owner, Jestings, and can smooth the way a bit."

"I like the plan, but I'd like the chief to sign off on it. Stand by, and I'll call you back in twenty minutes."

"Standing by. Can you send me to Archelotta?"

"Hang on."

The lieutenant of the IT division, also the only fellow officer Sam had dallied with romantically, picked up on the third ring. "Archelotta."

"Hey, it's Holland."

"How's it going? Heard you caught a homicide."

"Yeah, Willie Vasquez."

"No way. No *fucking* way."

"Can you see if you can get a signal from his phone? It wasn't on him when we found him."

"Sure. Whatever I can do."

Sam gave him the number.

"I'll call you as soon as I have anything. Might take a

while though. I heard cell service has been interrupted in some sectors because of the riots."

"We'll take whatever we can get."

"Gotcha. I'll be in touch."

As long as she had some time, she stopped for a sandwich and treated herself to a rare diet cola. If there'd ever been a time for a caffeine boost, this was it. Thirty hours without sleep was beginning to make her muzzy around the edges. While she ate in the car, she placed a call to her dad's house.

"We were wondering when we'd hear from you, Sam," her stepmother, Celia, said. "Long night?"

"Very long and not over yet. We're still at it."

"Lord. What an awful thing and all over a ball game."

Wait until Celia heard the rest of what'd happened because of a ball game. "My thoughts exactly. Is my dad handy?"

"Hang on just a minute, honey."

Sam smiled at the endearment. She enjoyed being mothered by the sweet nurse who'd married her paralyzed father on Valentine's Day. She thought about her own mother, who'd recently reappeared in her life. Her mother was looking to heal the rift that had festered between them since the day after Sam graduated from high school and her mom left her dad for another man. Some rifts could never be healed, or so she liked to think. As long as she went with that line of reasoning, she wouldn't have to deal with her mother's desire to spend some time together.

"Lieutenant," Skip said when he came on the line. "How goes it?"

"It's been better. After the city was torn apart last

night, we found Willie Vasquez dead in a Dumpster behind Air and Space."

"Come on…"

"Sad but true. Stabbed through the heart."

"Oh, for Christ's sake."

"Just had to tell his wife. Totally sucked."

"Always does, baby girl. I don't envy you that."

"First time I've ever caught a murder when the entire city had motive."

"That's a tough one, but I have faith in you. You'll get to the bottom of it. Poor Scotty. He'll be crushed."

"I know. Nick is getting him from school and taking him to the office for the afternoon."

"It'll help him to be with his dad."

"It's helping me to be with mine, even for a couple of minutes."

"Aww, kid, you sure know how to pull your old man's heartstrings."

Sam smiled at the gruffly spoken words, fortified by the sound of his voice and his reassurances. "I'll come by in the morning."

"I'll be here. Tell your boy to come see me when he gets home."

"I will."

"Let me know how I can help with this one."

"I'll do that too. Talk at ya later."

Malone called back ten minutes later than planned. By then Sam was on her way to dozing off in the car. "I talked to the chief," he said. "He gave the plan a green light. Hit me with a text when you're in with the team, and we'll call the press conference. We're deploying people all over the city in case there's more rioting, and we're sending Crime Scene to the ballpark. The minute you let us know you're with the team management, they'll descend on the locker room and anywhere else Willie might've been after the game. This way the team won't have time to prepare for their arrival. If they've got anything to hide, our guys will find it. Sound good?"

What it sounded like was a couple more hours before she could find a horizontal surface. "Yeah. I'm heading for the ballpark right now. I've got to wait for Hill, though, so give me half an hour."

"You got it."

"Also, before you go public, check in with Cruz to make sure Vasquez's family in the Dominican Republic has been notified."

"Will do."

Sam ended that call and placed another to Hill, who agreed to meet her at the ballpark's VIP parking lot. She drove to the ballpark, rehearsing what she would say to the team's owner and management as she drove. She glanced at the clock. Two-thirty. Nick would be picking Scotty up at school and breaking the unbelievable news about Willie. Sam would give everything she had, including the gold badge she'd worked so hard to earn, to spare the boy she loved from anything that could ever hurt him.

So this is motherhood. Her heart ached as she imagined how upset he'd be when he heard about Willie. Nick would take care of him this afternoon, and together they'd get Scotty through this.

SIX

Nick waited outside the gates to the Eliot-Hine Middle School, watching the flood of kids emerge at dismissal time. When Scotty let them know over the summer that he wished to live with them full-time, they'd had only a couple of weeks to apply for temporary custody from the commonwealth of Virginia's child welfare authorities and to figure out where to enroll him in school.

Nick and Sam had gone round and round about the pros and cons of public versus private school. Both of them products of public school, they'd leaned heavily in that direction from the beginning, but worries about security had them visiting a couple of the city's more prominent private schools.

After a couple of sleepless nights and many long debates over their first major parenting challenge, they'd decided to let Scotty make the final decision because they felt confident he'd do well at any of the schools they'd visited. He'd declared the private schools too fancy for him and had asked to attend the same school as the other kids in their Capitol Hill neighborhood. Nick had been pleased by the way the boy approached the decision and agreed with his reasoning.

Nick waited in the spot where Shelby met Scotty every day, where he'd met Scotty himself for the first week of school until he was certain the boy was settled into the new routine. It had taken tremendous schedule juggling to be free at two-thirty every day for a week, but he'd done it happily.

He'd waited a long time to be a father and to have the family he now cherished. And while he loved the career he'd inherited from his late best friend John O'Connor, his family came first. Always.

Scotty emerged from the school in a gaggle of boys who were talking and laughing, pushing and shoving, and doing all the things kids did after a long day cooped up in the classroom. Scotty wore a grin that stretched from ear to ear, and Nick smiled as he watched him, thrilled that he'd made new friends so quickly.

Although he shouldn't have been surprised. Scotty had a way about him that drew people into his orbit. It was a trait he shared with Nick, who'd always made friends easily, despite the hardscrabble, austere upbringing with his grandmother as reluctant guardian. His friends and their families had saved his sanity, and he still kept in touch with most of the guys he'd grown up with in Lowell, Massachusetts.

Trailing behind Scotty at a close but respectable distance were the two agents assigned to his detail. They spotted Nick immediately and nodded to him. The area around the school was a madhouse of buses, minivans, crossing guards, pedestrians and bicycles.

Nick waved to Scotty and delighted in the way the boy's eyes lit up at the sight of him. Was there anything better than the surprised but thrilled look on his son's face when he realized Nick was there to get him? Other than Sam, no one had ever loved him as much as Scotty did.

Scotty said a quick goodbye to his friends and rushed over to hug Nick, who loved that Scotty didn't care if his friends were watching. Nick supposed that would matter greatly in a year or two, but for now, Nick was a happy recipient of the spontaneous affection.

"This is a surprise," Scotty said.

"I thought you might be up for an afternoon on the Hill."

"That'll be cool." He'd been to work with Nick before so he could see his office and meet the staff. "What's the occasion?"

"We'll talk about it when we get to the office." Before Scotty could question what they had to talk about, Nick said, "Did you have a good day?"

"Boring. As usual." He said the same thing every day, and by now it had become a joke between them.

"Come on," Nick said, giving him a nudge, as he helped Scotty into the back of the SUV. Scotty's detail would follow behind them in a second SUV. Nick longed for the days of driving himself around the city and hoped the need for protection would end as soon as the election was over. "I'm sure *something* interesting happened."

"I did hear a word I'd never heard before."

"In which class?"

"Lunch," Scotty said, grinning at him. "Best class of the day."

Laughing, Nick followed him into the vehicle. Scotty's backpack landed with a loud thunk on the floor.

"So what's this word you learned?"

"Blow job. What does that mean?"

Nick nearly fell out of the car in shock. "Who the heck said that?"

"This kid Ethan who always acts like he knows everything. He was talking about his football that someone stole, and that if the kid who took it didn't give it back, he was going to give him a blow job. The other guys were laughing, but I didn't know what it meant, and I didn't want them to think I was dumb. So I figured I'd ask you."

Christ almighty, Nick thought. *What the hell do I do with this one?* "Well, um, first of all it has nothing to do with footballs."

"So what does it mean?"

"It's, ah, sort of a sex thing."

Scotty's entire face folded into a grimace that nearly made Nick laugh. "Eww, gross."

"Right, so you might not be ready to hear about it."

"I'd still like to know."

"Trust me, buddy. I don't think you want to."

"Please? I hate when all the other guys know something I don't know. It makes me feel stupid."

Like he didn't already have a big enough minefield to walk through with the boy this afternoon? And now this! He yearned for Sam's common sense approach to things. Where was she when he needed her? He told himself Scotty was twelve, soon to be thirteen, and certainly old enough—or getting there quickly—to know the truth about certain things. Whether or not Nick was old enough at thirty-six to be having this conversation was another story entirely.

"You're really going to make me say it, huh?"

"'Fraid so," Scotty said with the adorable grin Nick had fallen for the first time he met him.

"It's when a girl kisses you, you know… Down there."

For the first time since Nick had been forced to accept protection, he was glad he wasn't allowed to drive so he could have the special joy of watching Scotty's eyes bug with realization. "Come. On. They don't really do that!"

"Yeah, they do. If you're lucky."

"Oh my God, that is the grossest thing I've ever heard!"

Nick suppressed a huge laugh that he knew Scotty wouldn't appreciate. *Someday you won't think so*, he wanted to say, but somehow managed to refrain from sharing the thought.

"And you actually *like* that?"

Nick wanted to die on the spot. Nothing in his life could've prepared him for this conversation. "I take the Fifth on that."

"What does that mean?"

"I refuse to answer on the grounds that I might die of embarrassment."

"That means you *do* like it. That's so disgusting. What's wrong with you?"

"Um, nothing?"

"Yes, there is."

Nick's eyes watered from the effort it took to hold back the hysterical laughter that was busting to get out. He couldn't wait to relay this conversation to Sam. "Listen, buddy, I told you the truth because you asked me an honest question, and I always want to tell you the truth, but you shouldn't talk about this at school with the other guys, okay?"

"But I know something they don't know now."

"True, but a grown-up guy keeps stuff like this to himself. And I think you're a pretty grown-up guy."

"You do? Really?"

"I wouldn't have told you if I didn't think you were grown-up enough to handle it."

Scotty glowed with pleasure at the compliment, which made Nick glow on the inside.

"So why did you pick me up? Is something wrong?"

"Not with anyone in our family."

"Then who?"

"Let's get some ice cream at the Senate Dining Room and talk about it."

"Okay."

Always intuitive, Scotty was subdued as they arrived at the Capitol and were escorted by their agents to the dining room, which was largely deserted in the middle of the afternoon. After they ordered ice cream sundaes, Scotty remained unusually quiet. "Is there something wrong with the adoption?"

The question hit Nick's heart like an arrow. Was Scotty worried about that? "No, buddy. There's nothing to worry about there. The social workers are recommending approval, and we're just waiting on a court date to make it official. Anytime now." Because of who he was, Nick had been assured the date would be sooner rather than later. It was the first time he'd deliberately used his status and clout to get what he wanted, and he was perfectly fine with using it for this very good cause. "Have you been worried about it?"

Scotty shrugged. "Not really."

Nick waited for the boy to look up at him and saw the truth in his expression.

"Kind of."

He reached for Scotty's hand and held on tight. "There's nothing to worry about. I promise. If there was, I'd tell you."

"You would? Because I was thinking you wouldn't tell me cuz you wouldn't want me to worry."

"I don't want you to worry, but I promise right here and right now that I'll always tell you the truth about important stuff like this—and when you ask me about stuff like..."

"Blow jobs?" Scotty asked with the irascible grin that was much more in keeping with what Nick had come to expect from him.

"That too," Nick said with a grimace that made Scotty laugh.

Fortunately, their ice cream arrived and he was saved from having to revisit that unsettling topic.

"So what's going on?" Scotty asked between huge mouthfuls of ice cream and hot fudge and whipped cream.

Nick picked at his ice cream, unable to eat with what he had to tell Scotty weighing on him. "Remember when I said you're a grown-up kind of guy?"

"Uh-huh."

"Sometimes when you're a grown-up, things happen that aren't easy to understand or explain."

"Is this one of those times?"

"Yes, and it's really hard for me to tell you this, but Willie Vasquez was found dead this morning." Nick would never forget the moment his words registered with Scotty. His spoon fell into the bowl with a loud clank.

As his face crumpled, Nick pushed back from the table and reached for him.

Scotty threw himself into Nick's arms and broke down into heartbroken sobs that brought tears to Nick's eyes.

When the waiter approached the table, Nick held up

a hand to hold him off so he could devote his full attention to Scotty.

"I'm sorry, buddy. I know you admired him so much."

After a long period of silence, Scotty finally raised his tearstained face from Nick's chest. "Is it because he missed the ball?"

"We don't anything yet. Sam is working on the case, and she'll do her best to figure out what happened."

"So many people are mad at him. The kids were talking about it at school today. I tried to tell them it wasn't his fault, but they said someone who plays professional baseball should be able to catch a basic fly ball. I sort of agreed with them, as much as I feel bad for Willie."

"And that's probably true, but as long as a ballplayer, even a professional ballplayer, is a human being and not perfect, he'll make mistakes just like the rest of us do."

"You don't make mistakes."

"Sure, I do," Nick said, surprised. "I make them all the time."

"Like when?"

Nick tried to think of an example he could share. "You want to know the biggest mistake I ever made in my whole life?"

Scotty's eyes were still watery and his face red from crying, but he nodded, and Nick was happy to share his regrets if it would help his son to feel better.

"The first time I met Sam was six years before we got married. We had a really good time together. She gave me her phone number, and I called her because I wanted to see her again. When she didn't call me back, I was really bummed, and I assumed it was because she didn't want to see me again. Turns out, that wasn't true."

"How did you find out?"

"When I saw her again many years later we talked about it. Turns out her roommate never gave her my messages because he liked her too."

"Oh wow. That's totally lame."

"Right? She ended up very unhappily married to him for four years. The biggest mistake I ever made in my life was not going to find her to ask why she never called me back. I regret that we lost so much time together because of that. So everyone makes mistakes, even me and even professional ballplayers."

"One of the kids at the old house used to say 'shit happens.' I know that's a swear word we're not supposed to say, but…"

"It's true. Shit does happen, and sometimes there's no good reason for it, such as that ball sailing over Willie's head last night."

"And now he's dead, probably because of it."

"Sam would tell you it's easy to jump to that obvious conclusion, but who knows what really happened?"

"I'm glad she's the one who's going to find out. If anyone can do it, she can."

"I agree. I have to ask you a favor—you can't talk about what happened to Willie until the police make it public. Sam and I decided I should tell you so you wouldn't hear it somewhere else. I'm sure it won't be long before the entire city is talking about it, if they aren't already."

"I understand. I won't say anything."

Nick patted his back and kissed his forehead. "I hated having to tell you that."

"I know."

"You want to finish the ice cream?"

Scotty shook his head. "I don't feel like ice cream anymore."

"Neither do I."

HILL WAS WAITING for her when Sam pulled into the VIP lot. When he came over to open the car door for her, she wanted to tell him to knock it off. But he was a Southern gentleman down to his bone marrow and probably didn't think a thing of opening a car door for a woman, even if she was perfectly capable of opening her own damned door.

"Get any sleep yet?" he asked.

"Nope. You?"

They flashed their badges to security and were waved in.

"Nope. Helluva thing, huh?"

"What's the word for beyond insane?"

"Outrageous."

She kept an eye out for any sign of the Crime Scene Unit, but didn't see anyone yet. They were probably gathered on the other side of the building. "That's a good word."

"Guy misses a fly ball, and he's dead twelve hours later? Makes me wonder what kind of world we live in."

Before he could hold another door for her, she snatched it open and strolled into the palatial foyer. "You and I know all too well what kind of world we live in."

"True." He seemed to know exactly where he was going as they entered an area of the ballpark that looked more like the lobby of a fancy office building than a baseball stadium. At the reception desk, he gave his name and asked to see Ray Jestings.

"He's not accepting visitors at the moment," the young woman at the desk said. "I'd be happy to give him a message for you."

Hill glanced at Sam, and in a moment that was far more in keeping with her groove with Cruz, they placed their badges on the counter, right next to each other.

The woman's eyes darted between the two badges. "FBI and Metro PD," Hill said. "Let us up."

"I need to make a call first."

"Make it snappy," Sam said. "We don't have all day." The receptionist scurried into a back room, keeping her gaze fixed on them through a plate glass window as she placed the call.

While they waited, Sam looked around a reception area decorated with life-sized photos of Federals players as well as the ballpark and a large portrait of the team's handsome young owner.

"What if we discover that your childhood friend ordered Vasquez killed when he blew the biggest game in franchise history?"

Hill chuckled. "Are you impugning my professionalism, Lieutenant?"

"Never."

"Right… Do you want my help or not?"

"As much as it pains me to admit it, I need all the help I can get with this one."

The receptionist returned about two seconds before Sam was going after her. Sam's body was about an hour from full shutdown mode. She needed to get as much done as she could before her gas tank hit empty.

"You can go on up to Mr. Jestings' office."

"Gee, thanks," Sam said. "It took ten minutes to arrive at that foregone conclusion?"

"I'm sorry," the young woman said, her chin quivering. "We're all very upset today. No one more so than Mr. Jestings."

Oh for crying out loud, Sam thought as she followed Hill onto an elevator with no buttons. Apparently, it had one destination only.

"That poor girl," Hill said as the elevator whisked them upward. "You turned her into a quivering wreck."

"I hate receptionists. They're always standing between me and the people I want to talk to."

"You're endlessly amusing, Holland."

"Need I remind you that you're not allowed to be amused by me?" If he was going to be around again, Sam wanted to set the boundaries early on.

His smile faded. "No reminders necessary. I'm painfully aware of your blissful marital status."

Hill's use of the word "painful" left her feeling uneasy as they stepped into the office suite that housed the Feds' top management. As she followed Hill to a hallway lined with team memorabilia that ended with yet another receptionist, Sam dashed off a text to Malone, letting him know they'd cracked the Feds' inner sanctum.

This receptionist was male, mid-twenties and looked like he'd been crying. "Agent Hill," he said. "It's so nice to see a friendly face on a rather glum day around here. We were so close. *So* damned close."

Little did he know, Sam thought, that the team was about to have much bigger problems to contend with than a lost ball game.

"A tough loss for sure. Could I talk to Ray? I won't take much of his time."

"Yes, of course. I told him you were on your way up." He glanced at Sam and then back at Hill.

"This is Detective Lieutenant Holland from the Metro PD."

"The senator's wife."

Whereas she'd revealed her marital status willingly to Carmen Vasquez, here it bugged her. She loved being Nick's wife, but on the job she preferred being known for her own accomplishments rather than who she'd married. "Am I? I had no idea."

The young man frowned at her. "Go on in. He's expecting you."

On the way past, Avery patted the younger man on the shoulder. "There's always next year."

"That's what we've been telling ourselves all morning."

In one of the biggest offices Sam had ever seen, Ray Jestings was the picture of devastation. He sat in a gigantic leather executive chair behind his desk, staring out at the ballpark to his right. Beyond the park, Ray's view of the city extended past the Capitol and into Maryland.

"Hey, Ray."

"Avery." Jestings got up and came around the desk to hug his old friend. He was tall and lean with dark hair beginning to turn gray and looked like he hadn't slept yet either. "What brings you here?"

"This is Lieutenant Holland from the Metro PD. I'm afraid we've come with some bad news."

"I don't know if I can take any more bad news." He spoke in the same honeyed South Carolinian accent as Avery's.

"This is a lot worse than a lost ball game," Sam said,

earning a frown from Hill. Maybe she was getting a tad cranky after the night without sleep.

"What's going on, Avery?" Ray asked, his gaze bouncing between Sam and Hill.

"I'm sorry to have to tell you this, but Willie Vasquez was found murdered this morning," Hill said.

Ray stared at them, unseeing, as if trying to process what Hill had said.

"Ray? Why don't you sit down?" Hill put his arm around the other man and led him to the arrangement of chairs that overlooked the ballpark below.

"Someone killed Willie?" he asked, seeming genuinely shocked and devastated by the news.

"I'm afraid so," Avery said. "I'm so sorry."

"People were mad about what happened last night. But that someone could *kill* him..."

A knock on the door preceded Ray's assistant as he came into the office, white-faced and wide-eyed. "Mr. Jestings, there're cops all over the building demanding entrance."

Ray's dark eyes narrowed with rage that he directed at Sam. "I run a clean organization here, Lieutenant."

"If that's the case, then you have nothing to worry about. Let my people in so they can do their jobs."

He nodded to the assistant, who scurried from the room, closing the door behind him.

"You can look all you want but you won't find anything to tie this organization to what happened to Willie. He's a valued member of this ball club."

"Even after what happened last night?" Sam asked.

"Especially after what happened last night. No one wanted that win more than Willie did. He was a fierce competitor, a superior athlete and teammate. We all felt terrible for him, but no one felt worse than he did. The poor guy was in tears after the game." He dropped his head into his hands. "I can't believe he's dead."

"I'd like to speak to your general manager, team manager, security director and anyone else who had access to Willie after the game last night."

Jestings looked to Hill, seeming to seek guidance. "Get them up here," Hill said. "The more you do to aid in the investigation, the less we'll need to look at you and your team."

"Me and my team? You know me, Avery. You know I could never hurt anyone, let alone a ballplayer I loved and respected."

"Who cost your team its first trip to the World Series," Sam interjected.

Once again, Ray's furious gaze landed on her. "And you think I'd put that ahead of a man who had a wife and two small children at home? That I'd put winning ahead of his health and safety?"

"I don't know you at all. So you'll have to forgive me if I don't have the answers to those questions just yet. But your friend Hill is right. The more you cooperate, the more your people cooperate, the less time we'll spend here when we could be out finding the person who did this."

After a charged moment of silence, Ray got up, went over to his desk and made a call. Weariness clung to him as he leaned against the desk. "Aaron, will you please ask Bob and Jamie to come up? Thank you." He returned to the sofa. "I've asked our manager, Bob Minor, and trainer, Jamie Clark, to join us. They were with Willie longer than I was last night. Our general manager, Garrett Collins, is out today. The security director, Hugh Bixby, is dealing with police at the moment."

"You were with Willie after the game?" Sam asked as she made a note to pay Collins a visit at home.

"For a short time. He was inconsolable. We kept the media out of the locker room so he wouldn't have to face their questions."

"Walk me through everything that happened from the time Willie was brought off the field by team security," Sam said. "I need to know who was with him, what was said, when he left, how he left."

"Bob and Jamie will be able to speak more to that than I can. I was with him briefly in the training room after the game."

"Who were his friends on the team?" Hill asked.

"Again, Bob would be better able to speak to that, but from what I observed, Willie was friends with everyone. His teammates respected and admired him. We all did. Have you seen Carmen?"

"Yes," Sam said. "My partner is with her, and her brother is on the way from the Dominican Republic."

Ray closed his eyes but was unable to keep a tear from leaking out the side of his right eye. He brushed it away and opened his eyes. "She and Willie were very devoted to each other. I can't imagine what she must be going through. We'll reach out to make the team's resources available to her." He looked at Hill. "I've been in the business world my entire adult life, but nothing like this has ever happened before. I don't know what I'm supposed to do."

"First and foremost cooperate with the investigation," Hill said. "Ensure that everyone in your organization does the same."

"Of course. That goes without saying."

"Mr. Jestings, prior to last night's error, do you know of anyone who had a beef with Mr. Vasquez? Anyone he argued with or had problems with?"

"No. Like I said, he was very well liked. Here's Bob now. You can ask him. He'll tell you the same thing."

The gray-haired manager was stocky and thick through the middle with a ruddy, sunburned complexion. He wore a Feds ball cap and team jacket with jeans. "How come there're cops all over the place?" Bob asked Ray.

He gestured to Sam and Avery. "This is FBI Special Agent Avery Hill, an old friend of mine from Charleston, and MPD Lieutenant Holland."

Bob shook hands with both of them and sat next to Ray. "What can we do for you folks?"

"Mr. Minor," Sam said, "I'm sorry to have to tell you that Willie Vasquez was found dead this morning."

"*What?* Dead?" Bob looked at Ray, who nodded grimly. "Oh my God. What happened?"

"He was stabbed in the chest," Sam said.

"Where did this happen?"

"We're not sharing those details at this time."

"We have the right to know what happened to our friend and colleague," Bob said, a hint of temper flashing in his blue eyes.

"And we have the right to protect our investigation," Sam replied. She loved when people talked about their rights, as if they trumped the rights of the victim. In Sam's world, nothing trumped the rights of her victim du jour. "We need to know every move Mr. Vasquez made, from the time he was escorted off the field by your security personnel until the time he left the stadium."

Ray got up again and went to his phone. "Aaron, get Hugh up here, will you please?"

"Mr. Minor," Sam said, "when we spoke with Mrs. Vasquez, she told us she repeatedly tried to call you and all the other players last night when her husband didn't come home. She said she was unable to get through to anyone other than Mr. Jestings, which led her to believe all their former friends had turned their backs on them in light of Willie's error."

Bob's face got even redder than it was naturally. "That's not true! I got seven *hundred* phone calls last night. That's seven *zero zero*. I turned off my phone before the game and didn't turn it on again until this morning. If Carmen Vasquez called, that's news to me. I'm sure our players were dealing with the same thing—a barrage of calls from their management and media requests and old friends wanting to commiserate."

"How would you explain that none of their spouses took Carmen's calls either?"

"Lieutenant," he said in a patronizing tone that grated on Sam's tired nerves, "people were upset about what happened in the game. Willie's error cost this team a trip to the World Series. No matter how much we all liked him, that's a fact. People were upset."

"Was anyone upset enough to kill him?"

He maintained his composure, but his outrage at the question came through loud and clear to her. "No one on my team was upset enough to kill him."

After a knock on the door, a tall, blonde woman came into the room. Her blue eyes were red and raw from crying. Like the rest of the city, these people were taking a lost ball game a little too hard. "I got a message you wanted to see me?" she said to Ray.

He introduced Jamie Clark to Sam and Hill. "Jamie is the team's trainer." To Sam, he said, "Um, should I tell her?"

"Go ahead." That made one less person Sam had to tell.

"Tell me what?" Jamie asked, looking from Ray to Bob.

"Willie was killed last night," Ray said.

Her legs buckled. "No. No, no, *no*."

Ray reached for her and caught her in his arms when she would've fallen. Bob scooted over to make room for Jamie on the sofa.

Sam glanced at Hill and caught his eye. It was interesting, she thought, that Jamie's response to the news had been almost exactly the same as that of Carmen Vasquez. Very interesting, indeed. She'd worked with Hill enough by now to conclude that he too found the reaction odd, based on the way he'd tuned into Jamie's intense reaction as well as the subtle lift of his eyebrow.

"Ms. Clark," Sam said after water had been brought in for the other woman, "we're very sorry for your loss. As you can imagine, we have a lot of ground to cover in our investigation and it would help to know anything you can tell us about Mr. Vasquez's movements after he was escorted from the field."

She took a tissue from the box Ray offered and wiped her tears. "I'm not sure what transpired between the field and the training room, but I was with Willie last night after the game. I might've been the last member of the Feds organization to see him alive."

"Why do you say that?" Sam asked.

After she took another full minute to pull herself together, she spoke softly. “Willie has battled hamstring pulls this season, so we’ve worked closely over the last few months and became friends. I usually take the Metro home to Adams Morgan after the games, but he offered to give me a ride because the city went nuts after the game.” Her voice broke, and she paused to deal with a new influx of tears. “It had to be two hours or more after the game ended when we finally left. Team security walked us to his car. Do you need the information about his car? He just got a new Lincoln a couple of weeks ago.”

“We have it,” Sam said. “But thank you.”

“When you left,” Hill said, “were there still a lot of people around the stadium?”

“Some, but most of the craziness had started to move away from the stadium by then.”

“So no one other than the security personnel saw you leave with him?” Sam asked.

She shook her head. “I didn’t see anyone I knew in the player parking lot when the security detail walked us out.”

“Any unhappy fans hanging around, hoping for a glimpse of Willie?” Sam asked.

“Not that I saw. But that doesn’t mean they weren’t there. I was focused on Willie. He was so upset. I was worried he shouldn’t be driving, but he assured me he’d see me home safely.”

“Did he mention his wife or family?” Hill asked.

“He said he was sad that he had to face them as a failure. I tried to tell him he wasn’t a failure, that he’d had an amazing season and that no one would blame him for one mistake. He scoffed at that and said of course they should blame him. Who else should they blame? Nothing I said seemed to help him."

"Help me to understand something, Ms. Clark," Sam said. "Here's a ballplayer who is by all accounts well-liked and well-respected by his teammates. And yet, he's leaving with you rather than one of his so-called friends on the team. Explain to me why he was with you and not one of the other players."

Sam could tell the other woman was dying to say something snippy but refrained, probably in deference to the law enforcement officers as well as her bosses. "After the…the error, Willie came off the field and went directly to the training room. He didn't set foot in the locker room until everyone else had left. He couldn't bring himself to face his teammates. When the game ended, I went back to my office in the training room. I found him there, so I stayed with him until he was ready to leave. I thought that was the right thing to do. Wasn't it, Bob?"

He patted her knee in an almost paternal gesture. "It was the right thing to do. Ray and I were in the training room with them for a short time after the game ended. But we both had other concerns to see to, and since nothing we said seemed to help Willie, we left to deal with the press and the rest of the team."

"I'm wondering why he was allowed to leave without security," Sam said to Ray.

"He refused our offer of an escort home. He said this was his city and these people were his fans, and he wasn't going to hide from them."

"Why didn't you insist?" Sam asked.

"Things were happening very quickly all around us," Ray said. "The fans were rioting. Every member of our security team was dealing with what was happening in the stadium and outside of it. I had bigger concerns at that moment than arguing with a player who didn't want my help. Believe me, I wish now that I had insisted."

"I'd like a moment alone with Ms. Clark, please," Sam said.

"Why?" Ray asked.

"Because."

When he seemed to get that Sam wasn't going to tell him, he got up and gestured for Minor to do the same.

After the two men left the room, Sam focused in on Jamie. "You referred to your professional relationship, assisting Mr. Vasquez with his various injuries. Was your relationship with him strictly professional?"

Her gaze darted between Hill and Sam. "I'm not sure what you mean. I said we'd become friendly. We worked together closely all season."

"What I'm asking," Sam said as bone-deep fatigue set in, "is whether you were romantically involved with Mr. Vasquez."

Clark's face got very red, and her eyes widened.

When Jamie finally responded, her words were sputtered rather than spoken. "He was *married* with *children*."

"So?"

"So, the answer to your disgusting question is *no*, we were not involved in any capacity other than professional and personal in the sense that we chatted during our training sessions."

"Chatted about what?"

"The team, his performance on the field, the pain he was experiencing with the muscle pulls, his kids. The usual stuff people talk about."

"The conversation was focused solely on him and his work, family, etcetera?"

"Most of the time, yes."

"Are you married?" Sam asked.

"No."

"Engaged, boyfriend, any of the above?"

"I'm not sure what relevance that has to what happened to Willie."

"That's for us to decide."

"None of the above," she said.

"Did you have feelings for Mr. Vasquez that went beyond your professional relationship?"

All at once, Jamie was crying again in deep sobs that made it impossible for her to speak. Sam wanted to yell at her to answer the questions so they could get the hell out of there. Instead she had to wait until Jamie could speak again.

"I cared about him as a friend," she said between sobs. "He was my friend."

"You can let the others back in," Sam said to Hill.

He got up and opened the door for Ray and Bob.

"What happened after you left the stadium?" Hill asked when everyone was settled again.

"The traffic and the crowds were really bad. He'd have to go pretty far out of his way to take me all the way home and that was going to take a lot of time, so I got out at a Metro stop."

"Which one?" Sam asked.

"I, um… I guess it was L'Enfant Plaza."

Sam made a note to get video surveillance from the area around the Metro station. "Around what time would you say he dropped you off?"

"It was a little before midnight. I was worried about

making the last train, but Willie said they'd probably keep them running later than usual because of the game."

"Was he concerned about your safety in light of the rioting?" Hill asked.

She nodded. "He didn't want to drop me off, but I knew he was anxious to get home to Carmen, so I insisted I'd be fine. I never imagined that he wouldn't be."

"Did you see him pull away from the curb?" Sam asked.

She thought about that. "No. I darted for the station and never looked back."

Sam handed her a card. "If you think of anything else we should know, you can call my cell number." She rose and Hill followed suit.

"You'll keep us informed, won't you?" Ray asked, directing the question primarily to Hill.

"We'll do our best," he said. "If you could ask your people to cooperate with the investigation, it'll save us some time."

"You have my word that you'll get their complete cooperation."

"Your general manager," Sam said, consulting her notes.

"Garrett Collins," Ray said. "What about him?"

"You said he isn't in today. If you could get us his address, we'd like to speak to him."

Ray pressed a button on his desk. "I'll have Aaron get it for you."

"And your security director?"

"Hugh Bixby," Ray said.

Aaron came into the room.

"Can you get Garrett's home address? And where the hell is Hugh?"

"He's in the locker room dealing with the cops," Aaron said, his gaze darting nervously around the room.

"I'll wait around to talk to him if you want to take Collins," Hill said to Sam.

"Sure, I've probably got one more interview left in me before I fall flat on my face. Meet me at HQ at zero seven hundred?"

"I'll be there."

Sam headed for the door, but stopped when the floor seemed to move beneath her. And then Hill was there, gripping her arm, which was the only thing that kept her from falling over.

"That's it, Lieutenant," Hill said, as he guided her to the elevator. "Shift's over."

Sam tugged her arm free. "Let me go. I'm fine."

The elevator opened, and they stepped in. "You're not fine. I'll drive you home."

"That's not happening."

"Don't be stupid. You're too tired to do anything but cause more work for your colleagues by wrecking your car on the way home. I'll drive you, and then I'll come back and talk to Bixby."

Her vision was swimming, and her muscles refused to cooperate with her fervent desire to be rid of him. "What about Collins?"

"I'll take care of him too."

"We need to get the surveillance footage over to my third-shift people, Carlucci and Dominguez."

"I'll make sure they get it and let them know what they're looking for."

"No, you won't. I'll take care of my own people."

"Fine. Whatever you want."

"What I want is to have a great big argument right now, but I don't have the energy."

"We can have the fight tomorrow. I'll look forward to it."

He escorted her to his car and held the passenger door for her, closing it when she was settled. As he walked around the front of the car, she thought about her own car and wanted to ask if it would be okay in the lot overnight, but that would take energy she couldn't muster at the moment.

Determined to stay awake until she got home and could fall face-first on her bed, Sam tipped her head back against the cushioned headrest. That was a mistake, because the next thing she knew, Hill was opening the car door and acting like he was going to lift her out of the passenger seat.

"Hands off," she said, smacking at him. "I can walk."

"Fine."

"Yes, I am fine. Thanks for the ride."

"Do you want me to pick you up in the morning?"

"No, I do not want you to pick me up in the morning. Go away. You were supposed to go away."

"I'm sorry if my promotion has inconvenienced you."

"It has inconvenienced me, now get the hell out of here before my husband comes home and thinks you're moving in on his territory—again."

"Honestly, Sam, we're all adults here. I'm not moving in on anything."

"Try telling him that." Sam told herself to stop talking, to walk away and into the house before she could make an uncomfortable situation worse than it already was.

The front door to her house opened, and Shelby came

out wearing one of her litany of pink tracksuits and sparkly pink running shoes. She came down the ramp to the sidewalk.

"Agent Hill," she said, smiling brightly. "Nice to see you again."

"You too."

"Are you okay, Sam?" Shelby asked, taking a close look at her.

"I will be when I get some sleep. Later." Sam dragged herself up the ramp and into the house, leaving the door propped open for Shelby. She trudged upstairs and headed for the shower.

Before she hit the sack, she called Nick, anxious to hear how his talk with Scotty had gone.

"Hey, babe. We're on our way home. Where are you?"

"Home with about two minutes of consciousness left in me. How's the boy?"

"He's been better, but we had a good talk. Not that anything I say can make sense of it for him."

"I'm sure you were great with him. My dad wanted to see him. Would you mind dropping by there when you get home?"

"Sure, no problem. You wouldn't believe what else we talked about."

"What?"

"I'll save that for when you're wide-awake," he said with a laugh, letting her know it was nothing serious.

"I'll look forward to hearing all about it. Tell him I'm sorry I won't see him tonight. I can't stay awake."

"That's okay. Go to sleep. Love you, babe."

"Mmm, me too." With her final bit of energy, she put her phone on the bedside charger and turned on the TV to check what was being said about Vasquez. She forced her eyes to open when she realized that Farnsworth was about to begin a press conference she'd figured was long over by now. They must've been delayed by something.

Cameras captured Chief Farnsworth, looking pale and exhausted, as he walked to the courtyard located outside the main doors at HQ. The local media had gathered, waiting like hungry dogs on the scent of a meaty bone. Every time she went anywhere near them, Sam's hackles went up as if she were an angry dog. Angry dog versus hungry dog was never a good combination. What a relief it was to not have to deal with them this time.

The chief stepped up to the podium. "At zero eight thirty this morning, a body was found in the area of the National Air and Space Museum at Independence and Seventh Avenues. It has been determined that the victim, a Hispanic male in his late twenties, had been stabbed once in the chest. The victim has been identified as Willie Vasquez."

He paused for the collective gasp that went through the crowd.

They immediately erupted, shouting questions at the chief.

Sam knew from experience that he couldn't understand any of them over the roar of voices.

He held up his hands to quiet them. "As you can probably imagine, we've got a very big job ahead of us to determine where Mr. Vasquez was killed and by whom. We've got an entire city enraged with Mr. Vasquez over an error in a baseball game. Our goal will be to quickly bring the killer to justice while keeping the city from erupting into violence again. I'll take a couple of questions."

"Do you know yet when he was killed?" Darren Tabor from the *Washington Star* asked.

"Not yet. Dr. McNamara and her team are working to establish time of death as we speak."

"Can you say more about where he was found?" another reporter asked.

"Not at this time."

"Has the team been notified?"

"Yes."

"How many arrests were made overnight?"

"The latest number I heard was more than three hundred. We've filed numerous charges, ranging from arson to vandalism to malicious mischief. Our Special Response Team, along with every member of the MPD, our colleagues with the FBI and the National Guard helped to contain the violence before it got further out of hand."

He paused and seemed to be considering his words carefully. "I want to add that in addition to the sorrow we all feel over Mr. Vasquez's untimely death, I find it totally appalling that supposed fans of our hometown baseball team reacted to the team's unfortunate loss with violence. It would be my hope that in the future our citizens might consider the health and safety of their city before they take to the streets to vent their frustrations about a game. That's all."

"Well stated, sir," Sam whispered as she turned off the TV and reached for her phone to give Carlucci and Dominguez their marching orders. She got Gigi on her cell phone. "Listen up," Sam said, her eyes closed as she told them about the video surveillance and what they were looking for. It would make for a long, boring shift for the detectives, but it needed to be done. "Make sure Patrol continues to look for the blood and the car."

"We'll take care of it, LT."

"Thanks." She ended the call and dropped into the abyss.

SEVEN

"Is Sam okay?" Shelby asked oh-so-hot Avery Hill, who'd watched Sam walk away with an odd expression on his face.

"She will be when she gets some sleep. She was getting kind of loopy, so I drove her home."

"That was good of you. So how've you been?"

"Good. Fine. You?"

"Great. Loving the new job."

"And how's your other 'project' going?"

Shelby frowned at the reminder of their earlier conversation when he'd come to interview her fertility doctor in an investigation and discovered that she was trying to have a baby. "Nothing to report, unfortunately."

"Sorry to hear that."

She shrugged. "It'll happen if it's meant to." She couldn't think about the alternative. One way or the other, she was going to be a mother. Having Scotty around had gone a long way toward easing the craving, but she had to remind herself every day that he wasn't hers. "Sam said you might want to get together for coffee sometime."

"Um, sure, if you'd like to."

"I thought you were supposed to be moving."

"That was the plan, but the director had something else in mind for me that will keep me in town."

"I'm glad you'll be sticking around."

"Oh. Well, I ought to get back to work."

"Thanks for bringing Sam home."

"It was no problem."

Shelby faced a rare bout of indecision. Should she push him to commit to the date or let him leave and try again the next time? He was so good-looking. Dreamy. Those eyes, that hair, that *accent*… She wanted to jump all over him, a thought that nearly made her giggle.

"Well, I'll be seeing you," he said.

"Don't you want my number?" she asked, the words falling from her lips before she could decide whether it was a good idea to be any more forward than she'd already been with him.

His face became expressionless as he studied her for long enough that she nearly squirmed. "Sure," he finally said. "That'd be good."

"You thought about it long enough."

"It's not you—"

Shelby couldn't help but laugh. "You're supposed to say that *after* we go out. Not before."

That drew a small smile from him that did wonders for his stern countenance. "I'll have to remember that."

She withdrew her phone and clicked on the text function. "What's your number? I'll send you mine."

He recited his number.

"Got it. Next move is yours, Agent Hill."

"I appreciate your candid explanation of the rules."

"At my advanced age, I find myself rather tired of the gamesmanship involved with dating. I far prefer candor."

"It is rather refreshing."

Shelby smiled and was in the midst of forming another witty comment when Nick's Secret Service detail came around the corner on to Ninth Street and pulled up to the curb in two big black SUVs.

Avery stood beside her to watch the proceedings as the agents escorted Nick and Scotty from the first of the two cars.

Nick took one look at Avery and his normally genial expression hardened with displeasure.

What was that about? Shelby wondered as Nick and Scotty approached them.

"What're you doing here, Hill?" Nick asked.

"Senator, nice to see you too. I gave your wife a ride home."

"Why did she need a ride?"

"She was dead on her feet. I didn't think it would be safe for her to drive."

Nick eyed the other man warily. "Is that right?"

Avery's lips tightened with displeasure, and Shelby could tell there was something he was dying to say but refrained.

"How was the Capitol, buddy?" Shelby asked Scotty, hoping to ease the tension.

"It was cool. We had ice cream in the Senate Dining Room."

"Wow, that sounds like fun."

"I've got to get back to work," Avery said. "I'll see you."

"Hill?" Nick called after the agent.

"Yeah?"

"Thanks for giving Sam a ride."

"No problem."

After Avery got into his car and took off, Shelby glanced at Nick. "What was that all about?"

"I don't like that guy."

"How come?" Shelby asked, surprised by the unusual hostility she sensed in him.

"I just don't."

"You should have a reason for not liking someone," Scotty told his dad.

"I have my reasons."

Shelby would love to know what they were, but decided not to push it any further, especially with Scotty watching their every move. She put her arm around the boy, who was already two inches taller than her. "Ready for some dinner?"

"What're we having?"

"How does spaghetti sound?"

"Awesome." He said what she expected but the single word lacked his usual enthusiasm for all things Italian.

"Go wash your hands. I'll be right in."

Scotty took his backpack from Nick and trudged up the ramp to the house, his head bent.

"Is he okay?" Shelby asked Nick.

"Have you heard about Willie Vasquez?" Nick asked.

"No, what about him?"

"It was just on the radio so I suppose I can tell you that he was murdered overnight."

"Oh, no. Oh, Lord."

"Scotty took the news hard. He thought a lot of Willie, especially after he met him at camp last summer."

"What a tragedy. All because he missed a fly ball."

"Sam would tell us not to leap to any conclusions until we know more."

"Is she working the case?"

He nodded. "As soon as she gets some sleep, she'll be back on it."

"Could I ask you something else?"

"Sure."

"Agent Hill asked me to have coffee with him." Nick didn't need to know that she'd actually done the asking a while ago. "Would it bother you if I went?"

"Hell, no. Go. Have a great time. By all means." He started toward the ramp. "I'd better get in there and check on Scotty."

Confused by Nick's contradictory statements, Shelby followed him inside. *Men*, she thought, wondering if she'd ever understand what made them tick.

THE STUDIOS OF WFBR-FM were located adjacent to the stadium on Potomac Avenue. Home of "Feds Baseball Radio," the station broadcast all the team's games and hosted regular interviews with the players and management. WFBR had become a critical part of the team's presence in the city over the last three seasons.

At the reception desk, Gonzo asked to speak to the general manager and was escorted into the office of James Settle. He introduced himself and flashed his badge.

"What can I do for you, Detective?"

"Willie Vasquez was found murdered this morning."

Settle stared at Gonzo, as if he hadn't heard him correctly. "Christ," he whispered. "How?"

"He was stabbed in the chest."

"What is it you need from us?"

"We heard the Big Ben show this morning and were interested in speaking with him."

"I'll see if he's still in the building."

While Settle made a call, Gonzo looked around at the team memorabilia on the shelves and walls.

"He's on his way up," Settle said. "He's not in any trouble, is he?"

"I'd like to talk to him about some of the callers this morning."

They waited in uneasy silence until Big Ben came into the room. True to his name, Ben Markinson was big and burly with a headful of unruly curly hair and a beard that grew untamed. "You wanted to see me, Jim?" he asked in a voice made for radio.

Settle gestured to Gonzo. "This is Detective Gonzales with the Metropolitan Police Department. He'd like to speak to you about this morning's show."

Hands on hips, Big Ben scowled as he glanced at Gonzo. "What about it?"

"Willie Vasquez was found murdered this morning."

"Is that right? Probably had it coming after that piss-poor performance last night."

Gonzo stared him down, incredulous. "So you think murder is an appropriate punishment for failing to catch a fly ball?"

"An *easy* fly ball."

"Pardon me," Gonzo said, his tone thick with sarcasm. "An easy fly ball."

Ben shifted from one foot to the other. "Well, I'm not saying he deserved to die, but jeez, Detective, how could he *miss* that?"

"As I wasn't on the field at the time the ball was hit, I couldn't say. No one can really say what was going through his mind at that time, could they?"

"I guess not," Ben said begrudgingly.

"A lot of your listeners had plenty to say this morning."

"They're pissed off—and rightfully so."

"Any of them pissed off enough to commit murder?"

"How the hell should I know? I talk to a lot of them regularly on the show, but I don't actually know most of them."

"Have you met any of them in person?"

"Here and there at events, but what do I know about whether or not they killed him?"

"Are any of them regular callers who are familiar to you?"

"A lot of them are."

Gonzo held out his notebook and pen. "I'd appreciate a list of any that seemed angry enough over the game to commit murder."

Ben snatched the notebook out of his hand. "Hope you've got plenty of time because just about everyone who called this morning was pretty pissed off."

"I've got all the time it takes."

"Give him what he needs, Ben," Settle said.

Ben took the notebook to the conference table and made a big production out of sitting down. "You may as well get Marcy up here too." For Gonzo's edification, Ben said, "She's my producer."

"I'll call her," Settle said.

Gonzo sat across from Ben, resigned to being there a while.

SINCE GARRETT COLLINS lived somewhat close to Sam on Sixth Street, Avery decided to stop to talk to him on the way back to the ballpark. As general manager, Collins oversaw everything having to do with the players and their contracts as well as the coaching staff. The person in charge of fielding the team that had come so close to a championship season was probably angrier than most about the ball Willie had missed.

Was he angry enough to commit murder? That remained to be seen.

Collins lived in a row of high-end brick-front town houses. Avery parked in front of number 26, behind a black Mercedes SUV with a Feds decal on the back window. He noted that all the blinds were drawn inside the house, as if the occupant wanted to keep out the daylight. He strode up the steps that led to the front door and rang the doorbell.

When no one answered, Avery tried the metal knocker. After that failed to yield results, Avery called Ray Jestings on his personal cell phone.

"Avery? Do you have some news for me?"

"Your GM is ignoring his doorbell. Can you reach out and get him to let me in?"

"Yeah. I'll do it right now."

"Don't tell him about Willie. I want to do that."

"Okay."

"Thanks."

Avery leaned against the wrought-iron rail, arms crossed. As he fought off the fatigue that made him feel dull around the edges, he thought about the way Nick Cappuano had looked at him, as if he'd like to gut him right there on the sidewalk. Avery suspected they might've gotten into it if the boy hadn't been watching his father's every move.

He ran his fingers through his hair wearily. Despite his best efforts to forget about her, he was just as fascinated with the gorgeous Sam Holland as he'd been the first time he met her, long before he knew she was married to one of the country's most popular senators.

And now, supposedly, he had a tentative date with Sam's assistant. Fantastic. Like that wouldn't further complicate an already complicated situation.

The sound of locks disengaging inside the townhouse had Avery standing up straighter.

Garrett Collins looked like hell. There was no other way to describe his appearance as he opened the door to Avery.

"Mr. Collins, I'm Special Agent Avery Hill with the FBI." He flashed his badge to Collins, who eyed it warily.

"What can I do for you?"

"May I come in for a minute?"

"Um, that's probably not a good idea."

"Why's that?"

"The place is a bit of a mess."

"I'm sure I've seen worse." When Collins hesitated again, Avery said, "You can either let me in, or I'll take you into custody for a ride downtown. Your call."

The statement generated the first spark of life Avery had seen yet in the other man's eyes. "Take me into custody? What the hell for?"

"The murder of Willie Vasquez, to begin with." Avery tossed that out there, wanting to see what kind of reaction he'd get.

"Willie's dead?" Collins asked in a voice that was barely more than a whisper.

"Can I come in, or shall we do this at my office?"

Reluctantly, or so it seemed to Avery, Collins stepped back and admitted him into a living room that had been smashed to smithereens. Mirrors, lamps, the television… Nothing had been spared. A wooden baseball bat leaned against the wall, leading Avery to conclude it had been used to inflict maximum damage.

Avery turned to Collins. “What the hell happened here?”

“I was kind of…frustrated when I got home a little while ago.”

“So you smashed the shit out of your own home?”

“Better than going after the people who put me in the mood to smash things, wouldn’t you say?”

“Yes, I suppose so.”

“What happened to Willie?”

“He was stabbed in the chest. That’s all we’re saying at this time. Did you see him after the game last night?”

“I did not.” This was said through tight lips, and it didn’t take much to deduce that Willie’s error had led to the smash-fest.

“Had you spoken to him?”

“No.”

“Did you try to reach him?”

Avery followed Collins deeper into the townhouse to the kitchen where he went about the motions of making coffee. He held up the can, asking Avery if he wanted some.

“I won’t say no to a caffeine boost.”

“I didn’t try to call him because I didn’t have anything to say to him. Sixteen million dollars a year, and all he had to do was *catch the goddamned ball*.” Collins turned to Avery. “How could he miss an easy fly ball? The guy is a future Hall of Famer, for crying out loud.”

“Was.”

“Excuse me?”

“He *was* a future Hall of Famer.”

“Yes,” Collins said with a sigh. “He was. He needed

a few more seasons to get there." He started the coffeemaker and turned to Avery. "Don't get me wrong. I'm sorry he's dead. He was a nice guy. I liked him. I respected what he brought to the game and the clubhouse. But I'm pissed off that he missed that easy catch. I'll never get how that could've happened."

"Did you know of any problems he was having on or off the field?"

"He'd grappled with hamstring issues all season, but that was under control. Did you talk to Jamie?"

"Earlier. She was extremely broken up when she heard the news about Willie. Her reaction led us to wonder if there wasn't something more to their relationship."

"What do you mean?"

"Was there anything romantic between them?"

"I don't know. They spent a lot of time together. People talked, because that's what people do."

"Any other issues or problems in Willie's life that you knew about?"

"I don't get why you're asking questions like this when it's obvious a disgruntled fan took him out."

Avery nodded and accepted a mug of strong-smelling black coffee. "We're not paid to deduce the obvious. Do you know of anything that might be relevant to our investigation?"

"Carmen's brother has been in some trouble in the Dominican Republic. Willie bailed him out a couple of times, but then he cut off the money, which made Carmen's family mad. Marco made some threats toward Willie."

"What kind of threats?"

"The kind that resulted in Willie getting a restraining order against the guy to keep him away from his family."

"Has the brother-in-law been here?"

"I believe there was an altercation last winter, during the off-season. I don't have the details on that, but I was notified that he had a personal issue with the brother-in-law and stadium security was aware of it too in case the guy tried to gain access to him there."

Avery took notes as Collins spoke.

"You're really going to look into the brother-in-law after what happened last night? You gotta figure this was someone pissed about him losing the game for us."

"We're looking at everything. How long did you stay at the stadium last night after the game ended?"

"I was there until about five o'clock this morning."

"What did you do during that time?"

"Bob Minor and I met with the media. That was fun. Kind of like having a root canal without Novocain. After that, I spent some time in the locker room with the team, and then I met with Ray Jestings, the team's owner."

"Did you encounter anyone who was mad enough about Willie's error that they might've wanted to harm him?"

Collins stared at him, incredulous. "*Everyone* wanted to harm him. People were furious."

"Was anyone furious enough to act on the urge?"

"I'd like to think not, but who knows? This was as close as any of them have ever come to a World Series. They wanted it badly."

"Was anyone particularly vocal in regard to Willie?"

"Rick Lind was pretty pissed. He'd gotten us two

outs. He needed one from Willie, and Willie let him down."

Avery wrote down Lind's name and circled it. "If you think of anything else that might be relevant, give me a call." He handed over his business card and drained his mug. "Thanks for the coffee."

"No problem."

On the way out, glass crunched under his feet as he passed through the wrecked living room. He liked sports as much as the next guy, but this was over the top by anyone's standards. Who smashed up their own home over a baseball game? That question was on Avery's mind as he returned to the stadium to speak with Hugh Bixby.

In the foyer to the office portion of the stadium, Avery asked the same receptionist to direct him to Bixby.

"I'll see if I can find him," she said.

While he waited, Avery made a call to his deputy, Special Agent George Terrell. Since Avery had been promoted over Terrell to lead the division, his deputy had been cooperative and professional, but an undercurrent of resentment existed between the two men.

"What's up?" Terrell said.

"We're assisting the MPD with the Vasquez investigation."

"How'd we get roped into that?"

"I know Ray Jestings, the team owner, so I offered our assistance. With an entire city full of motive, they need all the help they can get."

"That's the truth."

"The club's GM mentioned a problem Vasquez had

with his brother-in-law in the last year or so. Could you look into that for me?"

"Sure. What's the guy's name?"

"The GM couldn't remember the name. Just that there was a restraining order in place to keep the guy away from Vasquez and the stadium."

"I'll see what I can find out."

"Thanks."

The line went dead, and Avery stashed the phone in his coat pocket. So he and his deputy would never be the best of friends. They could still work together when need be. It wasn't his fault that Director Hamilton had chosen to promote him rather than Terrell. Avery hoped that eventually Terrell would realize that.

"Mr. Bixby is in the locker room," the receptionist said.

"Where can I find the locker room?"

"Let me get someone to cover the desk, and I'll show you."

Ten minutes later, the young woman led him through a winding maze of hallways and down several flights of stairs that led to a tunnel. Outside a red door, she punched in a code that gave them access.

Inside the locker room, Metro PD's Crime Scene Unit was rifling through lockers and equipment as a man in a shirt and tie watched them. He had close-cropped blond hair and his build indicated he might've been an athlete in another life. If his red face was any indication, Mr. Bixby was enraged.

"Excuse me, Mr. Bixby—"

"What do you want? I'm busy here."

The receptionist recoiled from the harshly spoken words. "This is Special Agent Hill from the FBI."

The FBI acronym did the trick, as it usually did. Bixby's hands dropped from his hips and his expression slackened a bit. "Maybe you can tell me what *the hell* is going on here."

To the receptionist, Avery said, "Thank you for showing me the way."

"No problem." She scurried away as if someone had set her rear on fire.

Avery found it interesting that she was somewhat intimidated by Bixby. "You haven't spoken with Mr. Jenkins?"

"He called, but I was busy with cops invading my stadium, so I missed the call."

"Willie Vasquez has been murdered."

"Murdered."

"That's what I said."

"How?"

"Stabbed in the chest."

Bixby took in the scene unfolding in the locker room. "So that's what this is about."

"Yes."

"What're you looking for?"

"We won't know until we find it."

"If you're insinuating that a member of our organization had something to do with it—"

"I'm not insinuating anything. I'm investigating a murder, starting with the last place Mr. Vasquez was seen alive. When was the last time you saw him?"

Bixby blew out a deep breath. "Believe it or not, it was when he missed the ball. After that, I was extremely busy getting my people ready for exactly what happened."

"Have you been here all night?"

Nodding, he said, “I never left.” He glanced at Avery. “So why’s the FBI involved in this?”

“We offered our assistance to the Metro PD, and they accepted. It’s a big job to catch a murderer when an entire city has motive.”

“I bet it is. Do you need me for anything else? I have to go brief my staff about what’s happened.”

“Not at this time, but I’d appreciate if you’d remain available for the duration of the investigation.” Avery handed him a business card. “Call me if you think of anything that might be relevant.”

“I will.” He studied the business card for a moment. After taking a look around to make sure no one could overhear them, he glanced at Avery. “If I tell you something I heard, it won’t come back to bite me in the ass, will it?”

“I’ll do everything I can to keep that from happening, but I can’t make any promises.”

Bixby pondered that, seeming somewhat tormented. “Last night,” he began slowly, “after the dust settled, I overheard some of my guys talking about Lind.”

“What about him?”

“He was pissed at Vasquez. Seriously pissed. Apparently, he was ranting about how he’d done his job and Vasquez should’ve closed the deal for them. The loss and the blown save got charged to Lind when they should’ve been charged to Vasquez. That kind of thing.” He gestured to overturned chairs in the far corner of the room, including one that looked like it had been smashed against the cinder block wall. “Supposedly Lind made firewood out of that chair among other things.”

Avery looked up from his notebook. "What other things?"

"I didn't hear everything they said."

"Could you ask the people you heard talking about it to come down here?"

"That could lead to me getting bitten in the ass."

"I'm sorry, but this is a murder investigation. All bets are off."

Sighing, Bixby reached for the radio that was attached to his belt and summoned several people to the locker room with orders to drop what they were doing and come. "They'll be here momentarily."

Avery and Bixby coexisted in awkward silence as they watched the CSU detectives comb through every inch of the locker room. Seven minutes later, four men came in through the tunnel. Of varying heights, they were all ripped with muscles and seemed annoyed to be called from whatever they'd been doing.

"What's up?" one of them asked.

Hill nodded to Bixby, giving him permission to fill them in. "This is Agent Hill with the FBI. He's notified me that Willie Vasquez has been murdered."

The four men exchanged glances.

"What's that got to do with us?" the same guy asked. He seemed to be the spokesman for all of them.

"What's your name?" Avery asked.

"Jim," he said tentatively, glancing at Bixby who nodded.

"Jim what?"

"Morris."

"I heard you talking about Lind last night," Bixby said. "About how pissed off he was at Vasquez."

"You don't think—"

"We don't think anything," Avery said. "We just want to know what you might've heard him saying about Vasquez."

"He was fucking furious and rightfully so."

"Can you tell me, specifically, what you heard Lind say or what you saw him do?" Avery asked.

"Will he find out I talked to you?" Jim asked. "I don't want to piss him off."

"You have to understand, Agent Hill," Bixby said. "Our job is to protect and secure the ballpark as well as the players and to ensure the fans have a safe, enjoyable experience here. It goes against everything we believe in to speak to an outsider about one of the players."

"I understand and respect your position. However, a man has been murdered—a man who was loved by this organization yesterday, a man who has a wife and two young children who are counting on us to give them answers. If you know something that will help us get those answers for them, this is no time to be worried about pissing someone off."

"He said if he had a gun, he'd shoot Vasquez himself," another of them said.

"Your name?"

"Kyle Davidson."

Avery made a note. "You heard Lind say those words?"

"Yes, sir. He was running around the locker room, slamming doors and swearing. He was totally out of control, so Minor asked us to get down there in case there was trouble."

Interesting, Avery thought, that Minor had failed to mention the incident with Lind during their conversation. He made another note.

"Did you have to get involved?"

Kyle shook his head. "We stood by in case we were needed, but Lind wore himself out before we had to intervene."

"Were any of the other players spouting off?" Avery asked.

"Cecil Mulroney was pretty pissed too," Jim said. "He's the left fielder who grabbed the ball after Vasquez missed it."

Avery knew who Mulroney was, but didn't interrupt to tell him that.

"He kept saying he couldn't believe Willie missed the ball, and how he ought to go back to Little League and learn how to catch a ball."

"Did any of you see Vasquez after the game?" Avery asked.

"I did," Kyle said. "I was in the detail that brought him off the field."

"Was anything said?"

He shook his head. "What was there to say? We led him in here, and he went straight to the training room, slamming the door behind him."

"Did you see him again after that?"

"No, he didn't come out before I was called to the stadium to deal with the fans."

"So he was left here unprotected?"

"He was in a locked room. I didn't think he'd be in any danger." Kyle looked at Bixby and then at Avery. "It didn't happen here, did it?"

"No," Avery said. "We've been able to trace his movements as far as the L'Enfant Metro station. He drove there with Ms. Clark and dropped her to catch the train."

Jim and Kyle exchanged subtle glances, but Avery saw it.

"Something else you want to add?"

"Those two were awfully cozy," Jim said. "Spent a lot of time together, supposedly working on his hamstring issues. People talked."

"What did these people say?" Avery asked.

"That they seemed cozy. Speculation was that there was more to their relationship than met the eye."

"Did you suspect a romantic relationship or something else?"

"I never suspected anything," Jim said, holding up his hands. "I said other people did the suspecting."

"People thought they were messing around," Bixby said. "But to my knowledge, no one ever confronted either of them about it." He shrugged. "They're both adults, and if they wanted to get it on, as long as it didn't affect their work, who cared?"

"If it got out, something like that could cause a lot of trouble for Willie and the team," Avery said. "I find it hard to believe their relationship was common knowledge and no one cared."

"Maybe the front office cared," Bixby said. "But we aren't paid to care about who the players are screwing. If we were, our jobs would be a whole lot more complicated than they already are."

The other men nodded in agreement.

"So the players keep busy in that regard?" Avery asked.

More nervous glances followed the question.

"There's no shortage of women who are interested in spending time with them," Bixby said.

"How diplomatic," Avery replied. "We'll leave it at

that for now, but I reserve the right to delve deeper into that line of questioning at a later date if need be." He doled out cards to the four men. "If you think of anything else that might be relevant to the investigation, please call me."

"You guys can go on back to work," Bixby said.

"Thanks for your time," Avery added.

When they were alone, Bixby said, "Are you going to look at Lind for this?"

"We're certainly going to have a conversation with him."

"Will you tell him we pointed you in his direction?"

"I don't see the need to mention that. I'm sure there were plenty of witnesses to the meltdown. Anyone could've told us."

"Good," he said, seeming genuinely relieved. "That's really good."

"Are you afraid of Mr. Lind for some reason?"

"Not physically, if that's what you mean. He wields a lot of power around here. Has the ear of the front office. If he wanted to, he could cause trouble for me and my staff."

"I understand. I'll do everything I can to keep your names out of the conversation."

"I'd appreciate that, and so would they."

Avery shook hands with Bixby. "Do you have a card in case I need to get in touch?"

Bixby produced a business card from his wallet. "Will you keep me posted?"

"To the best of my ability."

"Thank you."

"Hill."

"Yeah?"

"Lind… He's a bit of a hot head. Something's a little off with him, if you ask me."

"Good to know. Thanks again for your help." Avery left the locker room and followed the exit signs through the twisting maze of tunnels that eventually led to a parking lot. Unfortunately, it wasn't the lot where he'd left his car. As he walked around the outer shell of the stadium, he thought about what a difference twenty-four hours made. The silence was in stark contrast to the roar of the crowd and the rage of the fans that followed Vasquez's unfortunate error.

Avery hadn't been at the game, but he'd watched it on TV from his hotel room. One of these days, he needed to get busy finding a permanent home in the District. After this case, he told himself. Then he'd take care of getting settled.

In the meantime, he placed a call to the MPD, asking for the detectives' pit when he reached Dispatch.

"Detective Dominguez."

"This is Agent Hill. I was wondering if I could pass along some information to aid in the Vasquez investigation."

"Of course. What've you got?"

"We need background checks, including financials, on Garrett Collins, the team's general manager and Rick Lind, closing pitcher."

"Anyone else?"

Avery thought about it for a second. "Let's do Jamie Clark, team trainer, and Bob Minor, the manager too."

"You got it."

"Anything back on Vasquez's financials?"

"Not yet. We're hearing there's been a hang up with

the banks in the Dominican Republic. We're working on it."

"Anything on the video surveillance?"

"Not yet."

"How about his car? Any sign of it?"

"Still looking for that and the blood."

"I'll let you get back to work. Thanks for the update."

"No problem. Thanks for the leads. Will you be attending the meeting at zero seven hundred?"

"I'll be there."

"See you then."

Even though he'd love to go have a conversation with Rick Lind, he wanted to talk to Sam first. Tomorrow was another day, and zero seven hundred would be upon him far too soon. In desperate need of food and sleep, he got into his car and drove "home" to his hotel.

EIGHT

BY THE TIME Nick finally got Scotty settled and into bed it was ten o'clock. After a visit with Skip and Celia, Nick had spent the entire evening with his boy, talking about Willie and what had happened to him. Scotty was a deeply sensitive kid, an old soul in many ways, and Nick had answered as many of his questions as he could. But some questions would never be answered satisfactorily, even if Sam and her team were able to piece together what'd happened to Willie.

Nick had brought home a huge briefing book that he was supposed to go over before morning meetings, but by the time Scotty ran out of questions, he was out of steam. He planned to do a quick review in the morning before his meetings.

Christina had spent all day rearranging two days of campaign events so Nick could accompany the president on the top-secret trip to visit the troops in Afghanistan. In light of the Vasquez murder and Sam's involvement in it—as well as Scotty's despair—Nick wished he hadn't committed to the trip. He hated to be away when so much was going on at home, but he had a job to do too. He couldn't pass up the chance to visit with the troops from Virginia who were stationed in Afghanistan.

He'd never admit to Sam about the tiny bit of anxiety he'd experienced when Nelson's staff first pitched the idea of the trip to him. Flying into a war zone on a gigantic plane with the U.S. flag all over it was not something he'd ever thought he'd do. But much of his life these days was made up of moments he'd never expected to experience, and flying on *Air Force One* would be one more unforgettable thing in a year of unforgettable things.

He took a shower and shaved before he slid into bed next to Sam, snuggling up to her, wishing she would wake up but not wanting to disturb her. As his hand connected with a wool sweater, he realized she was still fully dressed. She was so tired she hadn't even bothered to undress. At least she'd removed her shoes.

His breath caught when she turned over and reached for him, mumbling in her sleep. Nick put his arm around her and ran his other hand over her hair. "Shhh, it's okay, babe," he whispered.

"Time is it?"

"Almost eleven."

"Oh, thank God. I thought it was time to get up."

"Sorry if I woke you."

"You didn't. My bladder did."

"Why don't you go take care of that, and I'll keep your spot warm."

"Okay." She dragged herself out of bed and into the bathroom. When she returned a few minutes later, Nick was ready for her.

"Let's get you out of those heavy clothes so you're more comfortable."

"Are you coming on to me?" Laughing, he said, "Not this time."

"That's disappointing."

"You need sleep more than you need sex."

"Who says?"

He helped her out of her sweater and jeans. "Your husband, who always knows what's best for you." When she was down to just underwear, he moved back in the bed to let her in.

She joined him in bed and snuggled up to him. As warm, naked breasts pressed against his chest, he realized she'd shed the underwear too. He told himself that this night was about sleep and nothing else. *Keep telling yourself that*, he thought as his hand glided up and down her back while her hand caressed his belly.

His reaction was instantaneous and predictable when she was in the vicinity. "Samantha…"

"What?"

"Go back to sleep."

"I will. I've got hours and hours before I have to be at HQ. Plenty of time for sleep." As she spoke, her hand drifted downward and all his efforts to keep his mind off sex fell to the wayside when the back of her hand made contact with his erection.

"*Sam*."

"I didn't do anything."

"You did too. You know exactly what you did."

"I can't help if being naked in bed with you makes me think of things that have nothing to do with sleep."

"I should've slept downstairs so I wouldn't bother you."

"No, you shouldn't have. You belong right here with me."

He turned on his side to face her, and she took advantage of the opportunity to lay a hot, wet, sexy kiss on him. "You brushed your teeth."

"So?"

"So this was a deliberate attack."

"Guilty as charged."

"Since you went to all that trouble…" What else could he do but kiss her back? When she smiled against his lips he held her closer. But no matter how close he got to her it was never close enough.

As if she read his mind, she wrapped her arms and legs around him, imprisoning him in her web of soft, supple flesh and the scent of vanilla and lavender that never failed to stir him. It was the scent of *her*, of his woman, his only love.

Without breaking the kiss, he cupped her breasts and ran his thumbs over her nipples, making her moan. And then she sucked on his tongue, and his need became urgent. He moved them as one so he was on top.

As always, Sam welcomed him with her legs hugging his hips. He'd never felt completely at home anywhere until he found his home with her. Mindful of her need for sleep, he moved things along faster than he preferred, entering her in one smooth flex of his hips that took him straight to paradise.

She turned away from the kiss and drew in a deep breath.

"Are you okay?" he asked, relying on rigid control to remain still long enough for her to reply.

"Mmm. So okay. Love this. Love you."

"Love you too. More than anything."

They moved together like they'd been lovers for years rather than months, but then again they'd had a lot of practice since they'd reunited just before Christmas. He bent his head and found her nipple, tugging and sucking, which always drove her wild.

Her internal muscles tightened around his cock, letting him know she approved of what he was doing. So he did it again and again and again, until they were swept up together in a tumultuous release that felt like it went on forever, at least from his side of things. He had no idea what made her so different from the other women he'd done this with. Nothing in his life could compare to the overwhelming need she inspired him, the passion, the desire, the craving. If he lived a thousand years, he'd never get enough of her.

"Sleep is so overrated," she said after a long period of satisfied silence.

"You always say that until you don't get enough, and the rest of us are made to suffer."

She pinched his rear, making him startle and slide deeper into her. Sam gasped and dug her fingers into his ass, wanting to keep him there.

"Enough, you sex-crazed wench. You're only getting it once tonight."

"Is that right?"

"Yes. I am the husband, and I am in charge." He said the words, knowing they would infuriate her, and hopefully take her mind off sex and put it back on sleep.

"And I am the little woman who does exactly what she's told at all times."

Amused by her response, he slid his hands under her, squeezing her cheeks in a reminder of some of their recent activities in bed. Ever since he discovered that his lovely wife lost her mind when she was spanked, he'd taken full advantage of every opportunity to drive her wild. "Not quite yet, but we're working on your obedience issues."

The comment was met with another internal squeeze

that had him rock hard again, despite his best intentions to the contrary.

As she laughed, her lips brushed against his ear, further firing him up. It might be a good idea to admit he was entirely powerless where she was concerned. But he didn't have to admit anything. She already knew. How could she not when the proof was growing harder inside her by the second?

She ran her hands over his buttocks, dipping her middle finger between them in a move that nearly finished him off a second time.

"Sam, God, what're you doing to me?" he asked as she pressed several times against his entrance before moving further down to stroke the back of his balls.

"Just proving that you're not always in charge."

"As if we needed proof."

"Think of it as a reminder." She dipped her tongue into his ear as her finger moved back up to tease him some more. They'd been getting more and more daring with every passing month, and just when he thought things between them couldn't get any hotter, she proved otherwise by pressing her fingertip inside him.

Every thought was cleared from his mind, replaced by a haze of passion that had him taking her hard and fast, which he had the presence of mind to suspect had been her goal all along. He was coming again in no time, more intensely than the first time. Thankfully, she was right there with him because she'd completely demolished what was left of his energy.

As he lay on top of her, still pulsating in the aftermath, she did that thing to his ear again and nearly had him begging for mercy.

"Let me know when you want to be in charge again," she whispered in his ear, making him laugh.

"You made me your bitch."

That got another laugh out of her. "I really did, didn't I?"

"You know exactly what you did to me."

"Nothing you haven't done to me."

"You've got me thinking of revenge."

"Do your worst."

"I'll have to give that some serious thought." He raised his head from where it rested on her chest and kissed her. "You need to go back to sleep."

"I know," she said, brushing the hair off his forehead in a gesture that never failed to stir him. No one had ever loved him the way she did. "But this was time very well spent."

"You won't hear me complaining." Reluctantly, he withdrew from her and flopped on to his back, reaching for her.

She came into his arms, her head on his chest and her hand flat against his belly. "Are you going on the big trip with the president?"

"Looks that way."

"Oh. Okay."

He squeezed her tighter. "It will be, babe. I promise."

"If you say so. How's the boy?"

"Full of questions and disbelief. It was a tough afternoon and evening, but we got through it."

"I'm sorry I couldn't be here to help."

"He knew where you were and what you were doing. At one point, he said he was glad you were the one looking for Willie's killer because if anyone could find the person who did it, you can."

"I hope I don't let him down. We've got such a mountain to climb with this one. Where do we even begin when so many people were mad at him?"

"I suppose you work it the way you always do and wait for something to pop, as you would say."

"Yeah, I guess. Hopefully something popped overnight that will give us a direction in the morning."

He kissed her forehead and caressed her face. "Shut off that brain of yours and get some more sleep while you can."

"I will, but first tell me about the funny thing that happened earlier with Scotty."

Nick laughed. "You won't believe what he asked me about."

"What?"

"Blow jobs."

Sam lifted her head off his chest, and he wished the light were on so he could see her expression. "Are you freaking kidding me? Where the hell did he hear about that?"

"School. Where else?"

"I knew we should've sent him to the Quakers. I bet they don't talk about that stuff there."

"*All* boys talk about that stuff, no matter what school they go to."

"He's too young to be thinking about blow jobs."

"He's not too young, but luckily, he's not thinking about them the way we do. When I told him what it means he was totally grossed out."

"So you told him the actual truth?"

"Of course I did. He's too old to be treated like a baby."

"I suppose that's true. What exactly did you say?"

"That it's when a girl kisses you down there."

"Ack!" She let out a squeak of protest and pressed her face to his chest. "I'm dying. Dying. Dying. *Dying*!"

His finger combed through her hair. "Don't do that. I need you too much."

"So it grossed him out, huh?"

"Yep. He said anyone who likes that has something wrong with him. I said there's nothing wrong with me."

"You did not! Oh my God, Nick! Now he'll know we do that. Or that *I* do it."

"So what? It's part of life. Why should we act like that doesn't happen between us?"

"God," she said with a sigh, setting back on his chest. "I'm so not cut out for motherhood."

"Sure you are," he said with a chuckle. "The challenge is that we're going right from the frying pan to the fire of adolescence without years to prepare ourselves. We've gotta be ready for this stuff. It's coming fast and furious, whether we like it or not."

"I'd like to unsubscribe from the vocabulary conversations."

"No problem," he said, smiling. "How about I handle anything in the penis department?"

"That'd be awfully good of you. Were you freaking out when he asked about that?"

"Totally and trying not to die laughing at the same time. The faces he was making were hysterical. I wished you'd been there to help me out."

"I doubt I would've been much help. I would've been too busy screaming. I never thought I'd be so thankful that a murder kept me away from home."

Laughing, he held her close to him, thrilled by her, by them, by their son and their life. He had everything he'd ever dreamed of, and it was so much more than even his vivid imagination could've come up with. "Love you, babe."

"Mmm, love you too."

Long after she drifted off, he lay awake enjoying the simple pleasure of having her sleep all over him.

SAM WOKE MUCH LATER, roused by a sound coming from the hallway. She dragged herself out of bed, pulled on a robe and went to investigate. As she left her bedroom, she nearly tripped over Scotty's huddled form outside the door.

Sam squat next to him and rested a hand on his back. "Hey, buddy, what's wrong?"

"I had a bad dream," he said, sniffling.

She wondered how long he'd been there. "You should've come in."

"I didn't want to bother you."

"You wouldn't have bothered us." Sam reached for him, and he lunged at her, breaking down into sobs that brought tears to her eyes. She'd never seen him so upset. "It's not possible for you to bother us. Anytime you need us, you come in. All right?"

He nodded and clung to her. In that moment, Sam realized that while he might be growing up quickly, he was still a little boy in many ways and still in bad need of a mother. She was thrilled to fill that role for him.

"How about we get you back in bed?"

Shaking his head, he tightened his grip on her.

"I'll stay with you."

"You will?"

"Sure, I will. Come on. It's cold out here." She helped him up and got him tucked back into bed under the Red

Sox comforter he'd chosen after much debate between sports and superheroes. The walls of his room were plastered with the posters he hadn't been allowed to have in the state home. Nick had insisted on as many posters as the walls could hold. In the glow of the night-light, Spider-Man stood watch over them from the ceiling. "Move it on over, mister. Here I come."

He giggled as she made a big production out of getting in bed with him, "accidentally" hitting a few of his most ticklish spots in the process, which made him laugh some more. She much preferred the laughter to the tears that were so unlike him.

"Snuggle me," she said. "I'm cold."

He curled up to her, and Sam put her arms around him. Her cheek rested against his silky hair.

"Want to talk about it?" she asked.

"No."

"There's nothing to be afraid of. You're safe. You know that, right?"

"I know."

"Was it about Willie?"

"Sort of…"

"I'm sorry you're sad. What happened to Willie shouldn't happen to anyone."

"I don't understand how someone could kill him for missing a ball."

"I don't get it either, but people are so invested in sports. They take it way too far and lose all perspective."

"I read online that he has kids. Little kids."

Sam winced. "Yes."

"Did you meet them?"

"One of them. Miguel. He's four."

"It's so sad that he won't remember his dad. My mom and grandpa died when I was six, and I barely remember them. He's only four."

Moved by his compassion as much as his grief, Sam hugged him tighter. "I wish there was something I could say to make you feel better."

"The snuggling makes me feel better."

Sam smiled. "It makes me feel better too. You ought to try to get back to sleep so you're not super-duper tired tomorrow."

"Do you promise you won't leave?"

"I promise. And I'll let you in on a little secret."

"What's that?"

In a conspiratorial whisper, Sam said, "You're a much better snuggler than Nick is." In truth, no one did snuggling better than her husband, but Scotty didn't need to know that.

He laughed, which she'd hoped he would.

"You can't tell."

"I won't. Don't worry." As he relaxed into her embrace, Sam rubbed his back in small circles.

"Sam?"

"Hmm?"

"It's really nice to have a mom again."

Oh God, he was going to make her cry! "It's the very best thing *ever* to have a son as sweet as you. I never knew how great sons could be." She kissed the top of his head. "Love you, buddy. Try to go to sleep. I'll be right here. I promise."

She kept rubbing his back until long after he released a deep breath and fell asleep in her arms.

WHEN SAM'S ALARM went off at six, Nick realized he was in bed alone. Running his fingers through his hair, he stretched out the kinks and got up to find a pair of sweats before he went looking for his wife.

In the hallway, he noticed Scotty's door propped open and peeked inside to make sure the boy hadn't kicked off his covers the way he did most nights.

Nick was stunned to see Sam wrapped up in Scotty, both of them sound asleep. He stared at them for a long time, overwhelmed by the sight of her sleeping with the boy they both loved. As he ventured into the room, he wondered what he'd missed during the night.

He bent to kiss her cheek. "Sam." When she didn't rouse, he kissed her again. "Samantha." He kept his voice down so he wouldn't disturb Scotty.

"Mmm."

"It's six, babe," he whispered.

"No, it isn't."

"Yes," he said, chuckling, "it is." He smoothed her hair back. "What happened?"

"He had a bad dream. I heard him whimpering in the hallway. He didn't want to come in and bother us."

Scotty never stirred as they spoke in whispers.

"Oh, poor guy. He should've come in."

"That's what I told him too."

"What time was this?"

"I have no idea. Maybe we should let him sleep in a bit this morning. Shelby can take him to school when he wakes up."

"Sounds like a good idea. You need to get going to your meeting."

"I promised him I wouldn't leave."

"I'll tell him you stayed until you had to leave for work. He knows you've got a job to do."

Seeming reluctant, Sam disentangled from Scotty

and got up. She resettled the covers over him and pressed a kiss to his forehead. "At times like this, I hate that I have a job that requires so much of my time."

In the hallway, he hugged her. "I've said it before, and I'll say it again—I always hate your job."

"I know, I know." She went up on tiptoes to kiss him. "Gotta hit the shower."

"Want some company?"

She smiled at the perfectly innocent expression he attempted to pull off. "Are we talking about you, or do you have someone else you're going to send in?"

"Very funny, Samantha." He gave her a swat on the rear and steered her into the bathroom where he pushed the lock on the door—just in case. "Speaking of 'someone else,'" he said as he watched her remove the robe while he dropped his sweats onto a pile on the floor. "I saw your pal Hill last night after he brought you home."

"He's not my 'pal.' He's my colleague." She leaned into the shower to turn on the water, giving him a spectacular view of her spectacular ass. "And he brought me home because I was too tired to drive safely. Nothing more to it than that."

"For you anyway."

She turned to him, nude and furious and absolutely gorgeous. "What the hell is that supposed to mean?"

He went to her, put his arms around her and yanked her in tight against him. "It means I do not like that guy, as you well know."

"And as you well know, I have no control over who Director Hamilton puts in charge of his criminal investigation unit."

"You don't, but I could probably do something about that."

Her mouth fell open, and her eyes narrowed with rage, which he'd fully expected. "Don't you *dare* mess with his career! That's beneath you."

It wasn't beneath him in this case, but he wisely chose not to share that thought with his wife when he'd already managed to piss her off. Nick scowled at her back as he followed her into the shower. "I hate when you ruin my fun."

"I hate when you act like a jealous fool over nothing. And P.S. he's interested in Shelby, not me."

"He's interested in *you* and going out with her because she's close to *you*."

"Please, for the love of God, don't tell her that. I think she genuinely likes him."

"Someone's gotta."

"You're an ass hat, you know that?" She raised her hands to his chest, tweaked his nipples and tugged on his chest hair, bringing tears to his eyes.

"Ow. That hurt!"

"Good. Who am I naked in the shower with? Him or you?"

"You'd better not be naked in the shower with him."

"Ugh, you are driving me crazy! Stop acting like a jealous ass. I can't stand it."

"I can't stand the idea of some other guy lusting after you. That drives me crazy."

"I've said this before, and I'll say it again and again and again until you *hear* it, you big lughead—he's *nothing* to me. Stop manufacturing trouble where there is none and make love to your wife before you say something else that's going to get you into a shit ton of trouble."

"I don't want to make love to my wife. She's mean and calls me names."

She rolled her gorgeous blue eyes to high heaven. "Is that a challenge?"

"Take it any way you want to," he said with feigned disinterest. He loved goading her and making her mad. He filled his hands with soap and closed his eyes to wash his face. And then her lips made contact with his shaft and he swallowed a mouthful of soapy water that made him gag and cough. Blinking the soap out of his eyes, he found her on her knees. "Holy shit! What the hell?"

"All that talk of blow jobs last night gave me ideas."

"Sam, wait…"

"Shut up. You had your chance to do it your way, but you said you didn't want to, so now I'm in charge."

"Sam…" Oh God, she was seriously good at that with just the right amount of suction and tongue and hand action. Christ, she was totally making him her bitch *again*, one tug of her lips at a time, and that was before she opened her throat and took him deep. "*Fuck*," he muttered, clinging to control by a hair.

She cupped his balls and squeezed, sending him into orbit. After she licked him clean, she stood and eyed him triumphantly. "Wasn't much of a challenge. You might want to fight a little harder next time."

"I'll keep that in mind," he said, still breathing hard as she conditioned her hair and finished getting washed.

"Gotta get to it, Senator. Have a good day."

"Sam."

"What?"

He reached for her. "Come back."

With a quizzical expression, she moved closer to him. "Why?"

He bent his head and kissed her softly. "I love you."

"I know you do. I love you too, even when you're being an ass hat lughead."

"I don't give a shit about Hill, and I know you don't either."

"Then why do you insist on pushing my buttons where he's concerned?"

"Because pushing your buttons is always fun." He waggled his brows for emphasis.

Her mouth fell open in disbelief. "So wait, did you just totally play me here?"

Smiling, Nick shrugged. "Now, babe, that'd be awfully devious of me, wouldn't it?"

Her eyes narrowed into a glare as she poked him in the belly and stepped out of the shower. "This means war," she called over her shoulder.

"I'll look forward to that."

WELL INTO HIS tenth month of sobriety, Terry O'Connor cherished his new routine. He'd all but moved into the Adams Morgan home of his girlfriend, Dr. Lindsey McNamara. He loved nothing more than waking up to her gorgeous face on the pillow next to his. Some mornings, like today, they lingered in bed for as long as they could, laughing, talking and making slow, sweet morning love that left him completely sated but with no time for the AA meeting he attended most days before work.

He'd catch the noon meeting on the Hill or another after work if he got tied up in the office. Terry tried to make a meeting every day, but because of his crazy schedule during the campaign, he occasionally missed a day. Not many of them, though.

His hard-won sobriety was one of the most important things in a new life that was so much better than his worthless old life there wasn't even a word to describe how different it was. The relationship with Lindsey was by far the best part, with his job as Nick Cappuano's deputy chief of staff ranking a very close second.

After a shower and shave, he found a bag from the dry cleaner in the closet Lindsey had cleared out to make room for his suits. Though he still had an apartment of his own, he went there rarely these days to water a couple of lonely plants, pick up the mail and pay the bills.

He was knotting a red silk tie when she came into the bedroom bearing coffee fixed just the way he liked it—dark with a hint of sugar. "Thanks, hon, and thanks for picking up the dry cleaning. You're too good to me."

She patted his cheek and kissed him. "You're just as good to me," she said with a wink that was a not-so-subtle reminder of the bonus orgasm he'd treated her to before he let her out of bed.

"Did the papers come?" He'd had his subscriptions to all the major papers moved to her house, since he spent most mornings there.

"They're on the kitchen table. What's up later?"

"We've got a campaign meet and greet in Arlington after work. I shouldn't be too late if you want to grab dinner."

"That sounds good. Byron is on the early shift this morning, so I'm working until seven anyway."

"Perfect." He took her by surprise when he looped an arm around her waist and pulled her in close so her back was snug against his chest. He nibbled on her neck and made her tremble. "Have I told you yet today that I love you?"

"Only a couple of times."

"I'm slacking off."

"I've been meaning to talk to you about that."

Terry had never been in a relationship like this one. They talked and laughed and poked fun at each other. They made mad, passionate love and even laughed in bed too. Underneath it all was a foundation of respect and mutual admiration that humbled him. Every day he tried to make sure he deserved her. The thought of losing her respect or her love kept him sober. It was that simple.

She turned in his arms and raised her hands to his face. "I love you too."

Looking down at her, he took note of her bright green eyes, the dusting of freckles across her nose and the pink lips that were slightly swollen from his kisses. He fisted her long red hair and gave a gentle tug to position her for another kiss. "When I think about the way I was living a year ago… I had no idea life could be this sweet."

"My life was perfectly fine before, but this is *so* much better than perfectly fine."

They shared a warm smile that nearly made him forget all about the day of meetings and campaign business to attend to. "After the election, I want to get out of town for a week or so. Would you be game for that?"

"Yes, please. I haven't had a vacation in so long that I forget when the last one was."

"Let's get something booked ASAP. I'll look into it." He released her hair and let it flow through his fingers as she reached for his hand and led him to the kitchen. "Any preference on where we go?"

"Hot sand. Umbrella drinks. Very clear blue water."

"Got it," he said, smiling at her quick reply. He expected nothing less from her. "I like the way you think."

"Bagel?" she asked, holding up the bag from their trip to the market the night before.

"Sure. Thanks." While he waited on the toaster, he scanned the headlines in the *Washington Post*, *Washington Star*, the *Wall Street Journal* and the *New York Times*. He opened the *Star* to peruse the political news, and an item on page two caught his attention: Fire in Thailand Linked to U.S. Company.

He skimmed the story about the factory fire that killed more than three hundred young women over the summer. An investigation had uncovered a connection between the factory and U.S. textile giant Lexicore.

Terry gasped in shock as the name Lexicore jumped out at him. "Oh no, no, no," he whispered. "Holy shit."

Carrying two plates with bagels slathered in cream cheese, Lindsey came over to where he was standing at the counter. "Terry? What is it? What's wrong?"

"Remember the fire in Thailand last summer when all those girls were killed?"

She nodded. "Didn't they have the doors barred from the outside or something?"

"Yes."

"So horrible. What about it?"

"The factory is owned by Lexicore."

"As in Lexicore the big U.S. company?"

"One and the same. My dad is close to the company's president, and he's a huge stockholder. When my brother died, he left a two-million-dollar life insurance policy to Nick, and my dad invested most of it for him—some of it in Lexicore."

"Oh no," Lindsey said, properly stricken. "Oh God."

"Oh yes, and the press has made the connection to Lexicore this close to the election." He pulled his cell phone from his pocket and found his dad's number on his list of favorites.

"Good morning, son," Graham said. "This is a nice surprise."

"Dad, we've got a huge problem."

NINE

SAM ARRIVED AT HQ fifteen minutes before the meeting she'd called, raring to dig into the investigation after a decent night of sleep. Despite the interruptions, she felt rested and recharged and determined to make serious headway.

Her first stop was in the pit to talk to third-shift detectives Carlucci and Dominguez. "What've we got, ladies?"

"Good morning, Lieutenant," Carlucci said, choking back a yawn. "Autopsy report and photos from Dr. McNamara that came in last night. Vic died of a single stab wound to the chest that punctured his aorta. She puts the time of death between two and four yesterday morning."

Sam opened the envelope, flipped through the photos and scanned Lindsey's report, frowning when she saw that it contained nothing else she didn't already know.

"We watched security footage all night," Carlucci continued, "and were able to isolate the drop off of Ms. Clark in the area of the L'Enfant Plaza Metro station. He pulled back into traffic on Maryland Avenue, and that's where we lost him."

"Heading in which direction?"

"Toward Georgetown."

"So whatever occurred, it happened between L'Enfant and Georgetown."

"That's a lot of ground to cover," Dominguez said. "Any sign of the car or the blood?"

"Neither," Carlucci said. "Based on his interviews with team personnel last night, Agent Hill asked us to do background and financial checks on a number of the key players."

It irritated her that he'd asked her people to do something for him, but to say so would be childish and counterproductive, so she held her tongue. "Anything pop on that?"

"The general manager, Garrett Collins, is up to his eyeballs in debt." Carlucci handed Sam a printout that detailed a dire financial situation.

"Well, well, what've we got here?" she asked as she scanned the three-page list of creditors. "The guy makes seven figs and doesn't pay his cable bill?"

"We said the same thing."

Acting on a hunch, Sam said, "Go pick him up for further questioning."

"What about the meeting?" Dominguez asked. "You can join us already in progress if you get back in time. Before you go, print me out a picture of Willie alive and in uniform, will you?"

"Sure thing."

Carlucci produced the photo about two minutes later and headed out with her partner to pick up Collins.

Right after they left, Hill came into the pit looking perfectly put together in a dark suit with a lavender tie. Another guy might've looked effeminate in a tie that color, but there was nothing effeminate about him. He looked her over in that intense way he did so well. "You seem rested, Lieutenant."

"Rested and ready to hit it hard. I just sent Carlucci and Dominguez to pick up Garrett Collins."

He seemed taken aback by the news. "Why? I met with him yesterday and didn't pick up the murderer vibe at all. He's alibied up the wazoo too. He was at the ballpark until five in the morning after the game."

"That's after our estimated time of death, but he's also in debt up the wazoo," Sam said, handing him the printout of Collins' financials.

"Whoa," Hill said as he read over the info.

"I thought it was worth another conversation."

"Agreed. After I left your place, I went to his house on Sixth. He'd taken a baseball bat to his living room. Everything that could be smashed was—even what looked like a very big and very expensive flat-screen TV."

"What the hell? Did he say anything about it?"

"Just that he took his frustration out on things rather than people."

"Based on that and the financial report, I'd say he had some sort of stake in the game beyond the obvious professional interest."

"It's a thought worth pursuing. Collins mentioned the restraining order Willie had against Carmen's brother. I took the liberty of asking my deputy to look into that further. I'll let you know what we uncover."

Sam wasn't sure how she felt about him taking liberties with her investigation, but she chose not to express the thought since he had been quite helpful.

"We also need to take a look at Rick Lind," Hill said.

"The closer? How come?"

"From all reports he was infuriated about Vasquez

missing the catch, which put the loss and blown save on Lind's record."

"How infuriated?"

"He made firewood out of some of the furniture in the locker room and was ranting for quite some time after the game. Lots of witnesses."

"We'll talk to him after the meeting."

"Mind if I tag along?"

How did she tell him she did mind? The less time she spent with him the better—for everyone involved. "We've got it from here. I really appreciate your help with Jestings and the team yesterday, but you've probably got better things to be doing than dealing with dead ballplayers."

"Not at the moment. Things are kind of slow in my office."

Before Sam could come up with a polite way to give him the brush-off, Freddie came in looking completely wiped out.

"Did you sleep at all?" she asked.

"A few minutes here and there. Carmen's brother, parents, aunts and cousins got in around five. I was up all night with her. It was a tough night."

"Her brother is here? Which one?"

"Eduardo."

"Oh," Sam said, disappointed. Too bad it wasn't Marco. That would've made things easier for her. "Go home."

He eyed Hill suspiciously. Her partner didn't like the agent any more than her husband did. "That's okay. I can put in a few more hours."

"No need. We've got everyone else back at full speed

today. Get some sleep and report back tomorrow morning."

"All right. If you're sure."

"I'm sure."

"So," Hill said after Freddie walked away, "looks like you're in need of a partner for the day."

"Looks like." She headed for the conference room, determined to ignore him and the weirdness that lingered between them to focus on the job.

"Lieutenant," Jeannie McBride called from the pit.

"What's up?"

"They found Vasquez's car—or what's left of it."

"Where?"

"On New York Avenue. IT got a hit on his cell phone that led to the car. It's been pretty well picked over apparently."

Great, Sam thought. "Let's get CSU up there to process it. Do they have it roped off?"

"Yes, I asked."

"Go on up there and keep an eye on things. I don't want any mistakes."

"Yes, ma'am. I'll take care of it."

"Take Tyrone with you," Sam said, referring to Jeannie's partner.

Sam went into the conference room and headed directly to the dry-erase board where she tacked up photos of Willie in his uniform and the photos from the Dumpster as well as the autopsy pictures. She was well into detailing the timeline when people began filing in. Detectives Gonzales and Arnold were there along with Assistant U.S. Attorney Charity Miller. Her stilettos clicked on the tile floor as she came into the room.

Sam nodded to the prosecutor who was also a friend. "Welcome, Ms. Miller."

"Thank you, Lieutenant. Just looking for an update."

"Me too," Chief Farnsworth said as he came in with Captain Malone.

"Gonzo, go," Sam said.

"I met with James Settle, the general manager of WFBR, and Big Ben Markinson, the morning on-air guy who was inciting a verbal riot on the airwaves yesterday morning. He gave me a list of people who were particularly enraged, but a lot of them are first names, so it's going to be hard to track them down."

"See what you can do, but don't spend too much time on it." She turned to Hill. "You can go ahead and brief on what you did yesterday."

"After the lieutenant and I met with team owner Ray Jestings, manager Bob Minor, and the trainer Jamie Clark, I went by myself to meet with general manager Garrett Collins at his home on Sixth Street." Avery told them about the condition of Collins's home and the info they later uncovered about his financial situation.

"The financials lead us to believe he had more than just a professional stake in the game," Sam added. "Detectives Carlucci and Dominguez have gone to bring him in for a more in-depth conversation."

"I went over the financial reports for Minor and Clark," Gonzo said. "I don't see anything out of the ordinary on either."

"How about Vasquez?" Sam asked.

"Still waiting on the banks in the D.R. to get back to us."

Sam glanced at the chief. "Who do we know who would have some sway there?"

"I might be able to help with that. I'll talk to Forrester," Charity said, referring to the U.S. Attorney.

"Let me know," Sam said.

"I also met with Hugh Bixby, the team's security director," Avery said. "He mentioned Willie's brother-in-law, who he was apparently having some sort of issue with. There was a restraining order in place to keep the brother-in-law away from the stadium. I've got my deputy working on that."

"The brother-in-law in question is Marco Peña," Sam said, making a note about the restraining order. "I'll have Carmen fill us in on what was going on there. We'll see her when we're done here."

"Shouldn't the team's security director know the name of someone who has been legally barred from having contact with one of the players?" Gonzo asked.

"I got the sense from Bixby that there's a lot of drama among the players with women," Avery said. "He made a comment about how tracking the players' romantic exploits would take an army. Perhaps there are dozens of restraining orders in place, which is why he couldn't recall the brother-in-law's name."

"I could look into the other ROs related to the team," Malone said.

"That would help, thanks," Sam said as another thought occurred to her. She went to the phone on the wall and dialed an internal extension. "Hey, Archie, thanks for the help with finding Vasquez's phone. You didn't happen to do a dump on it, did you?"

"I sure did. I was just going to bring it down to you."

"Excellent," Sam said. "Thanks. While I have you, I could use some people reviewing security film today. We're looking for any sign of Willie's Lincoln MKZ or the man himself. We're still in need of a murder scene, and we're tracing his steps over a wide swath of the city. Can you spare anyone?"

"Send up the film, and I'll put all my available people on it."

"You're the best. Thanks again." She hung up and returned to her place at the head of the conference table. "I love working with people who think one step ahead. Archie dumped Willie's phone and is bringing us the data." To Detective Arnold, she said, "I want you on that today, and get all the remaining video footage that Dominguez and Carlucci didn't get to up to IT. They'll be taking over."

"Yes, ma'am."

"Gonzo, I want you to get with Patrol and find me a crime scene. Willie was killed somewhere between L'Enfant Plaza and Georgetown. See what you can do to move that along."

"Will do."

"I wanted to mention a couple of other things Bixby's people brought to my attention," Hill said. "I already told the Lieutenant that Rick Lind bears looking into. He was furious with Vasquez, busting furniture in the locker room, slamming doors. He said if he had a gun he'd shoot Vasquez himself. Bixby also mentioned that Cecil Mulroney was particularly vocal about his displeasure with Vasquez. The other thing the security guys told me is that everyone suspected a more-than-professional relationship between Vasquez and Clark, the trainer, but no one did anything about it."

"I'd think that would be a boatload of bad PR for Willie and the team if it came out that he was fooling around with his trainer," Farnsworth said.

"My thoughts exactly," Hill replied. "Willie had a reputation as a hardworking family man, and an affair would kill his image, not to mention his endorsement deals."

"Speaking of endorsement deals," Sam said, "we need to look at what companies he was working with and what a colossal fuckup on the field would do to those deals. When I talk to Carmen, I'll find out who his agent and manager were. We also need to have a more in-depth conversation with Ms. Clark about the true nature of her relationship with Vasquez. Maybe if we can get her alone without her bosses outside the door she'll be more forthcoming. But first, I'd like to go back to Ray Jestings and find out whether the alleged affair was common knowledge at his level. If it was, I want to know why he didn't do anything about it—and I want to know why he didn't mention it yesterday."

"I'd like to know that too," Hill said.

"We'll go there first."

NICK HAD BREAKFAST with Scotty but let Shelby take him to school so he wouldn't be late for his nine o'clock meeting with the Democratic caucus. Scotty had been a little better but not quite back to his usual self.

He hoped Scotty would shake off the despair over Willie's murder in a couple of days, but he worried the incident had triggered the boy's memories of the dark days that followed the deaths of his mother and grandfather. He planned to call Scotty's former guardian, Mrs. Littlefield, at some point during the day to see what she thought of the situation.

Nick walked into his office at eight thirty and found Christina and Terry waiting for him, both looking grim.

"What's up?" he asked as he dropped his bag on top of the desk that had once belonged to John O'Connor.

"We've got a little problem," Christina began.

"It's a big problem," Terry said, launching into a detailed explanation of Lexicore's connection to the factory in Thailand where all the women were killed last summer.

"What's that got to do with me?" Nick asked. "Remember when you asked my dad to invest the money John left to you?"

All at once, Nick figured out where this was going, and his stomach turned with dismay. He sank into his desk chair as he tried to process the overwhelming implications. He owned a piece of the company that in turn owned the factory where more than three hundred women had died in a fire while working under deplorable conditions. "Christ," he muttered.

"My dad is on his way in," Terry said. "He's beside himself. He had no idea that Lex was tied to that factory until it was in the paper this morning. According to Trevor," Terry said of their communications director, "Twitter is going crazy over the fact that Lexicore has been tied to the factory. Lexicore and Thailand are both trending at the moment."

"What'll happen when my name is tied to Lexicore?" Nick asked, not wanting to think of the campaign, his reputation or his rising star in the party when so many lives had been lost. But how could he not think about those things two short weeks before the election?

"I wish I knew," Terry said. "The good news, if there is good news, is that I suspect the tie to the factory in Thailand is going to come as a surprise to most of Lexicore's investors."

"First order of business is to unload the stock," Nick said.

"You'll take a huge financial hit if you do that," Christina said. "The value has plummeted since the news broke this morning."

"Who cares about the money? It's lost to me either way. I've got to unload that stock before the press jumps all over me."

"It might be too late for that," Graham O'Connor said as he strode into Nick's office looking frazzled. "This is all my fault, Nick. I had no idea Lexicore was into factories in Thailand. I failed in my due diligence on your behalf."

"How much did you invest with Lexicore?" Terry asked his father.

"A million of Nick's," Graham said, seeming ashamed, "and a couple million of my own."

The news hit Nick like a punch to the gut. Half the money John had left him might be gone.

"I'm so sorry, Nick," Graham said, his voice wavering. "I'll make it up to you. Somehow."

"I don't care about the money." Nick hated seeing his good friend so upset. "That's the least of my concerns. My first concern would be why a major U.S. corporation is allowing those kinds of conditions to exist in a factory it owns. My second question—and this is a distant second to the first one—is what're we looking at politically?"

"It's hard to say," Terry said. "The way I see it, we've got a couple of options. You could take a mea culpa and get out ahead of the story. Say you had no idea that Lexicore was involved with the factory and say you dumped the stock as soon as you found out about it."

"What's my other option?"

"Say nothing. Maybe your name will never come up."

Nick thought about both options and the potential fallout from each. His nature was to be honest and forthcoming in all his dealings, but if he admitted to the connection to Lexicore it could cost him the election. But if he didn't admit it and the press caught wind of it, that could cost him the election too. A hell of a dilemma.

"Let me fall on the sword," Graham said.

"What do you mean?" Nick asked.

"I'll issue a statement that you turned your inheritance over to me to manage for you, and you've been so busy that you totally trusted me to handle it. You knew nothing."

"Doesn't that make me look like sort of a dolt for not paying attention to what became of my money?"

"I could say that you were so upset by how you came to have the money that you didn't want to know what I did with it."

"Which is sort of true," Nick said. Other than a quick glance at the monthly statements, he didn't have anything to do with the management of the account.

"It's not a bad idea," Terry said.

"I don't like the idea of you fighting my battles for me," Nick said to Graham.

"I have nothing to lose."

"Only your sterling reputation," Nick reminded him.

"Eh," Graham said with a shrug. "Who cares? I'm not running for anything, and you are."

"I think Senator O'Connor's idea is your best bet," Christina said.

"I'm leaving tomorrow for a quick trip with the president," Nick said. "If we go with Graham's plan, let's wait until I'm gone. If I'm out of the country with the president and unreachable, the story might die before it gets legs under it."

"Good thinking," Terry said. "We could say that we aren't authorized to comment on the senator's personal affairs."

"Don't use the word 'affair,'" Graham said with a guffaw.

Nick laughed. "Yes, please think of a different word so you don't get me in trouble with my wife."

"Duly noted," Terry said with the first hint of a smile since the tense conversation began.

"You really think this'll work?" Nick asked Graham.

"I can't think of a better idea."

"Neither can I. All right, I'll let you fall on the sword with my thanks."

"Aw hell, I got you into this situation. I'll get you out of it."

Nick glanced at his watch. Ten minutes until he was due to the meeting.

"Could I have a moment alone, Senator?" Graham asked.

"Of course." To Terry and Christina, Nick said, "Thanks, guys. Appreciate your input."

After they left the room, Nick came around the desk to sit in the other visitor chair next to Graham. "What's up?"

"I got a call from Thomas's lawyer yesterday," he said, referring to his grandson who was now in jail for killing his father, Senator John O'Connor.

"What'd he have to say?"

"Thomas wants to see me."

"Oh. Wow. How do you feel about that?"

"I don't know. I can't imagine what he has to say to me. He blames me for everything. If I hadn't forced his father to keep Thomas and his mother a secret none of this would've happened. Hell, I blame myself. Keeping them apart was the biggest mistake I've ever made."

"Don't be too hard on yourself, Graham. Those were different times. You did what you thought was right at the time."

He glanced over at Nick, and for the first time, he looked like an old man. "I knew at the time that it wasn't right to keep John from his child. I knew it, and I did it anyway because I was afraid—for myself and for him. I loved this job. I loved everything about it. I went too far to protect my career at the expense of the people I loved. John paid for my mistakes with his life."

Nick leaned in to rest his hand on the other man's forearm, "John paid for his own mistakes, not yours. Thomas was angry about his father cheating on his mother. That's why he killed him."

"But if I hadn't forced John to live apart from Patricia, maybe they would've had a more normal life, and he wouldn't have felt the need to cheat on her."

"I don't think—" Nick stopped himself, mindful of his respect for Graham and his desire to protect John's legacy—always.

"What? Just say it. Whatever it is."

Choosing his words carefully, Nick said, "I don't think John had it in him to be monogamous with any woman, even Patricia."

"Maybe so. I never understood how he became such a skirt-chaser. He wasn't raised that way."

"To me it always seemed like he was looking for

something he just couldn't find no matter how hard he searched."

"He never found what you have with Sam or what I have with his mother. It makes me sad to think that he missed out on that."

"He led a very full life, and he wouldn't want you to be sad when you think of him."

"I know. Still… When I think about how I threatened to disown him if he had anything to do with them, it makes me sick. As if I ever could've actually disowned him."

Nothing he could say would make Graham feel better about what was now ancient history. "What'll you do about Thomas?"

"Go see him, I suppose. He is my grandson after all."

"Want me to go with you?"

Graham visibly brightened. "You'd do that?"

"Of course I would."

"After the election," Graham said. "Let's get you safely reelected, and then we'll see what he wants."

"Sounds like a plan. I hate to say it, but the caucus is meeting at nine. I need to get going."

Graham stood. "Can't keep your colleagues waiting." He rested a hand on Nick's shoulder. "I'll get you out of this Lexicore mess and get your money back."

"Don't sweat the money. Being a millionaire wasn't as much fun as it would've been with John around to help me spend the dough."

Graham smiled. "I'll be having a conversation with my broker about this entire situation. I'll make sure the rest of your money is safe and sound, but I wouldn't blame you if you decided to cut me out of the loop."

"That's not happening, so don't even talk about it."

"Where're you going with the president?"

"Can't tell ya," Nick said with a smile.

"Ahh, well, I can use my imagination to figure out your most likely destination, so I'll just say be safe, Godspeed and God bless."

"Thank you." Nick hugged him. "Take care and give my love to Laine."

"Will do."

SAM ALLOWED HILL to do the driving because she wanted time to think over everything they'd discussed in their meeting. On the way to the stadium, they listened to Big Ben Markinson on WFBR as he worked his listeners into a frenzy speculating about what might've happened to Willie Vasquez.

"I'm sorry," one caller said, "but the bastard had it coming to him. He totally screwed us out of a trip to the World Series."

"And you think he deserved to die for that?" Big Ben asked.

"Let's put it this way—no one will mourn his passing."

"Not even his wife or his two little kids or his parents?"

"You know what I mean, Ben. Why are you getting all sentimental? You were as mad as anyone yesterday."

"That was before I knew someone killed the poor guy. I know we're all bummed about the game, but Willie is dead. I mean… I'm sorry, but I don't think he deserved to die for not catching a baseball."

"You've gone soft, man."

"Your opinion. Get me someone else, Marcy."

The next caller wasn't much more forgiving, but did express a bit of empathy toward Willie's wife and kids.

"People are seriously fucked up," Sam said. "Seriously."

When they arrived at the stadium, the same receptionist from the day before sent them right up to the executive offices in the elevator that had no buttons.

"How does it know where to go?" Sam asked, studying the panel of red lights that meant something to someone. They meant nothing to her.

"I think it's only got one destination."

"Let me do the talking in there."

"Of course, Lieutenant. I wouldn't have it any other way."

His sarcasm wasn't lost on Sam, but she refrained from commenting. She missed Freddie and his sucking up. Tomorrow they'd get back to normal.

The elevator doors opened. Ray's assistant, Aaron, was waiting for them. "Right this way."

"What's with the VIP treatment?" Sam asked.

"Ray asked us to fully cooperate with your investigation," Aaron said. "That's what we're doing."

"It's very refreshing," Sam said. "We don't get a lot of cooperation in our line of work."

Aaron knocked once and entered Ray's office. He was seated at his conference table with Bob Minor. Sam was glad to see them both there, as she had questions for Minor too.

"Do you have news?" Ray asked, looking to his friend Hill. Ray had aged overnight and looked like he still hadn't slept at all.

"No, but we have more questions," Sam said.

"I have a question too—why did you arrest my general manager?"

"He wasn't arrested. He was brought in for questioning."

"Why?"

"There were some irregularities in his financial records that we needed to have explained."

"What kind of irregularities?"

"The all-but-broke kind."

"How is that possible?" Ray asked, incredulous. "He makes several million dollars a year."

"That answers one of my questions."

"When I went to speak with him yesterday," Hill said, "I found his home all smashed up. He'd taken a baseball bat to anything that could be smashed. Why would he do that?"

"Other than losing the biggest game of his career due to an error by one of his highest-paid players?" Minor asked, his tone thick with sarcasm.

"Is it possible Collins wagered on the game?" Sam asked.

The two men exchanged glances. "I wouldn't have any information about that," Ray said.

"Me either," Minor said. "If he bet on the game, he was risking his job and his career. That's one quick way to get banned from the game for life."

Sam knew there was more to the Collins story, but she wasn't going to get anywhere on that here. "Let's talk about Jamie Clark and her relationship with Willie."

"What about it?" Ray asked, taken aback by the question.

"We're told it was somewhat common knowledge

around here that there was more to it than just a trainer-player relationship."

Ray's face slackened with shock. "Told by whom?"

"That doesn't matter," Hill said. "Was it common knowledge to you?"

"Not to me," Ray said.

All eyes fell on Minor who squirmed and then wilted under the intense glare of the team owner.

"Did you know about this, Bob?" Ray asked.

"I suspected there was something going on," Bob said haltingly. "They spent an awful lot of time together."

Ray's face got very red. "*And you never said anything?*"

"I didn't think it was any of my business."

"None of your business," Ray said, astounded. "Like we'd need that kind of scandal with one of our marquee players, who is known for being a devoted family man?"

"It was because of his family that I kept my mouth shut," Bob said. "People like Carmen. No one wanted to see her hurt by her husband's stupidity."

"Is Ms. Clark here today?" Sam asked.

"No," Bob said. "She took a personal day."

"We'll need her address."

"What for?" Bob asked.

"What do you think?" Sam asked, beginning to be annoyed by him.

"She had nothing to do with this," Bob said.

"And you know this how?"

"I know her! She's not a killer!"

"If that's the case, then she has nothing to worry about. But you'll pardon me if your assertions aren't enough to keep us from looking more closely at her and her relationship with Willie." To Ray, Sam said, "Can you please get me her home address?"

"Yes, of course," Ray said, reaching for his phone.

"Get Rick Lind's while you're at it," Avery said.

"What the hell do you want with him?" Bob asked.

"We'd like to talk to him about the meltdown he had in the locker room after the game, for one thing," Sam said. "You know, the meltdown you failed to mention to us yesterday?"

Bob's ruddy complexion darkened with rage. "He was rightfully pissed off! The loss gets pinned on him along with the blown save. But that doesn't mean he killed Willie."

"Maybe not, but it would've been nice to hear about the incident from you when we asked if anyone had spouted off after the game," Sam said.

"I told you to be forthcoming," Ray said, visibly displeased with his manager.

"I didn't think a thing of it!" Bob said. "Of course Lind was pissed. A lot of people were."

"Including Mulroney?" Hill asked.

"What did you hear about him?" Bob asked.

"Just that he had a lot to say about Vasquez after the game," Hill said.

Bob glared at Hill. "Do you have the *first clue* what Willie denied his teammates by missing that ball? Do you have any idea how hard we'd all worked to get to that moment? All he had to do was catch the goddamned ball! *We pay him sixteen million dollars a year to catch the goddamned ball!*"

"That's enough, Bob," Ray said. "People were understandably upset. I think that goes without saying."

"Perhaps it does," Sam said, "but when we asked you

yesterday if anyone was particularly vocal, this was the information we were looking for."

"We apologize for our failure to provide that information," Ray said. "We were shocked by the news of Willie's death on top of the shock of the loss. Yesterday was a rough day around here, to say the least. I hope you'll accept my apology on behalf of my organization."

Sam appreciated a good suck-up as much as the next cop, but this guy was a little much. Just as she was about to say so, the office door opened and a tall, model-thin blonde breezed into the room like she owned the place. *Ah*, Sam thought, *the wife*. Elle Kopelsman Jestings—socialite, philanthropist and newspaper publisher, who did, in fact, own the place. Right behind her were two tall, muscular men, who appeared to be identical twins. They stood like lumps of meat right inside the door, keeping a close watch on Elle.

Very interesting, Sam thought, that she had such obvious security.

She went right to Hill, who stood to greet her with a hug.

"Nice to see you again, Avery." She spoke with a cultured, upper-crust voice that sounded rich—if a voice could sound rich. "Dreadful circumstances."

"Nice to see you too, Elle. I don't believe you know Lieutenant Holland from the Metro PD?"

Elle turned her formidable blue-eyed gaze on Sam. "Everyone knows Lieutenant Holland and her very handsome senator husband."

Sam wasn't sure she liked the almost predatory way Elle described her husband. It was all right for her to say that about Nick, but anyone else..." Good to meet you," Sam said, returning the handshake.

"I'm *thrilled* to meet you. I was just saying to Ray last week that we need to get you and the senator to one of our dinner parties."

"We're a little busy investigating a murder and running for reelection to be talking about social events," Sam said.

Judging by the surprise that registered in her expression, Elle was unused to being rebuffed when extending a coveted social invitation. "My apologies for interrupting. I came over to find out if there's any news about Willie. It's such an awful tragedy."

"Yes, it is," Sam said. "If you wouldn't mind, we'd like to conclude our meeting with your husband and Mr. Minor." Sam would never say so out loud, but she very much enjoyed the moment when it registered with Elle that Sam was asking her to leave.

Ray got up and went to his wife. With a hand on her lower back he guided her to the door.

"Why are they bothering you when it's clear that a crazy fan killed him?" Elle asked, loudly enough to ensure that everyone heard her.

"They're being thorough, honey. Give us a few minutes, and I'll be right out."

"Fine," Elle said in a frosty note of displeasure that spoke of entitlement and all the things Sam hated most about rich people who thought they owned the world. She wondered if poor Ray, who seemed like a nice enough guy, would be made to pay for his audacity in showing her out of a room her father had put him into in the first place.

The two hunks of meat followed their boss out of the room like faithful dogs.

Ray returned to his spot behind the desk. "Sorry about the interruption."

"Were you aware of the problem Willie was having with his brother-in-law?" Sam asked, unwilling to waste any more time with pleasantries.

Both men nodded.

"One of Carmen's brothers is a troublemaker," Ray said. "He's had issues with drugs, multiple arrests. He was always after Willie to bail him out. During spring training, Willie cut off the money and got a restraining order to keep the brother-in-law away from him, Carmen and the kids. Apparently, Willie's refusal to give him more money caused a big rift in Carmen's family because her parents felt that she and Willie ought to be helping the brother."

"Did it cause a rift between Willie and Carmen too?" Sam asked.

"That I don't know," Ray said.

Bob shrugged. "He didn't talk about it beyond notifying team security about the restraining order."

"How many of your players have restraining orders in place?"

Ray glanced at Bob, who shrugged.

"I'd say all of them have at least one," Bob said. "If they spend a night with a woman, she's got them married with three kids by the next day. Some of them don't get the brush-off message without legal intervention."

Sam made a note that pushed getting the details on the various restraining orders attached to members of the team to the top of her to-do list. "That's all for now," she said, standing. "I'd ask that you both remain in town and available for additional questioning should the need arise."

"For how long?" Bob asked.

"For as long as it takes."

TEN

ARMED WITH HOME addresses for Jamie Clark, Rick Lind and Cecil Mulroney, Sam and Hill left the stadium and headed for Carmen Vasquez's home in Georgetown. On the way, Sam left a message for Captain Malone, asking him to push the restraining order report to the top of his priorities.

"Why does Elle have such obvious security?"

"She's had them since one of her father's enemies tried to kidnap her as a child. Boris and Horace have been with her for years."

Outside the main gates to Carmen's building, several bunches of flowers had been laid, a couple of candles flickered in the breeze and a picture of Willie in his Feds uniform had been taped to the brick wall.

"Sort of a pathetic display of grief," Sam said.

"Especially when you consider that if something had happened to him two days ago, there would've been a sea of flowers and mourners."

"No kidding."

Security around the luxury condo complex had eased up since the day before, and they were shown right in to the elevator that took them to Carmen's top floor home. A muscular Hispanic man answered the door and eyed them suspiciously.

"What do you want?"

"Lieutenant Holland, Metro PD, and FBI Special Agent Hill to see Mrs. Vasquez."

"She's not seeing anyone right now."

"She's seeing us." Sam engaged in a staring contest, which she won when he turned away, leaving the door open.

Inside, they found several adults of various ages in the living room with the Vasquez children. Toys were scattered on the floor, and the coffee table was laden with a wide variety of food. They spoke in rapid-fire Spanish that Sam was unable to follow, but the suspicious glances directed their way were easy to understand. These people were distrustful of cops.

The man who'd answered the door returned with his arm around Carmen. She looked at them with glazed eyes.

Seeing their mother, the two little boys let out shrieks and ran toward her. Family members scooped them up before they could get to her.

Carmen watched the scene with a detached aura about her, only glancing at her children when one of them began to cry.

"Has she been medicated?" Hill asked.

"The doctor gave her something to help her sleep."

"How long ago?" Sam asked.

"Around five in the morning."

Enough time had passed, she decided, that they might be able to have a coherent conversation with her.

"We'd like to speak to her in private," Sam said.

"I'm not leaving her," the man said in heavily accented English.

"And you are?"

"Her older brother. Eduardo Peña."

"Who are all these other people?"

"Our parents, two aunts and a cousin. They came with me last night to be with her and the children."

Realizing she wasn't going to be able to get rid of the brother, Sam said, "All right. Just you. Find us a private space."

"This way."

He led them to an office behind the kitchen and settled his sister into a chair before going back to close the door.

Carmen stared straight ahead, her face devoid of expression.

Sam sat across from her and dragged her chair closer to the other woman. "Carmen," Sam said, placing her hand on top of Carmen's freezing cold hand.

She glanced at Sam with dead-looking eyes. "Do you know who killed my husband?"

"Not yet, but we're working really hard to find out what happened. I need to ask you a couple more questions that I hope you'll feel up to answering."

She gave a small nod.

"You have another brother?" Sam asked.

"Yes," she said softly. "Marco."

"What does he have to do with anything?" Eduardo asked sharply.

"Mr. Peña, we're interested in speaking with your sister," Hill said. "Not you. Be quiet or leave the room."

Judging by the hostile stare he directed at Hill, Eduardo wasn't accustomed to being spoken to that way.

"Willie had some problems with Marco?" Sam asked.

Carmen bit her lower lip and nodded, her eyes filling with tears. "Marco has been in trouble, and Willie helped him out a few times with money and lawyers.

After the most recent situation, he said he was done helping him."

"What recent situation?"

"I don't see what this has to do with anything," Eduardo said.

Sam glanced at Hill, who was already showing the other man to the door.

"You can't just kick me out! This is my sister's home. You can't come in here and push us around. That's harassment."

"Unless you'd like to be arrested for interfering with a police investigation," Sam said, "I'd suggest you shut up and get out before I get pissed off."

"You don't want that to happen," Hill said. "She has a vindictive side." He opened the door and "helped" Eduardo into the hallway. "Give us a few minutes with your sister, and then we'll be on our way."

Eduardo started to say something else, but Hill closed the door in his face.

Sam returned her attention to Carmen. "The incident you referred to… What happened?"

"Marco got involved with some bad people, and he owed them a lot of money. I don't know all the details, except that Willie refused to give him any more money. Marco said they'd kill him if he didn't get the money, but Willie refused to give in."

"Did you agree with his decision?"

"I, um, well… No. I didn't agree. We argued about it. I didn't understand why Willie wouldn't help my brother. He had plenty of money."

Sam thought it interesting that she said Willie had plenty of money, not *they* had plenty of money. "What did he say when you tried to convince him to give Marco the money?"

"He got mad. He said it had to end at some point. He wasn't made of money, and just because he had a lot now, didn't mean he always would. He said he'd be lucky to play for ten more years, and if we spent all the money now, what would happen to us later?"

Sam had to agree with Willie's smart thinking. "Do you know how much he'd given Marco in the past?"

"Close to a million."

Sam had to hide her shock at the high number. Who could blame the guy for cutting off the leech? "What did Marco need with that kind of money?"

"He made some bad investments." Carmen seemed almost ashamed as she spoke of her brother's poor judgment.

"Was he in trouble with the police?"

She nodded. "He had problems with drugs. That was one reason why Willie said no more. He was afraid Marco was spending it on drugs."

"Was he?"

"I don't know. Willie hasn't let me see him in years."

"What happened when Willie refused to give him more money?"

"Marco got really mad. My whole family was mad with us."

"That must've made things awkward between you and Willie."

She cast her gaze downward. "Yes."

"I know this is very difficult for you, Carmen, but I need to know what was going on in Willie's life so I can rule out people he knew as possible suspects."

"What do you need to know?" she asked, her chin quivering.

"Were you and Willie fighting?"

Nodding, she said, "A lot. I wanted to give Marco the money so my family would stop being so angry with us."

"Was the fighting unusual for you and Willie?"

"We never fought about anything except for my brother and money. We have so much of it," she said, gesturing at the opulently furnished room. "What would it have mattered to us to give him some of it?"

"What led to the restraining order?"

"I don't know what that is."

"It's a court order that forces Marco to stay away from you and Willie and your family."

"He... I... I didn't know about that."

Sam wanted to shoot herself for being so ham-handed. "I'm sorry. I assumed you knew, which was insensitive of me."

Carmen broke down, shaking her head as tears spilled down her cheeks. "He went to court to keep my brother away from us?"

"I'm so sorry you had to hear it that way."

She continued to shake her head. "How could he have done that and not even told me about it? Marco made some mistakes, but he is my brother. He is *family*." Sam could easily see both sides of the issue but didn't share the thought.

"I'll never get to ask him why he did it. The last time I talked to him..." She choked on a sob. "We fought about the money. He said we'd talk about it after the game, but I knew we wouldn't. He never wanted to talk about it."

"Did you have a joint checking account?" Sam asked.

"Yes. Why?"

"Could you have written a check to your brother without Willie knowing about it?"

"I suppose so, but I wouldn't have done that. Willie would've been mad at me."

"Carmen, I know this is so painful, but I have to ask if Willie was ever violent with you."

"No! Never! He wouldn't do that. He loved me. We had a bad time over the situation lately with Marco, but before that, we were always happy. Always."

"One last question. Could you tell me who his agent and manager were?"

"His agent was George McPhearson. I'm trying to remember his manager's name. Charlie something. George would know."

"Do you know how we can reach George?"

"His agency is in New York. I think his name is the name of the company."

"We'll find it. Thank you for talking to me and for helping us to figure out what happened to Willie."

"Do you think you will arrest the person who killed him?"

Under normal circumstances, Sam felt confident giving some assurance that the perpetrator most likely would be caught. In this case, however, she couldn't say for certain. "I hope so. We're doing everything we can. I promise."

"Thank you."

SAM AND HILL were quiet on the elevator ride to the lobby. They'd left Carmen in the care of her family, and Eduardo had thankfully kept his distance as they said their goodbyes.

"The brother is a bit of a thug," Hill said.

"I think he's used to getting his way and didn't like having us tell him what to do."

"Yeah, you're probably right about that."

"Seems like she has two thugs for brothers. Marco bears looking into."

"I'm one step ahead of you. My deputy did a run on him yesterday after I first heard about the restraining order." Reading from his phone, Hill said, "I just heard back from George, my deputy. Marco has quite a sheet in the D.R. Drugs and larceny, B&E, gang-related stuff. He's a busy dude. I can't believe Willie gave him close to a million bucks, and he came back for more. That takes some kind of nerve."

"And yet," Sam said, "I can see how Carmen wanted to keep the peace. Just give him the money, and make everyone happy."

"Willie was wise to think about the future. You hear so many stories about professional athletes who blow all the money during the salad years and leave themselves short for the golden years."

"Hard to believe that people with that kind of money could ever be short on cash."

"People who've never had money tend to go through it like crazy when they get it."

"True. So where can we find Marco Peña?"

"We were able to track him down in the D.R. My deputy was unable to find any sign of him leaving there in the last week. The last time he was in the U.S. was in April. One of us should probably go there to track him down."

"I hate to say this because I've always said I'd never be this kind of cop, but I can't go. Nick is heading out of town for a couple of days, and I can't leave my son. He took the news about Willie really hard and—"

"It's okay, Sam. You don't have to explain. I'll go."

"Are you sure? Do you have time? I mean, technically this isn't even your case."

"The director has given me wide latitude to decide what I want to work on personally and what I want to delegate. This interests me, especially in light of my ties to Ray. I don't mind going."

"That would be very helpful. Thank you." And it would save her limited travel budget from taking a big hit. It occurred to her that once again she'd be indebted to him. His chips were starting to pile up. She wondered when, if ever, he'd call them in.

"No problem," he said as they got into his car. "Where to now?"

"I want to see Jamie Clark again."

"What's the quickest way to get to Adams Morgan?"

"This time of day, take the Whitehurst to Rock Creek. Get off at Calvert Street."

"Um, okay. Whatever you say."

"I'll show you." Sam said, directing him as she pondered the meeting with Carmen and the next steps with Jamie. "I like Carmen. I don't want to think he was cheating on her."

"I know. I'd hate to have to tell her that."

"It would almost be worse than telling her he was killed," Sam said. She watched the city fly by through the passenger window as she went over the parts and pieces of what they'd learned so far. "If he was fooling around, let's hope that info never has to come from us."

"If this is a case of a random fan exacting revenge, we might never figure out who did it," Hill said after a long period of silence.

"That thought has occurred to me, but there was just enough chaos in Willie's life and in the lives of people involved with the team to make it worth our time to dig a little deeper into the people around him. If we're spinning our wheels, I guess we'll figure that out soon enough."

"I don't get the feeling that we're spinning our wheels."

"Neither do I," Sam said. "Willie missing that ball screwed something up for someone, and that someone was mad enough to kill him. Or it had nothing at all to do with missing the ball, and the error gave someone the opportunity to commit the perfect crime."

"Also a good possibility."

"I need to see where we are with Collins." As she reached for her cell phone it rang. She glanced at the caller ID to find Darren Tabor's number. Her first impulse was to ignore the pesky reporter, but he'd been good to her in the past so she took the call. "I'm busy, Darren."

"I know, and I'm sorry to bother you. I just need you to confirm one detail before I run it in an update to the online version of the Vasquez story."

"What detail is that?"

"Is it true he was found in a Dumpster?"

Sam's heart slowed to a crawl as she saw red. "Who told you that?"

"You know I can't reveal my sources."

"Tell me right now, Darren. Was it someone at HQ?"

"Might've been. So is it true?"

"Listen to me. Are you listening?"

"Yeah, yeah. Don't shoot the messenger, Lieutenant."

"We've withheld that detail because we might need it later. I'm asking you as a professional and as a colleague not to run that. We haven't told his wife about that either. I'd hate for her to hear it in the media."

"Aw, jeez, Sam. You're killing me here."

"How about this? When we close this one, I'll give you the exclusive. Do we have a deal?"

"Oh, all right. But don't forget you owe me."

"I won't," she said blowing out a deep breath. "Tell me one thing, Darren. Was it Stahl who called you?"

"I'm not saying. You know I can't."

"Fine. I'll be in touch." She ended the call muttering, "Motherfucker" under her breath.

"Got a leak?" Hill asked.

"More like a rat," Sam said as she dialed Dispatch and asked to be patched into the chief immediately.

"Lieutenant," the chief said. "Do you have news for me?"

"Nothing yet, but we're following a number of promising leads." Promising might be taking it a bit too far, but he didn't need to know that. "The reason I'm calling is we've once again got a leak at HQ. Darren Tabor just called me to ask if it was true that Willie was found in a Dumpster. We've kept that detail quiet in case we need it later, so I'd like to know how this is happening—again."

"So would I," he said in a tight tone that told her he was pissed too.

"You know as well as I do that it was Stahl. He'd love nothing more than to make me look bad by sabotaging my investigations. I don't want to tell you how to do your job—"

His bark of laughter halted her diatribe. "By all means. Don't let me stop you."

"Have Archie check the phone logs. I bet the call traces back to Stahl."

"You think he'd be stupid enough to place a call to a reporter from inside this building?"

"I think he'd be arrogant enough to assume he'd never get caught."

"You might be right about that."

"I'm always right about these things. Will you have Archie check?"

"Yes!"

"And will you tell me what he finds out."

"No way."

"That's not fair."

"Life isn't fair. Go back to work. Find me a killer."

"I'm on it." She slapped her phone closed. "I hope he nails that bastard."

"What's the deal with that guy Stahl anyway?" Hill asked as he navigated beastly midday traffic.

"I wish I knew. He hates my guts and always has. It didn't help when I was promoted to lieutenant and they gave me his command. He got sent to the rat squad," she said, referring to the Internal Affairs division, "and he's been a pain in my ass ever since."

"So you used to be under his command?"

"Yeah, and those were good times, let me tell ya. It's safe to say he was a pain in my ass then too."

Hill laughed. "I bet you were a pain in his as well."

"Me? A pain in the ass? I'm hurt."

"Sure you are," he said.

"He's a total boob. Couldn't find his own ass in a barrel of monkeys and had no business running a detective squad."

Laughing again, Hill said, "Where the hell did you hear that?"

"Hear what?"

"The thing about the barrel of monkeys."

"I made it up. You got the point, right?"

"You're a character, Holland. Truly."

"I hear that once in a while." Sam ventured a wary glance at him and found him watching where he was going. Perhaps it was possible, after all, for them to find their way to a collegial relationship that had no hint of romantic interest attached to it. She sure hoped so because if he was sticking around, she didn't need the headaches associated with that kind of drama.

"So what did you do to stir the ire of Lieutenant Stahl?"

"Well, first I was born to Skip Holland. They started out together, and my dad made it to deputy chief while Stahl never got past lieutenant. He always resented my dad for that. So when I came along and rose through the ranks pretty quickly, he was all set to hate me just because my last name was Holland. It didn't help, I suppose, that I was, you know, somewhat insubordinate while under his command."

"You? Somewhat insubordinate? I can't picture that either."

"Shut up. Yes, you can."

When they arrived in the Adams Morgan neighborhood, Sam directed him to Jamie's apartment building off Columbia Road. They parked and walked up three flights of stairs.

"I pictured something fancier for the head trainer of a Major League Baseball team," Hill said when they reached the third-floor landing.

"I know. This is nice but average at best."

"Right. And everything in her financials checked out?"

"I didn't see anything out of the ordinary."

Sam knocked on the door and pressed her ear against it, but didn't hear any movement inside. She knocked again, this time using a closed fist for greater impact, and heard the shuffle of feet on the floor.

"Who is it?"

"Lieutenant Holland," Sam said, holding up her badge to the peep hole, "and Agent Hill."

A series of locks disengaged and the door opened to reveal a woman who looked much different than the one they'd met yesterday. Judging from her puffy eyes, red nose and disheveled appearance, she was clearly in the throes of grief and hadn't slept at all.

"What're you doing here?"

"We need to speak with you again," Sam said. "Could we come in, please?"

"Um, sure. I guess. I'm not really dressed."

"We won't take much of your time."

Jamie stepped aside to admit them. The living room was simply furnished with a sofa, love seat and small entertainment center. No pictures, knickknacks, nothing of Jamie. Sam wondered if this was one of those places that came already furnished.

She and Hill took seats on the sofa while Jamie curled her legs under her on the love seat. "Have you found out what happened to Willie?"

"Not yet," Sam said. "We're still working on it. That's why we wanted to see you."

"Why me?"

"We've heard from several people associated with the team that you and Willie shared a particularly close relationship."

"So? I told you that yesterday. We were good friends."

"From what we've heard from others, it was common knowledge that you and Willie were… How shall I say it? Closer than friends."

Jamie's face went blank for a second and then a flush of anger flooded her cheeks. "They're saying we were having an affair."

"There is some speculation to that effect. Yes."

Jamie stared straight ahead and was quiet for a long moment. "Do you know what drives me crazy?"

"What?"

"That men and women can't be *friends* without people jumping to all sorts of incorrect assumptions."

"So you're saying there was no affair?" Sam asked.

"I said yesterday there was no affair."

"That was with your bosses outside the door. We were hoping you'd be more forthcoming away from work."

"There's nothing to say! We were friends! *Colleagues*. We worked closely together all season and then later when he was trying to stay healthy enough to finish out the postseason. I don't understand how that becomes an affair."

"People see two people spending a lot of time together, and they jump to conclusions," Hill said.

"There was no affair. He was devoted to his wife

and children. He was my friend, and I loved him. As a *friend.* Nothing more."

Sam was beginning to believe her. "Did he speak to you about his wife or his family or any issues they might've been having?"

"Here and there. I knew about the situation with Carmen's brother. That was weighing on him. He wanted to give him the money, but he was afraid he'd be throwing it into a bottomless pit. It had to stop somewhere, you know? He'd given him a lot of money."

"Do you know how much?" Sam asked, running on a hunch.

"I think it was close to a million."

"That's a rather personal detail to share with a colleague, isn't it?" Sam asked.

"He was torn up about the situation. He'd worked so hard to get where he was, to make the kind of money that most people only dream about. And everyone in his life wanted a piece of his pie."

"Who else besides Carmen's brother?"

"Her parents, her other brother, his parents, his siblings, his cousins, the friends he grew up with in the D.R. Everyone was after him all the time. It hurt him because it wasn't in his nature to say no to the people he loved. But he said he felt more like a banker rather than a ballplayer. Sometimes I got the feeling that he thought no one cared about *him*. They only cared about his money."

"Does that include Carmen?"

Jamie pursed her lips, as if she was trying to decide how much she should say. "Carmen enjoys the finer things in life. Willie was happy to provide them for her."

"But?"

"No buts."

"Did he include her among the people who wanted his money more than they wanted him?"

"I couldn't say. He didn't talk about her like that with me. He was always very respectful of her as the mother of his children."

"He loved his kids." The statement was intended to gauge Jamie's reaction to the mention of Willie's children.

Her eyes flooded with tears. "He adored those boys. He said everything he did was for them, so they could have a better life than he'd had."

"Did he grow up poor?"

"Extremely. He worked so hard. No matter what anyone says, he was the hardest working member of the team. No one wanted that win more than he did. I just… I don't know how he missed that ball. It was so shocking."

"Who were his friends on the team?"

"Until the other night, I would've said all of them. But he was closest to Chris Ortiz. They both grew up poor in the D.R. and found their way out with baseball. They had a lot in common."

"Do you know where we might find Ortiz?"

"Probably at his winter home in Fort Myers. He goes there the second the season ends and doesn't leave again until spring training. I think I have his number in my phone. I can check if you'd like."

"Yes, please."

Jamie left the room and returned a minute later with a piece of paper that she handed to Sam.

"If you think of anything else that might be relevant,

please call me," Sam said, handing her another card in case she'd lost the other one from yesterday.

"I will."

At the door, Sam turned back to Jamie. "I'm sorry for the loss of your friend."

"Thank you."

When they were back in the car, Hill said, "Where to?"

"Back to HQ for now to talk to Collins, and then I want to see Lind."

"You believed Jamie when she said there was no affair."

Sam found it interesting that he didn't pose a question, but rather a fact. "I do. How about you?"

"Yeah. And I was thinking, even if there was an affair, why would she kill him? Because he missed the ball? What would that have to do with her or what might or might not have been happening between them?"

"Right. Nothing to do with her beyond the team losing its chance to go to the World Series."

"So we can knock her off our list of suspects."

"I'm not ready to completely eliminate anyone." Sam dialed into the pit and reached Detective Arnold. "How's it going with the phone dump?"

"Slow. Lot of calls received before and after the game."

"Any outgoing calls?"

"Only to his wife."

"Are you near a computer?"

"Yep. What do you need?"

"A number for the George McPhearson Agency in New York City. A sports representation firm."

"Hang on a sec."

Sam could hear him clicking around on the keyboard as he did a search.

"Ready?"

As he rattled off the number, Sam wrote it down in her notebook. "Thanks. Let me know if anything pops on the phone log."

"Will do."

Sam ended the call and began to punch in the number for the McPhearson agency.

"You know," Hill said, "there's this marvelous new invention called a smart phone where you can search for things like phone numbers and then call directly from the website."

While she listened to the ringing phone, Sam said, "Why bother with a smart phone when I have smart people at my beck and call?"

"George McPhearson Agency. How may I direct your call?"

"To Mr. McPhearson."

"He's unavailable at the moment. May I send you to his voice mail?"

"Do not send me to his voice mail. This is Lieutenant Holland, Metro Washington, D.C. Police about the Willie Vasquez murder. Put me through to him. Now."

"Please hold."

"Another receptionist ripped to shreds," Hill said.

"My special gift."

"Mr. McPhearson's office."

"Lieutenant Holland, Metro Washington D.C. Police, about the Willie Vasquez murder. Please put me through to Mr. McPhearson immediately."

"I'm sorry but he's in a meeting and can't be disturbed."

"Let me tell you how this is going to go. Are you listening?"

"Um, yes…"

"I'm going to hang up with you and make a phone call to my colleagues in New York City. They're going to send over a couple of uniformed officers who will march into Mr. McPhearson's very important meeting. They will then handcuff him and take him into custody so we can ask him the questions we need to ask. *Or…* You could put him on the *goddamned phone right now.* Any part of that you don't get?"

"Please hold."

As he drove, Hill shook with silent laughter.

"Put me on fucking hold again."

The phone line clicked. "George McPhearson."

"Ahh," Sam said, "finally."

"I don't appreciate you intimidating my staff."

"And I don't appreciate being stonewalled by people who think a meeting is more important than getting justice for a dead man. In my world, *nothing* is more important than that."

"What do you want?"

"Tell me who might want Willie Vasquez dead for failing to catch that ball."

"Other than everyone in the Metro D.C. area and surrounding environs?"

"Yes, other than that. Sponsors, for instance, or angry agents who might've benefitted from a hefty new contract for a free agent after he won the World Series. We're interested in talking to those types of people."

"Are you accusing me of having something to do with this?"

"Should I be?"

"Of course not! He wasn't just my client. He was my friend too. I'm heartbroken over what happened to him—both on the field and afterward. He was one of the hardest-working, most dedicated athletes I'd ever had the pleasure to work with."

"Did your PR agency write that tidy little sound bite for you or did you come up with it all on your own?"

"*What the hell is your problem?*"

Sam held the phone away from her ear as he bellowed at her, wondering if he would've spoken to her that way if she'd been standing right in front of him. For his sake, she hoped not. "Murder is my problem, Mr. McPhearson. I want to know who in Willie's orbit might've had something to gain by the Feds winning that game, beyond the obvious. I'm thinking sponsors or perhaps a manager or agent who had a big deal riding on a trip to the World Series."

He was silent for so long that Sam wondered if he'd hung up on her. "Hello? McPhearson?"

"I'm here."

"And?"

"We all had a lot riding on that game, Lieutenant," he said in a far more weary, conciliatory tone. "There were deals lined up if the team made it to the World Series, not just for Willie but for several other players on the Feds as well."

"Who else do you represent on the team?"

"Lind, Mulroney, Hattie, Smith and Ortiz."

"Who among them had the most to lose?"

"Willie."

"Second?"

"Lind."

"Have you spoken to him since the game the other night?"

"I've left him a couple of messages. Haven't heard back from him yet."

"What about you? A lot to lose?"

"Of course, but I also represent six players on the Giants, so either way, I come out fine."

"Any of his sponsors stand to lose big-time because of Willie dropping that ball?"

"Not enough to kill him over it. They spread it out over the big names so they don't have all their eggs in any one basket."

"Just like agents, right?"

"Yes, I suppose you could say that."

"Why weren't you at the game with so many of your players in it?"

"I was there. I flew back to New York afterward."

Sam's phone beeped with another call that she ignored. "What about Willie's manager?"

"Charlie Engal. He's in Europe for a month with his wife, celebrating their thirtieth wedding anniversary."

"During the baseball play-offs?"

"He didn't manage baseball players when he got married. What do you want me to say?"

"I'd like to give you my number in case you think of anything that might be relevant to the investigation."

"Um, sure. Hang on while I get a pen. Okay, go ahead."

Sam gave him the number. "And you might want to train your people that when cops call for you, put them through."

"You'll have to pardon our ignorance. We don't get many calls from the police."

The phone beeped again, indicating whoever was trying to reach her was calling again. "I'll pardon it this time, but if I call you again and hit a brick wall, I won't be so forgiving. Thanks for your time."

Sam ended the call before he could say anything else. It pleased her to get in the last word.

"You told him," Hill said.

"I don't like when people get in the way of my investigation. They always think they've got something more important going on than I do." Speaking of that, she remembered the calls she'd ignored and checked her list of recent calls. Shit. They were both from Scotty's school. She called right back.

ELEVEN

"THIS IS SAM HOLLAND. I mean… Cappuano. You called me?"

"Ah, yes, Mrs. Cappuano. Your son Scotty is in the nurse's office. He's complaining of a stomachache, and he asked us to call you."

"Oh, um, okay, I'll be there to get him right away."

"We'll let him know. Thank you."

"Drive faster," she said to Hill. "My son is sick at school. I need to get him."

"Sure."

Sam's own stomach began to ache with anxiety. There were a lot of people she could call to pick him up—Shelby, either of her sisters, her stepmother, Nick, even Scotty's Secret Service detail could escort him home. But because Scotty had asked for her, no one else would do. At the last light before the parking lot to HQ, she turned to Hill. "You'll go to the Dominican Republic and work that angle?"

"Yes."

"Keep me posted."

"You do the same. Hope your son is okay."

"Thanks." Sam got out of the car and ran for the parking lot. Once inside her own car, she called Nick, but got his voice mail. "Hey, babe, just wanted to tell you I'm on my way to get Scotty from school. He's got a stomachache. I'll keep you posted. Love you."

Sam took a circuitous route to Capitol Hill, trying to avoid midday traffic. Her blood pressure was through the roof by the time she illegally parked outside the school and ran inside. In the main office, the receptionist was on the phone. Sam held back her inclination to use her usual receptionist skills on this one, until she realized the woman was on a personal call.

"My kid is sick," Sam said.

The woman had the nerve to hold up a finger.

Seriously? Sam wanted to reach out and snatch the phone out of her hand—and break the finger. The only thing that stopped her was the fact that Scotty would have to come back here tomorrow. "My kid is sick," she said again, louder this time.

This time the woman frowned at her. "I've got to go. Talk to you later."

"Where can I find the nurse's office?"

"I'll call down there for you. Your son's name?"

"Scott Cappuano." The sound of his new name rolling off her tongue made her smile—on the inside. She refused to smile at the receptionist.

She picked up the phone and dialed an extension. "Scott Cappuano's mother is here to pick him up."

Scott Cappuano's mother is here.

Her knees nearly buckled from the emotional wallop that accompanied five perfectly innocuous words that meant the world to her. When tears threatened, Sam turned away from the reception desk, fighting for composure. Her heart felt like someone was squeezing it. And then Scotty came into the office, dragging his backpack behind him, and nothing in the world mattered but whatever he needed. His Secret Service agents followed at a respectful distance.

"Hey, buddy," she said, reaching for him and starting for the door.

"You have to sign him out, Mrs. Cappuano," the receptionist said, pointing to a binder on the counter.

"Oh, right." Sam released Scotty, signed where directed and guided him from the office. Outside, she took a couple of deep breaths to regain her composure. Who knew that picking your kid up from school could be so fraught with emotion? She kept an arm around him. "What's going on?"

"Nothing."

The one-word answer was so out of character that Sam stopped walking and turned to face him. She was shocked to see his brown eyes brimming with tears. She rested her hands on his shoulders and bent to look him square in the eye. "What's wrong?"

He glanced at the school. "Not here."

Suddenly filled with anxiety, she said, "Come on." With a wary glance at the agents who followed them from the school, she shepherded him into her car and went around to the driver's side. She had him settled before they could insist on driving him home. "What happened?"

"Some kids were saying that Willie was a loser for not catching the ball. They said he deserved what happened to him."

"Oh, man." She could already see where this was going. "What did you say to that?"

"I told them he made a mistake, and no one deserves to die for that."

"That's right."

"They didn't agree with me. This one kid… Nathan Cleary…"

"What?"

"He punched me in the stomach."

"*What?* Are you kidding me? I'm going back in there to have a conversation with the principal." Not to mention the words she planned to have with his detail. What the hell were they doing letting another kid hit him?

Scotty grabbed her arm to stop her from getting out of the car. "No, Sam. No. You can't do that."

"What do you mean I can't do it? You were *assaulted* in school. You bet I can make a stink about that."

"If you do, the other kids will hate me. He's popular, and I'm still new. You can't make a stink. You *can't*."

Sam wasn't used to being told she couldn't do something, especially when it came to protecting her loved ones.

"Please?"

The single word, uttered in a small voice that was so not him, did her in. "Okay, fine, but if he hits you again, I'm getting involved."

"He caught me by surprise this time. If he hits me again, I'll hit him back."

"Yes, you will, and if they suspend you for that, we'll get ice cream and celebrate your first suspension."

That drew a hint of a smile from him.

"So you're not really sick."

He shook his head. "My stomach kinda hurts from being punched."

Alarmed, Sam said, "Should I take you to see Dr. Harry?"

"*No*," he said, full of preteen disdain.

Another thought occurred to her, one that she hoped would cheer him up. "Wanna come to work with me this afternoon?"

His eyes got very big. "Could I help figure out what happened to Willie?"

She started the car. "Absolutely. I could use all the help I can get, pal."

"So you're not mad that I pretended to be sick so you'd come get me?"

"I'm not mad because you were upset. But I don't want you doing that when you're bored. Got me?"

"Yeah, I got ya. I just couldn't stay there after what happened."

"I hope that bully Nathan is sweating his balls off worrying that he's going to get in big trouble when your badass cop mother finds out what he did."

Scotty snorted with laughter that warmed her heart. "That's two swear words in one sentence."

"*Balls* is not a swear word."

"It's vulgar. Mrs. Littlefield said so."

His former guardian had instilled some rather rigid values into the kid. Living up to them was proving to be a challenge for Sam. "If Mrs. Littlefield says so it must be true, but in my book, body parts aren't vulgar." They debated the vulgarity of various body parts all the way to HQ, laughing most of the ride. His detail followed behind in one of their signature black SUVs. Sam pulled into the parking lot and took her usual spot. "Stay here for a second, buddy. I'll be right back."

"Okay."

Sam got out of the car and walked over to the SUV, rapping on the window with her knuckles.

The window was lowered, revealing a female agent at the wheel and a male agent in the passenger seat. Sam couldn't remember their names, but their faces were familiar.

"Let me ask you something," she said.

"Of course, Lieutenant," the female said.

"How's it possible that my son manages to get punched in the stomach when he has *two federal agents* watching his every move?"

"We've been trying to keep our distance so he's able to have somewhat of a normal experience," the male said. "The incident with the other kid escalated very quickly. We regret that it happened and that we weren't close enough to stop it."

Sam could tell by his expression and his tone of voice that he did regret it. They both did. "I'm sorry. I don't mean to jump all over you, but I need to know he's safe at all times so I can function."

"We're sorry we let you down," the woman said. "It won't happen again."

"What're your names?"

They exchanged nervous glances, no doubt concerned that she was going to report them.

"I'm Toni, and he's Brice."

"Thanks for keeping an eye on Scotty, Toni and Brice. He'll be with me this afternoon. You're welcome to make yourselves comfortable in our reception area, but I can't have you in the back where we're working."

"We need to have eyes on him at all times when he's not inside your home," Brice said.

"Surely we can work something out as his mother is a police officer."

Toni shook her head, making her ponytail bob. "All times."

"Fine," Sam said with a huff of exasperation. She understood about having a job to do and how often it could be inconvenient for everyone involved. "But don't get in the way."

"We'll do our best to be unobtrusive," Brice said.

Sam was walking back to her car when Nick called.

"Hey, babe."

"What's wrong with the boy?"

"A fight in school."

"*What?* What the hell?"

"My questions exactly." She relayed a quick synopsis of the incident at school to her husband.

"How does that happen when he has a detail?"

"Apparently, they weren't close enough to stop a situation that escalated quickly."

"But that's their job."

"I think they walk a fine line between keeping him safe and allowing him a normal school experience. Don't worry. I ripped them new ones over it."

"I'll bet you did," he said, chuckling. "So where is he now?"

"With me for the afternoon. He's going to help me figure out who killed Willie."

"Do you have time for that?"

"Of course I do. He's my son."

"Yes, he is."

"It was kinda weird just now."

"What was?"

"Getting a call from school that he was sick and that he'd asked for me to come get him. And then the chick at the desk calls the nurse and says 'Scott Cappuano's mother is here to pick him up.' I got a little misty over that."

"Aw, babe. That's so sweet. You're a mom now."

"Finally."

"I wish I could give you a hug."

"That'd be nice. Rain check?"

"You got it. I have a thing after work, but I shouldn't be too late. I could use a hug too. This has been kind of a crappy day all the way around."

"What's wrong?" Sam asked, surprised to hear that. He was so endlessly upbeat and cheerful.

"I'll tell you when I see you. Love you. Tell my boy I love him too, and I'll beat up the kid that hit him if he wants me to."

Smiling, she said, "I already offered and was politely rebuffed."

"Maybe at the next school function you could do that thing you do with your hands on your hips with the badge and gun showing. Make sure the kid knows who he's screwing with."

"I believe I'll do just that, Senator. I like how you think."

"I feel like we should do something."

"I might give the kid's parents a call."

"That's a good idea. Make sure you say 'This is Lieutenant Holland with the Metro PD, and I'd like to talk to you about your son the bully.'"

"And some potential assault charges."

Laughing, he said, "That ought to get their attention. Hey, so maybe Scotty can come to my fundraiser tonight."

"I bet he'd love to. I could send him home with the detail to change."

"I'll pick him up around five thirty so we can go together."

"I'll tell him."

"See you after a while. Be careful with my family."

"I will. And P.S., I love you too." Sam ended the call and opened the passenger side door for Scotty. "That was Nick on the phone. He offered to beat up Nathan if you want him to."

"That might not be good for his campaign this close to the election," Scotty said dryly, already the politician's son.

They walked together toward the entrance to HQ. "Maybe not, but it sure would make him feel better. It would make both of us happy to give that kid a taste of his own medicine."

"It's cool that you guys are so mad about it."

"We're beyond mad. What's the next level after furious?"

"Um… I'm trying to think of this vocabulary word we had recently. In… Incense. Something like that."

"Incensed. That's a good word, but we need more umph. Something like freaking pissed sounds much better."

"Freaking is a swear."

"It is not!"

"Is too. Ask Mrs. L."

Sam expelled a dramatic sigh. "Her standards are way too high for me."

"No kidding, really?" he said, rolling his eyes at her.

"Are you making fun of me?"

"Yes, I think I am."

As Sam shared a grin with him, she was delighted to see him snapping out of the funk he'd been in when she picked him up. "Nick thought you might like to go to his fundraiser in Arlington tonight."

His eyes lit up with delight. He loved every second

he got to spend with Nick, even if they were doing something most kids would find boring. "I'd love to."

"You'll have to go home to change into your work clothes," she said of the khaki pants, blazer, dress shirts and assortment of ties they'd bought him for his appearances on the campaign trail. He had dubbed them his "work clothes," which they found hilarious.

"That's okay."

"I'll talk to the detail about getting you home to change. Nick said he'd pick you up at home at five thirty so you can ride there together."

In the lobby, they ran into Chief Farnsworth. "Hey guys," he said, eyeing the Secret Service agents who followed them. "How goes it?" He reached out to shake hands with Scotty.

Sam rested her hands on Scotty's shoulders. "I've got a deputy for the afternoon if that's all right with you."

"Of course. Everything okay?"

"He wasn't feeling too good at school, but he's a lot better now, right, buddy?"

The look of pure love he directed her way nearly made her knees buckle. "I'm a lot better now."

"How'd you like to come with old Uncle Joe to take a look at what's going on in the intake area? We could take your mug shot and fingerprints."

"Can I, Sam?" Scotty asked, his eyes glowing with delight.

Sam sent the chief a grateful smile. "Are you sure you have time?"

"I'm sure."

"Have fun and behave," she said to Scotty.

"I always behave," he said indignantly.

Yes, she thought as she watched him walk away with

the chief's arm around his shoulders, he was a good boy, which is why it hadn't occurred to him to hit back when the bully struck him. Next time, however, he'd know to defend himself. She'd make sure there wouldn't be a next time with that kid, but there were always others.

She went back to the detectives' pit where she was surprised to see Freddie. "What're you doing here?"

"Couldn't sleep, so I came back in."

"You look wrecked."

"Thanks. Appreciate that. I've been helping Arnold with the phone logs. Is there something else I should be doing?"

"We need to have a conversation with Garrett Collins, and then we've got to talk to Rick Lind, if you're up for it."

"I'm up for it."

"Give me a couple of minutes to get my shit together, and then I'll find you." She went into her office and sifted through a stack of messages that had nothing to do with the case so she pushed them aside.

A knock on her door had her looking up at Lieutenant Archelotta. "Got a minute, Sam?"

"That's about all I've got," she said. "What's up?"

He surprised her when he closed the door. "I was in the Lieutenants' Lounge earlier—"

"We have a Lieutenants' Lounge? Where the hell is that?"

"On the third floor."

"Why didn't anyone tell me that?"

"It's in the lieutenant's handbook."

"There's a *handbook*?"

"Honestly, Sam, you're a hot mess," he said, laughing.

"Yeah, I know. So anyway…"

"I heard Stahl talking about the Vasquez case and how Willie was found in a Dumpster."

Sam could feel her ire rising. "What did he say about it?"

"That it was symbolic and poetic. I believe those were the words he used. Then the chief asked me to check on whether any calls were made between here and the *Washington Star* today. I guess you could say I put two and two together."

"Was there a call to the *Star*?" Sam asked.

"One, from the extension in the Lieutenants' Lounge."

Sam surged to her feet. "We need to check the phone for prints."

"Already done."

"Excellent. You're good, Archie. Really, really good." The double meaning hung in the air between them until Sam cleared her throat and her dirty mind. "Are you willing to tell Farnsworth what you overheard?"

"If it means getting rid of Stahl, you bet your ass I'll tell him."

"We've got to play this right so we don't miss our chance to nail that bastard. Let's wait until you get the prints back, and we'll take the whole thing to the chief all sewn up in a neat package."

"Good plan."

"Could you see who he was talking to in the lounge?"

"Not without giving myself away," Archie said. "I'll keep you posted."

"Thanks for the heads up."

"No problem. I know he's been after you since they gave you his command, so I figured you could use a little ammo against him."

"You figured right."

"I can't believe he was stupid enough to call from a phone inside the house."

"Arrogance, pure and simple. He never thought he'd get caught."

"I hope we can nail him. I hate cops like him who make the rest of us look bad."

"Me too. Thanks again, Archie."

"Anytime."

Before she left the office, she called Gonzo's cell phone to check his status.

"Hey, LT. What's up?"

"Anything to report from the field?"

"Nothing yet. We've got Patrol officers fanned out looking for blood."

"Did you hear anything from Carlucci about the transport of Collins?"

"Just that he pitched a huge fit. Said he hadn't done anything wrong. He squawked about having an airtight alibi. The usual."

"Any talk of lawyers?"

"Not that she said. Beckett has him in interrogation two, waiting on you."

"Good, thanks. Keep me posted on the blood." Ending the call, she walked into the pit. "Cruz, let's talk to Mr. Collins."

"Fill me in."

Sam told him about Collins' financial situation as well as the state of his home when Hill visited him there the day before.

"Who smashes up his own stuff like that?" Cruz asked.

"Let's find out."

When Sam and Freddie burst into the room, Collins leaped to his feet. "What the hell is this about? I talked to Agent Hill yesterday—"

"Have a seat, Mr. Collins."

"I demand to know what is going on!"

"Have a seat, Mr. Collins," Sam said, more deliberately this time.

He flounced into the chair, still seething.

"Now, let's start over, shall we? I'm Lieutenant Holland. This is my partner Detective Cruz. He's going to record our conversation." She nodded to Freddie, who turned on the tape recorder that sat on the center of the table.

He rattled off the time and date. "Lieutenant Holland, Detective Cruz, interview with Garrett Collins, general manager of the D.C. Federals in the Willie Vasquez homicide investigation."

"I had nothing to do with what happened to Willie! I told Hill that."

"And he was inclined to believe you," Sam said.

"So what's this all about?"

"We'd like to know why the general manager of a Major League Baseball team is all but broke." She dropped the financial report on the table in front of him.

"How do you know about that?"

"We like to be thorough. Between this financial report and the damage Agent Hill witnessed at your home, we're wondering what you really had riding on that game."

He squirmed ever so slightly, but Sam saw it. "Did you wager on the game, Mr. Collins?"

"You know I can't do that. MLB players and employees are prohibited from betting on games."

"And yet that rule hasn't stopped it from happening in the past, has it?"

"No."

Sam let the silence fill the room, sending the message that she was waiting on him.

"You don't understand," he finally said.

"What is it I don't understand?"

"We were supposed to *win* that game. We *should've* won that game. All he had to do was catch the ball. Just catch the ball. Do you know what a difference that would've made for all of us?"

"What kind of difference would it have made for you?"

"The team I fielded would be going to the World Series."

"Beyond that?"

"There is nothing beyond that! I needed that to happen on every possible level."

"Why?"

"Because it was my chance to turn things around! You have to understand… I needed to win that game."

"So you've said. What you haven't said is why."

He took a drink from the glass of water on the table and wiped away a bead of sweat on his forehead. "I went through a really ugly divorce a couple of years ago. It wiped me out. I've been struggling to get back on my feet ever since."

"You make a lot of money, Mr. Collins. How do you find yourself unable to pay your cable bill?"

He dropped his head into his hands, his shoulders heaving as he broke down.

Sam glanced at Freddie, rolling her eyes. He didn't

engage, which was unusual, but then again, he was beyond exhausted.

"Do you have a gambling problem, Mr. Collins?"

"Yes," he said, his words muffled by his hands.

"And did you wager on the outcome of the National League Championship Series?"

His face still in his hands, he nodded.

"How much?"

"More than I could afford to lose, and now..."

"Now what?"

"I'm in really big trouble."

"What kind of trouble?"

"Every kind. I have to come up with a lot of money that I have no way of getting, or..."

"Or what?"

"I don't know, and I don't want to find out."

"Who are these people you're indebted to?"

"If I tell you that, I'm a dead man."

"You can either tell me who it is, or I'll set you loose so they can find you themselves. Then you can learn firsthand what happens when you screw them over."

"I can't tell you, and I can't go home, either."

"Did you have anything to do with the death of Mr. Vasquez?"

"No! What difference did it make to me after the fact if he was dead or alive? Killing him wouldn't have solved my immediate problem."

Inclined to believe him and running short on patience, Sam turned to Freddie. "Detective Cruz, will you please see about getting Mr. Collins a ride home."

Collins surged to his feet. "You can't do that! They're going to know where I've been and who I've been with. The minute you took me into custody, you put a mark on me. If you send me home, I won't live through the night."

"That's not my problem."

"*How is that not your problem?*" Spittle flew from his mouth, just missing Sam's face as she ducked aside. "Isn't cop an acronym for 'care of people'?"

"I do care about people—people who help themselves by giving me the information I need. Those are the people I care about."

"Fine!" He fell back into the chair, defeat resonating from him. "I'll tell you. Just don't make me leave here. Please."

Sam recognized genuine terror when she saw it, and this certainly qualified. "I'm listening."

"If I tell you, will you promise you'll protect me?"

"I'll do what I can. Depends on the quality of the information and whether it's credible or not."

"It's credible. I have a bookie who places bets for me. I have his name and a phone number."

Sam pushed her pad and pen across the table. "Write it down."

"I don't know the number off the top of my head. I need my cell phone. They took it from me when they brought me in here."

Sam got up and went over to Freddie. "Get the phone," she said in a low tone.

He nodded and left the room.

Sam returned to the table and reached for the pad on which Collins had written the bookie's name. Antonio Sandover. The name set off alarm bells, but Sam didn't know why. "I'll be right back," she said to Collins on her way out of the room.

Malone was in the hallway, apparently on his way

to see her. "I've got the info you asked for on the warrants related to the team. Hope you're not planning to sleep tonight. There're a lot of them."

"Great, can you leave it on my desk?"

"Sure."

"Why does the name Antonio Sandover ring a big bell with me?"

"The FBI is looking into him. Racketeering and other charges. We got a memo on it a couple of weeks ago."

Sam snapped her fingers. "That's it." She reached for her cell phone.

"Saw your Scotty getting fingerprinted by the chief," Malone said with a smile. "Took some pictures I'll send to your email."

"Oh, cool. Thank you."

"He's a cute kid. Always polite."

"I wish I could take some credit for that."

"He's probably lucky you got him later rather than sooner."

"That's funny. Hilarious."

Malone didn't try to hold back his mirth.

"You crack yourself up." Sam found Hill's number in her list of contacts and pressed send. When Hill answered, Sam said, "Talk to me about Antonio Sandover."

"What about him?"

"You guys have your eye on him?"

"Yes, we're building a case for gambling, racketeering and other potential charges. Why?"

"Collins is tied up with him. He's into him for a lot of money. He bet on the NLCS outcome."

"Are you kidding me? He risked a lifetime ban from baseball by betting on his own team?"

"Apparently, and now he's so afraid of what might happen to him that he's begging us to keep him in custody."

"Jesus. How do people get themselves into shit like this, especially when they make the kind of coin he does?"

"He's probably the type who's never satisfied no matter how much he has."

"We're going to need to put him in protective custody. And he might be useful to us. Let me make a couple of calls. I'll get right back to you."

"Thanks."

"The Feds want him," Sam said to Malone.

"So it's possible that Willie's murder might've saved Collins's life?"

"Quite possibly."

"We live in a strange and twisted world, Lieutenant."

"You're just figuring that out, Captain?"

They shared a smile before Sam went back into the interrogation room. "Here's the deal—the Feds are building a case against Sandover. You might be able to help them in exchange for protective custody."

"Help them? What does that mean?"

"Help them to build a case against Sandover."

"You're out of your freaking minds! Are you trying to get me killed?"

"Actually, I'm trying to keep you alive. You have two choices—assist the Feds in exchange for protective custody or walk out of here and fend for yourself with our best wishes."

"That's it? Those are my choices?"

"That's all I've got."

"Pretty sucky options."

"A smart guy like you probably should've considered these potential outcomes before you went into business with a known criminal."

"None of this would be happening if Willie had *caught that goddamned ball!"*

"Well, he didn't, so what's it going to be? Work with us or fend for yourself?"

Collins sagged into his chair. "Either way, I'm probably dead, so what does it matter?"

"Everything that can be done to ensure your safety will be seen to by the FBI."

"Pardon me if I don't find your assurances particularly comforting."

"I don't have all day, Mr. Collins. What's your decision?"

As he blew out a deep breath, the realization that life as he knew it was over seemed to settle on him. His shoulders slumped and his styled hair fell over his forehead. "I'll work with the Feds."

"I'll set it up. Sit tight."

"Yeah, sure. Like I have any other choice."

For once, Sam didn't feel the need to pour salt on open wounds, so she left the room and went back to her office to await Hill's call.

Freddie came in with Collins' phone in an evidence bag. "Am I still taking this to him?"

"Get Antonio Sandover's number off the phone."

Freddie let out a low whistle. "What's he doing messing with that cat?"

"What else? Betting on baseball."

"Seriously? He bet on his own team?"

"Apparently so."

"Are you looking at him for Willie's murder?"

"No," Sam said with a sigh. How nice would it have been to wrap this one up nice and neat by pinning it on the team's general manager who'd had far more than anyone knew riding on the outcome of the game? Unfortunately, nothing was ever that easy in her world. "He didn't kill Willie because that wouldn't have changed anything for him. Instead, he went home and beat the shit out of his house. Go get that number off his phone and put the phone back in the evidence locker. Then meet me here so we can deal with Rick Lind."

"Got it."

She took advantage of a free minute to run an internet search on Lind and printed out a few pages of information. When Sam's phone rang she took the call from Hill. "Speak."

"I'm sending over my deputy, Special Agent Terrell, to pick up Collins. He'll have three other agents with him for transport."

"I'll let Collins know."

"I'm on a five o'clock flight to the D.R. I'll be in touch after I've tracked down Marco."

"We're on our way to talk to Lind."

"I forgot to mention that Bixby told me Lind had issues."

"What kind of issues?"

"Anger, for one thing. Didn't take much to set him off."

"Good to know. Thanks again for making the trip."

"No problem."

She slapped the phone closed, stashed it in her pocket and went to find Cruz.

On the way out of HQ, she went looking for Scotty and the chief to let them know she had to leave.

Scotty lit up when he saw her coming into the intake area. “Sam! Check it out!” He held up his hands to show off the black smudges on his fingertips. “And here’s my mug shot.”

“Dude, you’re not supposed to *smile* when you’ve been arrested.”

“The celebrities smile in their mug shots because they know they’ll end up on TV, and they don’t want to look like dirt-bag losers.”

“Who told you that?”

“Uncle Joe.”

Sam smiled at the chief, who seemed more relaxed than she’d seen him in days. “You need to be home and ready by five thirty for Nick to pick you up,” she told Scotty, glancing at his agents, who nodded. “And make sure you get your homework done at some point.”

“I will.” He gave her a hug. “Thanks for coming to get me at school.”

As Sam returned his embrace, she wondered if she’d eventually get used to the overpowering love that came with having him in her life. “Anytime.” She kissed the top of his head and released him. “Thanks, Chief.”

“It’s been my pleasure,” he said with a warm smile for Scotty.

The man who’d never had children of his own had gotten himself an adopted grandson in Scotty and was clearly enjoying the new addition to their extended family.

“I’ll see you guys.”

TWELVE

LIND LIVED IN POTOMAC, an upscale Beltway community in Maryland. According to her research, he was married with three kids—two sons and a daughter. He'd come up through the University of California system and was drafted right out of college by the San Diego Padres in the third round. He'd bounced around on several National League teams before landing with the Feds during their inaugural season.

He'd come into his own as a closer with the Feds and had seen his star finally begin to rise in the last two seasons.

While Freddie drove, Sam read deeper into the pages she'd printed out where she found an arrest two years ago for a domestic issue that hadn't been adjudicated. She called Malone and asked him to get her the details. "Hang on," he said, clicking away on a keyboard. "Looks like his wife called the police because he was making threats toward her. They took him in, let him spend the night in the cooler but released him when she declined to press charges."

"Interesting. Thanks for the info. I'll let you know what he has to say."

"Sounds good."

As Freddie navigated traffic, Sam also took the time to flip through the stack of restraining orders that had been granted to Feds players. Most of them involved overly interested women who relentlessly pursued the ballplayers. Willie's order against his brother-in-law was a notable exception as it involved a family member rather than a fan.

"Why are you so quiet over there?" Sam asked her partner as she continued to scan the details of Willie's protective order against Marco Peña.

"I'm not quiet. I'm driving."

"You're quiet. What's wrong?"

"Nothing."

"Whenever you say nothing is wrong, something is always wrong."

"Quit acting like you know me so well."

Sam gave him a withering look. Other than his mother and maybe his girlfriend, Sam was fairly confident that no one knew him better than she did. "Shall we examine the evidence?"

"Here's a big idea—let's not."

"Come on, Freddie. What gives?"

"It was a rough night. That's all."

"Did she get to you?" she asked of Carmen.

"Of course she did. She'd just lost her husband and has two little kids to think about in a country that's not home to her. Her kids are American citizens, so she's torn about what to do now that Willie is gone. We talked some while we waited for her family to get there. It was... It was a long night."

And her sensitive partner would've been more affected than most by the young widow's grief. "It was good of you to stay with her, Freddie. Way above and beyond the call of duty."

He shrugged off her praise, as she'd known he would.

"Someone had to stay with her. All her friends abandoned her after her husband missed the ball."

"She was hurt by that."

"Extremely. The wives and girlfriends stick together, especially during the season when the guys are on the road so much. I got the impression that the other women had been a lifeline for Carmen as she raised her kids far away from her home and family. And then when she needed them most…"

"They deserted her."

"Yes."

"It's a sucky situation all the way around."

"I wish there was more I could do for her."

"Helping to find her husband's killer will go a long way toward getting closure for her."

"I can't believe you used the word 'closure.' You hate that word."

"True." She hated the word because there was never really closure for the families of murder victims, who lived in the shadow of violent crime for the rest of their lives. "We do what we can for them. We do the best we can."

"I know."

The best he could do wouldn't be enough for him, Sam suspected, vowing to keep a close eye on her partner over the next few days. They walked a fine line between their professional and personal relationships, and somehow managed to keep the balance. At times like this, however, she tended to think of him more as the beloved little brother she'd never had than the partner she'd trained and nurtured for years now. Not that she'd ever tell him that…

They rolled into Montgomery County and arrived in

Potomac, one of the wealthiest towns in the country. "I can't get over the real estate out here," Sam said. "Can you imagine living in a house like that?" She pointed to a Tudor monstrosity that would've occupied a full city block in the District.

"Not in this lifetime."

"Even if I could afford it, I'd never want to live way out here away from all the action."

"You'd go crazy out here."

Naturally, Lind lived in a gated community, and naturally, they had to fight with the rent-a-cop in the gatehouse to let them in.

"Just open the gate, Barney Fife, before I file a complaint with your supervisor," Sam said.

"Who the hell is Barney Fife?" the young man asked, baffled.

"Just open the goddamned gate. We're investigating a murder, and you're getting in our way."

"If I get in trouble for this—"

"You got two seconds or your little wooden arm is going to become my new hood ornament."

Giving her a filthy glare, the guy flipped a switch that raised the arm.

Freddie hit the gas and left a little dust in their wake. "Well done," Sam said. "I'm so sick and tired of the goddamned gatekeepers."

"Don't use the Lord's name in vain," he said with less conviction than usual, although Sam would've been more worried if he hadn't said it at all.

"My apologies."

"You could at least attempt a measure of sincerity when you apologize."

"What? Now I'm apologizing wrong too? I can't catch a break with you. I swear."

The friendly bickering was much more in keeping with their usual routine than his stony silence had been.

Rick Lind's house was yet another monstrosity made of sandstone with creamy white trim and a sleek black sports car in the driveway.

"Don't get too close to that thing," Sam said as Freddie pulled in next to the fancy car. "I bet the department's insurance wouldn't be adequate to cover even a scratch on whatever that is."

"I believe it's the latest Porsche."

"Hmm. How can you tell?"

"The decal on the back," he said, pointing as they got out of her boxy domestic car, which looked dumpy next to the glossy black thing.

"My poor car is suffering from an inferiority complex," Sam said. At the front door, she pushed the doorbell and listened to the chimes echo through the house. "Just like Christian Patterson's place. Remember that?"

"I remember him answering the door in his bathrobe during some midday nookie with his wife."

"I wonder if they're taking advantage of the once-a-month conjugals now that he's locked up."

Freddie snickered. "You would wonder that."

Sam pushed the doorbell again and again the obnoxious bells did their thing. "Imagine being asleep when that thing goes off. It must be like an air-raid siren during the war. Oh good, here comes someone."

The door swung open to reveal a stick figure of a woman with chestnut brown hair that curled at her shoulders as if she'd just stepped out of a salon. She was immaculately dressed in a tailored pink oxford shirt, formfitting jeans and leather boots.

"May I help you?"

They raised their badges for her inspection. "I'm Lieutenant Holland, Metro PD. My partner, Detective Cruz. We're looking for Rick Lind."

"Aren't we all?" she asked with a weary sigh.

Sam and Freddie exchanged glances. "What does that mean?" Sam asked.

"I haven't seen or heard from my husband since they lost the game the other night. When you said you were cops, I was hoping maybe you knew where he was and were coming to tell me."

"Have you reported him missing?" Sam wondered why she hadn't been told of a missing person report concerning a member of the Feds.

"Not yet."

"Why not?"

"Because he's done this before. When things don't go his way, he goes under."

"For how long?"

"Usually a day or so. This is the longest stretch so far."

"Any idea where he might be?"

"I've called everyone he might be with, but no one has seen him."

"What's your name?"

"Carla Lind."

Sam wrote the name in her notebook. "Is that his car?" Sam asked, gesturing to the black vehicle.

"Yes, his pride and joy," Carla said with a hint of bitterness.

"Do you mind if we come in for a minute?"

"Um, sure, I guess." She led them to one of those useless living rooms that were supposedly reserved for guests but never actually used by anyone.

"How does he get to and from the ballpark on game days?" Sam asked when she and Freddie were settled on one sofa and Carla on another.

"He usually drives but he hired a car service this time so he could drink if they won."

"Did you go to the game?"

"Yes. My children and I were in the owner's box with the other families."

"Did you see your husband after the game?"

"No. We left right after Willie's error. We were concerned about trouble. Turns out we did the right thing getting out of there."

"I assume your husband has a cell phone?" Sam asked.

"Yes, for all the good that's done me."

"When you call him, does it ring or go right to voice mail?"

"It rings."

Sam glanced at Freddie.

"Could we please get the number, ma'am? We'll have our IT detectives put a trace on it."

Carla's gaze darted between Sam and Freddie. "I don't know if that's such a good idea."

"Why is that?"

"When he gets into one of his…moods, it's better to leave him alone until he comes out of it."

"If your husband is in some sort of trouble," Sam said, "we could be running out of time to get a signal on the phone before it loses power."

With her elbows resting on her knees, Carla bit her

thumbnail as she seemed to ponder her options. "So you'd only use it to determine whether or not he's safe. Not for anything else, right?"

"What else would we use it for?"

"I don't want him to be embarrassed by whatever he might be doing."

"What do you suspect he might be doing?"

"He's been known to engage in some rather…shall we say…risky behavior when in one of his moods."

"Risky how?"

"He gets high for one thing."

"On what?"

"Cocaine is his drug of choice. We've managed to keep his…issues off the team's radar, and we'd like to keep it that way. We're handling it privately."

"Detective Cruz, I believe we have reasonable concern about Mr. Lind's safety to put a trace on his phone. Will you please contact Lieutenant Archelotta to get that going?"

"Yes, ma'am." Freddie got up and left the room. Carla watched him go with trepidation affecting her expression. "You'd never tell Rick that I told you to track him down, would you?"

"I don't see the need to do that. One of his teammates has been murdered. His name came up in the investigation."

Carla blanched at the word murdered. "Who was murdered? What're you talking about?"

"You haven't heard that Willie Vasquez was killed after the game?" Was she living under a rock?

"Oh my God! No! I knew there'd be nothing but anger and hate toward the team after the way they lost, so I've avoided everything the last few days. I haven't taken any calls or watched the news. I admit I've been hiding out a bit." She raised trembling hands to her face. "Poor Carmen. She must be beside herself."

"That's one way to put it. Are you friends with her?"

"We're friendly, but I'm not super tight with any of the wives. Who has time with three kids to care for and a husband with problems."

"You mentioned his moods. Is there a more technical term for them?"

"Probably," she said, her shoulders sagging a bit, "but we've never gone looking for an actual diagnosis. When you're a professional athlete with million-dollar endorsement deals, no one wants to hear that you're anything other than perfect. Rick fights his demons in private. We fight them together."

"A couple of years ago, you called the police about a domestic incident."

Her amiable expression hardened. "I never pressed charges. I don't see what that's got to do with this."

"Was he in one of his moods then too?"

She hesitated for a long moment, as if choosing her words carefully. "He'd blown a critical save, and it sent him into a tailspin."

"What did the tailspin involve?"

"Another cocaine binge and a couple of hookers—in my house. They wouldn't get out, so I called the cops. That got rid of the hookers, but needless to say, my husband wasn't too happy with me for making our private life public."

While the incident had happened years ago, Sam could see that the outrage hadn't lessened with time.

"I have to ask this—as a wife and a woman—why do you stay with him?"

"Because," she said with a sigh, "I'm the only reason he's still alive. When he's not out of his mind, he's sweet and loving and a wonderful father."

"You know that with the right medication—"

Carla held up a hand. "You're preaching to the choir. I've urged him for years to get help for his illness, but he's so afraid of it ruining his career. And with such a limited amount of time to make his mark in the game and to make as much money as he can, he's unwilling to risk it. So we live with his demons and do our best to keep them under control."

Freddie returned. "Archie's on it."

Sam turned back to Carla. "I have to ask you… Willie's error resulted in Rick being charged with the loss and the blown save. Would your husband have been upset enough to harm Willie?"

Carla opened her mouth to protest but nothing came out. "You… You think he *killed* Willie?"

"I asked if you thought he'd be mad enough to harm him."

"I… I don't know. I wish I could say absolutely not, but…" She broke down. "I don't know."

"Were they friends?"

"They were friendly. Good teammates, but they didn't hang out away from the ballpark or anything like that. Rick was quite a bit older than Willie. They didn't have a lot in common outside the game."

"You need to give me some ideas of where we might be able to find Rick."

She ran her fingers through her hair repeatedly. "It depends. He could be anywhere from a seedy hotel in Chinatown to the Ritz."

"Hopefully his phone will lead us to him." Sam

wrote her cell number on the back of her business card and handed it to Carla. "If you hear from him, call me. Anytime, night or day."

"I will."

"I'm also going to speak with the Montgomery County police to see about getting an officer stationed here in case he comes home."

"Thank you."

"Is there someone you could call to come stay with you until we get this sorted out?" Sam asked.

"I'll call my sister. She lives in Bethesda."

Satisfied that Carla would have support, Sam stood. "We'll be in touch."

Sam strode out of the house. "We need an APB on Rick Lind."

"I already got that ball rolling with Malone."

"Good job."

"And I contacted Montgomery County about sending an officer here to keep an eye out for Lind."

"Are you always one step ahead of me and I don't notice?"

"Often."

"I want to talk to Bob Minor and Ray Jestings. I want to know if the team knew they had a mentally ill player in their midst."

"How could they not know?"

"What do you mean?" Sam asked, taken aback by his vehemence.

"I haven't spent that much time with my dad since he's been back on the scene, but it's so obvious that he has a problem of some sort. I would've recognized that even if I hadn't already known his history, you know?"

"I do see what you mean. But your dad is doing okay now, isn't he?"

"He seems to be, but there are moments… Glimpses, I guess you'd call them, of the manic side from time to time that worry me. I know my mom sees it too, but we don't talk about it."

They got into the car with Freddie still driving. "Are you worried about him?" Sam asked when they were on their way back to the city.

"I'm more worried about my mom and what'll become of her if he has another breakdown. She's so happy—happier than I've ever seen her. I don't want anything to spoil that, you know?"

"Is he taking his meds?"

"As far as I know. It's not something that comes up over dinner. I'd love to ask him, but I don't have that kind of relationship with him."

"Would your mother ask him?"

"We don't talk about it."

Sam pondered the situation with a growing sense of unease. It had been a big gamble for Freddie and his mom to accept his dad back into their lives more than twenty years after he left without a word to them. He'd confessed to hiding his bipolar disorder from them. Freddie had struggled with the situation and had reluctantly—at first—allowed his dad back into his life. Sam would hate to see him hurt again if his father was unable to maintain the relationship.

Her cell phone rang and she took the call from Gonzo.

"I think I've got your murder scene."

"Where?"

He rattled off an address that Sam knew was close to the Office of Personnel Management on E Street.

"Head for Foggy Bottom," she said to Freddie. To Gonzo, she said, "Rope it off. We'll be there shortly."

"Already done. I'll be here."

On the way, Sam called Lindsey and asked her to come to the scene to get a sample of the blood so they could run the DNA to see if it was a match for Willie. Next she called Deputy Chief Conklin, who had all kinds of contacts within the federal government. "I need security film from OPM and surrounding buildings on E Street Northwest."

"I'll get right on it," Conklin said. "Assume you'll want CSU there too, so I'll take care of getting them dispatched."

"You're the best. Thanks." She hung up and called Ray Jestings. "Did you know Rick Lind was mentally ill?" she asked without preamble.

"Ah, well…"

"Yes or no. Did you know?"

"Yes, I knew."

"Who else knew?"

"The team physician, Dr. Leonard, and most of the team's upper management. What does that have to do with anything?"

"Lind hasn't been seen or heard from since he left the stadium the other night."

"Who told you that?"

"Mrs. Lind. She hasn't heard from him since the game."

"Why didn't she let us know that?"

"Do I really have to tell you why?"

Jestings let out a tortured sigh. "I don't know what

you want me to say. We knew he had problems. We knew he was managing his problems. The doctor paid close attention to his situation. What more were we supposed to do?"

"Do his teammates know about his condition?"

"They know he has anger issues, and they give him a wide berth, especially when he blows a save."

Once again Sam found herself marveling at the sports culture. The Feds had kept a lid on the situation and perhaps endangered his teammates, all because the guy threw a fastball like nobody's business. "How can I reach Dr. Leonard?"

"He's gone to his winter home in Jamaica. I can reach out to him and have him get in touch if you'd like."

"I'll let you know if I need to talk to him."

"Whatever we can do."

"I'll be in touch." Sam ended the call feeling exasperated by the case. "These people are ridiculous. They allow a man with significant anger issues to fill one of the most stressful roles on the team all the while they keep the fact that he has a significant mental illness a secret from his teammates."

"They know," Freddie said. "If they spend any time at all with him, they know something isn't right. As long as he gets the job done and doesn't direct his anger at any of them, they don't care any more than the management does about his 'issues.'"

"After we view the scene, my next call is to Chris Ortiz. He was Willie's closest friend on the team. He might be able to shed some light on the relationships between the players."

"We're spending an awful lot of time digging into

the team and the management. What makes you so sure it wasn't a deranged fan who attacked him?"

"It very well could be, but as I said to Hill when he asked me the same question, there was just enough chaos in Willie's life and in the lives of other people attached to the team that I'm running on a hunch."

"I'm glad your *other* partner thinks the same way I do."

The sarcasm came through loud and clear. "He's not my other partner, and he's nothing like you. I much prefer you."

"Right, because you can make me your bitch. Not as easy to do that to an FBI agent, is it?"

Sam fought the urge to squirm under the weight of his accurate assessment. "I do not make you my bitch." It occurred to her that Nick had used the same term to describe what she'd done to him in bed.

"Oh, please. Give me a break. Only every day."

"That's not my intention."

"Sure it isn't," he said, his words laced with humor.

"Am I a jerk to work for? Tell me the truth."

"Shut up, Sam. You know I'm yanking your chain. Don't go all serious on me."

"Answer the question."

"You're not a jerk to work for, but you do like to make me your bitch. I don't care what you say. You'll never convince me otherwise."

"It's our thing. Our groove."

"It's a good groove, and I wouldn't change a thing about it."

"You wouldn't?"

"Of course not. We're good together. We get the job done."

"Yes, we do. There's no one else I'd rather partner with. You know that, right?"

"Even Hill?"

"Especially Hill. He's a good cop, but he's no Freddie Cruz."

"Awww, shucks," he said laughing.

"Can I tell you something that you have to swear on a stack of bibles not to tell anyone else? Even Elin?"

"You know you can trust me."

"Yes, I do, but this is huge."

"Lay it on me."

"I think Nick is going to Afghanistan with the president tomorrow."

He took his eyes off the road for an instant to look over at her. "You *think*?"

"He can't tell me where he's going, which led me to my own conclusion."

"Wow. That's so cool. He'll get to ride on *Air Force One.*"

"That's the part he's most excited about too."

"Who wouldn't be?"

"Me, for one. I'd much rather stay home than fly on the president's plane—or any plane for that matter." She paused for a long moment. "It scares me to think of him on that huge target with the Stars and Stripes painted on the side."

"I'm sure they're counting on the element of surprise to get them in there without incident."

"No doubt. It's not the going in that worries me. It's the getting out. Whenever I think about that I break into a cold sweat."

"I'm sure it'll be fine, Sam. It's the president for

crying out loud. The guy has more protection than any human being alive."

"Still..."

He reached across the car to squeeze her hand. "He'll be fine, and the trip will do wonders for his campaign and his career."

"I know," she said, comforted by his assurances and the comfort of his hand covering hers. "Thanks for letting me tell you about it."

"Anytime."

They pulled up to E Street, across from the OPM building. Several squad cars were parked at the curb, and Sam was glad to see the Medical Examiner's van too. "Let's hope this is our crime scene," she said as she and Freddie ducked under the yellow tape one of the patrolmen held up for them.

Lindsey was on her knees collecting a sample from a huge puddle of blood that had darkened from exposure to the elements.

"What's the good word, Doc?"

Lindsey stood and took a series of photographs. "The consistency is what I'd expect after more than twenty-four hours, and the quantity is in keeping with a blow to the aorta. The proof will be in the DNA. I'll get it back to the lab and put a rush on it."

"We'd appreciate that."

As Lindsey walked away, Lieutenant Haggerty, who oversaw the Crime Scene Unit, approached Sam. "What've we got, Sam?" He eyed the blood puddle. A former Marine, he was built like a brick shithouse and wore his brown hair buzzed.

"We're hoping it's our Willie Vasquez crime scene. Can you have your people do a thorough search of the surrounding blocks? I'm almost to the point where I'd pay for a murder weapon."

"We'll see what we can find. What's this about Lind being in the wind?"

"We're not sure yet."

"Is he a suspect on Vasquez?"

"We don't know that either. I'll let you get to it. Keep me posted on what you find." As she walked away from him, her phone rang. "What now, Darren?"

"I heard on the scanner that you're looking for Lind."

"What about it?"

"Is he a suspect in Vasquez?"

Sam's head began to tingle and throb, a sign that she needed to get to her migraine medicine as soon as possible. "No comment."

"We're going to run the fact that you're looking for him. That's public info."

"Do what you gotta do."

"I still can't mention the Dumpster?"

"Not if you want the exclusive I promised you."

"You drive a hard bargain, Lieutenant."

"Gotta go, Darren." She stashed her phone in her pocket and checked the time. After five. She figured she had another couple of hours before Nick and Scotty would be home from the fundraiser.

"Where to?" Freddie asked when they were back in the car.

"HQ." They rode for a few minutes in silence while Sam mulled over her next steps in the case—among other things. "When we get back to the house, will you see if you can get me a phone number for a Cleary family in the Capitol Hill area. They have a kid named Nathan."

"Sure. What's that about?"

"The kid punched Scotty at school today."

"For real?"

"Unfortunately."

"I hope you're going to throw the badge around on that one."

"Maybe just a little."

Freddie grunted out a laugh. "If I get you the phone number, can I listen to the call?"

"I suppose that would only be fair."

"Awesome. These are the moments I live for."

They walked into HQ together, and while Freddie tracked down the Clearys' phone number, Sam called Chris Ortiz at his winter home in Florida. The woman who answered the phone didn't speak any English. Sam fumbled through her request to speak to Señor Ortiz.

"Un momento, por favor."

"Hello?"

"Is this Chris Ortiz?"

"Yes. Who's this?"

"Lieutenant Sam Holland, Metro PD."

"This is about Willie."

"It is. Do you have a few minutes?"

"Sure."

"Carmen said you were his closest friend on the team. Is that a fair assessment?"

"Yes. We came up together in the D.R. When we both ended up playing for the Feds it felt like a lucky break. It was nice to have someone from home there."

"Did you see Willie after the game the other night?"

"No. I asked where he was, and I was told he was in the training room waiting for the locker room to clear. I thought about going in there to see him, but I figured he wanted to be left alone. If it'd been me, I would've wanted to be alone too. I did try to call him a couple of times later that night, but his phone went right to voice mail. And then I heard what happened… I still can't believe it. It's so shocking. And sad. It's really, really sad. His kids are so young."

"People on the team were angry with him?"

"The whole thing is hard to fathom. Willie… He was one of the best center fielders in the game. Not much got by him, which is why it's so impossible to believe he missed an easy fly ball. Winning that game would've meant so much to all of us. It's the dream, you know?"

"Was anyone angry enough to want to harm him?"

After a long pause, Ortiz said, "You're looking at someone from the team for this?"

"We're looking at everyone."

"A lot of people were mad at Willie after that game—including a lot of people who didn't know him personally. How about the thousands of fans who took to the streets to express their anger?"

"We're looking at them too. What I need from you, however, is impressions about people close to Willie who might've been angry enough to harm him."

"Everyone was upset. People were stunned. How could this have happened? I heard that asked over and over that night. No one could make sense of it. Was there some anger? Hell, yes. I was pissed at him, and he's my friend. The public sees us as a bunch of overpaid jocks, and we are that. For sure. But we're also fierce competitors. We want to *win*. We're all going to relive that moment for the rest of our lives and ask why. Why didn't he catch that ball?"

"Anyone particularly angry?"

“I’m sure you’ve already heard that Lind was off the rails, as usual.”

“What do you mean ‘as usual’?”

“Something isn’t right with that guy. No one has ever clued me in on what it is, but you don’t have to be a doctor to know he has some anger problems, among other things.”

“What other things?”

He hesitated and cleared his throat. “Off the record?”

“If I need whatever you tell me to build a case it’s not off the record. If I don’t need it, it is.”

Sighing, Ortiz said, “He likes the ladies. At home he plays the part of the happy family guy, but on the road… That’s another story. He has a woman in every city.”

Sam thought of Carla Lind and what she’d been through trying to keep her husband healthy enough to play the game he loved, the same game that had made him wealthy. “Is that common among the players?”

“I’d like to say no, but there are a few who get around. No one quite like Lind, though. I’m not into minding other people’s business, but I feel sorry for Carla. She seems like a nice girl, and she’s totally oblivious to what he’s up to when she’s not around. I hate that.”

“Did Willie get busy on the road too?”

“Not that I ever knew about. That’s not how he rolled.”

“How did he roll?”

“He was a straight shooter. What you saw was what you got. I always like that about him. Even after he hit the big time, he was still the same guy I grew up with. I like to think that fame and fortune didn’t change either of us all that much. Outwardly, sure… We both have the homes and the cars, the *stuff.* But who we are underneath it all? That didn't change. At least not as far as I could see."

"There's been some talk of a possible affair between Willie and Jamie Clark."

"No way," Ortiz said, his scoff audible over the phone. "Whoever is saying that is full of shit. They were friends. That's it."

Sam had already come to that conclusion but appreciated his take on it. "Were you aware of the problems he'd had with Carmen's brother?"

"We talked about it a little. He asked me once if everyone in my family—and my wife's family—are after me for money all the time the way they were with him."

"Were they?"

"Not like Willie's family. My wife and I have a few in both our families who aren't shy about asking us for money, but Willie's family—and Carmen's—were over the top with it. They treated him like a bank, and after he cut them off, it got kinda ugly."

"How so?"

"He had a fight with her brother Marco at spring training. He came to our facility in Fort Myers and got into it with Willie as he was coming off the field. A couple of us had to get between them to keep it from escalating."

"Were the police called?"

"Yeah, I think someone from the team called them."

Sam made a note to get a copy of the report from the police in Fort Myers. "Did you hear anything that was said between them?"

"Marco was hassling him about what it meant to be family and how Willie had forgotten where he came from. Willie hung out with Marco when they were kids. That's how he met Carmen."

As that was something Sam hadn't heard before, she made a note of it. "Did he say anything to you about the confrontation with Marco?"

"Just that he was bummed about it, how they used to be friends before Willie became successful. Now Marco was all about the money."

"That must've been tough on him."

"It was. It's tough on all of us. You gotta understand—we're just regular guys who got really, really lucky to make it in baseball. A lot of guys we grew up with were just as good as we are but never made it to the big time. Those of us who did… Well, no one prepares you for how to handle being suddenly crazy rich, especially guys like me and Willie who grew up with less than nothing."

"Did you hear anyone on the team make overt threats to Willie's safety after the game?"

"Lind. He was pretty pissed, but then again he usually is. We don't pay much attention to his rants anymore."

"What did you hear him say?"

"That he'd kill that bastard if he could get his hands on him, and it was a good thing he was hiding out like the pussy he is. Stuff like that."

"Have you spoken to Lind since the game?"

"No, but that's not unusual. We aren't friends."

"Did you happen to see Lind leave the stadium after the game?"

"No, but everyone went their own way after the media crap was done."

"Did Lind meet with the media?" she asked.

"I believe he refused to, but don't quote me on that."

Sam made a note to check on whether Lind was interviewed after the game. "Anyone else spouting about Willie?"

"Cecil Mulroney was pretty mad too."

"Do you know where I might reach him in the off-season?"

"He's at his ranch in Texas. Hang on a sec. I'll get you the number."

While she waited, Sam realized she'd missed the boat by allowing the ballplayers to leave town while the investigation was still active. She might not have prevailed in keeping the whole team in the city, but not trying was another thing she could blame on the fatigue of a sleepless night.

"Ready?" Ortiz said when he came back on the line.

"Go." She wrote down the number. "Let me give you mine in case you think of anything else that might be relevant to the investigation."

"Sure. So you won't tell Mulroney who gave you his number, will you?"

"I can say I got it from the team."

"I'd appreciate that. We've got to play together again next year, and I don't need that kind of crap with my teammates."

"I understand, and I appreciate your time. I'm sorry for the loss of your friend."

"Thanks. It's crazy when you think about how someone probably killed Willie because of a baseball game."

"Crazy indeed. Call me if you think of anything else."

"I will."

Sam ended the call and sat back in her chair, feet

on the desk as she stared at the wall, rehashing everything she'd learned about Willie, the team, professional sports, the culture that surrounded the games, the family members and the missing teammate. None of it added up to murder.

She'd known all along that this investigation could end any number of ways. It could turn into a cold case in which the murderer was never found. It could lead to someone Willie had known—someone who was infuriated by his failure to catch that fly ball or perhaps a family member who felt entitled to share in Willie's riches. Or it could've been a completely random act of violence that occurred in the midst of a riot brought on by his error.

Over the years, Sam had learned to trust her instincts. They hadn't led her wrong yet. Everything in her was leading her to focus on the people around the slain ballplayer. There was just too much hate and discontent in his life to write off his murder as a random act committed by an aggrieved fan. That would be too simple. As mad as the fans had been, most of them weren't murderers. Despite that, however, she wasn't ready to rule out the possibility of a random act either.

And then there was the fact that the team was awfully new to the city for people to care enough to commit murder over a painful loss. Other far more established baseball teams had suffered much longer losing streaks, and no one had been killed over an error on the field. If Red Sox fans allowed Bill Buckner to live after his World Series error, surely the Feds fans wouldn't be out for blood from Willie, right?

She got up and went to the doorway to her office.

"Everyone in the conference room. Five minutes. Cruz, get Charity and Archie down here."

It was time to start over and go through it all one more time.

THIRTEEN

"WHERE ARE WE with Vasquez's financials?" Sam asked Charity when everyone was in the room.

"Forrester has been promised something by first thing in the morning. I'll let you know the second I have them."

"Good, thanks. Archie, how's it going with the film?"

"Nothing yet, but we're only about halfway through all of it. I've got three people on it, but it's slow going."

"We'll have more for you from what we think is our murder scene."

"Bring it up as soon as you have it. I'll put some second—and third-shift people on it." Sam glanced at Freddie, who nodded to let her know he'd take care of that.

"The restraining orders might be a dead end," Sam said. "Most of them involve overly enthusiastic women who wouldn't take no for an answer. The notable exception is Willie's brother-in-law, Marco Peña. Agent Hill has gone to the Dominican Republic to track him down and hopefully have a chat with him about his problems with Willie. I'm going to take one more look at the restraining orders tonight. We also learned this afternoon that Feds closer Rick Lind hasn't been seen or heard from since the game."

That news sent a low murmur through the room.

"Second vic?" Gonzo asked, echoing a thought Sam had also had.

“I’m not so sure.” Sam relayed what they’d learned from Lind’s wife about his illness.

“So everyone around him knew that he was seriously ill, but they kept it quiet because he could throw a hundred-mile-an-hour fastball better than anyone in the game?” Gonzo asked.

“Apparently.”

“This case is making me want to permanently swear off all interest in professional sports,” Gonzo muttered.

“So what’s our plan where Lind is concerned?” Malone asked from his usual post in the back of the room.

“We’ve got law enforcement in the Metro area looking for him, and his disappearance has hit the media. His wife couldn’t give us much insight on where he might be. I gathered from her that his disappearing acts aren’t new, and she never knows where he’s been when he resurfaces. I issued the APB only because of what happened to Willie, and because if we have a killer out to avenge the people who caused the loss, Lind might be on his or her list.”

“How do you figure?” Freddie asked. “Vasquez was the one who missed the ball.”

“Lind had plenty of chances to close out the game before that fly ball was ever hit,” Gonzo said.

“Right,” Sam said. “Most of the blame fell on Vasquez for missing an easy fly, but let’s not forget that Lind had ample opportunity to end the game and failed to get it done.”

“So if they’re both missing and say Lind is presumed murdered too, then that would rule out a random act by an enraged fan,” Freddie said.

“Exactly,” Sam said. “I’m going to have Carlucci and Dominguez track down the car service Lind used before the game to find out if they had any contact with him after. Someone had to see him leave the stadium. I'll reach out to the team owner and have him get with his security people to figure out who was the last one to see Lind after the game." She relayed the highlights of her conversation with Chris Ortiz. "I'll also be reaching out to Cecil Mulroney when I get a chance." To Arnold, she said, "Anything on the phone logs?"

"Nothing that stands out, but I'm only about halfway through the six hundred calls he received after the game."

"How do people get the phone number of a professional baseball player?" Jeannie asked.

"Our good friend Ben Markinson at WFBR did the post-game show and put it on the radio so fans could call him to express their displeasure with his performance," Gonzo said.

"There's got to be something we can charge him with for doing that," Sam said.

"I'll think of something," Malone said. "Jeannie, where are we with Willie's car?"

"CSU has gone over it and they're taking it back to the lab. We were able to retrieve his phone, and it's being processed for prints as well as GPS locations."

"We need a thread to pull," Sam said. "Let's hope this leads to one. Thanks everyone. Keep me posted."

While Sam gathered up her belongings, the others filed out of the room.

Jeannie hung back. "You sound frustrated," she said when she and Sam were alone. "That isn't like you."

"Funny, I feel like I'm usually frustrated in this job."

Jeannie smiled. "You hide it well. So, um, I was

wondering… Could I talk to you about something personal?"

Sam experienced a twinge of anxiety. She and Jeannie had been through a lot together, especially since Jeannie was kidnapped and raped during an earlier investigation. The detective had been doing much better, but Sam was always watchful for signs of ongoing post-traumatic stress. "Of course. Do you want to close the door?"

"That'd be great. Thanks." Jeannie closed the conference room door and turned back to Sam with a shy, hesitant look on her face. "This is awkward."

"Spit it out. Whatever it is, we'll figure it out the way we always do."

Rather than return to the seat, Jeannie stood behind it, her fingers digging into the vinyl. "Michael and I have set a wedding date."

"Oh, hey, that's great news. When's the big day?"

"July 18. We're going to do it out at Rehoboth Beach."

"That'll be really nice."

"I hope so. The thing is… You know how this job can be. It's all-consuming. It doesn't leave much time for a life or friends outside of work."

"You won't hear any argument from me on that."

"My sisters are going to be my matrons of honor, but I was sort of hoping that I might convince you to be an attendant too. You've become one of my best friends. I hope you know that."

"Oh, wow, well… That's very nice of you."

"You don't want to, do you?"

"I very much want to, and I'm honored that you would ask. I think of you as a good friend too. You know I do."

"But?"

"I'd be concerned about the message it would send to the rest of the squad if I make such a public statement of personal friendship with you."

"Of course. I understand. I'm sorry if I put you in an uncomfortable position."

"You didn't. And I'm not saying no. Since this is a first for me since taking command of the squad, let me run it up the flagpole and see what the brass has to say about it."

"I wouldn't want you to stick your neck out over it, Sam."

"I'm not." Sam got up and went around the desk to hug her detective—and her friend. "I'm very happy that everything has worked out for you and Michael."

"Thank you," Jeannie said, returning the embrace. "He was such a rock after what happened. It showed me everything I needed to know about who he really is."

"You know I'm one of his biggest fans, so no matter what, I'll be there with bells on for the wedding."

"That means a lot. I'd better get back to work. I'll keep you posted on what comes back from the car."

"And I'll let you know what the powers that be have to say about weddings and whatnot." Jeannie left her with a warm smile.

Sam walked out of the conference room feeling oddly elated by the conversation with Jeannie. Like Jeannie said—with so much time spent at work, there wasn't much time for outside relationships except with her husband, son, dad, stepmother, sisters and their families.

When she was younger, Sam had a lot of girlfriends but she'd fallen out of touch with most of them because of the endless demands of her job. Jeannie, Lindsey,

Charity, Faith and Hope were all colleagues, but they filled the void in some ways. Anytime she needed a female perspective, there was always one to be found at work, and they were all women she admired and respected. She supposed she should count Shelby among her new friends too. Despite the fact that she was their paid assistant, she had been a friend first.

Anxious to get home to her guys, she gathered up the stack of restraining orders and jammed the huge pile of paper into a tote bag that she unearthed from under her desk.

Cruz came in and handed her a slip of paper. "Nathan's home number. Parents are Patty and Dave."

"Thanks."

"Are you going to call now?"

"I suppose there's no time like the present. Close the door, will you?"

He pushed the door closed and took a seat in one of her visitor chairs.

Sam pressed the speaker button on her desk phone and waited for a dial tone before she punched in the numbers. As it rang, she glanced at Freddie and saw him watching the phone intently. He was such a good friend that he was as mad as she was about what had happened to Scotty at school.

"Hello?" a female voice said. She sounded like she'd run for the phone.

"Is this Mrs. Cleary?"

"It is. Who's this?"

"Lieutenant Sam Holland with the Metro Police."

"Oh, sure. I recognize your name. What can I do for you?"

"I'm not sure if you're aware of the fact that your

son Nathan punched my son Scotty in the stomach at school today."

"He did what? I didn't hear anything about that. The school never called me."

"Only because Scotty chose not to make it an issue at school. Since it was important to him that we not involve the school, I thought perhaps you and I might work this out between us."

"What's there to work out? They're boys. Boys scuffle. It's what they do."

Sam glanced at Freddie, who was now frowning. "It's also assault, and in my world, that's a criminal offense."

"Are you *threatening* me?"

"Not at all. I'm simply telling you to tell your kid to stay far, far, *far* away from mine. And you could also mention that Scotty's mother the cop won't overlook it next time."

"That sounds an awful lot like a threat to me."

"It's not a threat. It's a promise. If he hits my son again, we'll press charges—and I know how to make them stick. Any questions?"

After a very long pause, Mrs. Cleary said, "No. No questions."

"Another thing—if Nathan makes Scotty a social pariah because of this, I won't look fondly upon that either. Bottom line, tell your kid to leave my kid alone, and we won't have any further reason to speak to each other. Got me?"

"I got it." A loud click was followed by a dial tone.

Sam put down the phone. "I think that went well."

Freddie laughed. "You made your point, that's for sure."

"Scotty would be mad if he knew I'd done that."

"You can't let some other kid assault him and not do anything about it."

"Still..."

"You're a great mom, Sam. You did the same thing my mom or any other mom would do in this situation. Scotty might not want you to do anything about it, but he has to know you're not going to just let something like this go."

"Thanks for the support. I'm ready to get out of here. Go home and get some sleep. I'll see you bright and early."

"See you then."

Sam had just closed the door and was about to lock it when Archie came into the pit and pointed at her office. Her departure foiled, she went back into the office and turned on the lights. "Didn't I just see you?"

Archie followed her and closed the door behind him. "I got back to my office to find that we've got Stahl screwed every which way to Tuesday." He held up a flash drive. "Caught on camera at the time the call was made to the *Star* from the Lieutenants' Lounge. He's the only one in there."

Sam's heart beat faster as she absorbed the implications. "We have to take this to the chief."

"Right now?"

"I've got nothing better to do. Do you?"

They both did, but Archie smiled anyway. "Not a thing. Shall we?"

"After you."

As they walked to the chief's suite in silence, Sam had to force herself to keep calm as the thought of being rid of Stahl once and for all sent hope surging through her. *Don't get ahead of yourself*, she thought as the chief's admin waved them into his office.

"Lieutenants," Farnsworth said, rising as Archie closed the door behind him. "What can I do for you?"

"Lieutenant Archelotta has determined where our leak came from in the Vasquez investigation," Sam said.

"I was able to trace the call to the *Star* from the Lieutenants' Lounge. With the help of video surveillance, I determined who was in the lounge at the time the call was made." He held up the flash drive and gestured to the chief's computer. "May I?"

"By all means," the chief said, frowning as he stepped aside to make room for Archie.

Sam's palms were clammy as she waited for the video to pop up on the screen. When it did, Stahl was plainly visible and could be heard speaking about Willie Vasquez. "You didn't hear this from me," he said, "but they found the guy in a Dumpster. Someone decided to take out the trash."

Farnsworth's expression was positively thunderous when he reached for his phone. "Please ask Deputy Chief Conklin and Captain Malone to come in here. Thank you."

The three of them coexisted in tense silence until Conklin and Malone arrived.

"Lieutenant Archelotta, will you please tell Deputy Chief Conklin and Captain Malone what you told me?"

Archie went through the whole thing again, from the tip received by *Star* reporter Darren Tabor to tracing the call to the Lieutenants' Lounge to catching Stahl red-handed on the video, which was no less startling the second time Sam saw it.

"You gotta be kidding me," Conklin said.

"The guy's got balls," Malone added. "You gotta give him that."

Stone-faced, Farnsworth picked up the phone again. "Please ask Lieutenant Stahl to come in here immediately."

Stahl arrived ten minutes later with a knock on the door. "You wanted to see me, Chief?" His eyes narrowed with displeasure when they landed on Sam. "What's going on?"

"I'd like to know," Farnsworth said, "if you had anything at all to do with a tip that Darren Tabor from the *Washington Star* received about the Vasquez case regarding something we were intentionally withholding from the public."

Stahl's face turned the unhealthy shade of purple that Sam often inspired in him. "Did *she* tell you that?" He jabbed a thumb in Sam's direction.

"*Answer the question!*" Farnsworth roared.

"I had nothing to do with that," Stahl said indignantly. "Regardless of what Lieutenant Holland might've told you."

"Lieutenant Holland didn't tell me anything," Farnsworth said. "You did."

"Excuse me?"

"Lieutenant Archelotta," Farnsworth said, his steely stare fixed on Stahl. "Roll the tape."

Sam had worn the uniform for more than thirteen years. She'd had the satisfaction of nailing a lot of scumbags in her day. But nothing in her career would ever compare to the moment when it registered with Stahl that they could prove he had, in fact, made the call he'd just denied making.

Purple wasn't the right word for the hue that occupied his face. Naturally, all his venom was directed at her. "*She set me up!* She's been trying to get rid of me for years!"

Sam kept her expression completely neutral and let him dig his own grave.

"I'll take your badge, weapon, ID, radio and station keys," Farnsworth said, holding out his hand.

"You can't be serious! I didn't do anything that every other cop in this room hasn't done at one time or another."

"I urge you to refrain from any further comment," Conklin said. "You're being charged with interfering with a homicide investigation by releasing embargoed information to the media against the express wishes of the officer in charge of the investigation."

"*You're arresting me?*"

"You bet your ass I'm arresting you, and you're officially suspended with pay from the department pending a due process hearing."

Malone handed a pair of handcuffs to Conklin, who waited until Stahl thrust his badge, weapon, keys, radio and ID at the chief before he pulled Stahl's arms behind his back.

"I have rights! I want an attorney! You can't arrest me for making a phone call."

As Conklin cuffed him, Sam wondered if it was possible she was dreaming this whole thing. Even her fertile imagination never could've come up with this scenario.

"So you admit you made the call?" Malone asked. "Oh wait, we don't need you to admit it. We have it on film. Let's go." Malone tugged on Stahl's beefy arm, but he fought back, so Conklin grabbed the other arm and the two men all but dragged the shrieking lieutenant from the room.

"You're going to pay for this, Holland! You'd better watch your back, little girl! That stupid bitch set me up! This is all her fault!"

"Add threatening a public official to the list of charges," Farnsworth called after them. "That one's a felony." He seemed relish that last part.

"Sure is," Malone said.

None of them were sorry to see the last of Stahl. If only Sam believed they'd actually seen the last of him.

"Wow," Archie said, summing up Sam's sentiments.

"Good riddance," Farnsworth said. "But don't quote me on that. Good work, Lieutenants."

"Thank you, sir," Archie said.

Sam could tell he was trying to hide his satisfaction in the outcome of his mini-investigation.

"I'll need you both to file statements," Farnsworth said.

"That won't be a problem," Sam said.

"For me either," Archie said. "I need to get back upstairs and see where we are with your film, Sam."

"Thanks."

After he left, Sam wasn't sure what to say to the chief. Stahl's downfall had been swift and unexpected.

Farnsworth held Stahl's badge in his hand. "How could he be so foolish?"

"I've just come from speaking with Rick Lind's wife Carla. I learned that he suffers from some sort of mental illness. It's nothing that's been diagnosed or anything like that, but everyone around him is aware of it. I don't know if what Stahl suffers from is mental illness, per se, but something about him is 'off,' and we all know it."

Sighing, he lowered himself into his big leather executive chair. “I’m not at liberty to discuss personnel matters with you. However, I won’t deny what you say is true. All his venom is going to be centered on you. You know that, don’t you?”

“It has been for a while anyway.” Sam sat in one of his visitor chairs. “What will happen now?”

“He’ll be processed, arraigned and most likely released on bail, which is when you’ll really need to watch your back.”

“He doesn’t scare me. I’ve got Arnie Patterson and his followers targeting me.”

“Sam, you need to take this stuff seriously.” He tossed Stahl’s badge onto his desk. “What’s the story with the APB for Lind?”

“He’s gone missing.”

“Since when?”

“No one has seen him since the game. His wife hasn’t heard from him.”

“And she waited until now to tell us that?”

“Apparently, it’s not unprecedented when things don’t go his way. The people around him protect him when he’s in one of his ‘moods.’”

“Interesting.”

“It occurs to me that it’s possible Willie isn’t our only victim.”

“Oh, Jesus. Really?”

“I don’t know anything yet, but I’d like to find him. I’m going to head home now, but I’m taking work with me. I’ll be on the radio if anything comes across about Lind.”

“I’ll see you in the morning.”

She headed for the door, but something made her

turn around, which is how she caught him staring off into space. “Are you all right?”

“I’m disappointed and disillusioned at times like this, but I’m okay.”

“Don’t let Stahl get you down. There’re a lot more like us than there are like him.”

“Thank God for that.”

“Why don’t you go home and let Marti spoil you?”

“I just might do that.”

“Come on.” If she didn’t encourage him to leave, he’d find a reason to spend a couple more hours there. “Walk me out.”

“If you insist.”

“I do.” She waited while he said goodnight to his admin, who seemed shocked to see him leaving somewhat on time.

When they walked through the main doors, the media swarmed them.

“We’ll provide an update on the Vasquez case in the morning,” the chief said. “No comment until then.”

“Why is there an APB for Rick Lind?” one of the reporters called after them.

“No comment,” Farnsworth said. He was quiet until they reached the parking lot. “It might be time for me to retire.”

Shocked to the core by the unexpected statement, Sam turned to him. “What did you say?”

“Don’t look so astounded. I’m not as young as I used to be, and the job is wearing on me lately in a way it never did before. I don’t want to outstay my welcome.”

“You couldn’t possibly outstay your welcome. It’s been a rough couple of days. You can’t make a decision like that at a time like this.”

"True. I shouldn't have said anything. Consider it a weak moment."

"This place wouldn't be the same without you."

"Oh, sure it would. It was fine before me, and it'll be fine after me. You might have to follow the rules a little more closely without old Uncle Joe around to run interference for you," he added with a teasing smile.

Sam shuddered at the thought. "All the more reason for you to stick around."

He laughed, which she'd hoped he would.

"While I have you, let me run something past you," Sam said.

"Sure."

"Detective McBride asked me to be an attendant in her wedding. Since this is the first time one of my detectives asked me to be in their wedding, I had no idea what I should say."

"Do you want to do it?"

"I wouldn't be completely opposed. I think a lot of her. I guess you could say we're friends—as much as we can be anyway."

"I was going to say if you didn't want to do it, feel free to pin it on me."

"I like how you think," Sam said, laughing.

"It's easy to see why you'd be conflicted, but I'd be more concerned about a romantic relationship between a squad commander and a subordinate than I would about something like this. I'm sure by now it's no secret that you and Detective McBride are friendly."

"I guess you could say I'm friendly with all of them. I know I shouldn't be—"

"There's nothing wrong with being a friendly, compassionate leader, Sam. You get much more out of them with sugar than you'll ever get with vinegar. Just ask your old friend Stahl about that."

"Still, sometimes I wonder if I'm coloring outside the lines with them."

"As long as the lines never get blurred, you're fine. Don't look for trouble where there isn't any."

"Good advice, thanks."

"Please make sure I get pictures of you in pink taffeta."

"Um, hello, I don't have friends who'd have pink taffeta bridesmaid gowns." The very thought of pink taffeta made her want to barf, especially knowing it would make Shelby's life complete.

His ringing laugh made her laugh too.

"See you in the morning," she said. "Get some sleep."

"I'll try."

Sam got into her car and waited until he drove out of the lot before she followed him into traffic. The idea of the MPD without him at the helm was something she didn't want to think about. He'd been chief the entire time she'd been on the force. He'd guided and mentored her—and protected her at times. Of that she had no doubt.

While she certainly knew he couldn't—and wouldn't—work forever, she liked to think that his retirement date was years in the future. Now she had something else to worry about in addition to all the other issues on her mind at the moment.

When her cell phone rang, she answered it without taking her eyes off the road to check the caller ID.

"Holland."

"Hey, Sam."

"What's up, Tinker Bell?"

"I wanted to let you know that Tracy is here. She said she needed a place to hide out for a little while. She seems upset, and I thought you'd want to know."

"I'm on my way home. Thanks for the heads up."

"I was getting ready to leave, but I'll keep her company until you get here."

"I'd appreciate that. Thanks."

"Hey, um, I know you have a million other things on your mind, but I was wondering…"

"About?"

"Agent Hill. He said he would call, but I haven't heard from him."

"He's in the Dominican Republic for the Vasquez case."

"Ah, okay. That makes sense. Sorry to go all junior high on you."

Sam laughed. "No problem. See you in a few." Though she was anxious to spend some time with her dad, she went straight to her own Ninth Street home, vowing to see him later. Her oldest sister had been going through a difficult time with her seventeen-year-old daughter, Brooke. The stress had been wearing on Tracy for months, and Sam was anxious to hear the latest.

She parked in front of the house and took the ramp Nick had installed so her father could visit their home, which had been just another reason to love her thoughtful husband. Inside she found Shelby sitting next to Tracy on the sofa, handing her tissues and patting her knee.

Shelby seemed relieved to see Sam. She got up and came over to hand the box of tissues to Sam. "I'll let you take it from here."

"Thanks for staying, Tinker Bell."

"No problem. I love Tracy. I hate to see her so upset."

"So do I." As her sister was usually the one providing comfort, Sam hoped she could return many a favor. The front door clicked shut as Shelby departed, and Sam took a seat next to Tracy. "Hey, there."

"Hey. Sorry to show up uninvited."

"You're always invited. You know that."

"I needed a place to hide out. Ang is up to her eyeballs in poopy diapers, and Dad and Celia would worry. This seemed like my best bet."

"What's wrong?"

"What isn't wrong? The situation with Brooke is totally out of hand. Mike told me we have to do something about her or he's taking Ethan and Abby and going to his mother's. He doesn't want them around her, and I can't say I blame him. All she does is yell and scream and tell us to fuck off. Last night she told him to go fuck himself, that he's not her father and can't tell her what to do."

Sam tried to hide her shock but probably did a piss-poor job.

"How could she say that to him after the way he's stepped up for her for most of her life? Her own father didn't want her, but Mike always did. You should've seen his face. He was heartbroken."

Sam ached for the man who'd entered Brooke's life when she was just a baby and raised her as his own. "I can't say I blame him."

"That's the way she is lately. She goes right for the jugular."

"What in the world does she have to be so pissed off about?"

"It's mostly because we hate her friends and won't

let her hang out with them. She never drank or smoked or got high until she started running around with this one girl named Hoda, who's apparently the alpha bitch of a so-called girl crew that Brooke wants in on. We asked around a bit about Hoda and her pals and didn't like what we heard. We've prohibited her from hanging around with them, so she's coming at us with her claws out."

Sam handed her sister another tissue.

"I feel like a monster because I'm actually thinking about sending her away. She's ruining our lives. The other day, Ethan told me to fuck off. He doesn't even know what that means, but he's heard her say it so many times that he thinks he's being cool copying his big sister. Mike's right—Abby and Ethan can't live with her anymore, or she's going to ruin them too."

"Shit, Trace. I'm so sorry it's gotten this bad. I'd drag her ass over here, but we've got Scotty now, and we're not home enough to manage her."

"You're sweet to say that, but I wouldn't inflict her on my worst enemy let alone my precious baby sister. She's ruining my marriage too. All Mike and I do is fight about her. I keep telling myself we just have to get through this school year, and then she'll be in college, but I can't see how we can live like this for one more week, let alone a whole year. And her grades have gone to shit, so she probably won't even get into college. I don't know what to do."

Sam put her arm around Tracy and held her while she shuddered with sobs.

"She's my baby, but when I look at her, all I see is this person I don't even know. And God help me, I'm not sure I even love her anymore."

"Sure you do. You don't like her very much right now, but you'll always love her."

"She doesn't make it easy. I knew the teenage years would be tough, but this is something else altogether."

Sam had seen her niece in action enough times lately to appreciate some of what Tracy was dealing with.

"What about a shrink?"

"She's been seeing one for a year, and we've tried family therapy too, but now she refuses to go unless we let her see her friends. So we're at another standoff over that."

"Have you thought about sending her to boarding school?" Sam asked, only half joking.

"More often than I'd care to admit. I've even looked into it a little. I found the perfect program outside of Richmond. They run the place like a military academy, but it's not actually military. It's just what she needs."

"Do it, Trace. She might hate you now, but someday she'll see that you saved her life by sending her there."

"I'd do it in a minute, but it's twenty grand a year. We can't swing that."

"I can. Let me pay for it."

"No way, Sam. I could never let you do that."

"Why not? After Peter and I split and Dad got hurt, I lived there rent-free for two years. Nick won't let me pay for much of anything around here. My check goes in the bank and a lot of weeks I barely touch it because I'm too busy working to do much of anything. I've got the money. Let me help you the way you would help me if the shoe were on the other foot. Please, Trace. After all you do for me, this is the least I can do for you."

"I didn't come here hoping you would bail me out."

"To quote Ethan, 'fuck off.'"

That made Tracy snort with laughter that was quickly replaced by more tears. "It's too much. I can't let you do that."

Sam gripped her sister's hand. "Listen to me—who loves your kids more than you and Mike do?"

"Probably only you," Tracy said begrudgingly.

"And who has always loved Mike almost as much as you do?"

"You," Tracy whispered.

"I love all of you as much as I love anyone. If I can't help you, who can I help? You do so much for me. Please let me do this for you."

"If I let you do this, she'll hate you as much as she hates me. She knows we can't afford something like this."

"I can live with that if it means getting her back on track and keeping your family together."

"I don't know if Mike will go for it."

"Yes, he will, Trace. He wants her out of the house. This accomplishes that and puts her in a safe place where she'll be watched and monitored. He'll go for it."

"What about Nick?"

"What about him?"

"He'll stand by and let you give me twenty thousand bucks without blinking an eye?"

"He'd say, 'It's your money, babe. Do what you need to do.'"

Tracy offered a faint smile. "You sound just like him."

"Come here." Sam gathered her sister into a tight hug. "Let's get this done before things get any worse, okay?"

Tracy nodded. "Thank you. Thank you so much."

"I wish I could say it's my pleasure, but I hate that you're going through such an awful thing."

"So do I. It would certainly be a relief to not have to deal with her anger every day."

"Has she been seen by a doctor?"

"I dragged her to mine a couple of months ago. She chalked the whole thing up to hormones and teenage years and promised me she'd grow out of it. I wish I was convinced."

"She needs to get back into counseling."

"Group and individual counseling is part of the program at the school. That was one of the reasons it was so appealing to me."

"It sounds like where she needs to be. What do we need to do to make it happen?"

"I go there and fill out all the enrollment paperwork, pay the tuition and they come pick her up."

"Would you tell her this is happening?"

Tracy's eyes filled again as she shook her head. "If I did, she'd run away. That's my greatest fear."

"I know it feels awful to be doing this, but it's the right thing for her—and for you, Mike, Abby and Ethan. In your heart of hearts you have to know that."

"I do," Tracy said as tears spilled down her cheeks. "But I wish it didn't have to be so drastic."

"I worked with this cop on a detail once, and we were talking about his kids. One of them had big-time drug problems that the family had dealt with for years. The son had been arrested a couple of times, which is a huge embarrassment for any cop. They sent the kid to rehab three times, and every time they had hope. But then he'd come home and fall back in with the same crowd that got him into drugs in the first place, and the whole ugly cycle would start up again. He finally OD'd when he was twenty-five. You know what that dad told me?"

"What?"

"His single biggest regret in life is that he didn't move his son away from those kids when he'd had the chance. He thought all the time about how different their lives might've been if he'd just moved."

"I can't move. Not with Dad's situation, and you and Ang nearby. Our whole lives are here. Mike's job. The kids' school and their friends."

"If you can't move, you have to move her. Before this gets any worse."

"I know. You're right. I'll talk to Mike tonight, and I'll go there tomorrow to sign her up."

"I wish I could go with you, but I can't right now."

"Because of the Vasquez case. I know."

"Not just that. Nick is going out of town for a couple of days, and I need to be around if Scotty needs me. He's taking Willie's murder kind of personally since he met him last summer."

"I'm so happy you're getting to be a mom, Sam."

"So am I."

"Don't let what's going on with Brooke scare you. Hopefully, it's just a phase and she'll come back to us on the other side."

"Let's hope so. Do you want to ask Mike to come over here so you can talk to him without Brooke around?"

Tracy shook her head. "He won't leave Abby and Ethan home alone with her. I'll talk to him later when they're all in bed."

"Wait right here for a sec." Sam got up, went into the study and found her checkbook. She signed a blank check and tore it out of the book. When she returned to the living room, she handed the folded check to Tracy. "Whatever you need. There's plenty of money in the account. What's mine is yours."

Tracy stood to hug her. "Thank you so much. I can't tell you how much this means to me."

"I'm happy to help you for a change."

"Can I stay with you a while longer? I don't want to go home yet."

"Of course you can. Have you eaten?"

Tracy shook her head. "I don't think I could. My stomach has been a mess over all of this."

"Let's just sit and talk about nothing."

They resumed their positions on the sofa with Tracy resting her head on Sam's shoulder and holding her hand. "Tell me about the case."

"Do I have to?" Sam asked with a sigh. "It's a mess. About a million people wanted him dead. He had a chaotic personal life, and now another member of the team is missing."

"Who?"

"Lind, the closer."

"What's up with that?"

"I wish I knew. His wife says it's not unprecedented for him to go off and lick his wounds after a big loss, but it's starting to be a long time without anyone hearing from him."

"Do you think he's dead too?"

"I don't know what to think." Sam brushed at a ball of lint on her jeans. "Nick is going on a top-secret trip with the president tomorrow."

"For real? How cool is that?"

"Pretty cool for him. Not so much for me. Scares the hell out of me."

"Why? Where's he going?"

"He can't tell me, which means it's dangerous. I get this pain…" She pressed a fist to her breastbone. "Right here. Whenever I think about him being in danger."

"He lives with that same pain every day."

"I know, and I wish he didn't have to."

"So now it's your turn."

"I guess so."

"You know he'll be fine. He will be with the president and all his security. It'll be the safest trip he's ever been on."

"Keep telling me that. Maybe by the time he gets back I'll believe it."

"Awww, poor baby." Tracy squeezed Sam's hand.

"I feel like such a wimp when I say I couldn't live without him, but there it is."

"There's nothing wrong with feeling that way, Sam. Being madly in love with your husband doesn't make you any less of a badass. I promise."

"Really? It doesn't?"

Tracy's laughter made Sam feel better. "No, it doesn't. Who wouldn't love him? He's amazing."

"He is that. Things between us have been better than ever lately. Just when I think it can't get any better, it does."

"I wondered if having Scotty here would be tough on you guys. You haven't been married all that long, and it's a lot to take on a child when you're still figuring out the married stuff."

"Somehow it's all working perfectly. I keep waiting

for problems, but we both feel like Scotty has always lived here. It just works."

"I'm happy for you, Sam. After all you went through with Peter and the miscarriages, no one deserves to be happy more than you do."

"Thanks. I keep hoping I might get another chance to be pregnant. Despite significant effort, I still get the monthly event."

"It'll happen when it's meant to be."

"Is that so?"

"I'm your big sister, and I say it is so, thus it is so."

Snuggled up to her sister, surrounded by her love and understanding, Sam debated something else she wanted to ask her but didn't know how to say it. "Could I ask you something so personal it defies even the boundaries of sisterhood?"

"Since when does anything defy the bounds of our sisterhood?"

"True," Sam said with a laugh that belied the nerves that fluttered in her belly at the thought of broaching this particular subject—even with Tracy, who was probably her closest friend in addition to being her big sister.

Tracy nudged Sam with her shoulder. "Just say it. After fifteen years of marriage and three kids, you can't shock me."

"Have you and Mike ever… God, this is embarrassing."

"There's not much Mike and I haven't done, so spit it out."

"Have you done anal?"

"Oh yeah."

"Really?"

"Back when we were having sex—before Brooke

went ballistic and ruined a lot of things, including our sex life—we did it fairly regularly. It's been a few months since we did anything, though. At this point, plain vanilla is looking pretty darned good to me."

"I'm sure it is." Sam couldn't imagine going a couple of days without sex with Nick, let alone months.

"Are you guys talking about trying that?"

"We've almost done it a couple of times, but we always stop before it actually happens. It drives me crazy to know he's done it before, that he's done something with another woman that he hasn't done with me. Isn't that stupid?"

"It's not stupid that you want to be his one and only, Sam. How do you know he's done it before?"

"I asked him if he had, and he shrugged. He's too much of a gentleman to spill the dirty deets, but he didn't deny it. Knowing he's done it before, he's done *that* with someone else but not me… I can't stop thinking about it."

"It's not something you should do if you don't really want to. It's not for everyone."

"I think I want to." Sam's skin suddenly felt too tight for her body and her palms were sweaty just thinking about some of their recent encounters. "Sometimes I think there's nothing I wouldn't do with him."

Tracy fanned her face. "That's very hot."

"Tell me the truth, does it hurt like hell?"

"It's more uncomfortable than painful—at first. But the orgasms…*whoa*. Unlike any others."

"What makes it so much hotter than the regular way?"

"The fact that it's a little bit forbidden—not to mention illegal in some places. It's a huge leap of trust between partners, among other things, that you have to experience to appreciate. After the election, you should take him out to the cabin and rock his world."

"I'd rather do it right here. Did I tell you about what he did in the loft upstairs?"

"I don't think so."

"He recreated the beach in Bora Bora, right down to the palm trees and double lounge chair. We've had a lot of fun up there." Sam's face heated as she recalled some of the time they'd spent in their hideaway.

"He's one hell of a guy," Tracy said.

"He's the only one I'd want to do something like that with."

Tracy began to giggle uncontrollably. "What?"

"I'm trying to picture you doing that with Peter—"

"Stop! Don't put that picture in my head! It was all I could do to have regular sex with Peter once a month. He would've freaked out about anything more than straight missionary. He was all about keeping it clean and tidy."

"Why am I not surprised that he wanted to control you in bed too?"

"I don't even like to think about him. The years I spent with him seem like a bad dream since I've been with Nick. It's night and day."

"Have you heard from your lovely ex-husband lately?"

"Not since he tried to kill himself and listed me as his next of kin at the hospital."

"So creepy."

"That's Peter for you."

"All this talk about sex—with Nick, not Peter—makes me want to go home and make up with my husband, who has put up with way too much shit from my kid in the last year."

"You guys are solid, Trace. You'll get back on track."

"I hope so." She hugged her sister. "Thanks for being here for me."

"Happy to be here for you the way you always are for me."

The front door burst open and Scotty came in ahead of Nick.

"Sam, we had the best time. Nick made a ton of money, and all these people wanted to shake hands with me. It was so cool."

Sam and Tracy shared a smile as Tracy got up to hug her new nephew and her brother-in-law on the way out the door.

FOURTEEN

"WAS SHE CRYING?" Nick asked Sam as he sat next to her and leaned in to kiss her.

"I'll tell you about it later. Did you guys eat?"

Scotty sat across from them. "They had all this fancy stuff I didn't like too much. Nick said we could order pizza."

"That sounds good to me."

"I'll do it!" Scotty got up and ran for the kitchen where they kept the takeout menus.

"He seems like his old self again," Sam said.

"He's getting there. We had a good talk about what happened at school."

"I called the kid's mom."

Instantly amused, Nick tipped his head for a closer look at her. "And?"

"I made it clear that we won't put up with her kid pounding on ours."

"Define 'made it clear.'"

Sam laughed at his insistent tone. "I let her know we'll press charges if he hits him again."

Her laughter fueled his. "Oh my God, I love it! Good going, babe."

"You think so? I'm worried that Scotty will be pissed if he finds out about it."

"Then tell him so he knows."

"I'm scared to."

Nick laughed again as he put his arm around her and kissed the top of her head. "Watch out for mama bear. No one messes with her cub."

"You know it."

Scotty came bouncing back into the room. "Thirty-two bucks for a large, a small and a salad."

"How much of a tip is that?" Nick asked.

"Ten percent would be three dollars twenty cents and twenty percent would be six forty. So seven bucks?"

"Excellent." Nick withdrew his wallet from the front pocket of his suit coat and handed it to Scotty. "I know exactly how much is in there, mister."

Scotty seemed stricken by what Nick had meant as a teasing comment. "As if I'd ever steal from you when you've given me everything."

"I was joking, buddy. I know you'd never steal from me."

The regret she heard in Nick's voice made her ache.

"Just making sure," Scotty said tentatively.

Sam held out her hand to Scotty. "Come sit with us. I want to talk to you."

"Am I in trouble?"

"Don't be silly," she said as she settled him between them. "You're not in trouble." She met Nick's challenging glance over Scotty's head. "I wanted to tell you that I talked to Nathan's mom about what happened today at school."

He looked up at her, clearly distressed. "You did?"

Sam nodded.

"What did you say?"

"I told her what happened and that we were upset about it and didn't want it to happen again."

"You didn't go all Police Officer Barbie on her, did you?"

Sam once again met Nick's gaze over the boy's head and saw that he was choking back a laugh. "Maybe. A little." She fought the urge to squirm under the glare coming from a twelve-year-old. "But I was nothing like *Barbie*," she added with disdain.

"Tell me exactly what you said."

"That if he hits you again, we'll press charges. And that he's not to give you any grief in school. Or else."

"Sam! I told you not to do that!"

"Technically you told me I couldn't involve the principal, which I didn't do. I want you to know I truly respect your wishes, buddy, but he could've really hurt you. I can't let that happen again."

"Sam's right, pal." Nick to the rescue. "This time it was a punch to the belly. Next time he might push you down the stairs and break a bone or something."

"I hadn't thought of a next time."

"That's the way bullies roll," Sam said, thinking of Stahl. "When they get away with it they think they can do it again. They keep doing it until someone makes it stop. I'll bet if you ask around, you'll find you aren't the first one he's punched, but maybe you'll be the last."

Scotty seemed to be mulling that over.

"What're you thinking?" Nick asked him after a long moment of silence.

"I'm kind of scared to go back there tomorrow. What if he's mad at me and the other kids are mean to me because I got him in trouble?"

"I thought of that and made sure to mention to his mom that I'd be unhappy if that were to happen."

Scotty's lips curled into a small smile. "I like how you said you'd be 'unhappy.'"

"I thought that was funny too," Nick said. "The understatement of the century."

"You guys can make fun of me all you want," Sam said, "but I'm pretty sure that kid won't be bothering you again."

"Thanks, Sam, for getting mad and calling his mom and all that. It's cool that you did that for me."

Relieved that he wasn't angry with her for butting in when he'd asked her not to, Sam ran her fingers through his silky dark hair. "There's nothing I wouldn't do for you. There's nothing either of us wouldn't do."

He smiled up at her, and once again the love she felt for him bowled her over. And to think she hadn't even known him a year ago, and now he was her son, in her life to stay forever.

She looked away from him before she embarrassed herself. "Where's the chow? I'm starving."

Nick's hand on her shoulder steadied and reassured her. He got it. How could he not when he experienced the same emotions every day himself?

"They need time to cook it," Scotty said dryly. "Can I go play video games until it gets here?"

"As long as all your homework is done," Sam said.

"We did it in the car," Scotty said, scurrying into the study.

"*We* did it in the car?" she asked Nick when they were alone.

"I helped with math."

She curled into his embrace and sighed when his strong arms came around her. "How long do you think it'll be before he stops making me want to cry with gratitude six times a day?"

"A year, maybe two. If it's any consolation, he has the same effect on me."

"Best thing we ever did."

"Without a doubt."

"I wondered if it would be weird or hard or awkward once it was permanent, but it's none of those things. It's amazing and overwhelming and astonishing and infuriating when someone hurts him."

"I never had any doubt at all that you'd be the world's greatest mom. Now I know it for sure."

"You're a pretty good dad too. You 'help' with math."

"He did most of it. I just checked his work."

"Whatever you say, Senator. I have to tell you what happened today with my good friend Lieutenant Stahl. You won't believe it." Sam took great pleasure in relating the story of Stahl's downfall to her astonished husband.

"How could be he so stupid as to make a call like that from within HQ?"

"Who knows? Who cares? All that matters is he is done with the department."

"Is he blaming the whole thing on you?"

"What do you think?" she asked with a cheeky grin.

"Sam… Don't make light of it. He's a formidable enemy, and he's had it in for you for years. You need to be careful."

"He doesn't scare me."

"Still…"

"I also got asked to be a bridesmaid in Jeannie and Michael's wedding," she said, deliberately changing the subject before he could fret about her safety.

"Is that right? Are you going to do it?"

"I think I will. I talked to the chief about it and he said it's cool, so why not?"

"It was nice of her to ask you. When's the wedding?"

"In July out at Rehoboth. So what happened today that you said you'd tell me about later?"

Only because she was sitting so close to him could she feel every muscle in his body tighten with tension as he told her about the Lexicore stock and the company's connection to the fire in Thailand.

"Oh my God, Nick. What does that mean for the campaign?"

"Not as much as it means to our bottom line. Graham and I both dumped the stock today for a fraction of what we paid for it, so there goes about half the money John left me."

"Oh, um, this might not be the best time to tell you that I just gave my sister twenty grand."

His eyes bugged. "For *what*?"

Sam told him about Brooke and the school Tracy had found that might be the answer to their prayers. "I didn't know this had happened with your stock when I gave her the money."

"It's okay, babe. That's your money to do with whatever you want. There's plenty of mine left that wasn't tied up in Lexicore. Don't worry."

"Regardless, I probably should've talked to you before I wrote her a check."

"It's fine," he said, kissing her cheek and then her lips. "You did the right thing for her. She does so much for us."

"That's what I thought too. How could I not give it to her so she can get Brooke the help she needs?"

"I hate to hear that things with Brooke have gotten that bad. I had no idea."

"I've witnessed a few incidents in the last few months that were shocking, but I chalked it up to teenage craziness. I didn't know it was this bad either."

"Is that what we're in for with the boy?" Nick asked. "Lord, I hope not. I can't imagine that sweet boy turning into a two-headed monster."

"Me either." He combed his fingers through her hair, which went a long way toward relaxing and soothing her. "Listen, this thing with Lexicore… Graham is going to release a statement about how we owned the stock but dumped it—at a tremendous loss—as soon as we learned about the connection to the factory."

"That's probably the best strategy."

"He's going to do it while I'm gone and not available for comment."

"Oh."

"The press is apt to be all over you, which is my one worry with this plan."

"Nothing new there. They're always all over me."

"We don't really know what to expect with this, so I feel like I'm leaving you to deal with a potential nightmare on your own. I agreed to the plan but as the day went on, I started to worry about how it might affect you guys."

"Don't worry about us." She cupped his face and caressed the whiskers on his jaw. "If there's one thing I can handle, it's the press. I'm very good at giving them nothing they can use against me—or you. It's a good plan. Let Graham deal with it while you're gone, and hopefully by the time you're back it'll be old news."

"That's the goal."

"Are you worried about it screwing up the election?"

"A little bit. Wouldn't that be something after leading by such a big margin right up until the end?"

"You won't lose. Your constituents love you almost as much as I do." Sam loosened his tie and released the top two buttons on his shirt, caressing his throat before letting her fingers wander down to free the third button.

His hand on top of hers stopped her progress.

"Killjoy," she muttered.

"Two hours to get the boy fed, showered and into bed, and then I'm *all* yours."

"Two whole hours? That's ages from now."

"You'll survive."

Before she could object, the doorbell rang, and Scotty came running to pay the pizza deliveryman. The guys dove into the large pepperoni—Scotty's favorite—while Sam nibbled on her salad and eyed the pizza with envy. "One small piece won't make you fat, babe," Nick said, tuned into her thoughts as always.

"Yes, it will."

He used the pizza slicer to cut a big piece in half and lifted it onto her plate. "I like you with some meat on your bones, so eat up."

Scotty got up to refill his milk glass. It had taken a couple of weeks for him to feel comfortable helping himself to anything in their home, including the contents of the fridge, so it pleased her to see him pouring his own milk.

Sam took a delicious bite of the coveted pizza and wiggled a finger at Nick to bring him close enough to whisper in his ear. "You don't have to charm me with pizza. I'm a sure thing where you're concerned."

His smile was positively sinful and left no doubt that

if Scotty wasn't there, they probably would've made good use of the kitchen floor. It had happened before—more than once.

Suddenly, a couple of hours seemed like a really long time.

After dinner, Scotty suggested a game of video baseball, which Nick happily agreed to. Sam followed them into the study and took advantage of the opportunity to check her email. While she was sitting at Nick's immaculately appointed desk, she eyed the perfectly aligned frames that contained photos from their wedding, Scotty's most recent school picture and one of Sam and her dad that Nick had once told her he loved.

With a glance over her shoulder to ensure he was fully occupied with the game, she set out to turn each of the frames upside down. When one of them wouldn't stand upright in the new position, she rested it on its side. Then she got up and moved to the sofa to plow through the restraining orders relating to the Feds.

Almost every one of the marquee players had at least three of them attached to their name. All of the subjects were women, with the exception of Willie's brother-in-law. Out of curiosity, Sam read some of the complaints against the women and was appalled by lengths some of them went to while attempting to snag the attention of a big-time ballplayer. One of them had draped herself naked across the hood of Cecil Mulroney's car three times before he took action.

Another had befriended the mother of Ramon Perez hoping to gain access to him.

She read through the complaint Willie had filed regarding his brother-in-law Marco, who had threatened him physically after Willie refused to loan him the money he needed to pay off debts with dangerous people in the Dominican Republic. As she read, her vision swam and the words on the page became scrambled the way they did when she was tired and her dyslexia kicked in. A sure sign it was time to quit working.

Nick let out a shout and then a ringing laugh as one of Scotty's players hit a grand slam.

"That is totally unfair!" Nick said. "You cheated!"

Scotty gave him an arch look. "How do you figure?"

"You're better at this than I am. You know stuff I don't know."

"Don't be a bad sport."

"Bad sport? Did you call me a *bad sport*?" The "argument" descended into a heated wrestling match that had both of them laughing hysterically as Nick let Scotty beat the tar out of him. He was never anything but gentle, exerting just enough muscle to make the match a challenge for the boy, who had his dad in a headlock and was giving him a noogie.

"Give up yet?" Scotty asked, red-faced and sweating from exertion.

"Never." Nick ran his fingers over Scotty's ribs, knowing the ticklish spot would ruin his opponent's concentration.

"No fair!" Scotty said, screaming with laughter. Watching them, Sam's heart ached with love and contentment that was tinged with anxiety as she remembered the trip Nick would leave on in the morning, the trip that would take him far away from them and into danger she couldn't begin to fathom. A lump formed in her throat, and she got up to leave the room before she embarrassed herself by breaking down in front of them.

She loved him so much that it hurt to think about

being away from him for even the short time he'd be gone. But to picture him in any sort of danger made her crazy, which really wasn't fair when she considered what she put him through on a daily basis with her job.

In the kitchen, she fixed herself a glass of ice water and downed half of it before putting the glass on the counter. She stared into the darkness out the window over the sink, lost in thoughts she'd rather not be having. When Nick's hands landed on her shoulders and squeezed, she startled.

"Hey." He nudged her hair aside to gain access to her neck. "What's wrong?"

"Nothing."

"Samantha…"

No one else had ever called her by her full name. She'd been Sam her whole life until he made her his Samantha.

"Where's Scotty?" she asked, her voice sounding shaky and fragile to her own ears. She wondered how it sounded to her oh-so-observant husband.

"In the shower." With his hands on her hips, he compelled her to turn and face him.

At the look of concern on his face, her eyes filled with tears that infuriated her.

"What's wrong, Sam?"

"I'm scared about you going away and not coming back." She hated how vulnerable the statement made her, but it was the truth.

"Oh, baby, come on." He gathered her in close to him, so close she could feel his heartbeat as she breathed in his familiar scent. "I'll be fine. I'll be back before you have time to miss me."

"No, you won't." She rested her head on his shoulder, absorbing the sweet comfort that only he could provide. "I hate myself for this. I know I put you through far worse every day."

"I don't like to see you worried or upset, but knowing you love me enough to worry is very sweet."

"I love you too much."

"Not possible."

"It's not in my nature to be gushy, so maybe I don't say it often enough or show you—"

He stopped her with a soft, devastatingly sensual kiss. "Baby, you show me every day, in every look and every touch. I never wonder how much you love me. I always know."

Reassured by his words, she clung to him, needing him more than she'd ever needed anyone.

"I promise I'll be fine, and I'll be back before you know it."

She tightened her hold on him. "For the record, I'm disgusted by myself. It's so not like me to be a needy female."

His soft chuckle drew a hesitant smile from her. "You're my needy female, and I love you so much. I had no idea it was possible to love anyone as much as I love you."

They stood there, wrapped up in each other, for a long time, until the water turned off upstairs, and he released her with a kiss that promised sensual delights the moment they were able to be alone. "Let's get the boy in bed so we can spend some time together."

"What time do you have to get up?"

"I have to be at Andrew's by three."

"Is your detail going on the trip with you?"

He nodded. "Where I go, they go."

After they shut off the lights and locked the doors, they walked upstairs together.

Scotty was in bed when they got to his room, and they went in to say goodnight.

Nick sat on the edge of the bed. "So I won't see you tomorrow or Saturday, bud, but I'll be back early on Sunday."

"Is Mrs. Littlefield still coming up on Saturday to see me?"

"Yep," Nick said. "I talked to her today, and you're on for lunch and a movie."

"Cool. I can't wait to see her. Have a good time on your trip with the president, and make sure you memorize all the sick stuff about *Air Force One* so you can tell me about it after."

"I'll do that." Nick leaned forward to receive a tight hug from Scotty. "Keep an eye on Sam for me while I'm gone."

"I'll do my best, but she won't make it easy."

"I can hear you," Sam said dryly, which made them laugh.

"Dude, you're feeling my pain." Nick kissed Scotty's forehead and gave him another hug. "Have fun with Mrs. L. Tell her I said hi."

"I will."

Nick released him, and Sam moved in to pull the comforter up and over him, leaning in to kiss him.

"Come get me if you wake up during the night."

"I will. Thanks, Sam."

"Night, buddy."

"Hey, Nick?"

At the doorway, he turned back. "Yeah?"

"You'll be okay on the trip, right?"

The hint of anxiety in Scotty's voice touched Sam in the same place her anxiety dwelled.

"You bet. Nothing to worry about."

"Okay. Night."

"Love you, buddy. Sleep tight."

Knowing Scotty wasn't comfortable with the door closed tight, Nick left it propped open far enough to let in the faint glow of the night-light they'd bought when they discovered he was afraid of the dark. After Nick had found the door open and the light on in the closet one morning, he'd put two and two together and bought the night-light for the hallway.

They were all doing their best to navigate their new lives together, letting their love and affection for each other lead the way past any obstacles that might arise.

"What did we do before he lived with us?" Nick asked when they were in their room with the door shut and locked—for now.

"I have no idea, but it wasn't anywhere near as much fun as it is having him here."

"As I recall," he said, slipping his arms around her, "we had plenty of fun when it was just us."

That sexy smile of his always made her knees weak. "Yes, but this is better. We have us, but we have him too."

"I love our little family. It's the best thing to ever happen to me."

Sam combed her fingers through the silky strands of his hair. She never got tired of looking at him in all his glorious male perfection. "I'm so glad. I wanted that so badly for you."

He drew back from her to tug her shirt over her head and release her bra.

Sam took advantage of the opportunity to remove his shirt, and gasped at the exquisite sensation of her hardened nipples rubbing against his chest hair.

His arms encircled her, infusing her with his heat and his strength and his overwhelming love for her.

"You're everything to me," she whispered, needing him to know what was in her heart before he left.

He held her tight enough to cause pain, but it was the best kind of pain. "Sam, God, you're killing me tonight."

"I need you to know."

"I know, baby. How could I not know?"

"I'm not very good at saying the words."

"I don't need the words when I have the actions. You show me all the time, in a million little ways. Such as when you turn all my pictures upside down because you know it'll make me laugh when I find that you've left your mark on my desk—again."

Sam dissolved into laughter that went a long way toward relieving the tension that had gathered inside her as his departure drew closer. "I didn't do it."

"And then when you lie to my face," he said, his hands sliding down to cup her ass, which was still covered by denim, "it makes me hot."

"Everything makes you hot." She tugged at his pants, unbuttoning and unzipping so she could wrap her hand around the steely length that throbbed and grew as she stroked him.

His head fell back in surrender that touched her heart. "Everything about *you* makes me hot," he said through gritted teeth.

Sam dropped to her knees and had him in her mouth before he could gauge her intentions.

The groan that surged from deep inside him thrilled her as she sucked and stroked him to a fast, explosive finish.

"Christ have mercy," he whispered when she licked him clean in the aftermath.

She looked up at him, filled with female satisfaction at having had her way with him and breaking his control in the process.

His fingers in her hair gave a gentle tug, urging her up. He backed her up to the bed and laid her out before him, his eyes hot and needy despite the recent satisfaction. When he looked at her in that particular way, he could have anything he wanted from her—anything at all. Hoping to incite him, she raised her knees, letting her feet cling to the very edge of the bed as she spread her legs in blatant invitation.

He took the bait, all but pouncing on her in his haste to get rid of her jeans and panties. His suit pants came whipping off next and when he flung them across the room, Sam's sex clenched in anticipation. She loved him like this—wild, out of control and so hot for her he couldn't be bothered with his usual need for order.

She held out her arms to him, welcoming him into her loving embrace.

He came down on her, molding himself to her as only he could do. His lips and hands were everywhere, triggering all her senses as she tried to keep up with his seemingly ravenous need. The tug of his lips on her nipple had her hips arching off the bed, trying to get closer to the erection that lay already hot and full again on her belly.

She worked a hand between them, clasping him in

her tight grip and stroking him hard and fast, the way she knew he liked it.

His head dropped to her chest as he pumped into her hand. "I can't believe you're doing this to me again," he whispered roughly.

"What am I doing?"

"Don't act all innocent with me, Samantha." He pried her hand free, raised it up and over her head and then reached for her other arm, holding them together with one strong hand.

Captured by him, surrounded by him, overwhelmed by him, she waited breathlessly to see what he would do next.

He began with deep, drugging kisses, licking into her mouth in an erotic rhythm that had her squirming under him, looking for so much more. "Easy, baby," he whispered as he kissed her jaw and neck and then her ear, rolling her lobe between his teeth and biting down just hard enough to make her moan from the jolt of pure sensation that tightened her nipples.

Seeming to know what she needed, he shifted down ever so slightly, letting his erection slide through the slickness between her legs, bumping her clit on every pass.

Suddenly she wanted her hands free and fought against his tight hold.

"Wait," he said. "Let me love you."

"I want to touch you. I need to touch you." The need was so big, so huge it threatened to swallow her up. It mixed with the fear she'd been battling since she heard about the impending trip and made her tremble from head to toe.

He released her hands immediately. “Sam, honey, you’re shaking. What’s wrong?”

She wrapped her arms around him, bringing his head to rest on her chest. “I hate myself for feeling the way I do right now.”

His sigh was long and tortured. “I never should’ve agreed to this trip.”

“No, don’t say that. Everything in our lives is about me and my job. There’s nothing wrong with it being about you for once.”

“There’s something very wrong when it makes my strong, fearless cop shake with fear.”

“I’ll get over it. I promise.” With her hands on either side of his face, she urged him into another carnal kiss as she raised her hips in invitation.

“Not yet.”

“Yes. Now. *Please*.”

Responding to the urgency he heard in her plea, he entered her fully in one quick stroke that stole the breath from her lungs.

Her hands slid over his back and down to grip the tight, muscular ass that flexed under her hands as he went impossibly deeper.

Sam cried out from the sheer power they created together, every damned time.

He gave it to her hard and fast, the way she liked it best, and then he reached down to where they were joined to stroke her to an orgasm that seemed to go on forever. The first orgasm rolled into a second.

She came down from the incredible high to realize he was still hard, still moving, still possessing her with every deep stroke. And then he withdrew suddenly, and made her want to weep from the loss as he kissed his way down the front of her until he was kneeling on the floor next to the bed and her feet were propped on his shoulders.

Every muscle in her legs quivered with anticipation and aftershocks from the full-body orgasms he'd already given her. Deep down, she worried that nothing this amazing could last forever, not that she'd ever be stupid enough to share that thought with her devoted husband. She knew for certain that the only way it wouldn't last was if something happened to one of them. Since he told her about the trip, the fear of something happening to him had been as real and as palpable as her love for him.

"Why did you just get all tense again?" he asked, his lips soft and soothing on her inner thigh, even as she anticipated where his attention would soon be directed.

"Because I know what you've got planned, and I'm bracing myself."

"That's not why." His fingers slid between her legs, teasing and stroking. "Tell me the truth."

"I'm trying not to be afraid. I'm trying really hard."

"I must not be doing a good enough job getting your mind off it. Clearly, I need to work harder," he said, punctuating his words with searing strokes of his tongue over tender, sensitive tissues.

Sam fisted his hair to hold him there as one big hand clutched her bottom to anchor her for his fierce possession. Using fingers, lips and tongue, he reduced her to a trembling, needy, orgasmic disaster area and managed to wipe all worries and fears from her mind, one stroke at a time.

And then he withdrew his fingers and forced one of them past the tight barrier of her anus and sent her reeling into the strongest orgasm yet, crying out from the sheer power of it. She came back to herself to find he'd entered her again, surging into her over and over and over again, until he found his release deep inside her.

Sam wrapped her arms and legs around him, holding him as close as she could get him.

His lips moved softly against her neck, whispering words she couldn't hear but understood just the same. "I'll come back to you, Samantha." This was said so she could hear it. "I promise. I'll never leave you."

She blinked back tears and strengthened her already tight grip on him. "I'm sorry to be this way. I suppose I deserve it after what I've put you through over the last year."

"Yes, you do," he said, making her laugh, which of course had been his goal. He raised his head and looked down at her, his hazel eyes searing her with their intensity. "Anytime you feel afraid while I'm gone, I want you to remember I'm with the best protected person on the planet. They won't let anything happen to him, so nothing will happen to me either. Okay?"

She bit her lip and nodded.

"You have my heart and soul, Samantha, no matter where I am in the world, I belong to you. Only you."

Raising her hands, she caressed the face she loved more than any other. "I belong to you too, body and soul and heart and everything else I've got. If you'd asked me two years ago if I would ever say something like that to anyone, I probably would've sneered before I punched you. But you've laid me low and stripped me bare."

He pressed his hips against her, letting her know he was still lodged deep inside her—as if she needed any reminder. “I like you best stripped bare. I love you best when you’re not afraid to tell me how you feel.”

“They haven’t yet invented the words to adequately tell you how I feel about you or how you make me feel when we’re together like this. You turn me into someone totally different than I’ve ever been with anyone else.”

“That’s the most incredible thing you’ve ever said to me—in a year of incredible things.”

“I didn’t want you to leave with any doubts about what’s waiting for you at home.”

“I never have any doubts where you’re concerned. From that first second on a crowded deck, you’ve been mine. Always mine.”

She realized he was moving inside her again, fully recovered from the explosive release. “Turn over,” she said.

“Not this time.”

“You got your turn, now I want mine.”

With an exasperated growl, he managed to turn them and move them into the middle of the bed without losing the connection.

“I don’t know how you do that,” she muttered when she recovered her senses. “You must’ve had a lot of practice.” She knew almost nothing about the other women in his life, which hadn’t bothered her until recently, until she’d learned he’d done things with at least one of them that he hadn’t done with her.

“I don’t remember anyone but you, the only one who has ever mattered.”

Sitting astride him with his substantial erection throbbing and growing inside her, she couldn’t take the time to wonder about anything other than how best to drive any thought that didn’t include her right out of his mind. She raised herself up and slid back down on him slowly and torturously.

His fingers dug into her hips, and she knew he was resisting the temptation to take over.

She did it again and again until his head was thrown back and his throat exposed, making it too easy to lean down and sink her teeth into his pectoral, adding some suction so he would take her mark with him.

His hoarse shout was followed by a surge of heat deep inside her as he came violently, his hold on her hips ensuring he'd left his own marks, which was fine with her.

Sam collapsed onto his chest, sweaty and spent and sore and aching at the thought of him flying away from her in a few short hours.

He combed his fingers through her long hair, over and over again, until she started to drift off, still joined with him in every possible way. "We need to unlock the door in case Scotty needs us," she said.

"I'll do it."

The next thing she knew, he was kissing her awake. As his cologne filled her senses, she opened her eyes to find the bathroom light bathing them in a warm glow. He was fully dressed in a sweater and jeans. A garment bag sat on the bed next to him.

Sam's heart beat fast and hard as she realized he was leaving. She wanted to cry and beg him not to go, but she did neither of those things. Rather, she reached up to caress his freshly shaven cheek.

He turned his face into her caress, his lips warm and soft against her palm.

"Be careful out there," she said, stealing his usual line to her.

His smile was quick and perfect and so totally him. "Always am."

"That's my line."

"You're my girl." He gathered her into a tight, fierce hug, followed by a hot, erotic kiss intended to tide them over until he got back. "Love you, babe."

She clung to him and had to force herself to let him go when her every instinct was telling her to hold on for dear life. "I love you too. Be safe and hurry back. I won't be able to breathe until you're home again."

"Scotty and work will keep you too busy to worry." That wasn't true, but she kept the thought to herself because she didn't want him carrying the weight of her worries with him.

He kissed her once more and got up to shut off the bathroom light. "Go back to sleep for a while."

"I will."

"See you soon."

"I'll be right here waiting for you."

"Counting on that." He came back for one last kiss, lingering as if he didn't want to go any more than she wanted him to.

"Go on. You can't keep the president waiting." He squeezed her tight and released her.

She wished she could see in the darkness so she could watch him leave the room. Rather, she listened to him go down the stairs and rattle around in the kitchen. She heard the front door open and the rumble of his deep voice as he greeted his Secret Service detail. And then the front door closed, and the silence descended.

A car started up outside and pulled away, leaving more stillness and silence in its wake.

Sam stared at the red glow of the clock on the bedside table, which read two o'clock. Despite her fierce will, tears flooded her eyes and wet her pillow as she breathed in the scent he'd left on her hand. She saw every minute that passed until the alarm went off at six.

Sam felt like a fool for nearly forgoing a shower so she wouldn't wash his scent off her hand. "You're acting like a lovesick teenager," she muttered as she got up and dragged her aching, tired body into the shower. Everything she had hurt, more so than usual after a night of love with Nick.

Her back ached, her boobs hurt and her lips were raw and swollen. Overall, she was a mess. She stood under the hot water, letting it ease her aches. However, nothing could ease the pain in her chest that had started right around the time he left, and would probably remain until he returned.

Despite feeling ridiculous about her reaction to his departure, tears slid down her cheeks, washed away by the shower. She was determined to get them all out now before she woke Scotty and before she had to be at work. It was bad enough that she'd been a total wreck with Nick, but she wasn't about to inflict her fears on anyone else, especially Scotty.

She rinsed the conditioner out of her hair and glanced down to find the water tinted with pink. The realization was another shot to the heart, but at least it explained the excessive aches and pains as well as the tears that flowed more freely now that she knew another month would pass without conception.

Not for the first time she wondered if the baby she'd lost in February had been her last chance. And then she remembered what their doctor friend Harry had said about it taking months after the birth control shot wore off for conception to occur. It had only worn off a month ago, but now she could admit that she'd hoped to defy the odds and get pregnant again right away.

She yearned for Nick, the only other person who'd feel the same acute disappointment that she did. Finished with the shower, she wrapped a towel around her body and another around her hair, took care of the period situation, went to find her phone and was elated to find a text from him.

Slight delay but on the way now (3:45). AF1 is astonishing. Can't wait to tell you all about it. They're taking our phones until we're on the way home. If you need me in an emergency, call Derek. He'll know how to get word to me. Love you always. N

She sat on the bed, reading and rereading the text. He had to give up his phone. She couldn't tell him about getting her period until he got home. Until then, she'd have to bear the disappointment alone. The lonely feeling that overtook her reminded her a lot of the years she'd spent unhappily married to Peter when she'd thought a baby might cure what ailed them. Now she knew that nothing could've fixed them—not when she was meant to be with Nick.

Exhausted from the lack of sleep and feeling like she was wading through quicksand, she got dressed and went to wake Scotty. He was grumpier than usual, which made for a complicated hour together before Shelby arrived.

"Ready to go, sport?" Shelby said, full of cheerful enthusiasm. Today's pink sweater was accented with sparkly pink rhinestones. She'd yet to pick up on Sam's cranky mood but had tuned right into Scotty's.

Scotty put down his cereal spoon and pushed the bowl away. "I'm not feeling good. I think I should stay home."

Sam and Shelby reached for his forehead at the same time.

Shelby smiled at Sam and withdrew her hand.

"No fever," Sam said. "What're your symptoms?"

"My stomach hurts. I feel like I'm going to throw up."

Sam took the seat next to his and waited until he looked right at her. "Is this because you're afraid to see Nathan?"

He wilted under her scrutiny. "Maybe. A little."

"It's going to be tough to face him after what happened yesterday."

"What happened?" Shelby asked, taking one of the other chairs.

Sam nodded to Scotty, wanting him to say it in the hope that speaking the words might help him.

"I got punched in the stomach because I defended Willie Vasquez when the other guys were calling him a loser."

"Oh my God!" Shelby's blue eyes flashed with fury that made her a friend forever in Sam's world. She looked at Sam. "What're we doing about it?"

"I took care of it."

Shelby's smile was full of catty satisfaction. "I'll bet you did."

"That's what he's afraid of." Sam reached for Scotty's hand. "Here's what to do. If he says anything to you, give him the death stare. Do you know how to do that?"

He shook his head.

Sam narrowed her eyes and zeroed in on Scotty, making him retreat a bit in his seat.

"Wow. I hope you never do that to me for real."

"With you there, sport," Shelby said.

"Works wonders on guilty scumbags in the interrogation room. Now let me see you do it."

Scotty scrunched up his face, but nothing about his stare was deadly.

"No, like this." Sam went for her most sinister, intimidating glare. "You have to put some hate behind it."

"Mrs. Littlefield says we don't hate anyone."

"You hate what he did, right?"

"Uh-huh."

"Focus on that then. Let's see it."

Scotty's stare had a lot more menace behind it this time.

"There it is! Excellent. Now what will you do if he hits you again?"

"Hit him back?"

"That's right. You're allowed to defend yourself. But I don't want you to ever throw the first punch. You got me?"

"Yeah. I can see the difference."

"Now, give me a fist."

He rolled his fingers around his thumb and held up his hand.

"Dude, that is the fastest way to end up with a broken thumb. Like this." She manipulated his hand into a fist. "Lead with your knuckles."

"What if he comes at me from behind?"

"Stomp on the top of his foot," Shelby said. "Then spin around and clip him under the nose."

Sam nodded in approval. "Someone's had self-defense classes."

"When you're barely five feet tall and living in a city, you can't be too careful."

"Is your belly feeling better?" Sam asked Scotty. He nodded, showing more of his usual enthusiasm.

"Thanks for showing me what to do."

"You got it. Now go brush your teeth and comb your hair."

"I did comb my hair."

"The front looks good. The rest of it's a problem."

"Fine," he said, running off.

"Do you think less of me, as a Homicide detective, that I want to kill the kid who hurt him?" Shelby asked.

"Actually, I think more of you as a friend than I ever have before. Thank you for helping with that just now."

"You're a great mom, Sam. He's lucky to have you in his corner."

"That's nice to hear, thank you. I need to get to work. Do you mind making the drop at school and sticking around for a few minutes to make sure he's okay?"

"I'd be happy to."

"I'm going out to get the papers," Sam said. She was anxious to see if there was anything reported about Nick's connection to Lexicore ahead of Graham's statement.

Just as she was about to open the door, the doorbell rang.

She opened the door and was overtaken by a hulking form in a police uniform. Before she had time react, he had grasped her throat and was squeezing the life out of her.

FIFTEEN

THE FERAL SNARL from her attacker identified him as Stahl. Sam had been on the receiving end of that snarl often enough to recognize it. He had such a tight hold on her throat that she immediately saw stars and couldn't seem to get her hands to function properly to practice any of the self-defense strategies she'd just imparted to her son. The scene before her faded in the fog that filled her mind as she had enough capacity to wonder if she was going to die right there on her own doorstep.

As images of Nick and Scotty filled her mind, she found the wherewithal to slam her knee into his groin.

He shrieked and fell away from her, stumbling backward on the ramp.

Drawing in greedy gulps of cold air, Sam kicked at him, her foot connecting with his knee, drawing another grunt of pain from him.

And then Scotty's Secret Service agents were on him, pulling him down the ramp, kicking and screaming the whole way.

Sam bent in half, hands on knees as she took a series of deep breaths, willing her pounding heart into submission.

Shelby came to the door. "What happened? Oh God, Sam! Are you all right?"

"Yeah," Sam said. "Keep Scotty inside." When

Shelby hesitated, obviously torn, Sam said, "Go. Please. Close the door."

Shelby did as Sam asked, which was a tremendous relief to Sam, who didn't want Scotty to see her hurt.

"I called it in," one of the agents said as the other slapped cuffs on Stahl, who was calling her a fucking bitch and spitting his rage all over her sidewalk. "Ambulance is on its way."

"No ambulances," Sam said, her voice raspy from the attack. "I'm fine."

"It's for him."

"I'm so sorry that happened, Lieutenant," the agent said. He must've been new, because Sam hadn't seen him before. "He was in uniform and had your newspapers so we assumed he was a friend of yours."

"Not your fault," she said, still breathing hard as a MPD cruiser came screaming around the corner onto Ninth Street.

The agents turned Stahl over to the EMTs and patrolmen, who seemed a bit freaked out to be hauling away an Internal Affairs lieutenant. They looked to Sam for guidance. Ignoring the throbbing pain in her neck, she nodded to them and took extreme pleasure in watching them cuff a purple-faced, screaming Stahl to the gurney.

Sam took another minute to regain her composure before she went back inside. The entire incident had transpired in under ten minutes, but the seconds in which she'd been denied oxygen had felt like weeks.

Shelby rushed from the kitchen to meet her. "Are you okay? Tell me the truth."

"I'm fine. I don't want Scotty to know."

"Come," Shelby said, taking her hand, "quickly."

"Come where?" Sam allowed the tiny sprite to drag her through the kitchen to the mudroom where Shelby had to go on tiptoes to wrap a pink cashmere scarf around Sam's neck. "That bad, huh?"

"That bad."

Sam fingered the soft wool while turning her nose up at the color. "Desperate times call for desperate measures."

"Yeah, you're fine."

Scotty's footsteps were heavy on the stairs. He came back with his hair wet down and tamed into submission. Ignoring the runaway trembling that continued to rack her body, Sam held his backpack for him and turned him to face her, hands on his shoulders. "You're going to be fine." Despite the pain it caused her, she forced her voice to remain normal. "Right?"

He nodded. "Why are you wearing Shelby's scarf? You hate pink."

"Shhh," Sam said in an exaggerated whisper. "She gave it to me as a gift. I'm pretending to like it."

Scotty's lips curled with amusement.

"Let's see the death stare one more time."

His eyes narrowed into a positively sinister expression.

"That's my boy." She hugged him tightly. "Love you. If anything happens, use your cell phone to call me."

"We're not allowed to use them in school."

"Go in the bathroom and text me. I'll be there so fast they won't know what hit them."

His smile lit up his face and touched her heart. "Thanks."

She cuffed his chin. "Love you."

"Love you too."

Sam waited until he'd left with Shelby and the detail to let herself fall apart a little. She sat at the table and dropped her face into her hands, fighting back tears she refused to allow. Stahl had scared her. There was no doubt in her mind that he could've killed her. Her strength was no match against his rage, and in his addled mind, he had nothing left to lose.

She experienced a powerful longing for her husband's strong arms. In light of how angry he'd be over what'd happened on their doorstep—with Secret Service agents in close proximity—it was probably better for all of them that he was winging his way across the globe at the moment.

When the trembling finally subsided, Sam got up to collect her badge, gun and cuffs from the locked drawer in the kitchen where she kept them now that Scotty lived there. She went through the motions of securing her service weapon in the hip holster she wore on her belt and clipping her gold shield to the waistband of her jeans.

Because she knew her dad would be wondering what had happened to bring a police car screaming on to their street so early in the morning, she went down the ramp from her house and up the ramp to her childhood home, rapping on the door as she walked in. "Anyone home?"

"Back here," her dad called from the kitchen. Seated in his wheelchair, he was scanning the headlines in the morning paper. His wise blue eyes took a perusing look over her, settling on the pink scarf and widening with surprise. He hadn't seen her in pink since her toddler years.

Sam bent to kiss his forehead. "Anything in the news? I didn't get a chance to look at the paper." In light of recent events, the statement would've made her giggle if her throat hadn't been throbbing.

"Did you hear about Lexicore and the Thai factory?"

"Unfortunately, yes. Nick owned stock in Lex, and had to dump it at a huge loss yesterday."

"Ah shit. That's a bummer, but he doesn't need that sticking to him in the homestretch of the election."

"He's hoping it doesn't screw things up."

"Did he get off on the trip okay?"

"Early this morning."

"Are you going to tell me what just happened?"

"Do I have to?" Sam dropped into a chair and told him what had transpired the day before with Stahl. As she spoke, she watched her dad's usually genial expression harden with anger.

"So he blames you for the whole thing even though he was the one stupid enough to make the call at all, let alone make it from inside HQ?"

"That's the gist."

"And now he'll face an attempted murder charge on top of everything else."

"At least he'll never get bail after the stunt he pulled this morning."

"There is that." He glanced at her neck. "Take off the scarf. Let me see."

"No need. I'm fine."

"I didn't ask."

Sam reluctantly unwound the scarf from around her neck.

Skip winced. "Looks like it hurts."

"Doesn't feel great, but I'll live. I gotta get to work. They're going to want a statement about what happened with Stahl. Not to mention I've got one murdered ballplayer and another missing."

"Who's missing?"

"Lind, but we don't know yet if he's actually missing or off the grid licking his wounds. Apparently, that's his pattern."

"You sound frustrated, baby girl."

"I am. We need something to go on, and there's very little beyond the chaos in Willie's personal life. No one's jumping out at me as an obvious suspect." She got up, repositioned the scarf and leaned in to kiss her dad, surprised when he winced. "What?"

"Weird tingle in my leg."

"You're feeling something in your leg?" He'd been paralyzed from the neck down in an unsolved shooting almost three years earlier. To her knowledge, the only place he'd retained sensation was in his right hand.

"I don't know what it is."

"But it's something. Have you talked to the doctor?"

"I'm seeing him next week."

"What do you think it means?"

"I couldn't tell you. It's damned uncomfortable though. Like a bad case of pins and needles."

"Oh my God, Dad! You can't wait a week to get that checked!"

"Get what checked?" Sam's stepmother Celia asked as she came into the kitchen.

"Dad's got pins and needles in his leg."

"What?" asked Celia, who was a nurse.

"It's nothing," Skip said, his annoyance clear. "Just a weird ripple of some sort."

"A weird ripple that you can *feel*?" Celia asked.

"I don't know if I'm feeling it or dreaming it or what."

"And when were you going to tell me this?" his wife asked, hands on hips.

"Soon."

Celia scowled at him, but Sam knew she had to be as excited as Sam was. No one was more devoted to her dad than Celia.

"Will you call the doctor?" Sam asked her.

"Right away."

"Let me know what they say."

"Of course."

Sam leaned over to give her dad another kiss. "Do what Celia tells you to, got me?"

"Yeah, yeah. Go to work and catch me a killer." Sam squeezed Celia's arm on the way by. Wouldn't it be something if, after all this time, her dad regained some feeling in his paralyzed limbs? The idea of it was too tantalizing to entertain. Sam forced herself to put it aside until they knew more so she could focus on all the other more pressing matters at hand.

Anxious to hear how Scotty had fared at school, Sam took a call from Shelby. "How'd it go?"

"Perfectly fine. He ran into Jonah going in and was smiling by the time he got to the door."

"Oh, good. That's a relief. Thanks for taking him."

"No problem. I'll be there when he gets out."

"Thanks a million."

"Are you all right?"

"I'm fine. It's going to be a paperwork headache more than anything. Like I didn't already have enough to do today."

"Hang in there. Call if you need anything."

"Hey, Tinker Bell?"

"Yes?"

"It's really great having you around, except for the folding issue, that is."

Shelby's delicate laughter brought a smile to Sam's face. "Gee, thanks, boss. I'm enjoying the job very much. Thank you for trusting me with your home and your darling son."

"I'm glad it's working out. I'm at HQ." Sam's gaze landed on Avery Hill, dapper as always as he got out of his car and waited for her to park. "I'll talk at you later."

"Have a good day."

"You too." Sam got out of the car and approached Hill. "You're back." As soon as the words were out of her mouth Sam felt like an idiot for stating the obvious.

"So I am."

"And?"

"Marco's not our guy. He's been in the hospital for the last week with an emergency appendectomy gone bad."

"Why didn't Carmen tell us that?"

"She probably didn't know. His name was mud in her house, and Marco said he asked his parents not to further upset her by telling her he's been ill."

"I'm sorry you wasted your time going there."

"It wasn't a total waste." He tugged a sheaf of papers out of his bag. "Willie's financials."

"Excellent! We've been having the worst time with the Dominican bank. Appreciate the assist with this and the team and the trip."

"Mind if I stick around to see it through? I'm invested."

A few weeks ago, the question would've rankled and

annoyed. Now she understood that at some point he'd become a trusted—and often useful—colleague. "Sure. Since you were able to procure the financials, you can see that through. That'd help."

"Sure, happy to."

They walked toward the main door together. "Are you going to call Shelby?" Sam asked.

He eyed her warily. "Where'd that come from?"

"Just wondering—and so is she."

"Funny, I wouldn't take you for a girl-friendy kind of gal."

"I have girlfriends," Sam said, indignant that he thought he knew her so well.

He raised an eyebrow rife with skepticism. "Any who don't work here?"

"My sisters, and I suppose Shelby counts, not that it's any of your business."

He stopped short, and Sam had no choice but to stop too or run into him.

"You're right. It isn't my business. But here's the situation, Sam… You know I think a lot of you."

Since he'd all but confessed to being in love with her, Sam just nodded, afraid to do or say anything else and desperately afraid of where this might be leading.

"I'd like it if we could be friends. And if not friends, at least cordial colleagues who occasionally work well together."

He was offering her a way out of the uncomfortable tension that had surrounded them since she'd tuned into his crush on her, and Sam appreciated the overture. If he was going to be sticking around the District, their paths were bound to cross again, and there was no reason for their relationship to be antagonistic when their goals were often the same.

"That would be good. There's one thing you should know, though."

"What's that?"

How to say this diplomatically? "You have to be careful around Nick. He's… He's possessive of what's his, and he's in a position to make your life difficult if he chooses to."

Hill's lips got very tight with displeasure. "Has he made threats?"

"Of course not. But don't give him a reason to butt into your life. He's a perfectly rational guy. Most of the time."

"I stand warned." He started to stalk off, and Sam ran after him.

"Hill, wait." She grabbed his arm to halt his progress. "Hold on a second. I didn't say that to piss you off. I swear."

He glanced down at his arm and then at her. "Why did you say it?"

Sam let her hand drop away from him. "You've worked hard for your career. I respect that, and I don't want to have anything to do with messing it up." She was making a bloody mess out of this conversation. Nothing was coming out the way she intended. "That's all."

"Thanks for the heads up. I get it. If I were in his shoes, I'd be possessive of what was mine too."

His intense expression made her heart beat faster as a flash of fear went through her. Nick would kill him if he ever saw him looking at her that way. "I… Um…"

"Forget I said that." He extended a hand. "Friends?"

Sam eyed his outstretched hand warily before she reached out to shake it. "Friends."

"Let's get to work."

She released his hand and headed toward the main door, suddenly aware that the press corps camped outside HQ had witnessed the exchange with Hill. Fabulous.

"Lieutenant, any suspects in the Vasquez murder?" one of them asked.

"Nothing yet. Hope to have something for you soon."

"What's with the scarf?" Hill asked as they crossed the lobby.

"Had a little trouble with Lieutenant Stahl this morning," she said.

"What does that mean?"

Sam told him about what'd happened outside her front door.

"The guy's got brass balls going to your house, especially when you've got Secret Service all over the place."

"He's also got bruised balls. I managed to get off a good kick, but it's embarrassing to admit how quickly he overpowered me."

"He took you by surprise."

"Still…"

"Your pride is wounded."

"A little bit, but I feel better knowing his junk is wounded too."

Hill snorted with laughter. "You would."

Farnsworth waylaid them. "Lieutenant Holland. My office. Now."

Sam rolled her eyes at Hill. "Meet you in the pit."

"Good luck," Hill said.

Sam followed Farnsworth to his office.

He slammed the door and turned to her, furious. "Are you all right?"

Sam couldn't recall a time when she'd seen him so angry, and that was saying something since she often made him angry. "Yes."

"Let me see."

"That's not necessary. I'm fine."

"I said, *let me see*."

Aggravated by the bossy men in her life, Sam unwound the scarf and tipped her head so he could see what were probably angry bruises on her neck.

"God, Sam," he said, sagging. "He could've killed you."

"Well, he didn't and he's got bruised junk as a result of his trouble."

"That's the least of what he deserves. I just got off the phone with Forrester. He's going to throw the book at Stahl. There's nothing any of us hate more than dirty cops."

"So no chance of bail?"

"Forrester will fight it. He's handling the case personally."

"That's good. I can't help but relish the idea of Stahl in prison."

"I can't help but relish the last of him around here. He's been a pain in my ass for years."

"Mine too. I better get to it."

When someone knocked on the door, Farnsworth said, "Enter."

A sergeant with a camera came in. "I understand we need to document the lieutenant's injuries?" he asked.

"That we do," Farnsworth said. "Lieutenant…"

Resigned, Sam once again revealed the bruises and forced herself to remain still while the sergeant snapped photos of her from a multitude of angles. Just as Sam was about to snap at him to hurry up already, he said he had what he needed.

"Thanks, Sarge." After the sergeant left the room, Farnsworth said, "On behalf of the department, I apologize for what transpired at your residence this morning, Lieutenant."

"It was worth it if it gave us more ammo to use against him."

"I have to make a statement later today on Stahl's arrest and what happened this morning. I'd like you there."

"Sure. Just let me know when."

Sam left the chief's office and headed for the pit, anxious to dig into the latest on the Vasquez case.

"We think we've got a murder weapon," Cruz said when she walked in. "CSU uncovered a bloody knife in a garbage can six blocks from where Vasquez was found."

"Anywhere near the blood puddle?"

"More than six blocks in the opposite direction."

"Thank goodness our guys are thorough. Where is it now?"

"I sent it to the lab to be processed."

"Excellent," Sam said, finally feeling the buzz that came with progress. "Agent Hill was able to secure Willie's financial report from the bank in the Dominican Republic. He'll be digging into that today."

Gonzo came into the pit, accompanying a young woman who looked distressed. Petite with dark hair and eyes, she'd clearly been crying.

"Lieutenant, this is Liza Benjamin. She's a friend of Jamie Clark's. She came to the front desk asking for the officer in charge of the Vasquez investigation."

Sam gestured to the conference room and followed them in. She closed the door and turned to face the trembling woman, glancing at Gonzo, who turned on the recorder. Because she wasn't a suspect, they didn't need to inform her of the recording or advise her of her rights. "I'm Lieutenant Holland. I'm in charge of the Vasquez investigation. You've met Detective Gonzales. What can we do for you?"

"I… I don't know if I should be here, but I can't stop thinking about what happened to Willie."

Sam leaned back against the conference room table, the picture of relaxed competence when every nerve in her body vibrated with tension. Would this be the break they'd been waiting for?

"Take a deep breath and try to relax, Ms. Benjamin." Gonzo produced a bottle of water that he handed to her.

"Thank you," Liza said, her hands continuing to shake as she took a drink. "Jamie is my friend. We met at yoga class and fell into the habit of getting a smoothie after class. We got to know each other, shared confidences. That's how I knew about her friendship with Willie. She talked about him a lot. I started to wonder, you know?"

"About?"

"If it was more than friendship. I follow the team, so I knew he was married. I knew he had children."

"Did you suspect she was having an affair with him?"

"I know she was."

Sam gripped the conference table tighter. "How did you know that?"

"She told me."

"What did she tell you?" Sam hated interviews like this in which she had to pull every piece of information from the interviewee.

"That she was in love with him, and he loved her too. He was going to leave his wife after the season. They weren't getting along. They were fighting about money and how he wouldn't help her brother. He didn't want to be with her anymore. He wanted to be with Jamie, or so she said."

"Was she sleeping with him?"

Liza bit her bottom lip and nodded. "She said she'd never had sex like that in her life, but something happened a couple of days before the game."

"Do you know what it was?"

"He told her he couldn't leave his wife. As much as he wanted to be with Jamie, he was afraid he'd lose his kids if he left Carmen. She was devastated and furious. She'd made plans with him, and then he pulled the rug out from under her. She was very, very angry with him."

"It would help our investigation if you gave us a written statement," Sam said, glancing at Gonzo.

Liza's ravaged eyes widened with dismay. "Why? I just told you everything I know."

"We need it for the file."

"I... I don't know about that."

"If you weren't prepared to assist in our investigation, why did you come here?"

"I... I thought I should tell someone what I knew. I love Jamie. I don't want her to get in trouble, but she was so mad. She… She said she felt like she could kill him for putting her through this."

"Would you please write it down for us?" Sam asked, glancing at Gonzo who produced a yellow pad and a pen.

Tears rolled down Liza's cheeks as she waited for one of them to blink.

Neither of them did.

Sniffling, she picked up the pen and began to write. Sam went to the door and called out to the pit.

"Cruz!"

Freddie came into the room. "You bellowed?"

"Please stay with Miss Benjamin while she records her statement on the Vasquez case. Make sure she accurately depicts what Jamie Clark told her about her affair with Mr. Vasquez and how she wanted to kill him for putting her through such an ordeal after he ended things with her a few days before the game."

Freddie's eyes widened with surprise. "Will do. "Gonzo, let's go pick up Ms. Clark for additional questioning."

"You won't tell her what I said, will you?" Liza asked, dismay radiating from her.

"Of course we will," Sam said.

Liza blanched. "Oh my God."

"Keep writing."

Freddie sat at the table with her.

Sam strolled out of the conference room and into her office to get her keys and radio. She and Gonzo walked out to the parking lot together. "I wanted you to come with me so you can tell me what's going on with the custody case," Sam said as she pulled into traffic.

"Andy is trying to set up a meeting with Lori and her

lawyer." Andy Simone was Nick's good friend. Sam had asked him to help Gonzo with the case. "We're hoping we can work something out short of going to court."

"I hope so too."

"I suppose I'm going to have to share custody with her as much as I wish I didn't have to."

"She is his mother, Gonzo, and it seems like she's trying."

"I know."

"Have you told Christina about it yet?"

"I'm going to tonight. I wish it could wait until after the election, but Andy doesn't want to put off the meeting that long. He feels Lori and her lawyer might view it as stonewalling on our part."

"You should listen to him. He's a smart guy and knows what he's doing."

"The whole thing sucks."

"I know it's really hard, but you should try not to worry. You and Christina have taken such good care of Alex this year. That'll count for a lot."

"Thanks, Sam. I appreciate the support."

They arrived at Jamie Clark's apartment and took the stairs to the third floor.

"Not what I pictured for the head trainer of an MLB team," Gonzo said.

Sam pounded on the door. "I thought the same thing the first time I was here." When she didn't hear any signs of life from inside, she pounded again. "MPD, Ms. Clark. Open up."

Locks disengaged with loud clicks.

Suddenly uneasy, Sam rested her hand on her weapon.

The door cracked open and Jamie Clark eyed them

suspiciously. "What do you want? I told you everything I know."

"Is that so?" Sam asked, using her foot to push the door open wider. "We've just heard a whole other version of your story from a friend of yours."

"Who?"

"Liza Benjamin." Sam watched a wide array of emotions skirt across the other woman's face—fear, anger, disbelief and, finally, resignation.

"You asked me if I was having an affair with Willie. I was no longer involved with him when he died."

"The vagaries of your statement cast suspicion upon you," Sam said. "I hope you realize that."

Jamie broke down into sobs. "I was protecting Willie's kids. What would it matter now that we'd been together? That we'd fallen in love? I was protecting his memory."

"By lying to cops?"

"I'm sorry. I didn't want to lie, but I didn't know what else to do."

"We need you to come downtown to amend your statement."

"Am I under arrest?"

"Not at this time and not if you cooperate from this point on. We do have to cuff you for transport, however. Department policy."

Gonzo cuffed the crying woman.

"Can I at least put pants on?" She wore only an oversized T-shirt.

"We'll get you some pants downtown. Let's go." She cried all the way to HQ, but didn't say another word. In deference to her half-dressed state, Sam pulled into the parking lot at the morgue entrance and took her in that way, avoiding the media camped out front. "Get her into some clothes and put her in one of the interrogation rooms," she said to Gonzo. "Let me know when she's ready."

"Will do."

Sam walked into the pit just as her radio crackled with a call from Dispatch. "This is Holland. Go."

"Report of a possible homicide at the Capitol Motor Inn." The dispatcher provided an address on Massachusetts Avenue, one of the main arteries into and out of the city.

"Got it." She went into the conference room where Freddie was finishing up with Liza.

"Please stay available in case we need to reach you," Freddie said.

"Fine." She brushed past Sam and hurried toward the lobby.

"What did she think would happen if she came in here and told us all that about Jamie?"

"Not what did happen, that's for sure."

"We've got a body in a hotel room on Mass Ave. Let's go."

Sam had planned to use the morgue exit, but screaming coming from the direction of the lobby had her heading out there to see what was going on.

"What were you thinking, you stupid cow?" Jamie shouted at Liza as Gonzo forcibly restrained Jamie. "How could you do this to me?"

Frozen in place, Liza cried hysterically. "I had to tell them! Willie is *dead*."

"It's none of your fucking business!"

"Freddie, get Liza out of here. I'll meet you in the parking lot."

Sam went to help Gonzo, and between the two of them they dragged Jamie into central booking, screaming all the way.

"Sorry about that," Gonzo said. "She went off like a rocket when she caught sight of Liza. I've got it from here, but thanks for the help."

"We just got a report of a body in a motel on Mass Ave. Cruz and I are heading there now, so you can oversee her amended statement that includes the details of her sexual affair with Mr. Vasquez."

"I didn't kill Willie!" Jamie said, kicking at Gonzo, who let her connect with his shin and then smiled at Sam. "Give me a polygraph if you don't believe me!"

"Maybe we will, Ms. Clark," Sam said. "We aren't charging you with anything—yet. But technically, you just assaulted a police officer in front of other police officers, so don't try my patience."

"Go to hell. You don't understand anything."

"Ouch," Sam said. "That wounds me."

Gonzo's snicker of laughter followed her to the main door. She found Cruz in the parking lot, leaning into Liza's car.

"Are you okay to drive?" Sam asked her.

"I'm fine."

Sam nudged Freddie out of the way. "You did the right thing coming in today. Even if it cost you a friend, it was the right thing."

"If you say so," Liza said, dejected.

Sam stepped back so Liza could close the car door. When she pulled away, her tires squealed. "She can't wait to get away from us."

"Can't say I blame her."

"People are ridiculous," Sam said as they crossed the parking lot to the far end of the building.

"In general or in particular?"

Sam slid into the driver's seat. "In general. She comes in here with information about a woman who's banging our murder victim, and she thinks we're not going to do anything about that?"

"I don't think she gave it much thought beyond coming in and telling us what she knew."

"Clearly. Did you hear if Hill found anything in Willie's financials?"

"Nothing yet, but he was just getting started when I last saw him."

"Anything new with your dad?"

Freddie glanced over at her, seeming surprised by the sudden shift in conversation. "Elin and I had dinner with them last night. He's…very… I don't how to describe it. He's almost too enthusiastic about everything. Full of grandiose plans and ideas."

"You think he's manic again?"

"I don't know what to think," Freddie said with a sigh. "From everything I've read about the disorder, soaring highs and crushing lows are to be expected."

"What does Elin think?"

"She responds to him the same way my mom does."

"And how is that?"

"Like everything he does and says is fabulous. I feel like I'm the only one wondering if his behavior is normal. Elin thinks I'm looking for trouble where there isn't any."

"If you want my opinion…"

"I do. You know I do."

"You have good instincts about people and situations. Trust them. If your gut is telling you something is off, keep an eye on it as best you can."

"That's good advice. I wish I could talk to my mom about it without him around, but they're joined at the hip. They're even sharing her cell phone. Who does that anymore?"

"Does she seem happy?"

"I've never seen her so happy. Since he's been back, I feel like I'm seeing someone I've never met before in her. She never stopped loving him in all the years he was gone. I don't want to do anything to take away from her happiness. No one deserves it more than she does."

"But..."

"I'm worried about what'll become of her if he has another episode."

"That's a reasonable fear. All you can do is keep a close eye on it and be there for her if she needs you."

"Thanks, Sam. It helps to be able to talk to someone who doesn't think I'm ridiculous for being concerned."

"You're not ridiculous."

They arrived at motel to find it surrounded by police vehicles. The medical examiner's van pulled up a minute after they did. Lindsey walked with Sam and Freddie up the stairs to the second floor where a crowd had gathered outside room sixteen.

They entered the messy room where a Caucasian male, approximately six foot five or six inches, was lying facedown on the bed in a pool of blood. Lindsey handed Sam a pair of gloves. "Let's turn him over."

The two women worked together to turn the big man, gasping when they realized it was Rick Lind.

"Shit," Sam said, even though this discovery made her job slightly easier. Like Willie, Rick had been stabbed once in the chest, which connected the two murders and ruled out the possibility of a random attack by an outraged fan. “Cruz, get CSU over here.”

“Already on the way.”

SIXTEEN

SAM STEPPED BACK to allow Lindsey and her crew to prepare the victim for transport to the morgue. Glancing around the hotel room, she saw no obvious signs of struggle, which led her to believe Lind had been attacked in his sleep or by someone he knew. The room's surfaces were littered with pizza boxes, discarded takeout wrappers, beer cans and drug paraphernalia. Sam didn't touch any of it, leaving it for CSU to process. She peered under the bed and choked back a gag when she realized there were used condoms under there.

Rick Lind had gone on one hell of a bender after his team lost the big game.

She moved over to the door, which bore obvious signs of damage from whatever tool was used to pry it open.

A group of maids was standing outside the room in a tight cluster. One of them was crying.

"Was the door open when you found him?"

The one who'd been crying, who looked no more than sixteen or seventeen, nodded. "It was unusual for one of the doors to be standing open like that, so I looked inside and saw him."

"What's your name?"

Her gaze darted to one of the other girls, who was equally young, and the man who seemed to be standing guard over all of them. "Ginger," she whispered. She had mousy brown hair that might be pretty if brushed and world-weary hazel eyes.

Sam took a closer look at the young woman, who seemed familiar to her. “Do I know you from somewhere?”

Only because she was looking so closely at her did Sam recognize the second of stark, unadulterated fear that crossed her face in the instant before she said, “No.” The single word came out husky, and her tone was completely different than it had been only a minute before.

Acting on sheer instinct, Sam said, “I’ll need you to come downtown to make a statement.”

Ginger glanced at one of the other girls, the one who seemed equally afraid.

“You too,” Sam said to the second girl, a bottle blonde with blue eyes and bad skin.

Her big eyes took on a deer-in-the-headlights look. “What’d I do?”

“You were here. You might’ve seen something that would be helpful to the case.”

“I didn’t see anything.”

“Still, I need your statement.”

“We have to work,” Ginger said, a tinge of hysteria in her voice. “If we don’t work, we don’t get paid.”

“We’ll square it with the boss, don’t worry.” Sam was suddenly desperate to get them away from the hotel and the angry glares of the other maids and the man who was their supervisor.

Both girls cast anxious glances at the man, who didn’t look at either of them.

“Who are you?” Sam asked him.

“The manager.”

“Your name?”

"Bruce Jones."

"Is that your real name or did you make it up?"

His lip curled into a snarl that he wisely curbed. "Real."

"How long ago did the guest in room sixteen check in?"

"After the game."

"So you knew who he was?"

Bruce shrugged. "He was a frequent visitor."

"Do you have video surveillance of the premises?" Sam asked, gazing at the next closest establishment across the street, which would be too far away to get a good view of the goings-on at the motel.

Bruce pointed to a video camera above the doorway. Wires were hanging from the rusty metal that held it to the wall. "Used to."

"I'll need to borrow these two ladies for a while. I'm sure you understand that they're material witnesses, and as such shouldn't be penalized for any time they miss."

"Why you gotta take her?" he asked, nodding to the second one. "She said she didn't see nothing."

"I still need to question her."

"Fine. Just make sure you bring them back. They've got a job to do."

"I'll take good care of them."

While Freddie questioned people in nearby rooms about whether they'd heard anything coming from room sixteen, Sam accompanied the two trembling young women downstairs and helped them into the back of her car.

"I don't understand why you're taking us," the first girl said, her chin quivering as she fought back tears.

"You haven't done anything wrong. I promise you'll

be perfectly safe." To the second girl, she said, "What's your name?"

"Amber."

"Is that your real name?"

Amber looked at Ginger.

"My real name is Sam Holland. I'm a lieutenant in the Metro Police Department. I want to help you."

"You can't help us," Ginger said, her tone flat and full of despair. "No one can help us."

After thirteen years on the job, Sam had learned to trust her instincts and all of them were on full alert. "This might be your lucky day, because if anyone can help you, I can, but you have to trust me, okay?"

Amber reached for Ginger's hand and held on tight.

"Okay," Ginger said.

Amber nodded in agreement.

"Sit tight," Sam said. "I'll be right back." She shut the car door and gestured for Officer Beckett to join her. "Stay here and don't let anyone get near them, you hear me?"

"You got it, LT."

"If anyone tries to get them out of my car, shoot to maim."

The young Patrol officer's eyes widened with surprise at her orders. "Yes, ma'am."

Confident the girls were in good hands for the next few minutes, she went to help Cruz complete the canvas while Lindsey's team photographed the scene and removed Lind's body from the room.

"See you back at the house," Lindsey said to Sam as she headed downstairs.

Sam and Freddie knocked on every door in the seedy motel but didn't find anyone who'd heard a thing from room sixteen. They did, however, find a number of very young girls entertaining much older men.

"I need a shower," Freddie muttered as they took the stairs to the parking lot.

"No kidding," Sam said. She withdrew her cell phone from her pocket and placed a call to Malone. "The victim is Rick Lind," she said when he came on the line.

He released a low whistle. "No shit. Wow."

"We need Vice at the place where he was killed." She gave him the address of the motel. "Someone's running an underage prostitution racket here. I've got two of the younger girls in my car on the pretense of giving statements in the Vasquez case. I'm playing it cool for the moment, but we need to act fast before they bolt."

"I'll call it in right now. Good work, Lieutenant."

"While you're at it, do a run on a Bruce Jones. About forty, stocky, dark hair and eyes. He says he's the manager of the motel."

"Got it."

"We're going to notify Lind's wife, and then we'll be back to HQ with the girls."

"What's your plan there?"

"Not sure yet, but one of them looks really familiar. I had a feeling I needed to get them out of there."

"Your feelings are usually worth paying attention to. See you when you get back."

When Sam ended the call, Freddie let out a deep sigh. "Another wife to inform. I hate this case."

"Me too." Sam got into the car and turned to her passengers. After asking them to trust her, she didn't feel right about sending them to HQ with someone else. "We have an errand to do in Bethesda, and then we'll go to my office to talk, okay?"

Ginger nodded, her mouth set in a grim expression that belied her youth.

Taking her cues from Ginger, Amber followed suit.

"Just relax," Sam added. "You're not in any trouble. I promise." She had a million questions to ask them, but wanted to be careful with two obviously fragile young women, who might even still qualify as girls.

In deference to their passengers, Sam and Freddie were quiet on the ride to Bethesda.

"Who was the guy in the motel room?" Ginger asked, breaking the silence.

Sam glanced in the rearview mirror. "Had you seen him before?"

Ginger lowered her eyes as her face flushed with color. "Once."

Returning her attention to the road, she bit back the flood of questions she wanted to ask.

"Who was he?"

"Rick Lind, a relief pitcher with the D.C. Feds."

"Oh."

Sam looked in the mirror again and noted the sorrow etched into the young face staring back at her. She pressed harder on the gas pedal, wanting to get to Bethesda and back to HQ as soon as possible.

THE DRONE OF engines was the only sound in the guest section of *Air Force One* as it hurtled toward Bagram Air Force Base in Afghanistan. President Nelson and his entourage would meet with U.S. troops stationed in the war zone as well as the Afghani president. Nelson was locked in a dogfight with his Republican challenger, and the trip had been initiated to feature him as commander in chief in the waning days of the campaign.

Nick had never been on such a long flight, but the accommodations were so comfortable it was easy to forget he was on an airplane. He'd been given VIP treatment that included a tour of the president's quarters in the front of the plane, an amazing gourmet meal and an extra box of the souvenir M&M's signed by the president to give Scotty.

He couldn't wait to tell his son all about the amazing airplane that ferried the president around and had been making notes of things he didn't want to forget. Mostly he wanted to know how Scotty's school day had gone and whether he'd had any more trouble with Nathan the bully. Nick wanted to know how Graham's statement had gone over with the media and what Christina was hearing on the political front. And he really wished he could hear from his wife while he was away.

The lack of information was making him feel a bit twitchy, even though he understood the need for radio silence as the president jetted into a war zone. Despite what he'd said to Sam, Nick was a tiny bit anxious about the potential danger of landing in Afghanistan. They'd arrive under the cover of darkness, which offered a measure of comfort.

Nick heard a stir outside the guest cabin door before it opened to admit White House Chief of Staff Tom Hanigan. Roughly fifty with prematurely gray hair, Hanigan was intense and focused at all times.

"I apologize for disturbing you, Senator."

"You're not disturbing me."

"The president would like a few minutes."

Nick stood and ran his fingers through his hair, seeking to bring some order to it. "I'm wearing jeans. Is that okay?"

Hanigan spared him a rare smile. “So is he. Right this way.”

Outside the president’s suite, Hanigan stopped and turned to Nick. “How’s Derek?”

“Better.”

“We miss him. I hope he’ll come back to work after the election.”

“I think he will. He just needed some time to adjust to the new normal.”

“There are times when I hate this business,” Hanigan said. “Finding out what’d happened to Victoria—and why—was one of the worst moments of my career. And my life.”

“Mine too.”

“Let him know I’m thinking of him, will you?”

“I’d be happy to. I know he appreciates that you’ve held his job for him.”

“Of course we did. He’s the only one in the West Wing who can manage you people on the Hill.”

Nick laughed at the veiled insult, knowing it had been said in jest. “Ouch.”

Smiling, Hanigan knocked on the door to the president’s onboard office, which Nick had seen earlier, and led Nick into the room.

“Senator,” Nelson said, standing when Nick walked in. He extended a hand that Nick stepped forward to shake. To say it was surreal to be meeting with the president while in flight on *Air Force One* would be putting it mildly. “Thanks, Tom,” Nelson said. “I’ll take it from here.”

“As you wish, Mr. President.”

Hanigan departed, the door clicking shut behind him.

"Have a seat," Nelson said, gesturing to two upholstered chairs that sat adjacent to the desk. "Drink?"

"I wouldn't say no to some bourbon."

"That sounds good to me too."

The president poured them each a couple of fingers and handed one of the glasses to Nick. "Are you enjoying the trip so far?"

"It's an incredible thrill. Thank you for inviting me to come along."

"My pleasure." Nelson was tall with silver hair and startling blue eyes that reminded Nick of Sam's. He sat next to Nick. "I understand you're tied up in this Lexicore business."

"I take it Graham has made his statement."

"Indeed. You did the right thing dumping the stock as soon as you heard about it. I think you'll be okay with the voters. We're hearing most investors were unaware of Lex's ties to the factory in Thailand."

"It disgusts me to have been part of what happened there, even in an indirect way."

"Graham did a good job of conveying your grief over Senator O'Connor's death and the money you came into afterward. You don't have anything to worry about."

"And yet still I worry."

"I can't believe this is your first election. You're a seasoned pro."

"That's quite a compliment coming from you, Mr. President."

"Your family is well?"

"Yes, sir. The Secret Service is keeping a close eye on us in light of the threats Patterson's supporters made after his arrest."

"I understand you've added a son to the family."

Nick smiled, thinking of Scotty and the happiness he'd brought to their lives. "Yes, a twelve-year-old who was in state custody in Virginia. I met him on a campaign stop in Richmond and was instantly captivated. He's an amazing kid."

"You've done a wonderful thing for him."

"It's nothing when compared to what he's done for us."

"Nick… Do you mind if I call you Nick?"

"By all means. Please."

"I wanted to speak to you about something highly confidential. I hope I can count on your discretion."

"Of course."

Seeming troubled, Nelson took a drink from his glass. "Vice President Gooding has been diagnosed with a malignant brain tumor."

"Oh my God. That's awful. I'm so sorry."

"I am too. He and I go way back. I'm heartbroken for him and his family." He glanced at Nick, his gaze piercing. "He's going to resign after the election, which leaves me in need of a vice president. Your name has been mentioned many, many times, and I thought it was about time someone mentioned it to you."

Nick stared at him, flabbergasted. Was he dreaming this? "Well, I… I have no idea what to say."

"I can see I've blindsided you."

"Just a bit," Nick said with a laugh. And he'd thought being on the plane was surreal!

"Let me be honest with you, Nick. You're well aware of how brutal the reelection campaign has been. I think we'll win but not by much. There's still a lot I want to get done and only two years before the midterm elections. I don't want to spend half a year recovering from the election. Adding a vice president with your approval ratings would go a long way toward repairing some of the campaign damage."

"I'm honored to be considered."

"But?"

"You've met my wife," Nick said with a wry smile. "Can you picture her as the second lady of the United States?"

"The gun and cuffs might have to go," Nelson said, returning Nick's smile.

"We've just brought a child into our home. While the transition has been smooth, it's not without challenges. I'm not sure this would be the right time to ask so much of my family."

"All fair concerns. It is a lot to ask of our loved ones. At times, I wouldn't blame Gloria for hoping I lose the election. We're both exhausted from the endless campaign and the grueling four years that preceded it."

"It's not for the faint of heart."

"No, it isn't. Here's the thing, Nick. The party is impressed with you—and most of us are damned envious of your numbers. I have no doubt at all that you'll be a contender in four years, whether I win or lose next week. I'm sure I don't have to tell you that if you come on board as my VP, it all but assures your status as the party's heir apparent."

"And it doesn't matter that I've only been a senator for a year?"

"You've been in this business for more than a decade on the staff side, and you really struck a chord with people at the convention. We've done some polling, and your national numbers are exceptional. The people like you."

Nick's head spun as he attempted to process the enormity of what the president was asking of him—and what he was offering. They'd polled about him nationally? Unreal.

"Take some time," Nelson said. "Think about it. Nothing will happen until after the election. But I'll be looking to move quickly to fill the spot, and you're the guy I want." The president stood to indicate the meeting was over.

Nick stood and shook the hand he offered. "I'm truly humbled by the offer."

"Get in touch with Tom after the election. We'll be waiting for your call."

"Thank you, Mr. President."

He made his way from the front of the plane to the guest cabin, located just behind the wings.

Eric, one of the Secret Service agents, rose as he came into the cabin. "May I have a word, Senator?" He pointed to the empty back of the cabin and let Nick go ahead of him.

Nick was immediately on guard against whatever Eric might have to tell him.

"I received word from a member of your son's detail that there was an incident at your house this morning involving the Lieutenant and one of her MPD colleagues."

"What kind of incident?" Nick asked, trying to remain calm. Like there was anything he could do for his wife when he was on his way to the other side of the world.

Eric detailed the confrontation with Lieutenant Stahl.

"Is she okay?"

"She sustained abrasions on her neck and throat, but

Stahl got the worst of it. He was treated for a ruptured testicle and a broken kneecap."

Nick couldn't help the smile that found its way to his lips. "Good for her."

"She put a serious hurt on him."

"How was this able to happen with Scotty's detail on the premises?"

"With all due respect, sir, they're there to protect him, not her. You'll recall that she has repeatedly refused protection."

"Right, of course. I'm sorry. I don't mean to imply it was their fault."

"They provided assistance to her, but she didn't really need it."

"I bet she didn't. She ruptured his testicle, huh?"

Eric winced as he nodded.

"Trust me when I tell you, no one deserves it more."

"I'll have to take your word on that, sir."

"Thanks for letting me know."

"Of course."

Nick returned to his seat, buckled his seat belt and thought about what Eric had told him. He could only imagine Sam fending off Stahl and taking great pleasure in kicking her nemesis where he lived. But the idea of that guy's hands on her throat gave Nick the shakes. She'd had yet another close call. Thank goodness she was well versed in how to defend herself, but still… He hated how close she came to mortal danger and how frequently it happened. He'd yet to fully adjust to that part of his new reality. Hell, he'd probably never get used to learning that the woman he loved had been attacked—again.

Settling into his seat, he also tried to process his conversation with the president, but couldn't seem to bend his mind around that either. The last year had been a whirlwind of change and unexpected opportunities.

It had all begun with the murder of his best friend, John, the brother of his heart. Tapped by the party to complete the last year of John's term, Nick had done his best to live up to John's legacy and to the faith instilled in him by Graham and the Virginia Democratic Party. His so-called "fairy-tale" romance with Sam had cemented his popularity in Virginia, and his keynote address at the convention in August had put him on the national radar.

Everything had happened so fast that he sometimes felt like he'd stepped into a time warp and was being hurled forward at turbo speed. The fact that he had no political pedigree had helped. Even John had existed under the weight of his father's legacy. While Nick's connection to the O'Connors was no secret in Washington, he wasn't as attached to Graham as John had been. It was rare these days to find a politician who wasn't toting a ton of baggage with him, which was another reason his star had risen so quickly.

But vice president… Wow. Never in his wildest dreams had he imagined a scenario in which he'd be traveling aboard *Air Force One* with the president, let alone receive an offer like the one President Nelson had just made. Unreal.

When Nick thought of what Sam would have to say about it, he chuckled softly. He'd already asked a lot of her in the last year. His high profile had raised hers, which she chafed against actively. She preferred life far below the radar, not well above it. Her career was so much a part of who she was that he couldn't imagine her without the badge and cuffs.

How could he ask her to give that up when she'd worked so hard to get where she was? And she would have to give it up. There was no way the country's second lady could be out chasing down murderers, not without Secret Service protection that she'd never agree to.

He would mention the offer to her because he didn't keep things from her, but he didn't expect it to lead anywhere. Their lives were complicated enough as it was, and it was probably better to leave well enough alone.

But it had been nice to be asked.

AFTER A BRUTAL thirty minutes with Rick Lind's wife, Sam left her in the care of her sister with information about how to claim the body once the autopsy was completed.

Freddie, who had stayed with Ginger and Amber while Sam was with Carla Lind, was quiet as they made their way back to the city with their young passengers.

Amber had fallen asleep while Sam was in the Lind house, but Ginger continued to stare out the window.

Driving through afternoon traffic, Sam went over the case again from the beginning, thinking about who would have a reason to kill the players who'd cost the team a trip to the World Series. She kept coming back to the team management and ownership. Who else would care as much as they did?

Her cell phone rang and she took the call from Darren Tabor. "Nothing yet, Darren. I haven't forgot I owe you an exclusive."

"Your husband was tied up in Lexicore. Any comment on that?"

"Not a thing."

"His people are saying he's out of the country. Where is he?"

"I honestly don't know."

"Would you tell me if you did?"

"Probably not."

"You're nothing if not consistent."

"Thank you."

"Listen, there's something else I wanted to tell you, but I'm in a bit of a tight spot on this one."

"I'm listening."

"You have to promise you won't tell anyone you heard this from me."

"You have my word."

He hesitated, then cleared his throat. "The *Star* is hemorrhaging money. It's going downhill fast."

"I'm sorry to hear that." The *Star* was a D.C. institution, and as much as her dealings with the media rankled her, Darren was one of the few reporters who'd treated her fairly over the years—for the most part anyway.

"The internet has been annihilating the newspaper business for years now, but since Mr. Kopelsman died, it's gotten worse. His daughter is nowhere near the businessperson he was, and she's running the place into the ground."

"Interesting," Sam said. "How does that factor into the Vasquez case?"

"From what I understand, Elle was counting on the TV rights to the World Series and the influx of cash to bail out the entire company. Everything was riding on that."

"Is that so?"

"Since the team lost that game, everyone here is sweating their jobs. Myself included."

"This is very helpful, Darren. Detective Cruz is with me now, and I know I can count on his discretion."

"I understand. I don't want to think Elle or Ray could be behind something like this, but the company is in a lot of trouble, and protecting her father's legacy is the most important thing to her. I thought you should know that."

"You're racking up the points, Mr. Tabor."

Darren laughed. "Never hurts to be in good with the MPD."

"Thanks for this. I'll be in touch." To Freddie she said, "Well, that was enlightening. Did you catch the gist?"

"Sure did."

"This might be the break we've been waiting for. Will you get Ramsey from SVU to meet us in the pit?"

"Yep." Freddie made the call while Sam rang Shelby.

"What's up?" Shelby asked when she answered.

"How did Scotty make out today?"

"From what I can tell, it was a normal day. No interaction with Nathan and no trouble from anyone else."

"That's a relief."

"I agree."

"Is he there?"

"He just went over to have a visit with your dad."

"So Dad is back from the doctor? Did they tell you anything about what happened?"

"Celia said they want to admit him for a night to run

some tests to see if the bullet has shifted. That's happening next week."

Sam's stomach reacted predictably to that news. "Oh jeez. I wonder what that means?"

"Hard to tell, but try not to worry until you know more. Easier said than done. I know."

"Right. Thanks, Tinker Bell. I'll try to be home for dinner with the boy."

"I can stay if you're running late. Just let me know."

"Will do."

"What's up with your dad?" Freddie asked when Sam got off the phone.

She brought him up-to-date. "What do you suppose it means that they're admitting him?"

"Probably just being cautious."

"Yeah." Anything having to do with her gravely injured father made Sam's nerves go crazy. It had been a very long three years since he was shot and wounded during a routine traffic stop by an assailant who'd gotten away with it, despite the ongoing efforts of Sam and every member of the MPD. Skip had been three months shy of a retirement he'd worked so hard to enjoy.

Rather than fishing and cooking and doing all the things he loved to do, he'd been trapped in a wheelchair and reliant on others to care for his most basic needs. The idea that his situation could somehow get worse was more than she could bear to entertain.

"Don't go there, Sam," her partner said. He knew her as well as anyone and knew her dad was a weak spot for her.

She turned up the volume on the radio as the news began at the top of the hour, anxious for any word she could get on the president's secret trip overseas.

The announcer led with the growing scandal surrounding Lexicore and how several public figures, including retired U.S. Senator Graham O'Connor, had severed ties with the textile giant in wake of the news about Lexicore's ties to the factory in Thailand.

Sam was relieved when Nick's name wasn't mentioned as one of the public figures linked to Lexicore. "President Nelson surprised troops at Bagram Air Force Base in Afghanistan with a middle-of-the-night morale-boosting visit, which will be one of the president's final public appearances before the election. Nelson, who is locked in a tight race with Republican challenger Dominic Rafael, spent two hours on the ground with the troops and met with the Afghani president before departing ahead of daylight. The trip had been previously unannounced to the media.

"Reporters accompanying the president were not permitted to file stories on the visit until *Air Force One* was safely out of Afghani airspace. Virginia Senator Nick Cappuano, one of the public figures linked earlier today to Lexicore, is also with the president. Cappuano, running in the first election of his short but illustrious career, is considered a front-runner for the Democratic nomination in four years."

Overwhelmed with relief to know he was on his way home after safely landing and taking off in Afghanistan, Sam let out a long deep breath.

"Front-runner for the nomination," Freddie said. "That's crazy."

Sam couldn't even think about Nick running for president without her stomach hurting.

"I can't wait to hear about *Air Force One*," Freddie added.

"You sound like Scotty."

"It's way cool."

"Yes, it is."

"What happened?" Ginger asked from the backseat, reminding Sam that she still had a big issue to deal with where they were concerned.

"My husband is a senator, and he went on a secret trip to Afghanistan with the president."

"Wow," Ginger said, her tone dull and lifeless. "That's sick. He's lucky he got to do that."

"You're right," Sam said, able to agree now that he was on his way home, "he is lucky."

And so was she.

SEVENTEEN

THEY ARRIVED AT HQ to a huge media presence outside the main door.

"What the hell?" Sam muttered, heading for the morgue entrance. She feared the day they discovered her secret way into the building. As they walked in with Ginger and Amber, they ran into Lindsey McNamara. "What's going on out front?"

"I hear they're looking for you," Lindsey said. "Someone from the motel must've leaked the Lind connection to the media, and they want to know about Nick's ties to Lexicore."

"Great."

"Terry was really upset about that yesterday. He was worried about how it would affect Nick's campaign."

"Nick hopes the fact that most of Lexicore's investors were unaware of the ties to the factory will keep it from sinking his campaign."

"We all hope so," Lindsey said, giving Sam's arm a squeeze. "Who've you got there?" She glanced at Ginger and Amber, who were waiting for her with Cruz.

"Two of the maids at the motel where Lind was found. I got a funny feeling about them, so I made a big thing out of needing to question them here so I could get them out of there."

"You don't think…" Lindsey sighed, compassionate as always. "They're so bloody young."

"I know. We'll figure it out and get them some help. What've you got on Lind?"

"Just like Vasquez, a single stab wound to the aorta. Your killer knows where to aim to achieve maximum results."

"Time of death?"

"I'm estimating it to be early yesterday. I'll have my full report to you shortly."

"Thanks, Doc."

Sam and Freddie escorted the girls to the conference room in the pit, aware of the curious stares of coworkers they passed in the hallways. People were always curious about what she was up to—probably more so than usual today with word of her confrontation with Stahl winding through the corridors.

Agent Hill, who was working in the conference room, looked up when he heard them come into the room.

"Anything on the Vasquez financials?" Sam asked, watching his astute gaze take in the young women who'd arrived with her.

"Not a thing, and Lieutenant Archelotta was here while you were out to say that they haven't found anything useful on the video either. There was so much chaos in the streets that it's hard to tell what's going on in many cases.

"Could I have a word?" Sam asked.

"Sure." Hill gathered up his work and the suit jacket he'd slung over one of the chairs.

To Freddie, she said, "Give me one minute. I'll be right back."

She went out ahead of Hill, and waited until he'd closed the conference room door.

"What's up with the kids?"

"Nothing good." She gave him a condensed report on what had transpired at the motel, including the discovery of Rick Lind's body.

"Did either of them see anything regarding Lind?"

"I'm about to get into that with them. In the meantime, I need your help with something else—something you're not going to like."

"What's that?"

"I need you to run the financials on Ray and Elle and all their personal and business interests."

He seemed genuinely shocked by her request. "They didn't have anything to do with this, Sam. I've known him all my life."

"How long have you known her?"

"Fifteen, sixteen years? Something like that. A long time."

"I received a tip this afternoon that the *Star* is in big financial trouble. Elle needed the team to win because the World Series TV rights would've bailed out the entire company. She *needed* them to win."

"So what're you saying? She's going around exacting revenge on those who foiled her plan?"

"It's the closest thing to a motive I've seen yet."

"It's not them. They're not murderers."

"Are you able to maintain objectivity, Agent Hill?"

In that second she got to see what he looked like when he was very, very pissed. "Yes, I can, and I don't appreciate the implication."

"No implications. Just a question. I'll leave it to you to take a closer look at them while I talk to Ginger and Amber and try to figure out what's been done to them and what to do about it."

"Sam."

She turned back to him. "Yeah?"

"Good catch on the kids. You probably saved their lives."

"You would've caught it too. You're a good cop." She pushed open the door to the conference room. "Are you hungry?" Sam asked the girls.

Amber looked to Ginger to answer for both of them. "I could eat something," Ginger said.

Amber nodded in agreement. "How about pizza?"

Their eyes lit up with delight that even Ginger couldn't hide. "That'd be really good," Ginger said.

"Can we have cola too?" Amber asked.

"Absolutely." Sam handed Freddie two twenties. "Get enough for us too. And a house salad."

He rolled his eyes at her request and left to order the pizza. When he returned, he joined Sam on the other side of the table from where the girls were seated.

"Here's the deal, ladies," Sam said. "I'd like to know if you saw our murder victim around the hotel before he was killed. It would help us very much if there's anything you can tell us about him or the circumstances of his death. In return for your help and cooperation, we'll ensure that you never have to return to that motel or have anything further to do with Bruce."

Ginger let out a snort of disbelief. "And how will you pull that off? He's probably already here waiting for us to be released so he can take us back."

"He may be here, but it's not to take you back. Our officers are going into the motel and arresting everyone as we speak so we can figure out what's been going on there. You'll make our jobs a hell of a lot easier if you just tell us."

"What do you think has been going on there?" Ginger asked.

"If I had to guess, I'd say you're both runaways or perhaps you were abducted or somehow lured into a web of sex slavery and prostitution. Am I warm?"

Judging by Amber's bug eyes, Sam's assessment was spot-on.

"How do you know?" Amber asked in a whisper.

"Unfortunately, we've seen it before. We recognize women in distress when we see them. I brought you here because you were the two youngest women there, and I wanted to get you out while I could."

"We're not the youngest ones," Ginger said softly.

As Freddie sucked in a deep breath, Sam's stomach turned with revulsion. "Where are they?"

"There's a house," Amber said haltingly. "I'm not sure where it is. They blindfold us when they take us there."

"I can tell you where it is from the motel." Ginger closed her eyes and began to speak. "You leave the parking lot and take a left." She continued with a dizzying array of directions that Freddie frantically tried to keep up with.

"You memorized all that despite being blindfolded?" Sam asked.

Ginger opened her eyes and met Sam's gaze. "I've been going back and forth between the house and the motel for three years."

Sam had to fight to hide her shock and dismay from the girl who needed her help, not her pity. "How old are you, Ginger?"

"I think I'm sixteen, but I don't remember anymore."

"We're going to help you figure it out. I promise."

Freddie went to a map on the wall and used a highlighter to pinpoint the location of the house.

"Call it in to Vice and SVU," Sam told him.

"Call what in to SVU?" Sergeant Ramsey asked as he came into the room.

Both girls visibly shriveled at the sight of the big strapping man.

Sam got up and gestured for him to leave the room. She followed, closing the door behind her. "We've got a situation that we'll need your assistance with." She told him what they knew so far about the goings-on at the hotel and the house Ginger had led them to, despite being blindfolded on every trip.

Ramsey shook his head. "Fucking animals."

"No offense intended, but can you send one of your female officers down here to help with Ginger and Amber?" Sam had gotten the vibe in the past that Ramsey didn't like her, so she chose her words carefully. "As you can tell, they're uncomfortable around men."

"Absolutely. And I'll get my team over to the house to round up the rest of the kids."

"We're going to make a lot of parents very happy today." Sam couldn't think about what it might be like to not know where Scotty was for even a day, let alone years.

"They'll be happy until they realize the kid they're getting back bears no resemblance whatsoever to the kid they lost," he said with a sigh. "I'll take care of it."

Ramsey walked away, and Sam went back in with the girls.

Freddie went out to meet the pizza guy and returned

with the food, which the girls dove into like they were starving.

Sam could barely eat because she was so revolted by what she'd stumbled upon at the run-down motel, but she made an attempt to try to maintain some normalcy for the sake of the girls.

"Not hungry?" Freddie asked.

"Not anymore."

"I know. Me either."

Watching the girlish delight Ginger and Amber exhibited over the pizza gave Sam hope that maybe they weren't beyond a chance at a normal life. Even though she was pressed for time and dying to help Hill dig into Darren's lead, she forced herself to go slowly and to treat the girls with the kid gloves they deserved.

Ginger finished a second piece of pizza and washed it down with a long swallow of cola that she seemed to relish. "I've missed soda."

"I miss it too," Sam said. "I used to be a diet cola addict, but my doctor said I can't have it anymore because it was messing up my stomach."

"So you can't have it *ever*?" Amber asked.

"I'm not supposed to, but I sneak one every now and then."

"Is that right?" Freddie asked, drawing girlish giggles from both their guests.

"You guys are good friends," Amber said.

"I'm his boss," Sam said. "He has to do what I tell him to."

"But you're a girl," Amber said. "Girls don't get to be the boss."

"Around here, girls get to be the boss. In a lot of

places girls get to be the boss. Someday maybe you can be the boss too."

"Do you think so?" Amber asked, her voice full of yearning.

"I know so."

"You need us to tell you what we saw at the motel," Ginger said.

Sam wondered if the food had softened her disposition and made her more inclined to cooperate. "That would really help."

"He came in a cab after the baseball game," Ginger said.

"How did you know about the game?"

"Bruce watched it in the office. He was really mad when that guy dropped the ball. He said Rick would come to us after the game because he'd be too upset to go home."

"So he'd been there before?"

"He came a lot. He said it was the one place he could totally relax."

"What did relaxing entail for him?"

"Getting high, getting laid, getting drunk. All the things he couldn't do at home, or so he said."

"Did you have sex with him, Ginger?"

"Many times." This was said without a hint of emotion. "I was his favorite."

Sam recalled Lind's hulking size and tried to picture him with petite Ginger. The image made her sick. "Did he pay to have sex with you?"

"I don't know. You'd have to ask Bruce about that. If he did, I never saw any of the money."

"Was he nice to you?"

"Nicer than most of them."

"There were a lot?"

"Six or seven a day on a slow day."

Freddie gasped and then cleared his throat to cover it. "Have you had medical attention at all?"

"No."

Sam felt her composure wavering, but fought through the urge to punch something—or someone. "Did Rick have any visitors while you were with him?"

"Just one."

"Do you know who it was?"

"I don't know her name, but she has long blond hair. She was angry, and he asked me to leave so he could talk to her."

"Are you able to describe her in any more detail?" Sam realized that Ginger was most likely the second to last person to see Rick Lind alive.

"She was very pretty and skinny. Super skinny."

"You said she smelled rich," Amber reminded her friend.

"Right. She was wearing fancy perfume, and her clothes were expensive. Quality. I thought she might be his wife."

"Did he seem happy to see her?"

"No, he was mad she was there. He told her he had nothing to say to her. She said she had plenty to say to him."

"Had you seen her before?"

"Once. She came to the hotel earlier in the summer. He'd had another bad game, and I heard her yelling at him. And then I heard them having sex."

"How did you hear that?"

"I was in the room next door with another guy. The walls are really thin. I could hear them."

"Can you tell me what she was saying to him?"

"It was a long time ago, but I remember because she was so mean to him. She said she pays him to win, and she can't afford to lose. That everything was riding on this season."

"Could you hear what he said?"

"Not clearly. His voice was a low rumble. She was screaming though."

Sam got up and went to the murder board to remove the photo of Willie in his uniform. "Have you seen this man before?"

Ginger studied the photo.

"I have," Amber said softly. "He was a regular of mine."

Sam had to fight to keep her expression neutral. "When was the last time you saw him?" she asked.

"The other night after the game."

"How long were you with him?"

"A couple of hours, but then he said he had to go home. He never spent the night."

"Did he say anything about what had happened at the game?"

Amber shook her head. "He wasn't there to talk."

Sam expelled a deep breath as she pushed yellow pads across the table to them. "Will you please write down anything you can tell me about either man? How often they visited the motel, what they might've said or done, what kind of sex they liked to have. No detail is too small."

Amber glanced at Ginger, who nodded and handed her friend a pen.

"While you're working on that, I'd like to contact

your families. Is there anything you can tell us that would help us to find them?"

"I was abducted from a mall in Columbia, Maryland three years ago," Ginger said bluntly. "My parents are Justin and Deanna Moreland." She recited the phone number in a clear, calm voice.

"That's how I know you," Sam said, putting the pieces together. "Your parents have never stopped looking for you. They recently distributed a photo of what you might look like today, and it was spot-on."

"They're looking for me?" Ginger whispered, her chin quivering.

"They've never stopped. Your abduction was big news."

Tears rolled down her face. She swept them away, almost as if she was annoyed with herself for the emotional reaction.

"Do you remember your family, Amber?"

"I'm from Massapequa on Long Island. I got separated from my mom at a bus station in the city when I was nine, and they took me. My mom is Allison Tattorelli. People call her Alli."

"Do you remember her phone number?"

"I remember it started with 516, but I can't remember the rest."

"We'll find her, honey," Sam said, her heart breaking for the girls and their families and the ordeal they'd endured. "I'll be back in a few minutes. Detective Cruz will be here if you need anything."

She got up and left the conference room, shutting the door behind her. In her office, she dropped into the chair behind her desk and took a moment to get her emotions in check before she called Ginger's parents.

It was a phone call she couldn't wait to make but also dreaded at the same time.

Gonzo and Hill appeared at her door. "Everything okay?" Gonzo asked.

"The girls we brought in from the motel were abducted years ago."

"Oh, God," Gonzo said. "What can I do to help?"

Sam handed him the paper on which she'd written down the information about Amber's mother. "Can you find me a number for Allison Tattorelli in Massapequa, New York?"

He took the paper. "I'm on it."

"What can I do?" Hill asked.

"Find me a connection between the Capitol Motor Inn and Elle Kopelsman. One of the girls was able to put her with Lind before he was killed. The other one was probably the last to see Willie alive."

"He was there too?"

"He was a regular, just like Lind. Anything on the financials for Elle or Ray?"

"Nothing that stands out, but it's a complicated maze. You were right about one thing."

"What's that?"

"The paper is hanging by a thread, and it's dragging the rest of the family's holdings down with it."

"She would've been desperate to protect her father's legacy. She would've gone to any lengths to keep what he left her." Sam's spine tingled with the feeling she got whenever she was on to something. Everything was leading back to Elle Kopelsman Jestings.

"How would killing the ballplayers who lost the game for the team protect her father's legacy?"

"It wouldn't," Sam said, more certain by the second

that she was right about this. "But she would've been infuriated that they lost a game they should've won. She needed that win more than anyone else, and she would've blamed them for letting it get away." Sam snapped her fingers. "The goons!"

"What?" Hill asked, startled by the shift in conversation.

"The bodyguards helped her," Sam said, hearing clicking noises as the pieces began to fit together. "We've been looking for Willie's car on video from the wrong part of town. I've got to make a phone call, and then we need to go have a conversation with your friend Elle. Can you find out where she is tonight?"

"Yeah. I'll take advantage of my lifelong friendship with her husband to get that info for you."

"If you'd rather not, I'd be happy to call him."

"I'll do it."

When she was alone, Sam took another deep breath and dialed the number Ginger had given her. The phone rang five times before a woman answered. When her eyes filled with tears, Sam closed them, determined to get through this as unemotionally as possible. "Mrs. Moreland?"

"Yes, it is."

"This is Lieutenant Sam Holland, Metro Police Department in Washington, D.C. We've found your daughter."

THE NEXT TWO HOURS would forever go down as some of the most satisfying hours of Sam's career. Justin and Deanna Moreland arrived fifty-seven minutes after Sam called them, and their reunion with their daughter was full of tears and hugs and the kind of overwhelming joy that Sam didn't often get to experience as a Homicide detective.

Their joy brought her to tears more than once, but she made no attempt to hide them because everyone around her was in the same state. Even the formidable Agent Hill had wiped away a tear or two while watching the reunion of parents with the child they'd feared lost forever.

Ginger's tough outer facade crumbled the second her mother walked into the room, and she couldn't seem to stop hugging both her parents.

"I found Amber's mother," Hill said, drawing Sam's attention away from the drama unfolding in the conference room. He handed her a piece of paper.

"Thanks." Sam wiped her eyes, took a deep breath to calm her emotions and went into her office to call yet another parent who'd waited years to hear this news.

Like the Morelands before her, Alli screamed when Sam relayed the news and managed to stop crying long enough to tell Sam she was leaving right away to come to Washington.

Since she was looking at a long, late night at work, Sam called home while she had the chance.

"Hi there," Shelby said. "How's it going?"

"It's turned into an amazing day around here."

"How so?"

Sam filled her in on what'd happened at the motel and the reunions taking place between the missing kids and their heartbroken parents.

"Oh, Sam, oh my goodness! How wonderful!"

"Needless to say, I'm going to be here a while. If you need to leave, Scotty can have a sleepover at my dad's."

"I've got nothing going on tonight. I'm happy to stay here. Don't worry about us. We're just fine."

Sam nearly sagged with the overwhelming relief of having someone she trusted to help with Scotty. "I really appreciate it. I hope you know that."

"Of course I do. It's my pleasure to spend time with him. I suspect I love him almost as much as you do."

"He's pretty easy to love. Could I talk to him?"

"Sure, let me see if he's out of the shower yet. He talked me into pizza for dinner in exchange for taking his shower earlier than usual."

"You're a shrewd negotiator."

"I'm learning. Scotty, Sam is on the phone and wants to talk to you. Here he is."

"Hi, Sam, did you catch the bad guy yet?"

"Not quite yet, but we think we know who it is. I'll tell you all about it when I see you in the morning."

"I still get to go with Mrs. L tomorrow right?"

"Absolutely."

"She called tonight to see if I might like to have a sleepover at the house so I could see the kids. I told her I'd ask you and let her know tomorrow."

"That sounds like fun. If you want to stay, I can't see any reason why not."

"Will Nick mind if he gets home and I'm not here?"

"I bet he'll be so tired that all he'll want to do is sleep when he first gets home."

"That's probably true."

"How about you go with Mrs. L tomorrow, sleep over with the kids and we'll come get you Sunday afternoon? Maybe we can even stop at the farm and have dinner with the O'Connors on the way home." They had a standing invite to Sunday dinner that they rarely had time to accept.

"Could I ride the horses?"

"I'm sure that could be arranged."

"That would be the best weekend ever."

Sam smiled, delighted by his endless enthusiasm. "Shelby said things went okay with Nathan and the other kids today?"

"Yep. He didn't even look at me. I don't know what you said to his mom, but whatever it was, it worked."

"And the other kids didn't treat you any differently?"

"Nope."

"That's cuz they know your mom is a badass cop."

"Sam..."

"I know, I know," she said, holding back a laugh. The kid was too damned much.

"We need a swear jar in our house."

"What the heck is that?"

"We had one in Richmond. Every time you swear, you have to put in a quarter that I get to keep. I'll be rich living with you."

"Very funny! I need a full list of what counts as a swear if I'm going to have to pay for them."

"You know what counts."

"No, I don't. You're always adding new ones to the list." Had she ever enjoyed a conversation more? Not that she could recall. "Listen, buddy, I've got to get back to work. Behave for Shelby tonight and for Mrs. Littlefield tomorrow. We'll see you Sunday, and we'll call you while you're gone."

"I'll behave. Don't worry."

"Love you."

"Love you too."

Sam ended the call and held the phone to her chest for a long time afterward. She had no doubt at all that she, who had spent her entire adult life avenging murder victims, could easily kill anyone who dared to harm that boy. She'd loved fiercely in her life, but not much could compare to the fierce love that came with motherhood.

Hill came to the door. "Two ten-thousand-dollar checks were written from Ray and Elle's joint account the day after the game, one to each of her two bodyguards, signed by her. It's the only account of hers that has any money left in it."

Sam absorbed the new information, reached for her desk phone and asked Dispatch to connect her to the cell phone of Lieutenant Rango, the officer in charge of the Crime Scene Unit.

"Rango."

"It's Holland. How's it going at the motel?"

"Slow. This place is a DNA wonderland, a blue-light special of the highest order."

"Ugh, disgusting."

"Truly."

"I believe I have a suspect. She's a blonde with very long hair who got busy with Lind in the room. One thing I know about women with long hair is that they shed. I've got a pretty good case against her, but a long blond hair of hers from that room would help."

"I'll see what we can do. You might find her DNA in the sheets too. They were well used."

Sam grimaced. "We'll take what we can get. Keep me in the loop, and great job to your team on finding the knife."

"Any news from the lab on that?"

"Not yet, but we've got a rush on it. Have you heard anything about the processing of Willie's car?"

"We got a couple of partial prints off the steering wheel that one of our technicians is working on now."

"I could *really* use that info."

"Will see what I can do to move it along."

"Thanks. I'll be in touch."

To Hill, Sam said, "Were you able to figure out where your friend Elle is tonight?"

"She's attending a fundraiser at the Willard with Ray."

"Would you care to accompany me to the Willard or would you prefer to not have anything to do with arresting your friend's wife?"

"I'll go," he said tightly.

"Let me check on Cruz and the girls, and then we'll go."

As she stood up, Malone came to the door. "A moment, Lieutenant?"

"Ah, sure. Hill, I'll be right with you."

He left the room, and Malone came in, closing the door behind him.

Sam took a close look at her mentor, trying to figure out why he looked so different. "What's wrong?" She immediately thought of Nick, but tamped down that worry. He was on his way home. He was okay.

"There were twenty-six children at the house. The youngest was seven. The oldest was sixteen."

Disgust flooded every pore of Sam's being. "And the people holding them?"

"Six adults, all in custody. We're working now to locate the families."

Sam sighed and shook her head, filled with despair and relief and joy.

"A lot of families are going to be reunited tonight because you trusted your gut, Lieutenant."

Sam never had learned how to take a compliment. "Oh, well, I was just doing my job, sir."

"You once again went above and beyond the call of duty. I see another commendation in your future."

"Thank you, Captain." They were so rarely formal with each other, but the situation seemed to warrant it.

"Where are we with the Vasquez case?"

"I believe we've determined what happened to Willie Vasquez and Rick Lind."

"And that is?"

"They were killed by Elle Kopelsman Jestings, the wife of team owner Ray Jestings, because they lost a game that she desperately needed them to win." Sam explained about the financial troubles plaguing the *Washington Star* and how Elle had been counting on the TV rights to the World Series to bail out the company.

"How do you have her on the Vasquez murder?"

"I don't—yet—but I believe she paid her bodyguards ten thousand dollars each—some of the last money she had—to take out Vasquez. She took care of Lind herself after she got him drunk and high and pickled his brain with sex. She and the bodyguards must've talked about the perfect spot to stab someone to ensure they'd die as quickly as possible, thus the exact same wound for both victims."

"Hell of a way to go."

"Killing two of her marquee players also gets them off the team payroll. That might've been part of her motive."

Lieutenant Archelotta stepped into the office. "We've got something," he said, holding up a flash drive. "We finally got the film from the Smithsonian with footage of two guys tossing Willie in the Dumpster."

"Let's see," Sam said, buzzing from the thrill of connecting all the dots.

When Archie played the film on her desktop computer, Sam said, "We got 'em. Those are Elle's bodyguards. I've seen them so I can positively ID them." From the stacks on her desk, she produced a printout that included photos of the beefy twins that protected Elle—and apparently killed for her too. "Their names are Boris and Horace. Between this and Ginger's testimony that puts Elle in Rick Lind's hotel room close to time of death, we've got enough to arrest them."

"So what's your plan?" Malone asked.

"I'll use them against each other to get the full story of what happened to Willie. I'm pretty sure I know what happened to Lind. He outlived his usefulness. Thanks, Archie."

He handed her the flash drive when he removed it from her computer. "My pleasure," he said on his way out of the office.

"Well, it sounds like you've got everything under control, as usual," Malone said.

"Almost everything," she said with a wry grin. "Anything I can do?"

"Put some pressure on the lab to get back to me about the bloody knife CSU found, and we're going to need a nine-one-one DNA test done on Elle when we get her back here."

"I'll get on the lab and put Dr. McNamara on alert

about the DNA test." He was about to leave but turned back to her. "You're really all right after this morning?"

"I'm fine. A few bruises, but he got the worst of it."

"No one around here is sorry to hear that—or to see the last of him."

"I doubt we've seen the last of him."

"We have for now."

"I'll give you that."

"I'll let you get back to it."

In the conference room, Ginger had finished the statement they needed from her.

"The Special Victims detectives will be taking over from here, and they'll need to speak with you about the people who held you," Sam said. "For our part, we need you to stay available."

"Why?" Deanna Moreland asked. "Hasn't she been through enough?"

"She's a material witness in a murder investigation, among other things. We'll need her to testify."

"Oh, God."

Sam gestured for Ginger's mom to follow her outside the room and out of earshot of the girls. "There'll be other trials, Mrs. Moreland," Sam said. "Members of our team are out now rounding up everyone who was involved with the abduction of your daughter and numerous other children."

"There're more?" she asked.

"A lot more. And your daughter was instrumental in leading us to them. She's been amazingly strong and very helpful."

"That's my Sarah. She's been strong and capable all her life."

"She's been through a lot. It's going to take a long

time. I know it's difficult, but try to be patient and not expect too much too soon."

"Did they… Do you know…"

"The Special Victims detectives will make sure she gets the medical care she needs."

Deanna's face crumpled as Sam all but confirmed her worst fears.

As tears rolled down Deanna's face, Sam reached out to squeeze her hand. "She's alive. That's what matters most right now. You'll figure out the rest one day at a time."

"The other detective, Freddie. He said you knew something was off, and you got them out of there. I'll never have the words to properly thank you for finding my daughter."

Sam, who was fundamentally opposed to receiving affection from strangers, happily allowed herself to be hugged by the grateful mother. "I was just doing my job."

"You did much more than that today, Lieutenant, and our family will be forever grateful to you. Our prayers have been answered."

Sam patted Deanna's back. "If there's anything I can do for you over the next couple of months, don't hesitate to reach out."

"Thank you again." She stepped back and wiped her eyes. "I'd better get back to her."

Sam nodded and watched her return to her daughter, who was sitting close to her father, holding his hand tightly. Ginger—or Sarah—had lost her tough outer shell since her parents arrived, and Sam was optimistic that she'd be able to tap into her inner toughness to repair her life.

"Lieutenant?"

Sam turned to find a detective she didn't know waiting to speak with her. She was tall with sleek dark hair and model cheekbones. She took in the scene in the conference room, her eyes hard and uncompromising.

"I'm Detective Erica Lucas, SVU."

Sam shook her hand. "Good to meet you."

"Nice catch today, LT. You rescued those kids from a fucking nightmare."

Sam liked her no-nonsense attitude. "Thanks. We're ready to turn them over to you for the next steps in your end of the case."

"We're going to need to run rape kits and other unpleasant tests. Will they be able to handle that?"

"The dark-haired one is Sarah, but she was known as Ginger after she was abducted. She's tough. The other one, who goes by Amber, is far more fragile. Sarah is her touchstone. You might want to keep them together as much as possible."

"Good to know."

"Amber's mother is on her way from New York. She should be here in a couple of hours. I can get you her number so you can make her aware of your location when she arrives in town."

"That'd be great. Thanks."

"Take really good care of them, will you? They're good kids who've been to hell and back."

"I'll do everything I can for them."

"Thanks, Erica. Let me introduce you to them so you can get the ball rolling."

EIGHTEEN

An hour later, Sam had sent the girls off with Erica, promising to check on them soon. Freddie had graciously volunteered to stay with them a while longer while they warmed up to Erica. Her partner was never better than in situations that required a gentle touch, and she was enormously grateful for that quality in him. She'd have to tell him that the next time she had the chance.

Hill appeared in the doorway to Sam's office. "I've got something else. Elle was arrested last week by Fairfax County police after a tirade in Neiman Marcus at Tyson Galleria."

Sam's inner fashionista stood up to take notice when she heard the name of one of her all-time favorite malls. "What happened?"

"Apparently, her credit card was declined, and she raised holy hell about it. Mall security ended up calling Fairfax County police. She was charged with disorderly conduct and released on personal recognizance. She's due back in court next month to answer to the charges."

"Did you run her credit?"

His raised brow was the only change in his expression. "Honestly, Sam. Give *me* some credit, will you?"

"My apologies," Sam said, holding back a smile she knew he wouldn't appreciate. "Please proceed."

"She's in debt up to her eyeballs. Every card is maxed

out. All the money is gone. She's in big trouble. The paper is in trouble. The team is in trouble."

"What about Ray?"

"Miraculously, other than the one joint account that she tapped to pay the bodyguards, he kept his finances separate from hers when they got married. I can't help but think she and her father insisted on that to protect their money. But it ended up protecting his. He's not the fat cat the Kopelsmans are—or were—but he's hardly destitute. Other than the two checks from the joint account the day after the game, there is nothing out of the ordinary with any of his accounts."

"Do you think he knows about the hole she's dug for herself?"

"Probably not. Their marriage isn't what I'd call conventional."

"How do you mean?"

"She does her thing, and he does his."

"And the World Series rights would've solved all her problems."

"It would've bought her some badly needed time." He produced another piece of paper, detailing Elle's efforts to find investors to shore up the struggling company. "All of them bailed when the team lost the game. After I read about the investors, I called Bixby, the team's director of security, to ask if anything had happened in the owner's box that night. He said Elle flew into a rage, and had to be subdued by her bodyguards. They took her out of there. Bixby said it looked like they'd done it before."

"She's been escalating. Why didn't Bixby say anything about that when you talked to him before?"

"She's the owner's wife. He's interested in job security, and he figured it was just a tantrum. He said it didn't really register as anything important with his people. Her bodyguards handled it."

"It's time to pick her up, but we need to have another chat with Jamie Clark first." Sam gestured for him to head out of the pit, and after shutting and locking her office door, she followed him. "McBride and Tyrone, I'll need you to stick around for a bit. I'll authorize overtime."

"Sure thing, LT," McBride said. "What do you need?"

"Meet me in the lobby in ten minutes."

"We'll be there."

Hill followed her downstairs to the city jail where Jamie Clark was being held in a cell with six other women. She was sitting on one of the cots, tucked into a corner with her arms hugging her legs as if trying to be invisible. At the sight of Sam outside the cell door, she got up and rushed over, bumping into one of the other women on the way.

The woman pushed back, nearly knocking Jamie off her feet. "Watch who you're ramming into, bitch."

"Sorry," Jamie muttered, clearly fearful of the other women.

"I have another question for you," Sam said.

Jamie wrapped her fingers around the bars. "What?"

"You said that you and Willie were alone in the training room after the game."

"That's right. We were there for at least two hours, waiting for everyone else to leave so he could get his stuff and go."

"You said Ray Jestings and Bob Minor came in to talk to him during that time."

"Yes, they were both there for a short time before they left."

"Did anyone else enter that room? And I want you to think carefully and tell me the truth."

Jamie swallowed hard, her eyes darting between Sam and Hill. "One other person came in."

"Who?"

"Elle Jestings."

Bingo, Sam thought. That's exactly what she was hoping Jamie would say. "And you didn't mention this sooner because…"

Jamie glanced behind her. The other women had moved to the back of the cell, no doubt due to the presence of cops they wanted nothing to do with. Jamie lowered her voice. "I… She… She didn't know I was there, and I was afraid she'd be mad if she knew I saw her. Willie had asked for a few minutes alone, so I went into my office and sat in the dark, keeping an eye on him as best I could. She came in, shut the door and locked it. Then she walked up to Willie and smacked him across the face so hard it snapped his head back. I was so mad! How could she do that? Like he wasn't upset enough already. The poor guy. He started to cry, and he was apologizing, but she kept screaming at him."

"What did she say?"

"Stuff like 'Do you have any idea what you've done?' and 'How in the world did you miss that ball?' and 'You've ruined everything. Everything!'"

Sam wanted to scream herself when she thought about how much time Jamie could've saved them if she'd told them this the first time they met her. "Did he say anything?"

"No," Jamie said, shaking her head. Her chin quivered and her eyes filled. "He just kept crying and apologizing to her. I wanted to go out there and tell him to stop, that she didn't deserve his apologies. She was so awful to him. I didn't tell you because I was afraid of what she might do to me if she found out I was there."

"Has she ever threatened you or anyone you know before?"

"Not directly, but the players called her all kinds of names like Ice Bitch and Queen Frigid. That kind of stuff. No one likes her, but everyone loves Ray. People couldn't understand what he ever saw in her."

"This has been very helpful," Sam said. "I'll need you to make an official statement about the encounter between Elle and Willie in the morning."

"Please," Jamie said, "you have to let me out of here." She glanced over her shoulder at the women who were watching her closely. "I'm scared, and I'm sorry I lied to you and kicked Detective Gonzales. I shouldn't have, but I was trying to protect Willie and his kids. They were everything to him. I didn't want them to grow up hating him because of me."

Sam wanted to tell her there'd been other women, besides her, but she figured Jamie would hear that soon enough. It didn't need to come from her. She gestured to one of the guards. "Please move Ms. Clark to a private cell."

"Why do I have to stay here?"

"For right now, you're safer here than you'd be out there. Trust me on that. Stay put tonight, and we'll take care of the details in the morning."

"Are you going to charge me for lying to you?"

"We'll see how detailed your statement is and decide then."

Sam waited until the guard had moved Jamie before she headed back upstairs with Hill in tow.

"How'd you know Elle had been to see Willie after the game?" he asked.

"I didn't. I only suspected, and I needed Jamie to confirm it."

"You're good, Holland. Really, really good."

"I know."

"Nothing wrong with your ego either," he muttered.

"Healthiest part of me."

That got a big guffaw out of him as they entered the lobby where the chief was talking to McBride and Tyrone.

"The media is waiting for an update on your latest victim as well as the bust that went down at the motel. Are you prepared to give them a statement?"

"I could be." She was riding the high of rescuing the kids and figuring out what had been a baffling murder investigation. It was all coming together nice and neat, the way she liked it best.

"Damned fine work today, Lieutenant," the chief said, his pride evident in his affectionate gaze.

"Thank you, sir. We're on the verge of an arrest in the Vasquez and Lind case." She gave him a quick summary of what they'd discovered about Elle.

"Unreal," the chief said. "I knew her father a little bit. He always struck me as an upstanding kind of guy."

"By all accounts, he was until he made the mistake of dying and leaving his empire to her. I need your help with two things—a report from the lab on a bloody knife Crime Scene found and the partial prints one of the CSU techs was processing. I need them both—badly."

"I'll do what I can to move things along."

"Thanks." She glanced at the door and saw the horde of reporters gathered in the courtyard. "Shall we? I've got a fundraiser to get to."

"After you," Farnsworth said.

Hill, McBride and Tyrone accompanied Sam and the chief through the double doors to the courtyard. The reporters pounced immediately.

Sam waited for them to pipe down. "I've got a brief statement, and then I'll entertain a few questions." She paused for effect to make sure they were listening. "At sixteen hundred today the body of Feds relief pitcher Rick Lind was found at the Capitol Motor Inn on Massachusetts Avenue."

A murmur of shock rippled through the gathering. "Like Mr. Vasquez, Mr. Lind had been stabbed once in the chest, and his aorta was severed. While at the motel, MPD officers stumbled upon what appeared to be a sex slave operation involving numerous minors. Working in concert with the MPD's Special Victims Unit and Vice Squad, we were able to round up the perpetrators and rescue the children from a house where they'd been held away from the hotel. In all, six adults have been arrested and forty children—twenty-six found at the house and fourteen at the motel—are being reunited with their families tonight. Some have been missing for a number of years."

"Do you believe the perpetrators of the sex slave ring had anything to do with Lind's murder?" one of the reporters asked.

"No, we do not. We're continuing to work on establishing a connection between the Vasquez and Lind murders."

"Were you aware of your husband's ties to the Thai factory and the fire that killed three hundred workers?"

"I have no comment now or ever on my husband, his personal business or his career."

"But did you know he owned stock in Lexicore?"

"I have no comment now or ever on my husband, his personal business or his career."

"Did you know he was going with the president to Afghanistan?"

"I have no comment now or ever on my husband, his personal business or his career. Anyone left who doesn't get that?" When no one dared to ask another question about Nick, Sam said, "We're going back to work. We'll let you know when we have anything." This was said directly to Darren Tabor, who was in the back of the crowd. He nodded his understanding.

"Can you tell us what happened this morning with Lieutenant Stahl at your house?"

"I'm not at liberty to comment on an ongoing internal investigation."

Sam stepped away from the podium and gestured for Hill, McBride and Tyrone to come with her. As they went inside, Sam dropped back and gestured for Jeannie to walk with her. "So the thing you asked me about, it's cool with me and the department."

"Oh," Jeannie said, seeming surprised. "Are you sure?"

"I'm very sure, and I'm very honored to be asked."

Jeannie raised a brow. "Will you still think so when I'm dragging you to dress fittings?"

"Ugh. One fitting. That's all you're getting."

"I'll take it. Thanks, Sam."

Sam squeezed her detective's arm. "Sure thing."

Back in the pit, Sam turned to Jeannie and her partner, Will Tyrone. "We're heading to the W Hotel, Fifteenth Street entrance. I expect there to be a couple of muscular goons outside the ballroom, twins named Boris and Horace, of all things. Their job is to protect Elle Jestings. Your job is to arrest them for the murder of Willie Vasquez. I want you to call Patrol on the way and get them over there to back you up. I don't expect the goons to go quietly. I want them transported and held separately. They're not to have any time alone together."

"We're on it," Jeannie said, her eyes alight with the fiery passion that made her one of Sam's best detectives. "Meet you there."

ON THE WAY to the W, Sam contacted Charity Miller and laid out what they had on Elle.

"And you don't think the husband had anything to do with it?"

"No, only her and the bodyguards, one of whom killed Willie, but they were both there, and they both tossed him in the Dumpster. We've got that on film, and we can prove she paid them ten thousand dollars each to do her dirty work for her. Willie had ruined everything for her. She couldn't let him get away with that."

"It's a stretch without DNA and lab results," Charity said.

"I know, and that's why I'm going to get the three of them to roll on each other and make the DNA connection after the fact."

"What's the plan?"

Sam laid it out for her, step-by-step, and then waited to hear what Charity thought.

"Pick them up."

"On our way."

"You were pretty sure I'd go along with this," Charity said.

Sam could hear the smile in the prosecutor's voice. "I'm confident that I've got the right perps on the hook. I'll keep you posted."

"You could talk a dog off a meat wagon," Hill said after she hung up.

"Um, thank you. I think." Sam fiddled with her phone and placed a call to Darren Tabor.

"What's up, Lieutenant?"

"I'm about to arrest Elle Jestings and her bodyguards for the murder of Willie Vasquez. She did Lind on her own."

"Are you kidding me? Elle Jestings, the publisher of my paper, is being arrested for *murder*?"

"In about five minutes at the W."

"Holy shit."

"If you want to see her being marched into HQ, have a photog outside in about thirty minutes."

"Thanks for the tip, Sam."

"A promise is a promise. See you later." She closed the phone and pressed the accelerator, anxious to get this one closed.

"What's our plan at the W?" Hill asked.

"Are you willing to distract Ray so I can take care of her?"

"I can do that."

"Are you sure?"

"I said I'd do it."

Sam pulled up to the hotel and parked next to the bell stand.

One of the bellmen ran after her. “Hey, lady, you can’t leave that there!”

Sam flashed her badge without slowing down. “That’s lieutenant lady to you, and those are my colleagues.” She pointed to the car Jeannie had parked right behind hers. “Touch those cars, and I’ll toss your ass in jail.”

The young man stopped in his tracks.

“Ballbuster,” Hill said under his breath.

“Literally,” Sam said with a cheeky grin, still high off the damage she’d done to Stahl.

“Wince.”

Inside the hotel, a security guy tried to stop them from proceeding but was given the badge treatment.

“Out of the way,” Sam said.

“What do you want here?”

“Nothing to do with you or your hotel.”

“You’ll need to speak to the manager before you enter.”

“No, I don’t. Get out of our way, or I’ll happily arrest you for obstructing a homicide investigation.” As she spoke, Sam pushed by him and headed for the escalator that led to the mezzanine. With Hill, McBride, Tyrone and four Patrol officers in tow, Sam followed the music to the ballroom.

Two huge, stupid-looking guys in ill-fitting suits stood watch outside the main doors. Both were bald with muscles on top of their muscles.

Sam pointed to them, and Jeannie nodded.

“Over here,” Jeannie said to Tyrone and the patrolmen.

Confident that her people had the bodyguards managed, Sam and Hill entered the ballroom, which was filled with glitterati. Women in flashy gowns circulated with men in tuxedos as waiters passed champagne and fancy hors d'oeuvres. On the stage at the far end of the room, a swing band played a familiar tune with big brass sounds.

A woman in a slinky black gown approached them. "May I help you?" she asked, taking a perusing glance at Agent Hill.

"We're all set," Hill said, shutting her down as he fired off a text.

"The dress code is formal," the woman said as she looked down her nose at Sam's jeans.

"We're not here for the fundraiser," Sam said.

"They're in the front at a table," Hill said, heading in that direction.

Sam took off after him, yelling over the obnoxiously loud music, "How'd you know that?"

"I told you. I've got eyes on them."

She hated when he turned out to be so useful. "There," she said, grabbing his arm to halt his progress. She pointed to Ray and Elle sitting at a table, surrounded by people.

"Let me get Ray out of the way," Hill said.

Sam nodded, and stood back to watch him go over to the table and excuse his way toward Ray, who looked up at him, seeming surprised to see his old friend.

Hill tilted his head to ask Ray to join him away from the group.

Ray got up, said something to his wife and walked away with Hill.

The minute they cleared the dance floor and pushed through the double doors to the hallway, Sam made a beeline for Elle.

She tapped the woman on the shoulder and truly enjoyed the moment when Elle looked up and saw Sam hovering over her.

"What do you want? I'm busy."

Sam leaned in close to Elle's ear. "You're under arrest for the murder of Willie Vasquez and Rick Lind. You have two choices. Stand up and walk out of here with me, and I won't cuff you in front of all these people. I'll wait until we get outside. Second choice, put up a fight, and I'll cuff you right here and drag you out. Your call." As she spoke, the color drained from Elle's face and realization set in.

She'd never expected to be caught, Sam thought. It was a trait she shared with murderers everywhere.

"What's your decision?"

"Go to hell," Elle said, snarling through her teeth. "I'm not going anywhere with you. My lawyers will have your badge. Do you have any idea who I am?"

"You bet I do. You're a cold-blooded murdering bitch who's also flat broke, and you're under arrest." Sam grabbed her by the arm, hauled her out of the chair, turned and cuffed her before Elle ever knew what'd hit her.

Sam recited the Miranda warning in a clipped, no-nonsense tone and took great pleasure in dragging Elle kicking and screaming through the room. Tuning in to something happening, the band stopped playing, and the crowd parted to let them pass.

"Someone *do something*!" Elle shrieked. "This is police brutality! Lucien!"

Sam recognized the O'Connor family attorney, Lucien Haverfield, who watched the proceeding with a detached aura of amusement.

"Do *something*!" Elle screamed at him.

"May I ask what Mrs. Jestings is being charged with, Lieutenant?" Lucien asked.

"The murders of Willie Vasquez and Rick Lind," Sam replied, loud enough to make sure everyone around them heard her.

A gasp went through the gathering.

"I'm sorry, Elle," Lucien said. "I don't do murder."

Sam held back the urge to snort with laughter at his dismissive tone. "Let's go, Elle. You're done here."

Elle fought her the whole way, shrieking like a banshee. As they cleared the ballroom doors, she tried again to bust free of Sam's tight hold. "*Boris! Horace! Get this fucking bitch off me!*"

"They can't help you," Sam said, "because they've been arrested too."

"You won't get away with this," Elle said, seething as Sam dragged her onto the escalator.

"I already have. Keep fighting me, and I'll give you a little push." Sam slackened her hold on Elle, and the other woman screamed as she pitched forward on the escalator. Keeping a grip on the cuffs, Sam let her dangle precariously for a second before she pulled her back. Elle remained comically still for the remainder of the ride to the lobby.

A crowd had formed around the police cars, and smart phones held aloft recorded their emergence from the hotel. Sam would bet that Elle wished she'd worn her hair down tonight, because she had no way to shield her face from the cameras. "In you go," Sam said, putting her in the back of a Patrol car.

"You will *not* get away with this," Elle said once again.

Sam slammed the door in her face and walked away. That had gone well.

AVERY LED RAY to a hallway outside the crowded ballroom.

"What the hell is going on, Avery? What're you even doing here?"

"There's no easy way to say this, Ray. Elle is being arrested for murder."

Ray looked at him as if he'd spoken the words in a foreign language. "What in the world are you talking about? You don't think she had something to do with Willie…"

"Willie and Rick Lind."

His face went slack with shock. "Rick's dead too?"

"I'm sorry, but yes. He was found dead today at the Capitol Motor Inn."

"What's that got to do with Elle?"

"The company was in big trouble."

"We've had some problems, but big trouble is a bit of a stretch."

"She's completely broke. Every credit card is maxed out. The paper can't meet its payroll next week. Her house of cards was dependent on those World Series TV rights. In her mind, Willie ruined everything, and Rick didn't help by failing to close out the game when he had the chance."

"She wouldn't *kill* them. I mean, she's not always the warmest woman in the world, but she's not a murderer."

"Checks for ten thousand dollars each were written to Boris and Horace from your joint account the day after the game. Can you tell me what that was for?"

"I have no idea."

Avery let the statement speak for itself and watched as the realization hit Ray like a sledgehammer. "We believe she paid her bodyguards ten thousand dollars each to kill Willie. She took care of Lind herself."

"Why? Why wouldn't she get them to take care of him too?"

"Because Lind was personal."

"Personal? What does that mean?"

Once again, Avery let his silence do the talking, letting a moment pass during which the truth dawned on Ray.

"No. Elle and Rick Lind? Come on! That's not true. I don't believe it."

"I'm sorry, Ray, but we can prove it."

"How?"

"We have a witness that puts her in Lind's room. She heard them having sex once before. We believe the forensic evidence being gathered as we speak will prove recent sexual activity involving both of them in the room where Lind was killed."

Ray covered his mouth with his hand and turned away from Avery, his shoulders stooping a bit from the devastating news. "God, I was such a fool."

Avery rested a hand on his old friend's shoulder. "I'm so sorry."

Ray shook him off. "I don't want your pity."

"It's not pity."

"You never liked her, did you?"

"I never said that."

"You didn't have to. My mother always said I'd regret marrying her. People thought I was after her money. It was never about the money. I loved her."

"I know you did."

"I'd like to go home now."

"You're free to go."

Ray started to walk away, but turned back to Avery. "Thanks for getting justice for Willie. I really wish he'd caught that ball, but he certainly didn't deserve to die for missing it."

"No, he didn't."

Ray nodded in agreement and walked away.

Avery watched him go, sad for his friend and a little sad for himself too as another case came to a close. Who knew when he'd next lay eyes on the gorgeous lieutenant who'd occupied his thoughts far too often in recent months?

As he headed for the escalator, he knew he had to accept that he'd never have what he wanted from her. It was time to move on. With that in mind, he sent a text to Shelby asking if she had time for lunch tomorrow.

ELLE WENT BALLISTIC when she saw Darren and a *Star* photographer waiting outside HQ to document her arrival.

"*You're both fired! Don't you dare come to work tomorrow!*"

The photographer clicked away, capturing the tirade as Darren took copious notes of the venom that spewed from his publisher's mouth.

Sam took her time walking in as Elle once again fought her every step of the way.

An hour later, Elle and her bodyguards had been processed through central booking and settled in different interrogation rooms. Sam, Hill, Cruz, Malone and Charity Miller were watching them through one-way glass. Horace seemed nervous, Boris looked bored and Elle was still furious, pacing relentlessly from one end of the small room to the other.

Because they'd been working for close to fifteen hours by then and fatigue was setting in, Sam suggested they divide and conquer. She asked Hill to take Boris, Cruz had Horace and she would be going at Elle.

Lieutenant Rango stepped into the small room. "We found some of the blond hairs you needed in Lind's room, Sam." He handed her the evidence bag.

"Excellent! Charity, I need a warrant for her DNA."

"I'll get it for you."

"As an added extra," Rango said, holding up a second bag. "We've got some used condoms from under Lind's bed. We might be able to tie at least one of them to her."

"Lovely," Sam said. "Will you get them to the lab ASAP and put a rush on it?"

"On my way there now."

"Thanks, Rango. Good work. Cruz, will you let Lindsey's office know we're almost ready for them to swab her?"

"Yep."

"Any word from the lab on the knife?" Sam asked.

"They were working on it when I called earlier," Malone said.

"Great."

"Let's get this done," Sam said.

The others filed out of the room, leaving Charity and Malone to watch from the observation area.

"Hill," Sam said in the hallway.

He turned back to her.

"Are you okay?"

"Yeah, I'm great. I just helped arrest the wife of my childhood friend. Never better."

"I'm sorry it turned out to be her. Ray has to know you didn't enjoy that."

"Yeah, I'm sure he'll be all sorts of forgiving after I help put his wife away for the rest of her life." He shook his head. "Sorry. I don't mean to take it out on you. It's her I'm pissed with. She had everything, for Christ's sake."

"She didn't know any other way to live but rich and entitled. When that was taken from her, she struck out at the ones she blamed, never suspecting for a second that she'd get caught."

"I feel sorry for Ray," Hill said. "He's a hardworking guy who's put a lot of himself into running the team. Who knows where this will leave him?"

"Hard to say right now, but I'm sure it'll work out for him. People won't blame him for what she did. Let's get this done so we can get the hell out of here."

They joined Cruz at the far end of the hallway and entered the three rooms simultaneously.

"I'm not saying a word to you," Elle said when Sam walked in.

"You can just listen for now. Boris and Horace, your faithful henchmen, have told us everything."

"They wouldn't dare say a word about me to you!"

"Oh no? Funny how chatty they got when we told them they were looking at life in prison with no chance of parole unless they helped us to make a case against you. They told us everything—how angry you were with Willie and how you told them something had to be done about him, that he couldn't get away with ruining everything for you." Sam was spouting pure speculation, but judging from the reaction it drew from Elle, she wasn't far off the mark.

"They told us how you lured Willie to the seedy motel by blackmailing him with info about how he'd spent time there before with underage girls. How did you know that? Did your lover boy Rick tell you he'd seen Willie there before? Did you tell him you were going to call his wife, Elle? Is that how you got him there?"

Without skipping a beat, Sam continued. "Doesn't really matter how you got him there. Boris and Horace took over once he arrived, didn't they? They put him in a room with Amber, hoping to distract him with sex, before they killed him in one place, dumped him in another and took his car somewhere else and all but destroyed it. Did they use Willie's own baseball bats to destroy the car he'd loved so much? That would've been poetic, right? You must've been pretty pissed off with Willie to use almost the last of your available funds to pay Boris and Horace to do your dirty work for you."

"You have no idea what you're talking about," Elle said, a little less forcefully since Sam had offered a time line of how Willie's murder had gone down.

"Rick was a little more personal, since you'd been banging him on the side. You thought you could count on him to give you what you needed with the season on the line, but he didn't get it done for you either, did he? All he had to do was strike out *three* batters. *Three measly batters* and the Feds would be in the World Series, and you'd get the influx of cash you desperately needed to save your daddy's empire. But it didn't happen, did it? One of the best closers in baseball couldn't get it done for you, could he?"

Elle crossed her arms and raised her chin defiantly. "I want a lawyer."

"No problem. Who would you like us to call?"

She named one of Washington's top law firms. "Tell

them I want someone over here tonight to get me out of here."

Sam didn't bother to tell her there was no way she was getting out of there any time soon. She'd figure that out soon enough. "I'll give them a call. I'm sure they're standing by at the ready at this hour on a Friday night." She walked out of the room, letting the door slam shut behind her. A patrolman stood watch outside the door. "No one goes in or out of there without me knowing."

"Yes, ma'am, Lieutenant."

Sam went to the observation room to see how Hill and Cruz were making out with the bodyguards.

Horace was in tears, sobbing loudly as Cruz took him through the same scenario Sam had laid out for Elle.

"Ms. Elle," Horace said between sobs, "she said Willie had to go. He'd messed up everything, and why should he get away with that? Me and Boris, we didn't want to do it, but Ms. Elle, she said we had to or we'd get fired. We didn't want to get fired. We did it just the way she told us to. We just did what we was told to do."

"Nice work, partner," Sam whispered, beaming with pride as Freddie gently coaxed a confession from Horace.

Freddie pushed a yellow pad across the table. "Write it down, exactly the way it happened."

Horace dried his tears and reached for the pen with his left hand. As Lindsey and Byron had suspected, the killer was left-handed.

In the adjoining room, Hill worked over Boris. "Elle told us what you did. She said it was your idea to kill Willie."

"She said *what*? It wasn't my idea!"

"That's what she said."

"I don't understand. Why would she blame me? I just did what she told me to do. I always do what she tells me to."

"Have you killed for her before this?"

"No! I've never killed anyone before. It made me sick to do that to Willie. He wasn't a bad guy. He made a mistake. But Ms. Elle… She said he had to go. We couldn't let him get away with ruining everything."

Hill pushed a yellow pad across the table. "Write it down. Exactly the way it happened."

"Excellent," Sam said as it all came together.

"We've got enough to charge all of them with first-degree murder of Willie," Charity said. "I want the results of the DNA tests before we pin Lind's murder on her." She handed the warrant to Sam.

Sam grabbed the extension off the wall and dialed the morgue.

Byron Tomlinson answered.

"This is Holland. We've got the warrant. Can you get down here to take a swab for me?"

"On my way."

"Thanks."

While she waited for Tomlinson, Sam went into her office to look up the phone number for the law firm Elle had requested. She left a message with the answering service and then took a moment to check her own phone for messages. She was delighted to find a text from Nick.

On the way home. Heard you got into another scrape while I was gone. I can't leave you unsupervised for even a day. Missed you. See you in the morning.

Sam smiled as she reread the message. It felt like forever since she'd last talked to him. She couldn't wait to hear his voice and have his strong arms wrapped around her. The anticipation gave her a much-needed adrenaline boost.

Her desk phone rang as she was getting up to return to the observation area.

"This is Tim Russo returning your call about Elle Jestings."

"Yes, thanks for getting back to me. She's been arrested on murder charges and has requested an attorney from your firm to represent her."

After a long pause, he said, "I'm afraid that won't be possible. Mrs. Jestings has an outstanding balance on her account that exceeds fifty thousand dollars. We're unable to do any more work for her until the balance is settled."

Sam tried to imagine how this news would go over with Elle and couldn't help but smile. "I'll let her know. Thank you for returning my call."

"No problem."

Sam got up and went straight to the room where Elle was being held. "I just got off the phone with Tim Russo."

"He's on his way?"

"I'm afraid not. He said your account with his firm is in arrears to the tune of fifty thousand dollars, and until you've settled up with them, they're unavailable to do any more work for you."

"You can't be serious," she said, her face flushing with rage. "They were my father's attorneys for forty years! They wouldn't *dare* say no to me!"

"I believe they just did. Shall I call the public defender's office for you?"

In that moment it seemed to occur to Elle that she

was screwed. As she dropped into a chair, her silk dress billowed out around her before collapsing against her legs. "If it's that or nothing, make the call."

"Very good."

"You don't need to enjoy this so much."

"I don't enjoy anything about murder, except for catching the scumbags who did it and sending them away for life. That part I enjoy very much. You may as well get comfortable, Mrs. Jestings. You're going to be here a while."

By the time they got the DNA results back from the lab as well as the report on the knife that confirmed the presence of Willie's blood and Horace's fingerprints, as well as Boris's fingerprints on the steering wheel of Willie's car, it was after four in the morning. Sam, Hill and Cruz spent the next three hours typing up their reports and filing them.

At eight o'clock, Sam placed calls to Carmen Vasquez and Carla Lind to let them know arrests had been made in their husbands' murders. While it might have been cowardly on her part, she refrained from informing them that their husbands had been unfaithful. Both were still dealing with the grief of their sudden losses, and giving them the rest of the story at this time would've been piling on. They'd find out soon enough.

After she gave a brief statement about the arrests to the media, she was about to finally go home when she remembered she'd never filed a report on Stahl's attack. It took another hour to pound that out, and by then her eyes were gritty and raw. Although she was anxious to see Scotty before he left with Mrs. Littlefield at ten, she stopped first at her dad's house to update him on the case and to find out what had happened at the doctor's appointment.

"Are you crazy kids up yet?" she called out as she walked into the house to find her dad and Celia sitting at the kitchen table. "What's going on?"

"Have you been up all night, honey?"

"Just getting home now, but we got it sewed up." Celia held up the front page of the *Star* where a banner headline read "*Star* Publisher Elle Kopelsman Jestings Charged in Vasquez, Lind Murders." The picture of Sam dragging Elle into HQ was plastered under the headline.

"I can't believe she was involved," Skip said. "Her dad must be rolling in his grave."

"I suspect he's been rolling for some time as she drove his company into the ground."

"Want some coffee?" Celia asked.

"No thanks. I'm going home to crash." She sat for a minute. "I heard you're being admitted for some tests. What's up with that?"

"They think the bullet might be moving," Celia said grimly.

"What does that mean?"

"It may have to come out."

"But they said that would be too dangerous."

"Yes, and it would still be dangerous, but it might be more dangerous to leave it if it's moving."

Sam's exhausted mind struggled to process what her stepmother was saying. "If they take it out, will he regain feeling in his extremities?"

"They don't know," Skip said.

"But maybe?" Sam asked as a surge of hope shot through her.

"They don't know what to expect," her dad said

again. "It's a very unusual case. Has been from the beginning."

"When are you going in?"

"Next week. After the election, don't worry."

"Don't plan it around us! Do what's best for you!"

"It'll keep until then, baby girl," Skip said. "I want to see my son-in-law reelected before I steal the spotlight for a day or two."

"Are you sure it's okay to wait that long?"

"It's fine," Skip assured her. "Everything is going to be just fine. I don't want you to worry. Now come give your dear old dad a kiss and go home to bed. You're about to keel over from exhaustion."

Since Sam couldn't deny that, she got up and did as he asked, hanging on to him for an extra minute before she released him and went to kiss Celia's cheek. "Keep me posted."

"You know we will, honey."

Sam left her dad's house and walked the short distance to the ramp that led to her own home. Inside, she found Scotty having breakfast with Shelby. Judging from the chocolate smeared all over Scotty's face, Shelby had made chocolate-chip pancakes.

"Sam! You're home. Did you figure out who killed Willie?"

Sam bent to kiss his forehead. "I sure did. Three people are in jail right now."

"I hope they never get out."

"I doubt they will. Mrs. L will be here in a few minutes. You need to go wash your face and brush your teeth."

"Okay!"

"Grab your overnight bag too," Shelby called after him.

Sam took the seat he'd abandoned and tore off a bite of pancake from the stack on the table. "Thanks so much for staying here last night."

"I'm happy to do it whenever you need me."

"It's a huge help."

"I enjoy being with him. He's delightful."

Sam smiled. "Yes, he is."

"You look done in."

"I'm ready for some sleep."

"What time does your handsome hubby get home?"

"I'm not sure. He said sometime this morning."

"I'll get out of here so you two can have some alone time."

"Since we'll probably be unconscious for most of it, you don't need to rush on my account."

"I've got a wedding to check in on later today, and a hot date for lunch tomorrow." Her grin stretched from ear to ear. "I need to get my nails done and my hair colored."

"Ah, did a certain FBI agent finally call you?"

"Yes, he did. He wanted to go today, but I didn't want to be too available."

Sam laughed at her logic. "Good. I'm glad you heard from him. He's a nice guy. You could do worse."

"He's easy on the eyes. That's for sure."

"If you say so."

Shelby giggled as she got up from the table and made quick work of cleaning up the kitchen. "So why doesn't Nick like him?"

Taken aback by the question, Sam struggled to find an answer that didn't require the actual truth. "Who knows? Guys are so weird."

Thankfully, Shelby didn't choose to pursue it any

further and chatted about her night with Scotty as she finished loading the dishwasher.

Sam forced herself to stay awake until Mrs. Littlefield arrived to pick up Scotty for their outing.

He gave Sam a big hug before he left. "Tell Nick I'll see him tomorrow."

"I will, buddy. We'll be there to get you in the afternoon. Have a good time."

"We'll have a great time," Mrs. Littlefield said as she ushered Scotty out the door with his Secret Service detail in tow.

Shelby left a short time later, and Sam trudged upstairs, going directly to the shower where she nearly fell asleep standing up. As she was combing her hair, she caught her first glimpse of her injured neck. "Holy shit," she whispered as she took in the vivid blue marks.

She was glad to know her nemesis had gotten the worst of it, but Nick would flip when he saw her latest collection of bruises.

And how had he known about the altercation with Stahl anyway?

"Secret Service," she whispered to her reflection. Of course they had a direct pipeline to *Air Force One* and would've informed him of what happened in his absence. It had probably upset him to hear that she'd been hurt when he was too far away to do anything for her, which in turn upset her. She didn't like being the cause of his distress.

Sam dried her hair, secured it into a loose ponytail and wandered naked into the bedroom, eyeing the big bed with lust in her heart. Then she thought of the loft and decided that's where she wanted to be when he got home.

Still naked, she went upstairs, landed facedown on the comfortable double lounge chair and pulled a soft blanket over her. Sleep swooped down on her immediately. She fell asleep smiling, knowing she'd wake up to her husband's handsome face and get to spend an entire day completely alone with him. She couldn't wait to see him and to tell him all about what'd happened while he was gone.

NICK DROPPED HIS duffel bag inside the front door and laid his garment bag over the sofa to deal with later. He kicked off his shoes and took the stairs in stocking feet, anxious to lay eyes on his wife, even if she was sound asleep. He'd take what he could get. In the bedroom, he was surprised to find the bed empty and the blinds open to the late morning sunshine.

"Where the heck is she?"

And then he knew. Smiling, he took the stairs to the loft two at a time. She was curled up on her side, and the dip of the blanket revealed a bare shoulder, the graceful curve of her back and a tantalizing view of her gorgeous ass.

Nick licked lips gone dry and quickly shed his own clothes into a pile on the floor that was most unlike him. He'd showered and shaved on the plane before they landed so he wouldn't have to do anything when he got home but snuggle up to his beautiful wife in bed.

He'd talked to Scotty on the way home, so he knew she'd worked all night and managed to close the Vasquez and Lind cases. His Secret Service detail had filled him in on the arrest of Elle Jestings and her bodyguards.

Nick curled up to her warmth and pulled the blanket over both of them as he put his arm around her and breathed in the familiar scent of home.

She murmured in her sleep as her hand covered his, aware of his presence even in slumber.

He wanted her urgently but would never wake her after she'd gone so long without sleep. It was enough for now to hold her close, to feel her heart beating under the hand he'd rested on her chest and to enjoy the singular feeling of her naked body pressed against his.

The trip had been long and grueling. He'd slept only sporadically, especially after the conversation with the president had him running the different scenarios and failing to figure out how to fit the president's offer into their lives in a way that made sense for all of them.

Sam turned over and opened her stunning blue eyes.

"You're home." Her voice was hoarse with sleep and sexy as all hell.

His gaze traveled immediately to the angry bruises on her neck, which he traced with a light fingertip so he wouldn't hurt her. "I hope I never see that bastard Stahl again. I might have to kill him for doing this to you."

"Don't do that. I need you too much to have to arrest you for murder."

He brought her in tight against him and sighed when her arm curled around him.

"Missed you so much," she said. "I hated that I couldn't even talk to you."

"I hated it too. I was very anxious being so far from you guys with everything that's gone on lately. I couldn't wait to get home, especially after I heard about what happened with Stahl."

"So the Secret Service ratted me out on that, huh?"

"Yes," he said, chuckling, "they certainly did."

"Tattletaling—yet another reason to keep them far away from me. It was cool being on *Air Force One*?"

"It was an amazing experience. I wish you and Scotty could've come with me."

"As fun as it would be to fly to the other side of the world and back in two days, I'll have to take your word for it."

Knowing how much she hated to fly, he smiled as he kissed her. "Go back to sleep. We've got all day to lay around."

"You don't have anything for the campaign?"

"Not until tomorrow night."

"Two whole days together," she said with a sigh of pleasure. "I think I just died and went straight to heaven." As she said the words, she worked her leg between his and her hand moved from his chest to his belly and down to encircle his erection.

"Babe…what're you doing?"

"Saying a proper hello to my husband who I love so much and who I missed *so* much."

"While I love the way you say hello, you're too tired." She stroked and caressed him until he was on the verge of bursting. "I'm never too tired for this."

As much as it killed him to stop her, he wanted to be inside her when he lost control. "Wait. Let's do this together."

She turned onto her back and held out her arms, welcoming him into her loving embrace.

As he settled on top of her, he wanted to kiss and touch every inch of soft skin, but they were both in a rush after being apart for a few days.

"Hurry," she whispered, spurring his desire with the urgency he heard in her voice.

He entered her swiftly and then paused to relish the sweet relief of being joined with his love. "Samantha," he whispered, his lips brushing her neck and making her shiver. "I love you so much. I couldn't wait to get home."

"I couldn't wait for you to get home either. What's wrong with us that we can't bear to be apart for two days?"

"Nothing is wrong with us. Nothing other than being madly in love."

Smiling up at him, she caressed his back, her hands moving down in tantalizing circles until she gripped his ass and pulled him in tight against her as she came with a cry of pleasure that triggered his release. "God, baby," he whispered. "You're amazing. I can't get enough of you."

Her legs curled around his hips, keeping him lodged inside her. After a long spell of contented silence, she said, "I had another of those one-day periods while you were gone."

"Aw, honey. Shit."

She shrugged, showing nonchalance he knew she didn't feel. "We'll have to keep trying."

"That's certainly no hardship," he said, pushing against her as he kissed her. "It'll happen one of these months. We're a proven entity."

"Maybe. Maybe not. I'll be okay either way. I promise."

"I'm glad to hear you say that."

"Having Scotty with us has helped. I don't feel the same aching need to have a baby that I used to feel. If all I ever get is him, he'll be more than enough."

"For me too. We're so lucky to have as much as we

do." He withdrew from her and moved to his back, bringing her with him.

With her head resting on his chest and her hand caressing his belly, she caught him up on everything that'd happened while he was away. Nick was stunned to hear of the situation with her dad and the moving bullet.

"He says it's nothing to worry about, but still… It sounds like it could be."

"He's right that we shouldn't worry until we need to."

"I'm trying."

Anxious to get her mind off her worries about her dad so she'd be able to sleep, he said, "Tell me about the girls you rescued from the motel. I heard about it on the news on the way home."

"That was the craziest thing! I got one of my feelings. I can't even explain the sense I got that something was very wrong there." She told him about rescuing Ginger and Amber, how Ginger had led them to the house where dozens of other missing kids had been located and the tearful reunion between Ginger—who turned out to be Sarah—and her parents.

"I remember the story when Sarah went missing. It was big news around here."

"And all this time she was only an hour away in the District. Her parents were so happy and relieved. But they've got an awfully long road ahead getting her the help she'll need."

"That's amazing, babe. I'm so proud of what you did for those kids."

"Thanks. Everyone made a big deal about it at HQ."

"It's a huge big deal. You could've walked away from that hotel and their nightmare would've continued with no one knowing what was really going on. You saved them all by following your instincts."

"I'd only ever say this to you, because it sounds kind of arrogant, but…when things like that happen, I know I'm doing exactly what I was put on this earth to do. Does that make sense?"

"It makes perfect sense," he said, and it served to clarify his decision. Who was he kidding? There'd never been a decision in the first place. Her job defined her and gave her life meaning. He'd never ask her to give that up for him.

She let out a huge yawn. "I can't stay awake anymore."

"You don't have to, baby. I'll be here when you wake up, and we'll have all kinds of time to spend together."

"Can we stay right here in our loft and not leave until we have to pick up Scotty?"

"There's nothing I'd rather do."

"What's the latest with Lexicore?"

"You're supposed to be sleeping."

"I will after you tell me what's going on."

"Turns out most of their investors were blindsided by the connection to the factory in Thailand. We haven't seen any noticeable drop in the polls since the news hit that I was a stockholder."

"That's a relief."

"It's all thanks to Graham. He played it perfectly. As always, his instincts were spot-on."

"I'm glad. You deserve to be reelected. You work so hard." She relaxed into his embrace, and her breathing evened out, leading him to think she'd fallen back to sleep. "Nick?"

"Hmm?"

"Remember that thing we talked about doing together sometime?"

His recently satisfied libido stood up to take notice when he realized what she meant. "What about it?"

"I want to do it. I want to do everything there is to do with you."

He tightened his grip on her and kissed her forehead. "We'll get to it, babe. We'll do it all. I promise."

"Good," she said, yawning again. "Did you get to spend any time with the president on the trip?"

"We had a drink together in the middle of the night on *Air Force One*. It was incredible."

"That's so cool. Did anything else happen while you were gone?"

"No, honey. Nothing else happened. Go to sleep. I've got you."

EPILOGUE

SAM, NICK AND Scotty watched the election returns in a hotel suite across the street from the Greater Richmond Convention Center. The suite was full of family, friends and campaign staffers anticipating an easy victory for Nick in his first official election.

Graham worked the room like the seasoned politician he was, enjoying every moment of his adopted son's big night. Dressed in his "work clothes," Scotty followed Graham around, handing out cigars and shaking hands.

"Check out the next Senator Cappuano, already in training," Sam said to Nick. They sat together in front of the TV, watching the coverage and waiting to hear official results in the Virginia Senate race.

Nick smiled when Scotty shook hands with Virginia Governor Mike Zorn and his wife Judy, both of whom seemed charmed by the boy. They'd come by for a quick visit while they waited to see if he'd been reelected too.

"The kid is a natural," Nick said.

Sam reached for his hand and linked their fingers. "Just like his dad."

"I'll be glad when they call it," he said, glancing anxiously at the TV.

"It's in the bag, Senator. They probably had to invent a new way to count as many votes as you got."

"Shut up," he said in a teasing tone.

"Shut me up."

"I will. Later."

"Promises, promises. I just got a text from Trace. They're moving Brooke to the new school tonight. I guess it got kind of ugly when they told her what was happening."

"Let's hope things will be better for all of them with a little space."

"I can only hope so."

Graham came over to them, his blue eyes dancing with excitement and anticipation. He was in his element on a night like this and was clearly enjoying himself. He'd been glued to Nick's side all day, propping up the candidate during his first official election day.

"Could I have a word with the Senator-Elect?" he asked.

"Don't jinx him," Scotty said from behind Graham.

"You tell him, Scotty," Nick said.

"I'm just speaking the truth," Graham said.

Nick squeezed Sam's hand and released it. "Be right back, babe."

"I won't keep him but a minute," Graham said.

Sam reached out to Scotty. "Come sit with me."

As the two men walked away, Scotty plopped down next to her and focused on the election returns. "I wish they'd call it already."

Sam laughed. "You're a chip off the old block."

"What does that mean?"

"You're just like Nick. He said the same thing two minutes ago."

"Being just like Nick isn't a bad thing."

"It's a very good thing."

"This is all really cool, isn't it?"

"It's very cool, but I have to admit I'll be glad when

the campaign is officially over and we can go back to a somewhat normal life."

"Our life is never normal."

Endlessly amused by him, she said, "Already got that figured out, huh?"

"Yep. Didn't take long to figure out I'd never be bored with you guys for parents."

"Gee, thanks. I think…"

His smile was full of charm and mischief, but then it faded, and she could tell he had something on his mind. "Could I ask you something?"

"Anything."

"I heard you guys talking about Grandpa Skip having to go to the hospital next week. Is he okay?"

Sam winced. "Sorry you heard about it like that. It's possible the bullet that paralyzed him has shifted a bit. So they're going to do some tests to take a better look. Because he's sort of fragile, they want to admit him to do it. Nothing to worry about." She could see that he was trying to process the information.

"Is it possible that he might be able to walk again someday?"

"Oh, honey, I don't think we'll ever get that lucky."

"That sure would be awesome."

"Yes, it would. I wish you could've known him before he was hurt. He was impossibly big and strong and so full of life."

"He still is."

Moved to tears by three simple words, Sam held out her arms to him. "That's nice of you to say." She gave him a tight hug and let him go.

"It's nice to have a grandpa again."

"He thinks you're pretty great too."

"He does? Really?"

"Of course he does. What's not to love about you, Scotty Cappuano?"

Scotty's grin lit up his face. "There's nothing not to love about me."

"You said it, mister."

NICK FOLLOWED GRAHAM into one of the suite's two bedrooms. They left the door open so they could hear if there was any news.

"I just wanted a minute to say I'm proud of the campaign you ran, and I'm looking forward to the next seven years—and don't tell me I'm jinxing you. We both know you're going to walk away with it."

"Thank you for all your help. I couldn't have gotten this far without you."

"You could've done without the Lexicore hiccup," Graham said with a scowl.

"That's all it was—a hiccup. Thanks to your statement, the story of my involvement never got any traction."

"Well, it was the least I could do for getting you into that mess in the first place. I feel terrible that you lost so much money, though. I'll find a way to make it up to you."

"Don't give it another thought. I've still got more than half of what John left me, and I was hardly a pauper before John made me his beneficiary."

"True." Graham straightened Nick's tie and brushed some lint off his suit coat. "He'd be so proud of you, the best friend he ever had. He'd love this."

"I just wish he hadn't had to die to make it possible."

"He'd tell us both to quit fretting over him and enjoy

the moment. He was good at that—living in the moment."

"Yes, he was." *Maybe a little too good*, Nick thought, but he kept that to himself out of respect for his late friend and his late friend's father. "I had an interesting conversation with Nelson on the plane the other night."

"Interesting how?"

"You gotta keep this between us."

"Of course."

Nick told him about the vice president's diagnosis and his plans to resign after the election.

"Oh God. That's awful." Graham suddenly looked up at Nick, gasping. "He asked you to replace Gooding, didn't he?"

"Maybe."

Graham's eyes bugged. "You gotta be shitting me! That's amazing!"

"Before you get too excited, I'm going to turn him down."

"No..."

"Yes."

"*Why?* It would make you the absolute heir apparent in four years!"

"I know."

"So then why the heck are you saying no?"

Nick glanced at the open door, through which he could see Sam sitting with Scotty, their heads close together as they conversed. Her hair was long and curly tonight, the way he liked it best. She'd chosen a black silk dress that somehow managed to be both sexy and demure at the same time. The diamond key he'd given her as a wedding gift was nestled just above her full breasts, and her engagement ring sparkled as she ran a hand over Scotty's hair to straighten it.

Nick looked over at his friend and mentor, who had followed his gaze to Sam and Scotty. "I can't ask her to give up her career to support mine, Graham, and she can't be the vice president's wife and still chase down murderers. That's who she *is*. Asking her to be anyone else would be like asking her not to breathe. I can't do it."

"Surely some arrangement could be made."

"What kind of arrangement?" Nick asked with a smile.

"I don't know. Some kind." Graham looked like he might burst into tears at any second.

"I had an entire sleepless night on *Air Force One* to think about the various scenarios. I kept coming back to the same conclusion. It's not the right time—for her or for me."

"It *is* the right time for you," Graham insisted.

"If the time isn't right for her, it's not right for me either."

"What did she say when you told her about it?"

"I didn't tell her."

"Nick… *Come on!* You have to at least *tell* her about it. How do you know what she'll say if she doesn't even know?"

"I have no doubt that she'd give up the job she loves, the job that has defined her adult life, if I asked her to. I also have no doubt that she'd absolutely hate every minute of living in a gilded cage, surrounded by Secret Service all the time. I'm surprised she hasn't murdered a member of the details following Scotty and me over the last couple of months. That life isn't for her."

"She knew what she was signing on for," Graham said a bit petulantly.

"Neither of us could've imagined what this past year would bring. Now that the campaign is over, we're both looking forward to some downtime to spend with our new son. We're anxious for some peace. This last year has been unreal."

Graham screwed his face into what might've been a pout as he looked down at the floor. "You're killing me here."

Nick's laughter rang out, drawing Sam's attention in the adjoining room. He returned her smile. "I'm sorry. I probably shouldn't have told you."

"Nah, it's okay. I'll survive. Somehow."

"You won't say anything about it, will you?"

"You know you can trust me."

A huge cheer erupted from the adjoining room. Graham's big smile was back as he looked up at Nick.

"I think it's safe now to shake your hand and say congratulations, Senator-Elect Cappuano."

Nick returned the handshake and then hugged the older man. "Got a nice ring to it, doesn't it?"

"You bet it does. Keep making me proud, son."

"Always."

"Your lovely wife is looking for you, so let me get out of here and start pouring the bubbly."

On the way out of the room, Graham hugged and kissed Sam. "Congratulations, Mrs. C."

"Thanks, Graham. We'll be right out."

"Take your time. It's your big night. We'll wait for you."

Sam closed the door and turned to Nick, beaming with pleasure. "You did it!"

"So I hear." The roar from the next room was nothing short of deafening. "Come here." He waggled his finger at her and watched her come toward him, loving the way she moved, loving the way she looked, loving everything about her.

She stepped into his embrace, wrapping her arms around him inside his suit coat. "Congratulations, babe. I couldn't be more proud of you."

"Thank you. That means a lot coming from you."

"Your adoring public is waiting for you."

"They can wait a minute longer," he said, clinging to her.

"I bet they're kissing in there," Scotty said from outside the door, making his new parents laugh.

"As long as we're being accused," Nick said, looking down at her, "how about it?"

"Why not? I've never kissed a senator-elect before."

Smiling, he brought his lips down on hers, filled with love and confidence, knowing that as long as he had her and the son they both adored, he had everything he'd ever need.

* * * * *

Turn the page to read

After the Final Epilogue,

a never-before-published
bonus story from New York Times
bestselling author Marie Force!

AFTER THE FINAL EPILOGUE

THE ROAR OF the crowd in the ballroom had been so deafening Nick's ears were still ringing two hours after he and Sam had returned to their suite after celebrating with the campaign staff. It had been one hell of a great night, capping grueling months on the campaign trail that had him crisscrossing the commonwealth of Virginia more times than he could count.

It had all been worth it tonight, though, when the election had been called in his favor. Not that anyone had been surprised, because he'd been the frontrunner all along. But Nick hadn't taken anything for granted. That just wasn't his way. He'd chosen to run his campaign as if he had something to prove, which he still felt he did.

Almost a year after the murder of his best friend and boss, Nick still felt like an imposter, an understudy chosen to play a role until the star returned to full form. Except the star wasn't coming back. The role was now officially his, to make his own.

Since sleep was proving elusive, as it often was for him, Nick thought about the conversation with Graham, smiling in the darkness as he recalled his friend's pained reaction to President Nelson's offer. He'd known exactly how Graham would react—and Graham hadn't disappointed him.

Despite his mentor's assurances that something could

be worked out, Nick was comfortable with his decision to decline Nelson's offer to be his new vice president and to keep it from Sam. She would encourage him to take every opportunity that came his way, even if it meant sacrificing her own happiness.

He'd never ask that of her. He loved her too damned much. Running his hand over the naked expanse of her back, he loved how she slept all over him, sprawled on top of him like he was her favorite air mattress. Nick was more than happy to be anything she needed him to be.

She mumbled in her sleep, her hand moving from his chest to his belly, which stirred an immediate and predictable reaction. "Why are you still awake?"

"I've got this crazy hot babe sleeping naked in my arms. How do you expect me to sleep?"

Her hand continued down the front of him, encircling his erection. "I thought we took care of this."

"He never gets enough of you."

"What're you really thinking about?"

"The hot naked babe."

"Nick…"

"A lot of things—the campaign, the election, the next seven years, Scotty, you. Always you."

"What about me?"

"I just want to say, for the record, that I appreciate all the support during the campaign. I promised you one year and done in the Senate, and now we're signed on for seven more years."

She moved so she was fully on top of him.

He looped his arms around her, loving the feel of her warm naked skin against his.

"Have I told you how crazy proud I am of my senator husband?"

"I think you have."

"I don't know if you have any idea just how proud I am. Every day on the job people say to me, 'You're the senator's wife.' I act like it bugs me, but it doesn't really because I'm so proud. I love the way you stepped up after John died and pulled the staff together to continue his work. I don't think anyone else could've done what you did at that moment in time. People were shattered, and you put them back together with your quiet strength. We all rely on that strength more than you know."

"You humble me, Samantha, and I fear you give me too much credit."

"I don't give you anywhere near enough credit for what you do for me. I was a hot mess until you came along."

"You are hot. I'll give you that. But you were never a mess."

"Yes, I was. On the inside. My life was out of control. I was reeling from my dad's injury, the miscarriages, the divorce from Peter, the Johnson case gone bad. All of it. But the minute I saw you again, sitting in John's apartment on that awful day, I felt better. Calmer. Able to face whatever came my way because there you were again. I'd thought of you so often since the night we first met, and to find out that you'd thought of me, too…"

"I obsessed over you. I always knew you were it for me."

She surprised the shit out of him when she sat up and took him into her, coming down slowly.

Nick gasped, took hold of her hips and arched into her.

"And now we can do this, every day for the rest of our lives."

"Twice on Sundays," he said with a smile for her.

Returning his smile, she leaned in to kiss him. "Three times on Sundays."

"Whatever you want, babe."

Keep reading for a
Fatal Series Q&A with Marie!

FATAL SERIES FREQUENTLY ASKED QUESTIONS

How many books do you plan to write in this series?

I hope to write the series for as long as readers are enjoying it and for as long as it's fun for me to write. So far so good on the reader front. I'm extremely challenged by these books—not always in a good way—but I continue to be satisfied by the final outcomes. That keeps me engaged and coming back for more of Sam and Nick, who I adore writing. So no end in sight for now.

Will Sam and Nick from the Fatal Series ever have a baby of their own?

I honestly don't know. I'd love to give them what they want (as well as what readers want), but making Sam a mother to an infant would dramatically change the way she lives her life and would greatly alter the pace of the series. IF (and that's a very BIG IF at this point), they have a baby, I expect it would happen much later in the series, closer to the end.

Will Nick run for president, and if he does will Sam have to give up her job?

I don't know and I don't know! :-) I guess we'll have to see what life has in store for them. Look at it this way… We're at book six, and we still haven't lived a full year with them. The next election is four years away. That's a LOT of books between now and then.

Will we ever find out who shot Skip?

That's another question I get ALL THE TIME. Along with, "Do *you* know who shot Skip?" No, I don't know. I figure I'll find out when Sam does. I like that I don't know. I like that the possibilities are so endless. I like that it's frustrating to Sam that she's failed to find closure to that question. That's life, right? I do have some interesting stories coming up for Skip in future books that I'm looking forward to writing.

We'd love to read the story about the night Sam and Nick met the first time. Will you ever write that?

Yes! In fact, I'm already writing it. Watch for *One Night With You*, a Fatal Series Novella, in 2015. It will be included in the print edition of *Fatal Affair,* on sale in May, and in ebook format in June.

Do you have other questions that weren't answered here? Send them to Marie at *marie@marieforce.com.*

Thanks for reading!

ACKNOWLEDGMENTS

WHEN I WROTE *Fatal Affair* in 2009–2010, I never could've imagined how this series would take off with readers. I can't believe we're already at book six and going strong. Sam and Nick are such a joy to write—and so is their adorable Scotty. Hearing every day from readers who want more, more, *more* of them kept me going during the writing of *Fatal Mistake*. I have much more in store for the Cappuanos, their friends and family, and I hope you'll continue to come along on their wild ride.

My thanks as always to the many people who support me, especially "Team Jack," Julie Cupp, Lisa Cafferty, Holly Sullivan, Isabel Sullivan, Nikki Colquhoun and Cheryl Serra. They take very good care of me, and I so appreciate all they do to keep me sane. Julie also helps me with the Washington, D.C. details, which is a huge help. My agent, Kevan Lyon, is a wonderful supporter, partner and friend. Everyone at Carina Press and Harlequin, including my new editor, Alissa Davis, who have worked on this series—thank you for your enthusiasm for the Fatal Series. A huge thanks to my faithful beta readers Ronlyn Howe, Kara Conrad and Anne Woodall—I couldn't do it without you ladies and your awesome feedback!

Special thanks to my reader friend Stephanie Behill for her help with Spanish translation, and to financial advisor Joseph A. Medeiros, CFP®, CLU, ChFC, AIF,® who helped with information about buying and selling stock.

Every time I write a Fatal book, in the back of my mind I know I've got Newport, RI, Police Detective Captain Russ Hayes backing me up, which is a huge source of comfort. Thank you again, Russ, for keeping me honest and helping to ensure the police and investigatory aspects of the story are as close to real life as I can get them—while keeping them entertaining too!

Thanks so much to my family—Dan, Emily and Jake—who put up with me when I'm on deadline, and to my four-legged office mates, Brandy and Louie, who keep me company all day.

Finally, my most heartfelt thanks to my wonderful readers who make this magical life of mine possible. I'm thankful every day for each and every one of you. Thanks to your support, *Fatal Mistake* became the first book in the Fatal series to hit the *New York Times* bestseller list!

Want to chat with other fans who've read *Fatal Mistake?* Join the *Fatal Mistake* Reader Group at facebook.com/groups/FatalMistake/ *and the Fatal Series Reader Group at facebook.com/groups/FatalSeries*. Also, make sure you join my mailing list at marieforce.com to be notified when new books are available.

xoxo
Marie

SPECIAL EXCERPT FROM

Read on for a sneak preview of

FATAL JEOPARDY:

BOOK SEVEN OF THE FATAL SERIES

by New York Times *bestselling author*

MARIE FORCE

The game whizzed by so quickly Sam could barely keep up. Next to her, Scotty bounced with excitement as they watched Nick fly around on the ice with skill and stamina that astounded her. Although she shouldn't be surprised he was so good. Not only had he played hockey for years when he was younger but he regularly demonstrated his stamina in other important ways.

Chuckling at her own joke, Sam tried to keep her eyes on his white helmet and green jersey with number twenty-two on the back. With the campaign over and the election won, he had time now to rejoin the men's league he'd played in before his life had taken an unexpected turn almost a year ago.

That was when his best friend and boss, Senator John O'Connor, had been murdered. From that awful tragedy had come two interesting things—their relationship and his ascendancy into the Senate, where he now held the seat from Virginia in his own right after a resounding win in the election.

"He's so good," Scotty said, dazzled by Nick's skill on the ice. "I'll never be that good."

CARMFEXP00272

Sam hooked her arm around the twelve-year-old she and Nick were adopting out of state custody in Virginia and brought him close enough to drop a kiss on the top of his head. “Sure you will. Keep working hard and do what Nick tells you, and you’ll be up to speed in no time.”

“I don’t know,” Scotty said hesitantly, his eyes fixed on Nick. “All the other kids are way better than me.”

That was because they’d been skating and playing hockey for as long as they could walk, while Scotty had been well cared for but without the frills and extras most kids took for granted. “I have faith in you, and in Nick. If you guys keep practicing as much as you have been lately, you’ll catch up.”

Nick had spared no expense in outfitting Scotty with top-of-the-line hockey skates and all the required protective equipment. Sam had joked that the hockey bag was bigger than the kid, but Nick had assured her it was no bigger than anyone else’s. Hockey, she was learning, took a tremendous amount of time, equipment and money—not to mention the warmest coat she owned whenever she ventured into the ice rink.

“I hope you’re right,” Scotty said.

“I’m always right.”

Don’t miss
FATAL JEOPARDY:
BOOK SEVEN OF THE FATAL SERIES
by Marie Force, available in print September 2015!

www.CarinaPress.com

CARMFEXP00272

MARIE FORCE

00257	FATAL AFFAIR: BOOK ONE OF THE FATAL SERIES	___$5.99 U.S.	___$6.99 CAN.
00258	FATAL JUSTICE: BOOK TWO OF THE FATAL SERIES	___$5.99 U.S.	___$6.99 CAN.
00259	FATAL CONSEQUENCES: BOOK THREE OF THE FATAL SERIES	___$5.99 U.S.	___$6.99 CAN.
00269	FATAL FLAW: BOOK FOUR OF THE FATAL SERIES	___$5.99 U.S.	___$6.99 CAN.
00270	FATAL DECEPTION: BOOK FIVE OF THE FATAL SERIES	___$6.99 U.S.	___$7.99 CAN.

(limited quantities available)

TOTAL AMOUNT $________
POSTAGE & HANDLING $________
($1.00 for 1 book, 50¢ for each additional)
APPLICABLE TAXES* $________
TOTAL PAYABLE $________

(check or money order—please do not send cash)

To order, complete this form and send it, along with a check or money order for the total amount, payable to Carina Press, to: **In the U.S.:** 3010 Walden Avenue, P.O. Box 9077, Buffalo, NY 14269-9077; **In Canada:** P.O. Box 636, Fort Erie, Ontario, L2A 5X3.

Name: ________________________________
Address: ____________________ City: ____________
State/Prov.: ____________________ Zip/Postal Code: ____________
Account Number (if applicable): ____________________

075 CSAS

*New York residents remit applicable sales taxes.
*Canadian residents remit applicable GST and provincial taxes.

www.CarinaPress.com

CARMF00271BL